The Collected Supernatural and Weird Fiction of F. Marion Crawford Volume 5

The Collected Supernatural and Weird Fiction of F. Marion Crawford Volume 5

Including One Novel 'Greifenstein', and
Three Short Stories 'The Screaming Skull'
'The King's Messenger,' and 'Man Overboard!'
of the Strange and Unusual

F. Marion Crawford

LEONAUR

The Collected
Supernatural and Weird
Fiction of
F. Marion Crawford
Volume 5
Including One Novel 'Greifenstein', and Three Short Stories
'The Screaming Skull' 'The King's Messenger,' and 'Man Overboard!'
of the Strange and Unusual
by *F. Marion Crawford*

FIRST EDITION

Leonaur is an imprint
of Oakpast Ltd

ISBN: 978-0-85706-555-1 (hardcover)
ISBN: 978-0-85706-556-8 (softcover)

http://www.leonaur.com

Publisher's Notes

Contents

Greifenstein

CHAPTER 1

Frau von Sigmundskron was not really much past middle age, though the people in the village generally called her the old baroness. Her hair was very white and she was thin and pale; her bold features, almost emaciated, displayed the framework of departed beauty, and if her high white forehead and waxen face were free from lines and wrinkles, it must have been because time and grief could find no plastic material there in which to trace their story. She was a very tall woman, too, and carried her head erect and high, walking with a firmness and elasticity of step such as would not have been expected in one whose outward appearance conveyed so little impression of strength. It is true that she had never been ill in her life and that her leanness was due to the most natural of all causes; but these facts were not patent to the observer, and for reasons which will presently appear she herself would have been the last to mention them.

There was something, too, in the look of her blue eyes, shaded by long brown lashes which had retained their colour, that forbade any expression of sympathy. The least experienced of mankind would have seen at a glance that she was the proudest of women, and would have guessed that she must be one of the most reticent. She moved and spoke as though Sigmundskron were still what it had been in former days, and she had brought up her only child to be as much like herself, as it was possible that anything so young and fair could resemble what was already a type of age and gravity.

Poverty is too insignificant a word to describe the state in which the mother and daughter lived, and had lived for many years. They had no means of subsistence whatever beyond the pension accorded to the widow of Lieutenant von Sigmundskron, 'fallen on the field of honour,' as the official report had expressed it, in the murderous war with France. He had been the last of his name and at the time of his death had no relations living; two years earlier he had married a girl as penniless and as noble as himself, and had lived to see a daughter born, destined to inherit his nobility, his penury, and the bare walls of his ancestral home.

Sigmundskron had been a very grand castle in its day, and the half-ruined walls of the old stronghold still rose majestically from the summit of the crag. Indeed the ruin was more apparent than real as yet, and a few thousands judiciously expended upon the masonry would have sufficed to restore the buildings to their original completeness. Many a newly enriched merchant or banker would have paid a handsome price for the place, though the land was gone and the government owned the forest up to the very foot of the rock.

But the Lady of Sigmundskron would rather have starved to death in her vaulted chamber than have taken half the gold in Swabia to sign away her dead husband's home. Moreover, there was Greif, and Greif was to marry Hilda, after which all would be well again. Greif, with his money, would build and restore and furnish the old castle, and bring back the breath of life into the ancient halls and corridors. But in order that Greif might marry Hilda, it was necessary that Hilda should grow up beautiful, and to grow up at all, it was necessary that Hilda should be fed.

It had come to that, to the very question of food, of mere bread to eat. There was not enough for two, but Hilda must not starve. That was the secret which no one, not even Hilda herself must ever understand. During the first years, it had not been so hard to live. There had been a few poor jewels to sell, a few odds and ends that had brought a little money. While Hilda was a little child it had been easier, for she had needed but few clothes and, being little, had needed to eat less. But at last there had come a day when Frau von Sigmundskron, not so thin nor so pale as now, had seen a hungry look stealing into the eyes of the fair-haired girl. It was little enough that they had between them, but the mother said to herself that she could keep alive with less.

The careful economy which bought nothing not capable of sustaining life and strength could go no further. There were but so many pence a day for food, and to expend more today was to starve tomorrow. From that moment Frau von Sigmundskron began to complain of headache, and especially of loss of appetite. She could not eat, she said. She did not think there was anything the matter, and she would doubtless be better in a few days. But the days ran on to weeks, the weeks to months, and the months to years, and Hilda grew tall and fair, unconsciously eating her mother's portion of the daily bread. No hermit ever lived upon so little as sufficed for the baroness; no perishing, shipwrecked wretch ever measured out so carefully the ounce of biscuit that must maintain life from day to day; no martyr ever submitted more patiently and silently to his sufferings. But Hilda grew, and the years sped on, and Greif would come in time.

Greif, upon whom such great hopes were centred, was a distant cousin as well as a neighbour. The relationship was on the side of Hilda's mother, whose grandfather had been a Greifenstein, and who might have been expected to accept some assistance from her rich connexions, especially as she was quite willing that her daughter should marry their only son. But the baroness was a woman whose pride forbade her to accept under the pressure of necessity what had not been offered freely in other times.

It must be admitted also that the Greifensteins, though well aware that the Sigmundskrons were extremely poor, were far from suspecting that they were in need of bread. They knew that the castle was still the unhampered property of the two ladies, and they supposed that if things were really in a bad state, the baroness would raise money upon it. She never alluded to her affairs when she was with her relations, and excused herself from asking them to stay with her, on the ground of her poor health.

On rare occasions Greifenstein and his wife drove over to the castle, and were invariably admitted by the same soberly-dressed, middle-aged woman, who showed them into the same old-fashioned room, whence, having made their visit, they returned to the outer gate by the way they had come. That is all they ever saw of Sigmundskron. Twice in the year, also, Hilda and her mother were invited to stay a fortnight at Greifenstein, but no one would have supposed from their behaviour that the luxury of the latter place surprised them, or seemed in any way preferable to what they enjoyed at home. Hilda's education had not been neglected.

Among her earliest recollections was her mother's constant injunction never to make remarks upon what she saw in other houses. The child was not long in learning what the warning meant, and as she had inherited a plentiful share of her mother's pride she almost unconsciously imitated her mother's behaviour. Greif himself was the only person who might have known something of the true state of the case; but as he had been accustomed to be in love with his cousin ever since they had been children he would have feared to hurt her feelings by asking questions. For Hilda was reticent even with him, not from any shame at the idea of being thought poor, but because she was too proud to have it thought that either she or her mother could ever need the help of the Greifensteins.

Furthermore, if the baroness's reluctance to ask for assistance has not been sufficiently explained, there is one more consideration which might alone have sufficed to account for her conduct. Between her and Greif's mother there existed a great and wholly insurmountable antipathy. She could not understand how Greifenstein could have married such a woman. There was a mystery about it which she had never fathomed. Greifenstein himself was a stern, silent man of military appearance, a mighty hunter in the depths of the forest, a sort of grizzled monument of aristocratic strength, tough as leather, courteous in his manner, with that stiff courtesy that never changes under any circumstances, rigid in his views, religious, loyal, full of the prejudices that make the best subjects in a kingdom and the bitterest opponents of all change.

In appearance and manner Frau von Greifenstein presented the most complete contrast to her husband. She had been pretty, fair and sprightly in her youth, she was now a faded blonde, full of strange affectations and stilted sentiments. Possessing but indifferent taste, she nevertheless devoted much time to the adornment of her person. She was small of stature, but delicately made, and if her nervous desire to please had granted to her outward personality a moment's repose during the day, she might still have passed muster as a fairly good-looking woman. Unfortunately she was animated by an unceasing activity in trivial matters, and was rarely silent. Some women make one think of a printed page in which there are too many italics, and too many useless marks of exclamation.

At first, their constant cries of admiration and outbursts of enthusiasm produce a vague sense of uneasiness in the listener, which soon develops to a feeling of positive distress and generally ends in a real and deep-rooted dislike. At the beginning one looks about anxiously for the object which could produce so grotesque a smile. There is nothing, for the conversation has been as lead, but the smile does not subside; it only passes through the endless variations that succeed each other from the inane grin to the affected simper which is meant to be tender. The whole face moves perpetually, as the facial muscles of a corpse, excited by an electric current, seem to parody all the expression of living human sentiment.

But Frau von Greifenstein was not in reality so foolish as might have been thought. Her silliness was superficial. One part of her life had been full of strange circumstances, and if the whole truth were told it would appear that she had known how to extract a large amount of personal advantage from situations which to many persons would have seemed hopeless. She and her husband rarely left their castle in the Black Forest, and it might naturally be supposed that their life there was exceedingly dull and monotonous.

In her own heart Clara von Greifenstein recognised that her present luxurious retirement was a paradise compared with the existence she must have led if she had not known how to help herself at the right moment. During the earlier years of her marriage, the recollection of her antecedents had been so painful as to cause her constant anxiety, and at one time she had even gone so far as to keep a sum of money about her, as though expecting to make a sudden and unexpected journey. But five and twenty years and more had passed, without bringing any untoward incident, and she felt herself very secure in her position. Moreover a son had been born to her and was growing up to be very like his father.

Without Greif there is no knowing what turn affairs might have taken, for although Clara's husband maintained towards her the same stiffly considerate behaviour which had always characterised him in their relations to each other, he certainly admitted to himself that she was not growing old gracefully; and it is even possible that, in some remote glen of the forest, his grave features may have occasionally allowed themselves a look of sorrowful regret, or even of actual repugnance, when he thought of his wife's spasmodic smiles and foolish talk. Possibly, too, he may have sometimes speculated upon her probable condition before she had married her first husband, for he himself had found her a widow of apparently little more than five and twenty years of age.

But if any suggestion at all derogatory to Greifenstein had presented itself to his mind, his pride would assuredly have lost no time in smothering the thought. Was she not the mother of Greif? And besides, if all were to be told, was there not an unpleasantly dark spot in his own family, in the shape of his half-brother, Kuno von Rieseneck? Indeed the existence of Kuno von Rieseneck, concerning whom Clara knew nothing, was the reason why Greifenstein had lived for so many years in the country, only travelling outside of Germany when he travelled at all.

He wondered that his wife, being ignorant of the story, should be willing to share the solitude of the Black Forest without a murmur, and her submission in itself suggested that she, too, might have some good cause for preferring a retired life. But if he had been satisfied with what he knew of her five and twenty years ago, he was not the man to allow himself any dissatisfaction now that Clara was the mother of that stalwart young fellow who was heir to all the Greifenstein property.

In the month of July Greif was to come home from the University, and immediately afterwards Hilda and her mother were to come over for their half-yearly visit. The ancient place where this family meeting was convened was so unlike most castles as to deserve a word of description.

The Swabian Black Forest is literally black, save when the winter snow is heavy on the branches of the huge trees and lies in drifts beneath them, covering the soft carpet of fir needles to the depth of many feet. The landscape is extremely melancholy and in many parts is absolutely monotonous. At intervals of several miles the rock juts suddenly out of the forest, generally at places where the Nagold, more a torrent than a river, makes a sharp bend. Many of these steep and stony promontories are crowned by ancient strongholds, chiefly in ruins, though a very few are still in repair and are inhabited by their owners. The name of Greifenstein will not be found on any map of the district, but those who know that wild and unfrequented country will recognise the spot.

The tumbling stream turns upon itself at a sharp angle, swirling round the base of a precipitous and wedge-like cliff. So steep are the sides that they who chose the summit for a fortress saw no need of building any protection, save one gigantic wall which bestrides the wedge of rock, thus cutting off a triangular platform, between the massive bulwark and the two precipices that meet at the apex of the figure. This single fortification is a solid piece of masonry, enormously thick and of great height; its two extremities being surmounted by pointed towers, connected by a covered walk along the top of the wall, which, even at that height, is fully six feet wide and nearly a hundred in length.

This was the rampart behind which the Greifensteins had dwelt in security through many generations, in the stormy days of the robber barons. So sure were they of their safety, that they had built their dwelling-place on the other side of the bulwark in a manner that offered no suggestion of war or danger. The house was Gothic in style, full of windows and ornamented with spacious balconies and much fine stonework. The three-cornered platform was converted into a flower-garden, surrounded by a parapet. Protected on the north side by the huge wall, and fully exposed to the southern sun, the plants throve in an almost artificial spring, and in the summer jets of water played in the marble basins and cooled the hot, pine-scented air.

One narrow gate, barely wide enough for two persons to pass abreast, gave access to this paradise through the grey, window-less mass of masonry by which it was separated from the melancholy forest without. One small building only was visible on the side of the woods, scarcely fifty yards from the gate. This was a small, square, stone tower, half overgrown with brush and creepers, and evidently abandoned to decay. It was known in the family and neighbourhood as the 'Hunger-Thurm,' or Hunger Tower, as having been used as a place for starving prisoners to death, in the fine old days when the lords of Greifenstein did as they judged good in their own eyes.

Frau von Sigmundskron used to look curiously at the grey building when she was staying with her relations. She could have described the sufferings of the poor wretches who had perished there as well as any one of themselves or better. Not twenty miles from all the luxury that dwelt behind that lofty bulwark, she had been starving herself for years in order that her only child might live. And yet the well-fed woodmen touched their caps and their rosy wives and daughters curtsied to the 'Lady Baroness' who, as they told each other, spent her life in the towers of Sigmundskron hoarding untold wealth which would one day belong to the golden-haired Lady Hilda.

They knew, for the knowledge could not be kept from them

14

and their kind, how very few were the silver pieces which were ever seen in the hands of old Berbel, when she came down to the village market to buy food, and they naturally concluded that the baroness was a miser even like some of themselves, keeping her store of gold in a broken teapot somewhere among those turrets in a spot known only to the owls. It is also possible that Berbel—her name was Barbara—encouraged the idea, thinking it better that her beloved mistresses should be thought avaricious than poor.

The burgomaster of the hamlet, who had to take off his coat in order to sign his name when that momentous operation was unavoidable, but who was supposed to know vastly more than the schoolmaster, used to talk about certain mines in Silesia, owned by the Sigmundskrons; and once or twice he went so far as to assure his hearers that gold and even diamonds were found there in solid blocks as big as his own Maass-Krug, that portentous jug from which he derived inspiring thoughts for conversation, or peaceful satisfaction in solitude, as the case might be. All, however, agreed in predicting that things would go much better when the young gentleman of Greifenstein was married to the young lady of Sigmundskron.

On that warm afternoon in July when Greif was expected, his father took his gun, though there was little to shoot at that season, and sallied forth on foot along the broad road that led to the distant railway station. The portly gatekeeper smiled pleasantly as he stood looking after his master. For many years, whenever the student was to come home, old Greifenstein had gone down that road, in the same way, without a word to anyone, but having that same twinkle of happy anticipation in his eyes, which was never seen there at any other time. Very generally, too, the laden carriage came rumbling up to the gate with Greif's belongings, and an hour or two passed before father and son emerged on foot from the first trees of the forest.

Today also, the master had started betimes and it would be long before he heard the horses' bells below him in the valley. He walked quickly, as active men do when they are alone, and there is no one to hinder them, stopping now and then to see which way a hare sprang, or pausing to listen when his quick ear caught the distant tread of a buck. He knew that he might walk for miles without meeting a human being. The road was his, the land was his, the trees were his. There was no felling to be done in the neighbourhood, and no one but himself or his men had any right to be prowling about the woods.

In the perfect solitude his features relaxed a little and their expression changed. The glad anticipation of the meeting with his son was still in his eyes, but in the rest of his face there was a weary look which those who knew him best would not have recognised. He was thinking how different life would seem if Greif and he were to be the only inhabitants of the old home during the next dozen years. Then he stiffened his neck suddenly and strode on.

At last the far off tinkling of bells came up to him from the depths of the forest, with the dull thud of horses' hoofs that echoed among the trees. He quickened his pace, knowing at how great a distance the sounds could be heard. Ten minutes elapsed before the carriage came in sight, and then almost instantly a loud shout rang through the woods, followed by an answer from old Greifenstein, deeper, but quite as strong.

'Father!'

'Greif!'

Greif had leaped down from his place and was running up the hill at a pace that would have tried the horses. In a moment more the two tall men were in each other's arms, kissing each other on the cheek.

At three and twenty the student looked as much like his father as a young and fair man can look like an elderly dark one. Their features were the same, both had the same sinewy firmness of build and the same eyes; but Greif's close-cut golden hair and delicate moustache gave him a brilliancy his father had never possessed. He seemed to bring the light with him into the deep shade of the glen where they met. One looking at him would have felt instinctively that he was made to wear the gleaming uniform of a Prussian Lifeguard, rather than the sober garments of a civilian. As a matter of fact, he was dressed like an Englishman, and would probably have been taken for one, to his own intense disgust, in any European crowd.

'And how is the mother?' he asked in a somewhat formal tone, as soon as the first embrace was over. He had been brought up with dutiful ideas.

'Your mother is exceedingly well,' answered Greifenstein, whose manner also stiffened perceptibly. There was a moment's pause.

Perhaps it was in the hope of dissipating that awkward feeling which somehow or other always made itself apparent when the Lady of Greifenstein was mentioned, that her husband pulled out his case and offered Greif a cigar.

'I have brought you a pipe,' said the latter, and as the carriage came up to where they were standing he snatched his bag off the back seat. 'It will make you feel young again,' he laughed, as he took a paper parcel from the receptacle. 'It is a "Korps" pipe, colours and tassels and all.'

Greifenstein, one of whose favourite hobbies was the advantage of pipes in general, was as delighted as a boy with the little gift, and instantly produced a huge silver tobacco box out of the depths of his shooting coat, from which he began to fill the china bowl.

'Thank you, my boy,' he said as he drew the air through the unlighted pipe to assure himself that there was no obstruction.

Then he took out an old-fashioned flint and steel, lighted a bit of tinder with a practised hand and laid it upon the tobacco. He made a sign to the coachman, who urged his sturdy Mecklenburg horses up the hill and was soon out of sight. The two men walked slowly forwards and smoked in silence for a few minutes.

'When is Hilda coming?' asked Greif at last, when he thought he had allowed a decent interval to elapse before putting the question which chiefly interested him.

'She will come tomorrow, with her mother,' replied Greifenstein, not noticing, or pretending not to notice, the faint blush that rose in his son's face.

'I suppose we must wait another year,' remarked Greif with a sigh. 'It seems absurd that at my age I should not have finished my education.'

'You will be glad, when you are married, that you have your military service behind you.'

'I do not know,' answered the young man absently.

'You do not know!' exclaimed his father in surprise. 'Would you like to go and live with Hilda in a garrison town while you served your year as a volunteer?'

'I was not thinking of that. I have thought lately that, after all, I had better take active service. Would you object?'

Greifenstein was taken by surprise and would possibly have uttered a loud exclamation if he had not long ago schooled himself to be incapable of any such breach of gravity. But he did not answer the question.

'Father,' began Greif again after a pause, 'is it true that you ever had a brother?'

Greifenstein's tough face turned slowly grey.

'A half-brother,' he answered with an effort. 'My mother married again.'

Greif glanced sideways at his father and saw that he was oddly affected by the inquiry. But the young man had his own reasons for wishing to know the truth.

'Why have you never told me that I had an uncle?' he asked.

'He is no uncle of yours, my boy, nor brother of mine!' answered Greifenstein bitterly.

'I fought about him the other day. That is all,' said Greif.

'He is not worth fighting for.'

'Then the story is true?'

'What story?' Greifenstein stopped short in his walk and fixed his sharp eyes on his son's face. 'What story? What do you know?'

'A man told me that your brother had been discharged from the army with infamy—*infam cassirt*—and condemned to impris-

18

onment, for betraying some arsenal or armoury into the hands of the rebels in 1848. I told him—well—that he lied. What else could I say? I had never heard of the scoundrel.'

'You were quite right,' answered Greifenstein, who was very pale. 'I never meant that you should know, any more than your mother. That is the reason why we live in the country all the year. But I thought it would come—I feared that someone would tell you!'

'I do not think that any one will repeat the experiment,' observed Greif, turning away and looking down at the torrent, which was visible between the trees. 'And what has become of this Herr von Rieseneck, if that was his name?'

'He is alive and well. Rich, for anything I know to the contrary. He escaped from the fortress where he was confined and made his way to South America. I had not seen him for some time before that disgraceful affair. We had quarrelled about other matters, and he had entered the Prussian service.'

'I wish you had told me about him before.'

'Why should I? Do you think it is a pleasant subject for conversation? As his name was not mine, thank God, there was a chance that you might never know nor hear of him.'

'I see why you do not wish me to enter the army.'

'Yes,' answered Greifenstein laconically, and he once more walked forward.

For some time neither spoke. Greifenstein's profound hatred of his dishonoured brother was too deeply stirred to allow of his continuing the conversation, and in a different way the younger man was quite as much affected as his father. When the student with whom he had fought had cast in his teeth the evil deeds of Kuno von Rieseneck, he had unhesitatingly denied the story, thinking it a merely gratuitous insult invented on the spur of the moment. No one present during the altercation had thought fit to confirm the tale, and Greif had wreaked his vengeance upon his enemy in the most approved fashion, in the presence of the assembled 'Korps.' But the words had taken effect and he had determined to learn from his father's lips whether they had any foundation in fact.

Being satisfied of the truth of the story, however, his mood changed. No one who has not studied the character of the German gentleman—the old-fashioned Edelmann—will readily understand how directly he feels himself injured by the disgrace of a relative even very distantly removed. He has often little enough in the world but his name and his pride of caste, but as compared with the former he holds his life as of no value whatsoever, and where the latter is concerned he will suffer much rather than offend the exclusiveness of his class by derogating from the most insignificant of its prejudices. He is not afraid of poverty.

No one can maintain the position of a gentleman with more exiguous resources than often fall to his share. Rather than leave the smallest debt of honour unpaid, he will unhesitatingly take his own life. That a man should suffer himself to live after doing such a deed as had broken Kuno von Rieseneck's career seems to him a crime against humanity. He is often called avaricious, because, like Frau von Sigmundskron, he is often very, very poor; but he has never been called a coward, nor a traitor, by any man, or class of men, who knew him. All gentlemen throughout the world are brothers, it is true, for to be a gentleman is to be brave, honest, courteous, and nothing more. But the gentlemen of different nations are like brothers brought up in different schools.

An Englishman who should demand satisfaction by arms, of another Englishman, for a hasty word spoken in jest, would be considered a lunatic in the clubs, and if he carried his warlike intentions into effect with the consent of his adversary, and killed his man, the law would hang him without mercy as a common murderer. On the other hand, a German who should refuse a duel, or not demand one if insulted, would be dismissed from the army and made an outcast from society. And these things do not depend upon civilisation, since modern Germany is probably more civilised than modern England. They depend upon national character.

When Greif heard of his uncle's existence, and, at the same

time, of his disgrace, it seemed to him that a cloud had descended upon his own brilliant future. He had long nursed in secret his desire for a military life, and had often wondered at his father's unwillingness to discuss the matter. He now suddenly understood the true state of the case and realised, by the measure of his disappointment, the magnitude to which his hopes had grown. But there was something more than this in the despondency which seized upon him so quickly and would not be thrown off.

'Does Hilda know this?' he asked, at length giving expression to his thoughts.

Greifenstein did not answer at once.

'I do not think her mother would have told her,' he said after a time. 'But her mother knows.'

'And my mother does not?'

'No, nor never shall, if I can help it.'

If the two men spoke little on their homeward walk it was not for lack of sympathy between them. On the contrary, if anything could strengthen the strong bond that united them, it was the knowledge that they had a secret in common which they must keep together.

CHAPTER 2

To suppose that Hilda, at eighteen years of age, was like the majority of young girls as old as she, would be to imagine that human character is not influenced by its surroundings. She was neither a village Gretchen, such as Faust loved and ruined, nor was she the omniscient damsel of modern society. During the greater part of her existence she had lived without any companions but her mother and the faithful Berbel. But she had grown up in a wild forest country, in a huge dismantled stronghold, of which the windows looked out over the tumbling torrent, and across endless thousands of giant trees, whose dark tops rose like sombre points of shadow out of the deeper shade below. Even the sky was not blue. Half a kingdom of firs and pines and hemlocks drank the colour from the air and left but a sober neutral tint behind. The sun does not give half the light in the Black Forest that he gives elsewhere.

As Hilda had never, within her recollection, seen an open plain, much less a city, her idea of the world beyond those leagues of trees in which she lived was not a very accurate one. She could hardly guess what the streets of a great town were like, or what effect a crowd of civilised people would produce upon her sight. And yet she was far from ignorant. There were books enough left at Sigmundskron for her education, and the baroness had done what was in her power to impart such instruction as she could command. Hilda had probably read as many books as most girls of her age, and had read them more carefully, but she was very far from loving study for its own sake. Her time, too, was occupied in other ways, for she and her mother did most things for themselves, as was to be expected in a household where want reigned supreme over the hours of every day, from sunrise to sunset.

The necessity for maintaining appearances was small indeed, but such as it was, neither mother nor daughter could avoid it. No one could predict what day the Greifensteins would choose for one of their occasional visits, and in the time of the vacations no one could foresee when Greif might make his appearance, striding over the wooded hills with his gun and his dog to spend a quiet afternoon with Hilda in their favourite sunny corner at the foot of the dismantled tower. When poverty is to be concealed, his shadow must not be caught lurking at the door by chance visitors. Nor was it only out of fear of being surprised by her relations that the quiet baroness insisted that Hilda and even Berbel should always be presentable. Her pride was inseparably united with that rigid self-respect which, in the poor, alone saves pride from being ridiculous.

It was indeed marvellous that she should succeed as she did in hiding the extremity of her need from the Greifensteins, but it must be remembered that she had never been rich, and had learned in early youth many a lesson, many a shift of economy which now stood her in good stead. The Germans have a right to be proud of having elevated thrift to a fine art. From the Emperor to the schoolmaster, from the administration of the greatest military force the world has ever seen to the housekeeping of the meanest peasant, a sober appreciation of the value of money is the prime rule by which everything is regulated.

Frau von Sigmundskron had made a plan, had drawn up a tiny budget in exact proportion with the pension which was her only means of subsistence, and thanks to her unfailing health had never departed from it. The expenditure had indeed been so closely regulated from the first, that she had found it necessary to limit herself to what would barely support life, in order not to stint her child's allowance. Being by temperament a very religious woman, she attributed to Providence that success in rearing Hilda for which she might well have thanked her own iron determination and untiring efforts. If ever a woman deserved the help of Heaven in consideration of having bravely helped herself, the baroness had earned that assistance.

So far as the ordinary observer could judge, however, she had obtained nothing from the world save a reputation for avarice. Hilda was too much accustomed to the state of things in which she had grown up, to appreciate her mother's sacrifices, or to feel towards her anything like warm gratitude. She herself did all she could, and that was not little, in the struggle for existence. It is even possible that she was more grateful to Berbel, than to the baroness herself. For Berbel voluntarily shared privations, to which the two ladies were obliged to submit. Berbel was faithful, devoted, uncomplaining, cheerful; and she was all this, not for the sake of a servant's pay, since her wages were infinitesimally small, but out of pure affection for her mistress.

Berbel had been the wife of Lieutenant von Sigmundskron's servant, who had fallen beside his master, rifle in hand, his face to the enemy. Mistress and maid were left alike widows on the same day, alike young and portionless, the only difference being that Frau von Sigmundskron had Hilda, while poor Berbel was childless. Then Berbel refused to go away, once and for ever, and the officer's widow accepted the lifelong devotion offered her, and the three cast in their lot together, to keep themselves alive as best they could beneath the only roof that was left to them.

Frau von Sigmundskron had been very much surprised when, on a sunny June morning, three years before the time of which I write, Greifenstein had appeared alone, arrayed in the most correct manner, instead of being clad in the shooting coat he usually wore. She had been still more astonished when he formally proposed to her an engagement by which Greif should marry Hilda so soon as he had finished his studies at the University. He told her frankly why he desired the alliance. She knew of Rieseneck's disgrace, and she would understand that the story was an injury to Greif.

On the other hand he, Greif's father, had never done anything to be ashamed of, and the lad himself was growing up to be a very fine fellow and would be rich—Greifenstein did not state the amount of his fortune. He apprehended that his cousin would consider Greif a good match from a worldly point of view. Furthermore, though barely twenty, the young man was deeply attached to Hilda, who was just fifteen, The attachment was evidently likely to turn into love when both should be three or four years older. If Frau von Sigmundskron would consent, a preliminary, verbal agreement might be made, subject to the will of the two children when the right time should come, it being essentially necessary, as Greifenstein remarked in his stiffest manner, that two young people should love each other sincerely if they meant to marry.

The baroness opened her clear blue eyes very wide, as though she had seen a coach and four laden with sacks of gold driving through the old gates of the castle. But she was far too well bred to burst into tears, or to exhibit any embarrassment, or even an improper amount of satisfaction. She replied that she was much obliged; that she was poor, and that Hilda would inherit nothing whatsoever except Sigmundskron, a fact which her cousin must please to understand from the first; that, if the absence of any dower were not an obstacle, it was not for her to create difficulties; and, finally, that she believed Hilda to be quite as much attached to Greif, as Greif to her. Thereupon Berbel was sent to fetch a bottle of wine—there had been half a dozen bottles in the cellar thirteen years ago, and this was the first that had been opened— and Greifenstein refreshed himself therewith and departed, as stiffly, courteously and kindly as he had come.

Greif had come over as often as he pleased during his vacations, and had written whenever he liked during his terms. Never having seen any one at home or abroad whom he considered comparable with Hilda, he had grown up to love her as naturally as he loved the pine-scented air of his home, the warm soft sun, or the still beauty of the forest. Hilda was an essential part of his life and being, without which he could imagine no future. Year by year it grew harder to say good-bye, and the happiness of meeting grew deeper and more real. There was a pride in the knowledge that she was for him only, which played upon the unconscious selfishness of his young nature and gave him the most profound and exquisite delight.

At three and twenty he was old enough to understand the world about him, he had accomplished his year of obligatory service in the army, and had come into contact with all sorts of men, things and ideas. He was himself a man, and had outgrown most boyish fallacies and illusions, but he had not outgrown Hilda. She was there, in the heart of the forest, in the towers of Sigmundskron, away from the world he had seen, and maidenly ignorant of all it contained, waiting for him, the incarnation of all that was lovely, and young, and fair, and spotless.

He pitied his fellow-students, who loved vulgarly whatever came into their way. He could not imagine what life would be without Hilda. It was a strange sort of love, too, for there had been no wooing; they had grown up for each other as naturally as the song-bird for its mate. There had been no hindrances, no jealousies, no alternate hopes and fears, none of those vicissitudes to which love is heir. Nothing but the calamity of death could interfere with the fulfilment of their happiness, and perhaps no two beings ever loved each other from whom death seemed so far.

Hilda was happy, too, in her own way, for what she knew of the outer world was what she saw through Greif's eyes. To him the greatest of all blessings would be to come back to the forest and never to leave it again, and Hilda argued that the world could not be worth seeing, if the woods were so vastly preferable as he seemed to think. She felt herself to be what she was in his imagination, a part of the nature in which she had grown up, as much as the oldest and tallest fir tree on the hillside.

People who spend all their lives in unfrequented regions, feel a sense of property in the air, the earth and the water, which city-bred folks cannot readily understand. They have such an intimate, unconscious knowledge of the seasons, the weather, the growth of plants and the habits of animals, that it seems to them as though their own hearts beat in every corner of the world around them, and as though all the changes they see from day to day were only manifestations of their own vitality. They may not see, or know that they see, beauties which amaze the wanderer who visits their wilderness, but they feel them as he never can, and feed on them as he cannot feed.

Their senses, not dulled by daily close contact with thousands of indifferent and similar objects, nor by the ceaseless chatter of their fellow-beings, see sights and hear sounds altogether beyond the perceptions of gregarious man. The infinite variety of nature, as compared with the pitiful monotony of the works of humanity, produces in their minds an activity of an especial kind. They do not know what mental weariness means, nor the desire for nervous excitement. The succession of morning and evening does not bore them, for it is a part of themselves, like hunger and the satisfaction of appetite, thirst and the refreshing draught from the spring. They are good, though their virtues be negative, and they are happy, for they have never heard of unhappiness.

Their existence is the very opposite of ours, full where ours is empty, empty where ours is crowded to overflowing. They are never alone, for the world is their companion, they are never hurried, for they move with time itself, whereas our existence is but one long effort to outrun the revolution of the hours. They do not dream of fame, for they feel the eternity of perpetually renewed life in all that surrounds them; they have never heard of competition, for their only rival is God Himself.

Hilda's earliest recollections did not go back beyond the time when she had been brought to the Black Forest, and the singular simplicity of her life made the past years seem strangely short. Children whose first remembrances are full of new impressions, grow old quickly, while those to whose perceptions little is offered grow up more slowly, and more naturally. Other conditions being the same, these latter will be calmer, healthier and more reasonable. The best horse is not the one which is made to do the most work as a colt, though performing dogs must learn their tricks as puppies if they are to learn them at all.

Much in life depends upon the truth of our first impressions, and as this, in its turn, depends directly upon our ability to judge what we see and hear, it is clear that children may be injured permanently if too many things be brought within the sphere of their observation before they have learned the uses of hearing and sight.

The grand solitudes of the forest, the imposing calm of nature when at rest, the indescribable magnificence of the winter storms, had furnished Hilda with her first deep impressions. That death, of which her mother sometimes spoke, was the disappearance of all that lived beneath the soft, silent snow. That mysterious resurrection of the dead was nature's irresistible glad leap to meet the sun, as the noonday shadows shortened day by day; that happy life to come was the far-off summer, when the wind would sigh and whisper again among the branches he had so rudely handled in his wrath, when all the air would smell of the warm pines, when the mayflower would follow the hawthorn, and the purple gentian take the mayflower's place, when the wild pea-blossom would elbow the forest violet, and the clover and wild thyme and mint would spring up thick and crisp and sweet for the dainty roebuck and his doe. Hilda used to think that the souls of the blessed would at last take their bodies again, just as the wildflowers in the wood sprang up with their own shape and beauty, each according to the little seed that had lain dead and forgotten since autumn had sighed its dirge above their myriad tiny graves, burying the summer as sadly as men bury those they dearly love.

And yet Hilda never put any of those thoughts into words, though in her books she loved best those words that expressed her half-formulated feelings. Had she been removed to the noise and the whirl of city life, she would very probably have known how to define what she had lost, she might even have made others feel what she herself had so keenly felt. But in the silent towers of her home, or amidst that noiseless, ever-growing life that belongs to undisturbed nature, all she could have wished to express was expressed for her, in a grander language than that of man. She had no need of spending long hours in reverie and contemplation, as people do who are not used to their surroundings, or who compare their present with their past.

Constant occupation had become a part of her being, and unceasing small activity in household matters the condition of her life. Heaven knows, there was enough to do between making and mending everything she wore, keeping in order even the small part of the gigantic building which she and her mother inhabited, cultivating as best she could the plot of ground in the castle yard which was all the land left to her, the last of her name, and, in the midst of all this manual labour, in maintaining that prescribed amount of appearance, from which she had never been allowed to deviate since she had been a little child.

A spotless perfection of neatness was indeed the only luxury left within reach of the two ladies, and for that one available satisfaction there was no trouble they would not cheerfully undergo. But these manifold household labours did not vulgarise Hilda's character. If she enjoyed the luxury of Greifenstein during her half-yearly visits, it was not because she disliked or despised her own home life. She was too thoroughly conscious of the inevitable to groan over her lot, she was too strong in mind and body to desire luxurious idleness, and she never imagined that a woman could find occupation except in household duties. Her whole existence had made her so simple that she could never have comprehended that complicated state of mind which is so delightful to society.

Something of nature's own freshness, too, had been infused into the young girl's veins, refreshing and renewing the life in that old blood of which she was the last descendant. Blue eyes are rarely very bright. Hilda's seemed to have a special vitality of their own, which gave the impression that they must shine in the dark as some crystals do for a few seconds when they have been long exposed to the sun. They were of that rare type which appear to sparkle even when not seen directly, not merely reflecting the light as a placid pool reflects it, but making it dance and change as sunshine does in falling water.

Hilda's hair was yellow, and yellow hair is often lustreless as the pine dust in the woods; but hers glowed, as it were by its own colour, without reflection, out of the very abundance of vitality. Her features were delicate and aquiline, but were saved from any look of deficient strength by that perfection of evenly-distributed colour which comes only from matchless health and untainted blood, combined with a rare strength in the action of the heart. Hilda possessed one of those highly-favoured organisations which nature occasionally produces as normal types of what humanity should be. Such people bring with them a radiance that nothing can extinguish, not even extreme old age. Their beauty may not be of the highest type, but their vitality is irresistibly attractive, and spreads to their surroundings, undiminished by any effort they make.

When Hilda was told that if she and Greif loved each other they should marry, she was far less surprised than her mother had been when old Greifenstein had made his proposal. It seemed strange to the baroness that her daughter should not even blush a little on learning the news. But Hilda saw no reason for blushing and did not feel in the least disconcerted. To her it all seemed perfectly natural. She had always loved Greif, ever since she could remember anything. Why should he not love her? And if they loved each other, they would of course be married in due time.

It was but the fulfilment of her life, after all. There was surely nothing in the idea to cause her any emotion. Did not Heaven dispose everything in the best possible way, and was not this the best possible thing that could happen? Did the hawk mate with the wren, or the wild boar with the doe? But the baroness did not understand. She asked Hilda if she should be very unhappy if Greif died, or if he married someone else.

'God will not be so unkind,' answered the young girl simply.

Frau von Sigmundskron was silent. It was clear that Hilda, in her innocence, had never expected anything else, but her mother trembled to think of what might happen if that simple faith were rudely disappointed. It was characteristic of the devoted mother that she thought of her child's heart, and not of the worldly difference to Hilda between single life at Sigmundskron and wedded life at Greifenstein, between starvation and plenty, extreme poverty and the state of enjoying all that money could give. It was long before she could comprehend what had passed in Hilda's mind, or the process of reasoning by which the young girl had reached such a calm certainty of anticipation. When she at last saw that it was an extremely simple matter, she realised how completely her daughter had been shut off from the world since her birth.

At first she had doubted the reality of the girl's quiet manner in the circumstances, but she soon discovered that Hilda behaved during Greif's visits exactly as she had always done, meeting him gladly, parting from him regretfully, speaking with him as though there were no difference in their relations in the present, nor were to be in the future, excepting that Greif would always be present, instead of only coming from time to time. She knew that Greif himself was far from looking at the matter with such supreme calm. She saw the colour come and go in his fair face in a way that showed a constant emotion, and she feared lest such a very susceptible young man as he appeared to be should be entrapped, when away from home, by the designing mother, of whom every other mother sees the type in the background of her thoughts.

But Greif did not fall a victim to any such schemes. If Hilda had at all resembled most girls of her age, he could have compared her with them, and the comparison would not have been to her advantage. She could not have possessed their cheap accomplishments, their knowledge of waltzing, or their intimate acquaintance with their neighbours' affairs. She could not have put on their sentimentality with men, nor their cynicism with each other. She could not imitate their glances and she did not imitate their dress. She was a creature apart from them all. Deeply imbued as he was with all the prejudices of an exclusive caste, Greif could not have looked upon Hilda as he did, if she had been a peasant's child, even though she had been herself in all other respects.

There was that in her position which appealed to the romanticism of his nature. The noble but unfortunate maiden, the last of an ancient race, dwelling in dignified retirement in her half-ruined ancestral home, was vastly more interesting than any equally well-born girl could have been, who chanced to be rich enough to be marched into society as a matrimonial investment for young men of her station. But it was precisely because Hilda possessed that one point in common with all such eligible young ladies that Greif regarded her with a romantic devotion he could never have felt for a village Gretchen.

His pride in her nobility was indeed far less than his love for herself, but it made for that love a rampart against love's deadliest enemy, which is ridicule. He certainly did not tell himself so. He would have thought it an insult to Hilda to worship her for anything but her own self; but he was none the less aware that the pedestal upon which his idol stood was strong enough to withstand any assault. This being certain, it was the very impossibility of any further comparison that attracted him most. She was unlike any one whom he met, or was ever likely to meet, and his imagination invested her with many exceptional attributes, most of which she undoubtedly possessed in one degree or another.

Each time he returned and left the noisy train and the smart modern railway station behind him, to plunge into the silent forest, he felt more strongly that his real sympathies all lay between Greifenstein and Sigmundskron, and that his visits to the world were only disturbing dreams. They must be renewed from time to time, at ever-increasing intervals, but the real peace of his life awaited him in his home. He, too, like Hilda, was a child of the woods, and felt that the trees, the foaming streams and the changeless crags were all parts of himself, to lose which would be like forfeiting a limb of his body or a sense of his intelligence. The baroness need not have been afraid lest he should wander about the world to forget Sigmundskron or Hilda. Nature had made him constant, and circumstances had made him happy in his own place.

And so for years the lives of all these persons had run on, until the time was approaching when Greif and Hilda were to be married, and great changes were to be made at Sigmundskron. Greif had come home for the last time but one, and his next return would be final. During months and years the baroness and her daughter had been slowly preparing for the great event. The most unheard-of economies had been imagined and carried out in the attempt to give Hilda a little outfit for her wedding, just enough to hide the desperate poverty in which they had lived.

Many a long winter's evening had the two ladies spun the fine flax by the smouldering fire; many a long day had Hilda and Berbel spent at the primitive loom in the sunny room of the south tower; through many a summer's noon had the long breadths of fine linen lain bleaching on the clean grey stone of the ramparts, watered by the faithful servant's careful hand. Endless had been the thought expended before cutting into each piece of the precious material; endless the labour lavished upon the fine embroideries by Hilda herself, upon the minute stitching by her brave-hearted mother.

But the work had progressed well, and the finished garments that lay amidst bundles of sweet-smelling dried herbs in the great old press would have done credit to the spinning and weaving and handiwork of skilled craftsmen. It was fortunate that there had been time for it all, else Hilda would have made but a poor figure on the great day.

As for Berbel she believed that the forest itself had helped them, when she saw all that had been accomplished and remembered how she had bought the flax pound by pound at the market. Though a great share in the joint success was due to her own patient industry, the result seemed so fine as compared with the humble beginnings that she was much inclined to thank the Heinzelmannchen and their 'brownies' for the most part of it all. The baroness thanked Providence, and Hilda thought it was all due to her love for Greif. Perhaps they were all three right, and possibly each shared in some measure the views of the other two.

At least so far as the gnomes are concerned, most people who have lived long in forests and solitary places have discovered that their work, if they like it, is performed with a rapidity and skill which is marvellous in their own eyes, and if you do not call the little gentleman who comes at night and helps you by the name of Rubezahl, you may call him the Spirit of Peace. But as long as you receive him kindly and give him his due it matters very little how you christen him, for he is an affectionate spirit and loves those who love him for himself, and does their work for them, or makes them think he does, which, in fact, is just the same.

Unfortunately there are other spirits as busy as he in the world, and he has a way of taking himself off at the slightest alarm, which is often very distressing to those who love him; and some of those other spirits had chosen for their abode the Castle of Greifenstein and for their companions the persons who dwelt there. The unforeseen plays a very great part in our lives; for if it did not, we should most of us know exactly what to do at the right moment, and should consequently approach perfection at an unnatural rate.

While Greif and his father were slowly ascending the hill towards their home, while Frau von Greifenstein was looking at herself in her mirror and wondering whether she had not thrown away her youth after all, while Berbel was weaving and

Hilda embroidering and the old baroness stitching steadily along the folded linen—while all these people were thus quietly and peaceably engaged, an event was brewing which was destined to produce some very remarkable results.

And lest the justification of ordinary possibility should be required by the sceptical hereafter, I will at once state that the greater part of what follows is a matter of history, well known to many living persons; and that in writing it down I wish it to be understood that I am submitting to the judgment of humanity a strange case which actually occurred within this century, rather than constructing from my own imagination a mere romance for the delectation of such as will take the trouble to read it.

Chapter 3

'Oh! Is it not too delightful to see my dear, dear cousins!' screamed Frau von Greifenstein, throwing herself into the arms of the pale and quiet baroness. 'And dear Hilda, too! *Ach, ist es nicht herzig!* Is it not too sweet!'

She was wonderfully arrayed in an exceedingly youthful costume, short enough to display her thin, elderly ankles, and adorned with many flying ribbands and furbelows. An impossibly high garden hat crowned her faded head, allowing certain rather unattached-looking ringlets of colourless blonde hair to stray about her cheeks. She made one think of a butterfly, no longer young, but attempting to keep up the illusions of spring. Hilda and her mother smiled and returned the salutation in their quiet way.

'And how have you been at Sigmundskron?' continued the sprightly lady. 'Do you know? It would be my dream to live at Sigmundskron! So romantic, so solitary, so deliciously poetic! It is no wonder that you look like Cinderella and the fairy godmother! I am sure they both lived at Sigmundskron—and Greif will be the Prince Charmant with his Puss in Boots—quite a Lohengrin in fact—dear me! I am afraid I am mixing them up—those old German myths are so confusing, and I am quite beside myself with the joy of seeing you!'

Greifenstein stood looking on, not a muscle of his face betraying the slightest emotion at his wife's incoherent speech. But Greif had turned away and appeared to be examining one of the guns that stood in a rack against the wall. The meeting had taken place in the great hall, and he was glad that there was something to look at, for he did not know whether he was most amused by his mother's chatter, or ashamed of the ridiculous figure she made. The impression was certainly a painful one, and he had not attained to his father's grim indifference, for he was not obliged to assist daily at such scenes. He could not help comparing Hilda's mother with his own, and he inwardly determined that when he was married he would take up his abode at Sigmundskron during the greater part of the year.

Hilda looked at her hostess and wondered whether all women of the world were like Frau von Greifenstein. The situation did not last long, however, and half an hour later she found herself sitting beside Greif on a block of stone by the ruined Hunger-Thurm.

'At last!' exclaimed Greif, with a sigh of satisfaction. 'Is there anything so tiresome as the sight of affectionate greetings?'

'Greif—' Hilda paused, as though reconsidering the question she was about to ask.

'Yes—what is it, sweetheart?'

'When we are married, I must love your mother, must I not?'

'Oh yes—no doubt,' answered the young man with a puzzled expression 'At least, I suppose you must try.'

'But I mean, if I do not love her as much as my own mother, will it be very wrong?'

'No, not so much, of course.'

'Do you love her, Greif?'

'Oh yes,' replied Greif cheerfully. 'Not as I love you—'

'Or your father?'

'That is different, a man feels more sympathy for his father, because he is a man.'

'But I am not a man—'

'No, and you are not my mother either. That is again different, you see.'

'Greif—you do not love your mother at all!' exclaimed Hilda, turning her bright eyes to his. But he looked away and his face grew grave.

'Please do not say that to me, dear,' he answered quietly. 'Let us talk of other things.'

'Does it pain you? I am sorry. I asked you because—well, I wanted to know if it was exactly my duty—because—you see, I do not think I ever could, quite, as I ought to. You are not angry?'

'No, darling. I quite understand. It will be enough if you behave to her as you do now. Besides, I was going to propose something, if your mother will agree to it. When we are married, we might live at Sigmundskron.'

'Oh! Greif, are you in earnest?'

'Yes. Why not?'

'You do not know what a place it is!' exclaimed Hilda with an uneasy laugh. She had visions of her husband discovering the utter desolation of the old castle, but at the same time she felt a sudden wild desire to see it all restored and furnished and kept up as it should be.

'Yes, I know. But there are many reasons why I should like it. Of course it has gone to ruin, more or less, and there would be something to be done.'

'Something!' cried Hilda. 'Everything! The great rooms are perfectly desolate, no furniture, hardly any glass in the windows. We are so poor, Greif!'

'But I can put panes into the frames and get some furniture. We need not have so much at first.'

'But you will have to get everything, everything. You are used to so much here.'

'I should not need much if I had you,' answered Greif looking at her, as the colour rose in his own face.

'I do not know. Perhaps not.'

'I should be happy with you in a woodman's hut,' said Greif

earnestly.

'Perhaps,' replied Hilda a little doubtfully.

'There is no "perhaps." I am quite sure of it.'

'How can you be sure?' asked the young girl turning suddenly and laying her hands upon his arm. 'Did not your father say the same—no, forgive me! I will not speak of that. Oh Greif! What is love—really—the meaning of it, the true spirit of it? Why does it sometimes last and sometimes—not? Are all men so different one from another, and women too? Is it not like religion, that when you once believe you always believe? I have thought about it so much, and I cannot understand it. And yet I know I love you. Why can I not understand what I feel? Is it very foolish of me? Am I less clever than other girls?'

'No, indeed!' Greif drew her to him, and kissed her cheek. Her colour never changed. With innocent simplicity she turned her face and kissed him in return.

'Then why is it?' she asked. 'And none of my books tell me what it means, though I have read them all. Can you not tell me, you who know so much? What is the use of all your studies and your universities, if you cannot tell me what it is I feel, what love is?'

'Does love need explanation? What does the meaning matter, when one has it?'

'Ah, you may say that of anything. Would the air be sweeter, if I knew what it was? Would the storm be louder, or grander, or more angry, if I knew what made it? And besides, I do know, for I have learned about storms in my books. But it is not the same thing. Love is not part of nature, I am sure. It is a part of the soul. But then, why should it sometimes change? The soul does not change, for it is eternal.'

'But true love does not change either—'

'And yet people seem to think it is true, until it changes,' argued Hilda. 'There must be something by which one can tell whether it is true or not.'

'One must not be too logical with love, any more than with religion.'

'Religion? Why, that is the most logical thing we know anything about!'

'And yet people have differed very much in their opinions of it,' said Greif with a smile.

'Is it not logical that good people should go to heaven and bad people to hell?' inquired Hilda calmly. 'Religion would be illogical if it taught that sinners should all be saved and saints burnt in everlasting fire. How can you say it is not logical?'

'It certainly cannot be said if one takes your view,' Greif answered, laughing. 'But then, if you look at love in the same way, you get the same result. People who love each other are happy and people who quarrel are not.'

'Yes; but then, love does not only consist in not quarrelling.'

'Nor religion in not being a sinner—but I am not sure—' Greif interrupted himself. 'Perhaps that is just what religion means.'

'Then why cannot love mean something quite as simple?'

'It seems simple enough to me. So long as we are everything to each other we shall understand it quite enough.'

'Just so long—'

'And that means forever.'

'How do you know, unless you have some knowledge by which you can tell whether your love is true or not?'

'Why not yours, sweetheart?'

'Oh! I know myself well enough. I shall never change. But you—you might—'

'Do you not believe me?'

'Yes, I suppose so. But it always comes to that in the end, whenever we talk about it, and I am never any nearer to knowing what love is, after all!'

The young girl rested her chin upon her hand and looked wistfully through the trees, as though she wished and half expected that some wise fairy would come flitting through the shadow and the patches of sunshine to tell her the meaning of her love, of her life, of all she felt, of all she did not feel. She read in books that maidens blushed when the man they loved spoke to them, that their hearts beat fast and that their hands grew cold—simple expressions out of simple and almost childish tales. But none of these things happened to her. Why should they? Had she not expected to meet Greif that day? Why should she feel surprise, or fear, or whatever it was, that made the hearts of maidens in fiction behave so oddly?

He was very handsome, as he sat there glancing sideways at her, and she could see him distinctly, though she seemed to be looking at the trees. But that was no reason why she should turn red and pale, and tremble as though she had done something very wrong. It was all quite right, and quite sanctioned. She had nothing to say to Greif, nothing to think about him, that her mother might not have heard or known.

'I am no nearer to knowing,' she repeated after a long interval of silence.

'And I am no nearer to the wish to know,' answered Greif, clasping his brown hands over his knee and gazing at her from under the brim of his straw hat. 'You are a strange girl, Hilda,' he added presently, and something in his face showed that her singularity pleased him and satisfied his pride.

'Am I? Then why do you like me? Or do you like me because I am strange?'

'I wish I were a poet,' observed Greif instead of answering her. 'I would write such things about you as have never been written about any woman. However, I suppose you would never read my verses.'

'Oh yes!' laughed Hilda. 'Especially if mamma told me that they belonged to the "best German epoch." But I should not like them—'

'You do not like poetry in general, I believe.'

'It always seems to me a very unnatural way of expressing oneself,' answered Hilda thoughtfully. 'Why should a man go out of his way to put what he wants to say into a certain shape? What necessity is there for putting in a word more than is needed, or for pinching oneself so as to cut one out that would be useful for the sense, just because by doing that you can make everything fit a certain mould and sound mechanical—*ta ra tatatata ta tum tum!* "*Ich weiss nicht was soll es bedeuten*" and all the rest of it. There is something wrong. That poem is very sad and romantic in idea, and yet you always sing it when you are particularly happy.'

'Most people do,' said Greif, smiling at the truth of the observation.

'Then what is there in poetry? Does "I love you" sound sweeter if it is followed by a mechanical "*ta ra ta ra ta tum*" of words quite unnecessary to the thought, and which you only hear because they jingle after you, as your spurs do, when you have been riding and are on foot, at every step you take?'

'*Schlagend!*' laughed Greif. 'An annihilating argument! I will never think of writing verses any more, I promise you.'

'No. Don't,' answered Hilda emphatically. 'Unless you feel that you cannot love me in plain language—in prose,' she added, with a glance of her sparkling eyes.

'Verse would be better than nothing, then?'

'Than nothing—anything would be better than that.'

Greif fell to wondering whether her serious tone meant all that he understood by it, and he asked himself whether her calm, passionless affection were really what he in his heart called love. She felt no emotion, like his own. She could pronounce the words 'I love' again and again without a tremor of the voice or a change in the even shading of her radiant colour. It was possible that she only thought of him as a brother, as a part of the world she lived in, as something dearer than her mother because nearer to her own age. It was possible that if she had been in the world she might have seen some man whose mere presence could make her feel all she had never felt. It was conceivable that she should have fallen into this sisterly sort of affection in the absence of any person who might have awakened her real sensibilities. Greif's masculine nature was not satisfied, for it craved a more active response, as a lad watches for the widening ripples when he has dropped a pebble into a placid pool. An irresistible desire to know the truth overcame Greif.

'Are you quite sure of yourself, sweetheart?' he asked softly.

'Of what?'

'That you really love me. Do you know—'

Before he could finish the question Hilda was looking into his face, with an expression he had never seen before. He stopped short, surprised at the effect of his own words. Hilda was very angry, perhaps for the first time in her whole life. The brightness of her eyes almost startled him, and there was a slight contraction of the brows that gave her features a look of amazing power. Greif even fancied that, for once, her cheek was a shade paler than usual.

'You do not know what you say,' she answered very slowly.

'Darling—you have misunderstood me!' exclaimed Greif in distress. 'I did not mean to say—'

'You asked me if I were sure that I really loved you,' said Hilda very gravely. 'You must be mad, but those were your words.'

'Hear me, sweetheart! I only asked because—you see, you are so different from other women! How can I explain!'

'So you have had experience of others!' She spoke coldly and her voice had an incisive ring in it that wounded him as a knife. He was too inexperienced to know what to do, and he instinctively assumed that look of injured superiority which it is the peculiar privilege of women to wear in such cases, and which, in a man, exasperates them beyond measure.

'My dear,' said Greif, 'you have quite misunderstood me. I will explain the situation.'

'It is necessary,' answered Hilda, looking at the trees.

'In the first place, you must remember what we were saying, or rather what you were saying a little while ago. You wanted an explanation of the nature of love. Now that made me think that you had never felt what I feel—'

'I have not had your experience,' observed Hilda.

'But I have not had any experience either!' exclaimed Greif, suddenly breaking down in his dissertation.

'Then how do you know that I am so different from other women?' was the inexorable retort.

'I have seen other women, and talked with them—'

'About love?'

'No—about the weather,' answered Greif, annoyed at her persistence.

'And were their views about the weather so very different from mine?' inquired the young girl, pushing him to the end of the situation.

'Perhaps.'

'You do not seem sure. I wish you would explain yourself, as you promised to do!'

'Then you must not interrupt me at every word.'

'Was I interrupting? I thought my questions might help you. Go on.'

'I only mean to say that I never heard of a woman who wanted an explanation of her feelings when she was in love. And then I wondered whether your love was like mine, and as I am very sure, I supposed that if you felt differently you could not be so sure as I. That is all. Why are you so angry?'

'You know very well why I am angry. That is only an excuse.'

'If you are going to argue in that way—' Greif shrugged his shoulders and said nothing more. Hilda seemed to be collecting her thoughts.

'You evidently doubt me,' she said at last, speaking quietly. 'It is the first time. You have tried to defend your question, and you have not succeeded. All that you can tell me is that I am different from other women with whom you have talked. I know that as well as you do, though I have never seen them. It is quite possible that the difference may come from my education, or want of education. In that case, if you are going to be ashamed of me, when I am your wife, because I know less than the girls you have seen in towns and such places—why then, go away and marry one of them. She will feel as you expect her to feel, and you will be satisfied.'

'Hilda!'

'I mean what I say. But there may be something else. The difference may be there because I have not learned the same outward manners as the city people, because I do not laugh when they would laugh, cry when they would cry, act as they would act. I do not know half the things they like, or do, or say, but from what I have read I fancy that they are not at all simple, nor straightforward in their likings and dislikes, nor in their speech either. I do not even know whether I look like them, nor whether if I went to their places they would not take me for some strange wild animal. I make my own clothes. I have heard that they spend for one bit of dress as much as my mother and I spend in a whole year upon everything. I suppose they do, for your mother must wear what people wear in towns, and her things must cost a great deal. I think I should feel uncomfortable in them, but if we are married I will wear what you please—'

'How can you say such things—'

'I am only going over the points in which I am different from other women. That is one of them. Then I believe they learn all sorts of tricks—they can play on the piano—I have never seen one, for it is the only thing you have not got at Greifenstein,—they draw and paint, they talk in more than one language, whereas I only know what little French my mother could teach me, they sing from written music—for that matter, I can sing without, which I suppose ought to be harder. But they can do all those little things, which I suppose amuse you, and of which I cannot do one.

'Perhaps those accomplishments, or tricks, change them so that they feel more than I do. But I do not believe it. If I had the chance of learning them I would do it, to please you. It would not make me love you anymore. I believe that we, who think of few people because we know few, think of them more and more lovingly. But if I took trouble to please you, it would show you how much I love you. Perhaps—perhaps that is what you really want, that I should say more, act more, make a greater show. Is that it, after all?'

Her mood had changed while she was speaking, perhaps by the enumeration of her points of inferiority. She turned her bright eyes towards Greif with a look of curiosity, as though wondering whether she had hit the mark, as indeed she had, by a pure accident.

'It cannot be that—I cannot be such a fool!' Greif exclaimed with all the resentment of a man who has been found out in his selfishness.

'I should not think any the worse of you,' said Hilda. 'It is I who have been foolish not to guess it before. How should you understand that I love you, merely because I say good morning and kiss you, and good evening and kiss you, and talk about the weather and your mother's ribbands! There must be something more. And yet I feel that if you married someone else, I should be very unhappy and should perhaps die. Why not? There would not be anything to live for. Why can I not find some way of letting you know how I love you? There must be ways of showing it—but I have thought of everything I can do for you, and it is so little, for you have everything. Only—Greif, you must not doubt that I love you because I have no way of showing it—or if you do—'

'Forgive me, Hilda—I never doubted—'

'Oh, but you did, you did,' answered Hilda with great emphasis, and in a tone which showed how deeply the words had wounded her. 'It is natural, I suppose, and then, is it not better that I should know it? It is of no use to hide such things. I should have felt it, if you had not told me.'

It was not in Hilda's nature to shed tears easily, for she had been exposed to so few emotions in her life that she had never acquired the habit of weeping. But there was something in her expression that moved Greif more than a fit of sobbing could have done. There was an evident strength in her resentment, even though it showed itself in temperate words, which indicated a greater solidity of character than the young man had given her credit for. He had not realised that a love developed by natural and slow degrees, without a shadow of opposition, could be deeper and more enduring than the spasmodic passion that springs up amidst the unstable surroundings of the world, ill nourished by an uncertain alternation of hope and fear, and prone to consume itself in the heat of its own expression. The one is about as different from the other as the slowly moving glacier of the Alps is from the gaudily decorated and artificially frozen concoction of the ice-cream vendor.

'I am very sorry I said it,' returned Greif penitently. He took her passive hand in his, hoping to make the peace as quickly as he had broken it, but she did not return the pressure of his fingers.

'So am I,' she answered thoughtfully. 'I was angry at first. I do not think I am angry any more, but I cannot forget it, because, in some way or other, it must be my fault. Forgive you? There is nothing to forgive, dear. Why should one not speak out what is in one's heart? It would be a sort of lie, if one did not. I would tell you at once, if I thought you did not love me—'

Greif smiled.

'Ah Hilda! Since we have been sitting here, you have told me you thought I might change—do you not remember? Was what I said so much worse than that?'

'Of course it was,' she answered. 'Ever so much worse.'

Thereupon Greif meditated for some moments upon the nature of woman, and to tell the truth he was not so far advanced as to have no need for such study. Finding no suitable answer to what she had said, he could think of nothing better than to press her hand gently and stroke her long straight fingers. Presently, the pressure was returned and Greif congratulated himself, with some reason, upon having discovered the only plausible argument within his reach. But his wisdom did not go so far as to keep him silent.

'I think I understand you better than I did,' he said.

Hilda did not withdraw her hand, but it became again quite passive in his, and she once more seemed deeply interested in the trees.

'Do you?' she asked indifferently after a pause.

'Perhaps I should rather say myself,' said Greif, finding that he had made a mistake. 'And that is quite another matter.'

'Yes—it is. Which do you mean?' Hilda laughed a little.

'Whichever you like best,' answered Greif, who was at his wit's end.

'Whichever I like?' she looked at him long, and then her face softened wonderfully. 'Let it be neither, dear,' she said. 'Let us not try to understand, but only love, love, love forever! Love is so much better than any discussion about it, so much sweeter than anything that you or I can say in its favour, so much more real and lasting than the meanings of words. If you could describe it, it would be like anything else, and if you tried, and could not, you might think there was no such thing at all, and that would not be true.'

'You talk better than I do, sweetheart. Where did you learn to say such things?'

'I never learned, but I think sometimes that the heart talks better than the head, because the heart feels what it is talking about, and the head only thinks it feels. Do you see? You have learnt so much, that your head will not let your heart speak in plain German.'

Greif smiled at the phrase, which indeed contained a vast amount of truth.

'If you could make the professors of philosophy understand that,' he answered, 'you would simplify my education very much.'

'I do not know what philosophy is, dear, but if there were a professor here, I would try and persuade him, if it would do you any good. I know I am right.'

'Of course you are. You always will be—you represent what Plato hankered after and never found.'

'What was that?'

'Oh! nothing—only perfection,' laughed Greif.

'Nonsense! If I am perfection, what must you be? Plato himself? I do not know much about him, but I have read that he was a good man. Perhaps you are like him.'

'The resemblance cannot be very striking, for no one has noticed it, not even the professors themselves, who ought to know.'

'Must you go back to Schwarzburg?' Hilda asked, suddenly growing serious.

'Yes, but it is the last time. It will not seem long—there is so much to be done.'

'No. It will not seem long,' answered Hilda, thinking of all that she and her mother must do before the wedding. 'But the long times are not always the sad times,' she added sorrowfully.

'I shall be here for Christmas,' said Greif. 'And in the new year we will be married, and then—we must think of what we will do.'

'We will live at Sigmundskron, as you said, shall we not?'

'Yes. But before that we will go away for a while.'

'Away? Why?'

'People always do when they are married. We will go to Italy, if you like, or anywhere else.'

'But why must we go away?' asked Hilda anxiously. 'Do you think we shall not be as happy here as anywhere else? Oh, I could not live out of the dear forest!'

'But, sweetheart, you have never seen a town, nor anything of the world. Would you not care to know what it is all like beyond the trees?'

'By and by—yes, I would like to see it all. But I would like poor old Sigmundskron to see how happy we shall be. I think the grey towers will almost seem to laugh on that day, and the big firs—they saw my great-grandfather's wedding, Greif! I would rather stay in the old place, for a little while. And, after all, you have travelled so much, that you can tell me about Italy by the fire in the long evenings, and I shall enjoy it quite as much because you will be always with me.'

'Thank you, darling,' said Greif tenderly, as he drew her cheek to his, and he said no more about the wedding trip on that afternoon.

The shadows were beginning to lengthen and the cool breeze was beginning to float down the valley, towards the heated plain far away, when Hilda and Greif rose from their seat under the shadow of the Hunger-Thurm, and strolled slowly along the

47

broad road that led into the forest beyond. Whatever feeling of unpleasantness had been roused by Greif's unlucky speech, had entirely disappeared, but the discussion had left its impress far in the depths of Hilda's heart. It had never occurred to her in her whole life before that any one, and especially Greif, could doubt the reality or the strength of her love. What had now passed between them had left her with a new aspiration of which she had not hitherto been conscious. She felt that hereafter she must find some means of making Greif understand her. When he had said that he understood her better, she had very nearly been offended again, for she saw how very far he was from knowing what was in her heart. She longed, as many have longed before, for some opportunity of sacrifice, of heroic devotion, which might show him in one moment the whole depth and breadth and loyalty of her love.

CHAPTER 4

While Hilda and Greif were talking together the three older members of the family party had established themselves in a shady arbour of the garden, close to the low parapet, whence one could look down the sheer precipice to the leaping stream and watch the dark swallows shooting through the shadow and the sunshine, or the yellow butterflies and moths fluttering from one resting-place to another, drawn irresistibly to the gleaming water, out of which their wet wings would never bear them up again to the flower-garden of the castle above.

Frau von Greifenstein had seated herself in a straw chair with her parasol, her fan and her lap-dog, a little toy terrier which was always suffering from some new and unheard-of nervous complaint, and on which the sensitive lady lavished all the care she could spare from herself. The miserable little creature shivered all summer, and lay during most of the winter half paralysed with cold in a wadded basket before the fire. It snapped with pettish impotence at every one who approached it, including its mistress, and the house was frequently convulsed because there was too much salt in its soup or too little sugar in its tea.

Greifenstein's pointers generally regarded it with silent scorn, but occasionally, when it was being petted with more than usual fondness, they would sit up before it, thrust out their long tongues and shake their intelligent heads, with a grin that reached to their ears, and which was not unlike the derisively laughing grimace of a street-boy. Greifenstein never took any notice of the little animal, but on the other hand he was exceedingly careful not to disturb it. He probably considered it as a sort of familiar spirit attached to his wife's being. Had he been an ancient Egyptian instead of a modern German, he would doubtless have performed a weekly sacrifice to it, with the same stiff but ready outward courtesy, and prompted by the same inward adherence to the principles of household peace, which so pre-eminently characterised him.

The Lady of Sigmundskron had neither parasol, nor lap-dog, nor fan. Her plain grey dress, made almost as simply as a nun's, contrasted oddly with the profusion of expensive bad taste displayed in her hostess's attire, as her serious white face and quiet noble eyes were strangely unlike Frau von Greifenstein's simpering, nervous countenance. The latter lady would certainly have been taken at first sight for the younger of the two, though she was in reality considerably older, but a closer examination showed an infinite number of minute lines, about the eyes, about the mouth, and even on her cheeks, not to mention that tell-tale wrinkle, the sign manual of advancing years, which begins just in front of the lobe of the ear and cuts its way downwards and backwards, round the angle of the jaw.

There was a disquieting air of improbability, too, about some of the colouring in her face, though it was far from apparent that she was painted. Her hair, at all events, was her own and was not dyed. And yet, though she possessed an abundance of it, such as many a girl might have envied, it remained utterly uninteresting and commonplace, for its faded straw-like colour was not attractive to the eye, and it grew so awkwardly and so straight as to put its possessor to much trouble in the arrangement of the youthful ringlets she thought so becoming to her style. These, however, she never relinquished under any circumstances whatever. Nevertheless, at a certain distance and in a favourable light, the whole effect was youngish, though one could not call it youthful, the more so as Frau von Sigmundskron who sat beside her was, at little over forty, usually taken for an old lady.

For some moments after they had all sat down, no one spoke. Then Greifenstein suddenly straightened himself, as though an idea had occurred to him, and bending stiffly forward in his seat, addressed his cousin.

'It gives us the greatest pleasure to see you once more in our circle,' he said emphatically.

Frau von Sigmundskron looked up from her fine needlework, and gracefully inclined her head.

'You are very kind,' she answered. 'You know how happy we are to be with you.'

'Ah, it is too, too delightful!' cried Frau von Greifenstein, with sudden enthusiasm, covering the toy terrier with her hand at the same time, as though anticipating some nervous movement on his part at the sound of her voice. The dog stirred uneasily and uttered a feeble little growl, turned round on her lap, bit his tail, and then settled himself to rest again. The lady watched all these movements with anxious interest, smoothing the folds of her dress at the spot on which the beast was about to lay his head.

'Ah! my beloved, my treasure!' she murmured in a strident whisper. 'Did I wake you! Dear, dear Pretzel! Do go to sleep! I call him Pretzel,' she added, looking up with a wild smile, 'because when he is curled up, with his little legs together, on his side, he is just the shape of those little twisted rolls my husband likes with his beer. It is a vulgar name, yes—but this is a vulgar age, dear cousin, you know, and we must not be behind our times!'

'Is it?' asked Frau von Sigmundskron without taking her eyes from her work.

'Oh, dreadfully so! Is it not, Hugo? I am sure I have heard you say so.'

'Without doubt, the times are changed,' replied Greifenstein.

'But I suppose that what is modern will always seem vulgar to old-fashioned people.'

'Ah, you do not call me old-fashioned, dear husband? Do you? Really, if I am old-fashioned, the times must have advanced very, very quickly! Eh? Dearest cousin, he calls us old-fashioned! You and me! *Aber nein!* How is it possible!'

A fit of spasmodic, unnatural laughter shook her from the tip of her lace parasol to the toes of her small slippers, causing such a convulsion in the lap-dog's mind that he sat up on her knees and joined his cries with hers, until he had succeeded in attracting her attention, when he was instantly caressed and kissed and petted, with expressions of the greatest anxiety for his comfort. In about thirty seconds, however, the noises suddenly ceased, Pretzel went to sleep again and his mistress sat looking at the swallows and the flitting butterflies, her weary features expressing nothing that could be connected with mirth, any more than if she had not laughed for years. The repose could not last long, but Greifenstein felt that it was refreshing.

In five and twenty years of married life, by dint of never exhibiting any annoyance at his wife's way of expressing herself, he had grown hardened against the disturbing effect of her smile and voice until he was really very little affected by either. So far as her conduct was concerned, he had never had anything to complain of, and since he had chosen her of his own free will, he considered that one part of his duty consisted in suffering her eccentricities with patience and calm. The idea that a German who called himself a gentleman should not do his duty never entered his mind. On the other hand, his imperturbable manner sometimes irritated his wife, and in justice to her it must be allowed that his conversation in her presence was often very constrained.

'The next time you come to Greifenstein,' he said, leaning forward again and speaking to his cousin, 'it will be on the occasion of a very happy event.'

'Yes,' answered Frau von Sigmundskron with her gentle smile, 'I hope so.'

'I think that if you approve, and if your daughter has no objections—'

'Objections!' cried Frau von Greifenstein, suddenly waking from her reverie and turning her face to her companion's with an engaging simper. 'As if dear, sweet, beautiful Hilda could have any objections to marrying our Greif! Objections! Ah no, dear cousin, that youthful heart is already on fire!'

The words were uttered with such an affectation of softness that Pretzel did not move, as his mistress anxiously looked to see if he were awake when she had done speaking.

'No,' replied the other lady calmly. 'She has none. But I do not think that was what my cousin Greifenstein meant.'

'I meant that the marriage might take place early in the new year, if neither you nor your daughter had any objections,' said Greifenstein.

'But they have none—she has just told you so! Oh, Hugo, how dull men are, where love is concerned! Why should they object?'

'Indeed, I cannot see any reason why they should not be married in January,' said Hilda's mother. But there was a shade of annoyance in her face, and she bit her lip a little as she bent over her work.

'Very good, then,' pursued Greifenstein, as though his wife had not spoken. 'We will say the first week in January, if it is agreeable to you.'

'It seems to me,' observed Frau von Greifenstein with a fine affectation of irony, 'that I might be consulted too.'

The Lady of Sigmundskron looked up quickly, but Greifenstein seemed to grow calmer than ever.

'Pardon me, my dear wife,' he answered, with a rather formal inclination of the head. 'If you will be as kind as to remember our conversation of last night, you will call to mind that I asked your consent to the arrangement, and that you gave it at once.'

'Ah yes!' said Frau von Greifenstein. 'It is true. I daresay we did speak of it. Ah, you see, the multiplicity of my household cares drives these things from my head!'

Thereupon her face grew vague and expressionless and she looked again at the birds and the butterflies.

'Moreover,' said Greifenstein, now addressing his wife directly, 'I am sure you will recollect that we proposed to ask our cousin to stay with us until the young people return from their wedding trip.'

'Yes—yes. I believe we did,' replied Clara very vaguely and nodding her head slowly at each word. 'Indeed we did!' she exclaimed turning quickly with one of her unexpected smiles. 'Of course! Dear, dear! What could you do, all by yourself up there among those towers? Such a solitary life, and your only daughter, too! How I pity you!'

'You are very kind. But I am not much to be pitied. Many mothers lose their children altogether when they have married them. Hilda will always be near me, and we can see each other as often as we please.'

'Your room at Greifenstein will always be ready to receive you,' said the master of the house.

'Oh always, always!' affirmed his wife with great vivacity.

The conversation languished. It was impracticable to discuss anything seriously in the presence of Frau von Greifenstein, for her inopportune interruptions rendered any connected talk impossible.

Presently Greifenstein took a newspaper from his pocket and began to read the news of the day aloud to the two ladies. He did not read well, and the sound of his mechanical voice had a drowsy effect in the warm June air, like the clacking of an old-fashioned mill, dull, regular and monotonous. Neither of his companions, however, felt inclined for sleep. His wife watched the birds with a weary look, and his cousin plied her needle upon her fine work. During many hundreds of afternoons like this Frau von Greifenstein had sat in the same place hearing the same voice, and wearing the same expression. She rarely listened, though she occasionally uttered some exclamation more or less appropriate to what she thought she had heard. She was generally asking herself whether she had done well to accept the peace and the isolation that had fallen to her lot.

Her life was certainly neither happy nor gay. She had all that money could give, but there was no one to see that she had it. Like glory, wealth gives very little satisfaction unless there is a public to witness its effects, and the pleasure we derive from them. Frau von Greifenstein had no public, and to a nature that is fond of show the privation is a great one. She could dress herself as gorgeously as she pleased, but there was no one to envy her splendour, nor even to admire it. For years she had played to an empty house. If, by any fantastic combination of events, it were possible that a fairly good actress should ever be obliged to play the same part every night for five and twenty years in an absolutely empty theatre, and if she did not go mad under the ordeal, she would perhaps turn out very like the Lady of Greifenstein.

The stage was always set; the scenery was always of the best and newest; the vacant boxes and the yawning pit were brilliantly lighted; the costumes were by the best makers; the stage manager was punctual and in his place; the curtain went up every day for the performance; but Frau von Greifenstein's theatre was silent and untenanted, not a voice broke the stillness, not a rustle of garments or a flutter of a programme in a spectator's hand made the silence less intense, not an echo of applause woke a thrill of pride or vanity in the heart of the solitary performer. And the poor actress was growing old, wasting her smiles, and her poses, and her bursts of laughter, and her sudden entries on the empty air, till by mechanical repetition they had grown so meaningless as to be almost terrifying and more than grotesque.

It was no wonder that she seemed so very silly. Incapable of finding any serious resource in her intellect, she had devoted her energies to outward things in a place where there was no one to applaud her efforts or flatter her vanity. Many women would have given it up and would have fallen into a state of listless indifference; some would have become insane. But with Frau von Greifenstein the desire to please by appearance and manner had outlasted any natural gift for pleasing which she might once have possessed, and had withstood the test of solitude and the damping atmosphere created by a total absence of appreciation. It cannot be denied that her mind dwelt with bitterness on the hardness of her situation.

More than once she had thought of changing her mode of life to plunge into a pietist course of simplicity and asceticism. But when the morning came, the emptiness of her existence made the diversion of personal adornment a necessity. There was nothing else to do. And yet she never pressed her husband to go and live in town, nor to fill the castle with visitors. She had lost all hold upon the current of events in the outer world; and as she looked at herself in her mirror, and saw better than anyone else the remorseless signature of time etched deep in the face that had once been pretty, she felt a sharp pain in her breast, and a sinking at the heart, for she knew that it was all over and that she had grown old.

There were even moments when she feared lest she were becoming ridiculous, for she had not originally been without a certain acute perception in regard to herself. But the fear of ridicule is never strong unless a comparison of ourselves with others is possible, and Frau von Greifenstein lived too much alone to suffer long any such imaginary terrors. The time when she might still have made a figure in the world had gone by, however, and she knew it, and as any desire for change which she had formerly felt had sprung from the wish to be seen, rather than from the wish to see others, she was becoming resigned to her fate. She had reached that sad period at which half the pleasure of life consists in dreaming of what one might have done twenty years ago. It is a dreary amusement, but people who are very hopeless and solitary find it better than none at all.

Greifenstein read on, without much punctuation and with no change of tone. There was an article upon the European situation, another upon tariffs, the court news, the *gazette*, the festivities projected for a certain great event. It was all the same to him.

'In view of the solemnity of the occasion, his majesty has

deigned to grant amnesty to all political—'

He stopped suddenly and coughed, running his eye along the lines that followed.

'To all what?' inquired his wife with a show of interest.

'To all political offenders concerned in the revolutionary movements of 1848 and 1849,' continued Greifenstein, who sat up very straight in his chair and tried to read more mechanically than usual, though his voice grew unaccountably husky. What followed was merely a eulogium upon the imperial clemency, and he read on rapidly without taking his eyes from the printed sheet. Frau von Sigmundskron uttered a little exclamation. She had pricked her thin white finger with her needle. The Lady of Greifenstein saw the tiny drop of blood, and immediately exhibited an amount of emotion out of all proportion with the accident.

'Oh, what have you done!' she cried, and she was pale with anxiety as she bent forward and insisted on seeing the scratch. 'But, my dear, you have wounded yourself! Your finger is bleeding! Oh, it is too dreadful! You must have some water, and I will go and get you some court-plaster —do be careful! Bind it up with your handkerchief till I come!'

She rose quickly, and Pretzel for once was forgotten, and rolled from her knees to the grass, falling upon all-fours with a pathetic little squeak. But Frau von Greifenstein picked him up and fled towards the house in search of the plaster before he could make any further protest against such rough treatment.

'My wife cannot bear the sight of blood,' observed Greifenstein, who had lowered the newspaper and was looking over his glasses at his cousin's hand.

'The wound is not dangerous,' she answered with an attempt to smile, but her eyes fixed themselves on Greifenstein's with a look of anxious inquiry.

'He will come back,' he said, in a low voice, and the colour slowly left his face.

'Do you think it possible?' asked his cousin in the same tone.

'It is certain. He is included in the amnesty. He has hoped for it these many years.'

'Even if he does—he will not come here. You will never see him.'

'No. I will not see him. But he will be in Germany. It is for Greif—' he stopped, as though he were choking with anger, but excepting by the pallor of his stern features, his face expressed nothing of what he felt.

'Greif will live here and will never see him either,' said Frau von Sigmundskron. 'Besides, he does not know—'

'He knows. Some student told him and got a sabre cut for his pains. He knows, for he told me so only yesterday.'

'That only makes it easier, then. Greif will be warned, and need never come into contact with him. Hilda would not understand, even if she were told. What can she know about revolutions and those wild times? I am sure he will never attempt to come here.'

'He shall not sleep under my roof, not if he is starving!' exclaimed Greifenstein fiercely. 'If he had not been the dog he is, he would have made an end of himself long ago.'

'Do not say that, cousin. It was better that he should live out his life in a foreign country than do such a bad thing.'

'I do not agree with you. When a man has taken Judas Iscariot for his model I think he ought to follow so eminent an example to the end.'

Frau von Sigmundskron did not wish to argue the point. Far down in her heart there existed an aristocratic and highly irreligious prejudice about such matters, and though her convictions told her that suicide was a crime, her personal sentiment of honour required that a man who had disgraced himself should put an end to his existence forthwith.

'He will write, if he means to come,' she observed, by way of changing the current of the conversation.

'It would be more like him to force himself upon me without warning,' said Greifenstein, folding the paper with his lean strong hands and drawing his thumb-nail sharply along the doubled edges. The action was unconscious, but was mechanically and neatly performed, like most things the man did. Then he opened it, spread it out and looked again at the passage that contained the news. Suddenly his expression changed.

'I do not believe he is included in the amnesty,' he said. 'He was not convicted for a political misdeed, but for a military crime involving a breach of trust. He aggravated his offence by escaping. I do not believe that he is included.'

'But will he not believe it himself?' asked Frau von Sigmund-skron.

'It will be at his peril, then.' Greifenstein's face expressed a momentary satisfaction. Again he folded the paper with the utmost care, evidently reflecting upon the situation.

'I suppose he will be sent back to the fortress,' observed his companion.

'I would almost rather he were pardoned, than that,' answered Greifenstein gloomily. 'The whole scandal would be revived—my name would appear, it would be a fresh injury to Greif. And my wife knows nothing of it. She would hear it all.'

'Does she know nothing?' asked Frau von Sigmundskron, looking curiously at her cousin.

'Not a word. She never heard his name.'

'I could not help supposing that she left us just now because she was disturbed at the news—and she has not come back.'

'She is not so diplomatic as that,' answered Greifenstein with something like a grim smile. 'She forgets things easily, and has probably been detained by some household matter.'

Frau von Sigmundskron could not help admiring the way in which Greifenstein always spoke of his wife, excusing her more noticeable eccentricities, and affecting to ignore her minor peculiarities, with a consistent dignity few men could have sustained in the society of such a woman. It was a part of his principle of life, and he never deviated from it. It had perhaps been strengthened by the necessity of teaching Greif to respect his mother and to treat her with a proper show of reverence, but the prime feeling itself was inseparable from his character, and did honour to it. Whatever he might think of his wife, no living person should ever suspect that he could have wished her to be different. He had chosen her and he must abide by his choice.

But his cousin was a very keen-sighted person and understood him better than he guessed, admiring his forbearance and giving him full credit for his constancy. She had her own opinions concerning his wife, and did not like her; nor was she quite free from a disturbing apprehension lest at some future time Greif might develop some of his mother's undesirable peculiarities.

At present, indeed, there seemed to be nothing which could justify such fears; but she found it hard to believe that the young man had inherited nothing whatever from his mother. She could remember the time when Frau von Greifenstein had been younger and fresher, when her hair had been less dull and colourless, and when her complexion had possessed something of that radiance which was so especially noticeable in her son. And yet Hilda's mother felt instinctively that she could never dislike Greif, even if he became vain and foolish, which did not seem very probable.

For some minutes neither of the cousins spoke, and Frau von Sigmundskron sat doing nothing, which was altogether contrary to her nature, her work lying upon her knees and her hands joined one upon the other. As for Greifenstein, he had at last folded the paper to his satisfaction and had returned it to his pocket. Presently the sound of his wife's footsteps was heard upon the gravel path. She seemed less excited than when she had left her seat.

'I have kept you waiting,' she said, as she came up. 'I could not find what I wanted, and when I did that dreadful Pretzel was swallowing a pair of scissors and nearly had a fit, so that I had to give him a hot bath to calm him. He is such a care! You have no idea—but here it is, if it is not too late. I am so dreadfully sorry! I thought I should have died! Do let me put it upon your finger.'

The scratch had entirely disappeared, but Frau von Sigmundskron did not wish to appear ungracious, or ungrateful, and held out her hand without any remark. It would have seemed un-charitable to make Clara's errand look wholly superfluous be-fore Greifenstein. But he paid very little attention to what was passing, for he was preoccupied with his own thoughts, and be-fore long he rose, excused himself for going away by saying that he had some pressing correspondence, and left the two ladies to their own devices.

Frau von Sigmundskron felt rather uncomfortable, as she al-ways did when she was alone with her hostess. Today she had an unpleasant consciousness that she was in the way, and that, if she were not present, Clara would have already disappeared, in order to be alone. She resolved to make the interview as short as possible.

'The weather is very warm,' she remarked, as a preparatory move towards going into the house.

'Is it?' asked her companion as though she had been told something very unusual.

'It seems so to me,' responded the baroness, rather surprised that the fact should be questioned. 'But then, it always seems warmer here after Sigmundskron.'

'Yes—yes, perhaps so. I daresay it is. How very good of his majesty— is it not?'

'To grant an amnesty?'

'Yes, to forgive those dreadful creatures who did so much harm. I am sure I would not have done it—would you? But you are so good—did you ever know any of them?'

'Oh no, never. I was—' She was going to say that she had been too young, but she was stopped by a feeling of considera-tion for Clara. 'I was never in the way of seeing them,' she said, completing the sentence.

'As for me,' said Clara, 'I was a mere child, quite a little thing you know.' An engaging smile—poor woman, it was more than half mechanical and unconscious—emphasised this assertion of her youth.

Frau von Sigmundskron, in whom enforced economy had developed an unusual facility for mental arithmetic, could not refrain from making a quick calculation. Forty-eight from eighty-eight, forty—a young thing, perhaps ten—ten and forty, fifty. Clara was virtually admitting that she was fifty, and if she owned to that, she must be nearer sixty. In other words, she must have been well over thirty when she had married Greifenstein. She was certainly wonderfully well preserved. And yet Greifenstein had more than once told his cousin that he had married his wife when she was a widow five and twenty years of age. This was the first occasion upon which Clara had ever let fall a word which could serve as a starting-point in the calculation, and though the baroness was the best and kindest of mortals she would not have been a woman if she had failed to notice the statement, or to draw from it such conclusions as it offered to her ingenuity.

'The people who profit by the pardon will be old men,' she remarked.

'Old?' repeated Clara with a scarcely perceptible start. 'Not so very. They may be less than sixty—a man of sixty is still young at that age. I wonder whether any of them will profit by the permission to return. What do you think, Therese?'

The question was asked with every show of interest, and the baroness raised her quiet eyes from her work. She and Clara very rarely called each other by their first names. They generally avoided the difficulty by a plentiful use of the convenient designation of cousin. Frau von Greifenstein evidently meant to be more than usually confidential, and her companion wondered what was coming, and began to feel nervous.

'Really,' she answered, 'I do not know. I suppose that a man who has been expelled from his country and exiled for many years, would naturally take the first opportunity of returning. I should think it probable. On the other hand—' she stopped a moment, to smooth a stitch in her work.

'On the other hand?' repeated Clara anxiously.

'Well, I was going to say that in forty years, a man might learn to love an adopted country as well as his own, and might prefer to stay there. It would depend upon the man, upon his character, his tastes, perhaps upon whether he had gone into the revolution out of mistaken patriotism, or out of personal ambition.'

'Do you think so? Why?' Frau von Greifenstein seemed deeply interested.

'Because I fancy that a patriot would come back at any rate. His love of his country would be the strongest element in his nature. An ambitious man would either have found a field for his ambition elsewhere in forty years, or the passion would have died a natural death by that time.'

'Ah yes! There is truth in that! But what a dreadfully extraordinary position!' she exclaimed, with one of her unexpected bursts of laughter. 'What a novel! Do you not see it! Oh, if I were only a novelist, what a plot I could make out of that! Dearest cousin, is it not time to have coffee?'

CHAPTER 5

From that day the life at Greifenstein became even more drearily monotonous than it had been before, for all the party excepting Greif and Hilda. To any one not accustomed to the atmosphere the existence would have been unbearable, but humanity can grow used to anything by degrees. A stranger finding himself unexpectedly at the castle would have felt that the sweet air of the forest was poisoned at that one point by some subtle and undefinable element, that appealed to none of the senses in particular, but oppressed them all alike. The sensation was not like that caused by a vague anxiety, or by the shadow of a coming event creeping mysteriously onward, a mere uneasiness as to the result which must soon be apparent, but of which it is not possible to say whether it will be good or bad.

It was worse than that, for if there were to be any result at all, it must be very bad indeed. Greifenstein himself felt as he supposed a criminal might feel who was hourly expecting discovery. If his half-brother returned, the suffering caused by his presence in the country would be almost as great as the shame of having committed his crime could have been. Frau von Sigmundskron was more indifferent, for she had never known the man, and her knowledge of what he had done was less accurate than Greifenstein's. But she was nevertheless very uncomfortable when she thought of his appearance.

It had been judged best to acquaint Greif with the proclamation of the amnesty, in order that he might be prepared for any contingency, but the news made very little impression upon him, for he had learned the existence of his disgraced relative so recently that he had from the first feared his return, and had thought of what he should do ever since. Moreover he had Hilda with him, and he was very young, two circumstances which greatly diminished his anxiety about the future. He was very glad, however, that his academical career was so near its end, for he reflected that it would be tiresome to be constantly fighting duels about his uncle. For the present, he had abandoned the idea of taking active service in the army.

Greifenstein was more silent, and stiff, and severely conscientious than ever, and his daily habits grew if possible more unbendingly regular, as though he were protesting already against any unpleasant disturbance in his course of life which might be in store for him. When he was alone with his cousin, he never recurred to the subject of Rieseneck or his return, though the baroness constantly expected him to do so, and watched his inscrutable face to detect some signs of a wish to discuss the matter. For two reasons, she would not take the initiative in bringing up the topic. In the first place, as he was the person most nearly concerned, her tact told her that it was for him to decide whether he would talk of his brother or not. Secondly she was silent, because she had noticed something, and knew that he had noticed it also. Frau von Greifenstein's behaviour was slowly changing, and the change had begun from the hour in which her husband had read from the paper the paragraph relating to the amnesty.

From the first moment, Frau von Sigmundskron had suspected that Clara was affected by the news, and her first impression had very naturally been that she knew the story and had learned it from her husband. There was nothing improbable in the idea, and but for Greifenstein's words, she would have taken it for granted that this was the true state of the case. He, however, had emphatically denied that Clara was in the secret, and had evidently looked forward with pain to the moment when he should be obliged to communicate it to her. He was the most scrupulously truthful of men, and could not have had any object in concealing the point from his cousin.

And yet there was no doubt that his wife's manner had changed, and the baroness could see that Greifenstein was aware of it. Clara's vague absence of mind, which had formerly been only occasional, was increasing, while her fits of spasmodic laughter became fewer, till at last whole days passed during which her features were not disturbed by a single smile. There was indeed little to laugh at in her home, at the best, but she had laughed frequently nevertheless, because people had told her long ago that it was becoming to her style of beauty.

But she was growing daily more silent and abstracted, scarcely speaking at all, and not even pretending to be amused at anything. Greifenstein watched her for a week, and then inquired whether she were ill. She thanked him and said there was nothing the matter, but during some hours after he had asked the question she made an evident effort to return to her former manner. The effect was painful in the extreme. Her affected mirth seemed more hollow than ever, and her words more incoherent. Frau von Sigmundskron began to fear that Clara was going mad, but the latter was not equal to sustaining the effort long, and soon relapsed into her former silence. Her face grew suddenly very old. She moved more slowly. The wrinkles deepened almost visibly, and she became daily thinner. It was evident that something was preying upon her, and that the mental suffering was reacting upon her body.

Greifenstein said nothing more, and he told no one what he thought. If his cousin had not suggested to him that Clara must know the story, he would have supposed that she was ill, and would have sent for a physician. It would never have entered his mind that she could have understood all that the proclamation of the amnesty meant to him. He would have supposed it a coincidence that she should have been first affected by the malady on that particular day.

But the baroness's remark had had the effect of fixing in his mind what had immediately preceded it. He remembered how his wife had suddenly taken advantage of a most trivial excuse, to show an amount of exaggerated emotion unusual even for her. He remembered her long absence and her changed expression when she returned, her silence that evening and her increasing taciturnity ever since. The connexion between the paragraph and her conduct seemed certain, and Greifenstein set himself systematically to think out some explanation for the facts. In five and twenty years Rieseneck's name had never been mentioned in her presence. If she had ever heard of him it must have been before she had married Greifenstein.

It was possible that she might feel the disgrace involved in the man's return so keenly as to suffer physically at the thought of it; but Greifenstein's common sense told him that this was very improbable. In such a case it would have been far more natural for her to come to her husband and ask to be told the whole truth. It was easier to believe that her conduct was due to some other cause, that she had really never heard of Rieseneck's existence, and that there was some other person whose possible return, in consequence of the amnesty, she dreaded as much as Greifenstein feared the reappearance of his half-brother.

Many persons had been involved in the revolutionary move-ments of 1848 and had been obliged to leave the country in consequence. Clara's first husband had died of heart disease in Dresden in the year 1860, and consequently could not have been connected with the events of those times in any way to his discredit. She had shown Greifenstein the official notice of his death in an old gazette of the period. But it was not unlikely that in those unsettled times one of her relations might have got into trouble and been exiled or imprisoned.

At the time of her marriage however she had acknowledged no relative excepting an elderly aunt who had been present at the wedding, but who had died since, without ever paying a visit to the castle, and no other connexion of hers had ever appeared upon the scene. Greifenstein was well aware that he had hurried the marriage by every means in his power. He had been fascinated by Clara, and had been madly in love. They had met in the Bavarian highlands and had been married two months later in Munich, with very little formality.

Since that time Greifenstein had always avoided going to Dresden, on account of the painful associations the city must have for his wife, and had preferred not to visit Berlin, which had been the scene of his brother's crime and trial. The consequence was that neither of the two had ever been among people who had known them previously.

The idea that two disgraced persons might come back from exile, instead of one, was extremely disquieting to Greifenstein's peace of mind. He knew well enough what to do with Rieseneck if he appeared. He would shut the gates and let him shift for himself. But the other man would be in search of Clara. He wondered who he might be, and what their relations could have been, whether he would turn out to be a brother, an uncle, or merely some man who had loved her in former days, a mere rejected suitor.

Even should he prove to be her brother, he could not reproach her for her silence, since he found himself in exactly the same situation. That contingency, however, was remote. It was extremely unlikely that each should have a brother who had been convicted of evil deeds in the revolution, considering how short a time the disturbance had lasted. The theory that the man was a disappointed pretender to her hand was infinitely more probable. In any case, Greifenstein made up his mind that a person existed whose return Clara feared, and the prospect of whose appearance was so painful as to affect her health.

For some time he hesitated as to the course he should pursue. He was certainly free to tell her his suspicions, on condition that he told her of his own apprehensions at the same time. To get her secret without giving his in return would be unfair, according to his notions of honour, even apart from the consideration that if Rieseneck came back he would ultimately be obliged to confide in her. But, on the other hand, there was a possibility that Rieseneck might not come back, after all, and in that case, if he had told her everything, he would have submitted himself to a painful humiliation without necessity. He resolved to keep his own counsel and at the same time to ask his wife no questions.

Rieseneck was in South America, but Greifenstein had no reason for supposing that the person whose possible return so greatly disturbed Clara had betaken himself to so distant a country. He might be in Italy, in France, in England, anywhere within eight and forty hours' journey. He might therefore arrive at any moment after the proclamation.

But no stranger came, though the days became weeks, and the weeks months, until it was almost time for Greif to go back to Schwarzburg. Greifenstein began to think that the problematical personage was dead, though Clara evidently did not share his opinion, for she never regained her former manner. Under any other circumstances Greifenstein would have enjoyed the change, the absence of irrelevant interruption, the rest from her unnatural laughter, the gravity of her tired face. He was far from being satisfied, however, and his earnest mind brooded constantly over the possibilities of the unknown future. His situation was the harder to bear because he could not explain it to his son, the only human being for whom he felt a strong natural sympathy. It would have seemed like teaching the boy to suspect his mother of some evil.

Greif secretly wondered what was happening in his home. The atmosphere was unbearably oppressive, and if he had not been able to spend most of his time with Hilda he would have asked his father's permission to take his knapsack and go for a walking expedition in Switzerland, on the chance of falling in with a fellow-student. He had noticed the change in his mother from the first, and asked her daily if she were not better. Clara would not admit that she was ill, but she looked at Greif with an expression to which he was not accustomed and which made him nervous.

Hitherto he had never quite known whether she loved him or not. She had spoiled him as much as she dared when he was a child, but there had always been something in her way of indulging him which, even to the little boy, had not seemed genuine. Children rarely love those who spoil them, and never trust them. Their keen young sense detects the false note in the character, and draws its own conclusions, which are generally very just. Greif had found out when he was very young that his mother gave him everything he asked for, not because she loved him, but because she was too weak to refuse, and too indolent to care for the result. He had found her inaccurate in what she told him, and negligent in fulfilling the little promises upon which a child builds such great hopes, though she was always ready to pay damages for her forgetfulness by excessive indulgence in something else, when it was agreeable to her.

Greif had discovered that his father rarely promised him anything, but that if he did, it was something worth having, and that he was scrupulously exact in keeping his word about such matters, even at the expense of his own convenience. He consequently admired his father and was proud to imitate him; whereas he very soon learned to consider his mother as a person of inferior intelligence, who did not know enough to be accurate, and who did not respect herself enough to fulfil her promises. But for his father's influence he would probably have ended by showing what he felt. Greifenstein, however, exacted from him an unvarying reverence and courtesy towards his mother, and never, even in moments of the greatest confidence, permitted the boy to criticise the least of her actions.

To tell Greif of the suspicions which agitated his own mind was therefore contrary to Greifenstein's fixed principles, and consequently utterly impossible. In reply to his questions about his mother's health the only answer which was at once plausible and in accordance with truth was the plain statement that Clara denied being ill, but that she nevertheless appeared to be suffering from some unknown complaint. Greif was not satisfied, but his own ingenuity could discover no explanation of the facts, and he was obliged to hold his peace.

His mother's manner and her look when he spoke to her disturbed him. It was as though her uncertain and careless affection had suddenly developed into something more true and sincere. There was something wistful in the fixed gaze of her eyes, as though she feared to know what was in his heart, and yet longed for some more frank expression of his love for her than that mere reverential courtesy which he had been taught to show his mother since he was a child.

Being very young and of a very kind heart, Greif began to wonder whether he had not misunderstood her throughout many years. He possessed that kind of nature which cannot long refrain from returning any sort of affection it receives, provided that affection appears to be genuine. He gradually began to feel a responsive thrill in his heart when he saw that his mother's sad eyes watched his movements and lingered upon his face. The tone of his voice began to change when he addressed her, though he was scarcely conscious of it. His words became gentler and more sympathetic, as his thoughts of her assumed a kindlier disposition. He began to reproach himself with his former coldness, and he frankly owned to himself that he had misunderstood her.

It had always been his custom to go to his mother's *boudoir* in the morning, when he had not already left the house before she was visible. It was rather a formal affair. Greif knocked at the door and waited for her answer. Being admitted, he went to his mother and kissed her hand. She kissed his forehead in return. He asked her how she was, and she inquired what he was going to do during the day. After five minutes of conversation, he generally took leave of her with the same ceremony, and departed. He usually avoided being with her at any other time, and accident rarely brought them together in the course of the day, for Greif was always with Hilda or with his father.

Very gradually, he began to find this morning visit less irksome. He fancied that his mother would willingly have detained him a little longer, but that she felt how little he could care for her society as compared with that of Hilda. Then, too, she had grown so sad and silent as to excite in him a sort of pity. At last the feeling that was drawing them closer found expression.

Greif had made his usual visit one morning and was about to leave the room. Her sorrowful, faded eyes looked up to his, and slowly filled with tears. He felt an irresistible impulse to speak, and yielded to it.

'Mother,' he said, kneeling down beside her, and taking her hand affectionately in his, 'what is it? Why are you ill, and sad? Will you not tell me?'

She looked at him a moment longer, wonderingly, as though hardly believing what she saw. Then she broke down. The long restrained tears welled up and rolled over her thin cheeks, making lines and patches in the pink powder, at once grotesque and pitiful. The carefully curled ringlets of colourless hair contrasted strangely with the sudden havoc in her complexion. Perhaps she was conscious of it, for she tried to turn her face away, so that Greif should not see it. Then all at once, with a heartrending sob, she let her head fall forward upon his shoulder, while her nervous, wasted hands grasped his two arms convulsively.

'Oh Greif! I am a very miserable old woman!' she cried.

'What is it, mother? Oh, tell me what is the matter!' he exclaimed, not knowing what to say, but amazed at the outburst he had so little anticipated.

For some moments she could say nothing. Greif held her, and prevented her from slipping off her seat. Looking down, though he could not see her face, he could see well enough how the tears fell fast and thick upon the rough sleeve of his shooting coat and trickled down the woollen material till they rolled off at his elbow. He did not know what to do, for he had never seen her cry before, and was indeed little accustomed to woman's weeping.

'Dearest mother,' he said at last, 'I am so sorry for you! If you would only tell me—'

'Ah Greif-my son—if I thought you loved me—a little—I should be less unhappy!'

'But I do. Oh, forgive me, if I have never shown you that I do!' He was in great distress, for he was really moved, and a great wave of repentance for all his past coldness suddenly overwhelmed his conscience.

'If it were only true!' sobbed the poor lady. 'But it is all my fault— oh, Greif, Greif—my boy—promise that you will not forsake me, whatever happens to me!'

'Indeed, I promise,' answered Greif in great surprise. 'But what can happen? What is it that you fear, mother?'

'Oh, I am very foolish,' she replied with a hysterical attempt at a laugh. 'Perhaps it is nothing, after all.'

Her tears burst out afresh. Greif attempted in vain to soothe her, calling her by endearing names he had never used to her before, and feeling vaguely surprised at the expressions of affection that fell from his lips. All at once, with a passionate movement, she threw her arms round his neck and kissed him. Then, pushing him aside, she rose quickly and fled to the next room before he could regain his feet.

For some moments he stood looking at the closed door. Then his instinct told him that she would not return, and he slowly left the room, pondering deeply on what he had seen and heard.

The next time they met she made no reference to what had passed, and Greif's natural delicacy warned him not to approach the subject. Had there been such previous intimacy between the two as might be expected to exist between mother and son, an explanation could scarcely have been avoided. As it was, however, both felt that it was better to leave the matter alone. The bond between them was stronger than before, and that was enough for Clara. She experienced a sense of comfort in Greif's mere existence which somewhat lightened the intolerable burthen of her secret.

As for Greif himself, the situation appeared to him more mysterious than ever, and the air of the house more oppressive. It seemed to him that everyone was watching everyone else, and that at the same time each member of the household was concealing something from the others. He felt that it would be a relief to return to the thoughtless life of the University, even at the expense of a separation from Hilda.

Hilda had not failed to notice what was so apparent to everyone else, and had asked her mother questions concerning the evident depression that reigned in the household. But the good baroness had only answered that, whatever might be the matter, it was no concern of Hilda's nor of her own; and that when disagreeable things occurred in other people's houses it was a duty not to see them. Hilda's ideas about ill health were exceedingly vague, and she contented herself with supposing that Frau von Greifenstein was ill, and that sick persons probably always behaved as she did. At last the time came for Greif's departure.

The sense of impending evil was in some measure accountable for the unusual emotion exhibited at the parting. He had never taken leave of his mother so affectionately before, nor had he before seen the tears start into her eyes as she kissed him and said goodbye. Never before had the grip of his father's hand seemed to convey so much of sympathy, nor did he remember that his own voice had ever at other times trembled as though it were sticking in his throat.

Even Frau von Sigmundskron was a little moved and pressed his hand warmly when he kissed her, though she said nothing. Hilda was very silent, and never took her eyes from him. He had bidden her farewell before taking leave of the rest, at their old haunt by the Hunger-Thurm. There had not been many words, and there had been no tears, but it had been nevertheless the saddest parting Greif ever remembered. The day was cloudy and a soft wind was making melancholy music among the grand old trees. Their own voices had sounded discordant and out of tune, and the words that might have expressed what they felt would not be found, and perhaps were not needed.

But when the last minute was come the whole party went out together to the gate where the carriage was standing. Greif found himself with Hilda, separated for a moment from the rest. She laid her hand upon his arm and spoke in a low voice.

'Something evil is going to happen to you, Greif,' she said.

There was something in the accents that chilled him, but he tried to smile.

'I hope not, sweetheart,' he answered.

'I am sure of it,' said Hilda in a tone of conviction. 'I cannot tell why—only, remember, whatever happens—it will be something terrible—I shall always love you—always, always.'

The others came up, and her voice sank to a whisper as she repeated the last word. Greif looked anxiously into her face, and saw that she was pale, and that her flashing blue eyes were veiled and dim. He was startled, for he had never seen such a change in her before. But there was no time for words. He whispered a loving answer, but she seemed not to hear his words as she stood against the huge rough masonry of the gate, gazing down the drive in the direction of the Hunger-Thurm. As he was driven rapidly away, he looked back and waved his hat. The others had stepped forward upon the pavement on one side of the gate, but Hilda had not moved. Then as the turn of the road was about to hide the castle from view, he saw her cover her face with both her hands and turn back into the shadow of the deep gateway.

Greif settled himself in his comfortable seat, wondering what it all meant. It was very strange that Hilda should have so suddenly and so forcibly expressed the same idea that had agitated his mother a few days earlier. It was impossible that they could have talked together, or that they could be thinking of the same thing. There was no sympathy between them, and besides, if Hilda had learned anything from Frau von Greifenstein which Greif did not know, she would certainly have told him of it, especially as this impending catastrophe threatened him as well as his mother. He was too firmly opposed to all sorts of superstition to believe that Hilda had received any supernatural warning of an event about to occur.

But for the conversation that had taken place with his mother, he would unhesitatingly have told himself that Hilda was yielding to a foolish presentiment raised by the sorrow of parting. Persons in love are very apt to fancy each separation the last, and to imagine some dreadful disaster to be in store for the object of their affections. He flattered himself that his own common sense was too strong to be shaken by such absurdities, but he owned that the sensation was a natural one. Without giving way to presentiments he nevertheless always felt that something might happen to Hilda before his return, and it was not strange that she should feel the same anxiety in regard to him. The impulsive expression she had given to her fear was not in itself surprising, and if she had turned pale for the first time in her life, it was perhaps because her heart was really waking to something stronger than that even, emotionless affection she had hitherto bestowed upon him.

There was a similarity, however, between his mother's words and Hilda's, which was not so easily explained, and the coincidence was oddly in harmony with the oppressive constraint that had reigned at Greifenstein during the vacation. Greif could not help thinking very seriously of it all, as he drove rapidly through the forest to the railway station; so seriously indeed, that he at last shook himself with a movement of impatience, said to himself that he was growing superstitious as a girl, and lit a cigar with the strong determination not to give way to such nonsense.

Smoking did not help him, nor the prospect of meeting a fellow-student or two in the course of the afternoon. He tried to think of the life that was before him at the University, of the serious work he must do, of the opening festival of all the united Korps at the beginning of the term, of his own responsibilities as the head of the association to which he belonged, of the pleasant hours he would spend in discussing with youthful shallowness the deepest subjects that can occupy the human mind, deciding, between a draft of brown ale and a whiff of tobacco, that Schopenhauer was right in one point, and that Kant was wrong in another. But, for the present, at least, none of those things could by mere anticipation distract his thoughts from the matter which occupied them.

All through the long drive, Hilda's face was before him and her voice was in his ear, repeating her strange warning. She had said that she should always love him. His mother had implored him not to forsake her in her trouble, whatever it might be. At the same time, his father was in the greatest anxiety concerning Rieseneck's movements. Could there be any connexion between that affair and the conduct of the two women? Again his common sense rose up with an energetic protest, and displayed to him all the absurdity of the hypothesis. Could Rieseneck's possible return affect his mother more than his father? Could that doubtful event suffice to rouse Hilda's fears to such a pitch?

If the man came back, he would come as a suppliant, entreating to be received once, at least, on tolerance. He would come as a penitent prodigal might, to get a word of compassion from his brother, perhaps to borrow money. He could do no harm to any one, beyond the moral shame he brought upon his relatives by prolonging his wretched existence. He was certainly not a particularly dangerous person to Greif himself, and Hilda's warning had been essentially personal, having no reference to anyone else. He could not understand it, and grew impatient again, realising how deeply he had been impressed.

The forest looked unusually gloomy, and added by its melancholy solemnity to the depression of his spirits. He was glad when he saw through the trees the smart wooden railway station with its coloured signals, its metal roof, and its air of animation. He could not help thinking that the effect was something like that once produced upon him when he had come back to the University town from the funeral of an eminent person whom he had never seen. He had been obliged to attend the burial with the whole body of the students, and had stood more than an hour in the churchyard before he could get away.

He remembered how unusually bright and lively the town had appeared to him by contrast when he returned. Even the thought of Hilda could not now make the recollection of his home a pleasant one, for Hilda herself was intimately connected, by her last words, with the whole impression of funereal gloominess from which the busy railway station furnished him with the means of escape.

CHAPTER 6

The system of student life in Germany with its duelling, its associations into Korps, its festivals, and its rabid tenacity to tradition, has frequently been pronounced ridiculous by European and American writers, though it does not appear that those who laugh at it have entered into Korps life themselves, even when they have resided during a considerable time at a German University. There is, however, much to be said in favour of its existence in the only country where it has taken root as a permanent institution; and since it is necessary to follow Greif's history from the time when he was still a student, some explanation of a matter generally little understood may not be out of place at this point.

Everyone knows that a German University has no resemblance, even in principle, with what English-speaking people generally understand by the word University. The students do not live in communities, nor in any set of buildings appropriated for their dwelling. The University, so far as its habitation is concerned, means only the lecture-rooms. Instructors and pupils live where they please and as they please, according to their individual fortune or pleasure. The students are differently situated from other members of society in one respect. They are not amenable to the police for any ordinary offence, but in such cases are brought before the University authorities, and are liable to be confined in the University prison, attending the lectures belonging to their course, during the period of their detention, for which purpose they are let out and shut up again at stated hours. This corresponds to some extent with the English system of 'gating.'

A very large body of young men, of various ages, find themselves almost entirely their own masters, at an age when the English undergraduate is bound to be at home at twelve o'clock, to attend chapel and hall dinners, besides fulfilling the obligations imposed by a regular course of study. They live in lodgings, free of any supervision whatever, they eat where and when they please, if they do not choose to hear lectures there is no one to oblige them to do so, for they are supposed to possess enough common sense to know that the loss is theirs if they fail at their examinations. It is natural that under these circumstances they should form associations among themselves. In every University there will be a certain number of students from each of the country's principal provinces.

Fellow-countrymen will generally be drawn together when they are forced to live under similar conditions in one place. To this instinct may be traced the origin of Korps, and, generally, of all associations that wear colours, except the so-called Teutonia, which is probably the oldest of all, and which was originally a political institution having for its object the promotion of liberal ideas together with the unity of Germany. There are Korps of the same name, but the two are always quite distinct and their colours are generally different.

There are three classes of associations. The Burschenschaften, or fellowships, the Landsmannschaften, or fellow-countrymen's unions, and the Korps. The latter word is French, and was formerly spelt 'Corps'; as no better word could be found, or introduced, the German initial letter is used to distinguish the meaning when used in this sense. Besides these three classes of acknowledged associations, all wearing colours, and recognised by the University, there are usually a number of subordinate ones, termed contemptuously '*Blasen,*' which may be translated 'bubbles,' a designation given on account of their supposed instability.

Although admission to these unions is generally, and probably always, obtained by ballot, they are not clubs in any ordinary sense of the word. Each has a habitation or lodge, called a Kneipe, or drinking-hall, and a fencing-room, or a share in the use of one, but there is no set of apartments corresponding to a club, nor intended for the same manifold purposes. The organisation and object of the union require no such conveniences.

The Korps rank highest in estimation and are generally the most exclusive. In a country where caste prejudice has attained to such gigantic proportions as it has in Germany, its effects are felt very early in life; and in Universities where every advantage of education is placed within easy reach of the very poorest, a course of lectures for a term often costing but one pound sterling, it is impossible that there should not be circles formed, in a regular scale, by young men whose fortunes are more or less alike. Upon these social and financial distinctions the Korps have grown to be what they are.

Every Korps has three orders of members, and three regular officers, to each of whom, is assigned one department in the management of the associations. The orders consist of two regular and one irregular. The lowest and least important, is considered irregular, and those who are not admitted further have no claim to anything but a place in the drinking-hall, and the protection of the regular Korps. They may be men of any age, but are generally students who are prevented from fighting by some physical defect, or by the serious objection of their parents, without whose consent no one is supposed to be admitted to the full fellowship of the union.

The second order consists of novices, who are designated by the name of 'foxes.' The appellation is probably derived from the custom of playing a kind of game, at the opening of the term, which is called the fox-hunt, and in which the novices, riding astride of chairs, are made to run the gauntlet through the 'fellows' who are armed with blackened corks, and who, without moving from their places, attempt to smudge the faces of the youngsters as they hop past. These 'foxes' are young students who have just joined, and who are not admitted to the rank of fellows until they have fought a certain number of times. They are raised to the higher dignity after a ballot, at which they are not present, and the term of probation generally lasts six months, or one term.

The fellows, or Burschen, are full-fledged Korps students, eligible to become officers. The officers are three, and are called respectively the first, second and third, 'in charge.' The first is the chief, who presides at formal meetings and in the drinking-hall, where the Korps assembles officially on two evenings of the week. He also represents the Korps at the weekly meetings of all the representatives. The second in charge manages all affairs relative to fighting, and is personally responsible to the association for all formalities relating to the duels of its members.

If any fellow, or novice, has challenged, or been challenged by, anyone else, he must immediately report the affair to the second in charge, who arranges the meeting for him, and warns him, at least twelve hours beforehand, of the time appointed. The third in charge is secretary and treasurer; he keeps the minutes of all meetings, collects the dues from the members, pays the bills, and is responsible for the financial department and correspondence.

In well-conducted Korps, and there are many such, the president considers himself morally bound to see that all the members attend their lectures regularly. That the associations are not generally mere idle, riotous bands of students, is sufficiently shown by the fact that almost every prominent man in German public life has belonged to one of them, from the great chancellor downwards. Generally speaking, too, each novice is considered to be personally under the charge of one of the fellows, whose duty it is to keep him out of trouble and to see that he is not idle. It will be seen that the system of organisation is good, and that in reality it has a strong military element, like most organisations which find favour in Germany.

But if it is military it is also militant, and it is the fact that fighting is one of its chief objects, which has caused it to be so much abused by foreigners. It is necessary in the first place to understand the conditions of the sanguinary battles between the Korps, and the points by which they are distinguished from the more serious affairs which are occasionally settled by appeal to arms.

The ordinary student's duel is not a dangerous affair, though it is often far more serious than is commonly supposed. The weapon used is a long, light rapier, square at the point, two-edged and sharpened like a razor down the whole length of the front, and to about nine inches from the point at the back. The hilt is a roomy basket of iron, though in some Universities a bell-hilted sword is used, and in that case the guard is similar to the first position in sabre fencing or single stick. The blade is very pliable and not highly tempered, so that in unskilful hands it is apt to bend and become useless.

The law requires that the combatants should both wear an iron protection over the eyes, lest the loss of sight should render the student useless for military service. To protect life also, a heavy silk scarf bandage is placed round the throat, completely protecting the jugular vein and the carotid artery. The right arm, which in this peculiar fencing is used to parry the cut in tierce, is also protected by bandages, and the body is covered by a leathern cuirass, heavily padded, from the middle of the breast to the knees. It will be seen that the whole head, excepting the eyes, is exposed, as well as the chest and shoulders. Thrusting is forbidden as well as the cut in second, below guard, but the latter is permitted when either of the combatants is left-handed, owing to the difference of the position.

Novices' duels consist generally of fifteen rounds, the first being merely a formal salute. The fellows fight during fifteen minutes, unless one of them is severely wounded before the end of the time. An umpire has a stop-watch in his hand, and only the exact time of actual fencing is reckoned, which is rather a delicate and troublesome matter. Speaking is not allowed. If both combatants are good fencers and cautious it sometimes happens that neither is touched, but as many as thirty slight wounds are occasionally inflicted on both sides. A surgeon is always present and decides when a wound is too severe to allow of further fighting. This usually occurs when a large artery is cut, or a splinter raised upon a bone.

Meetings are generally arranged for novices, as soon as they have learned to handle the rapier, whether they have had any quarrel or not, and such encounters rarely lead to any result worth mentioning. The intention is to accustom the student to fighting for its own sake, and he must submit to the conditions or leave the Korps with ignominy. He learns to fence with coolness and judgment, in a way that could never be learned on the fencing ground with masks and blunted weapons, and he acquires from the first the habit of facing an armed man with little but his own blade to protect him.

It must be remembered that duelling is a social institution in Germany. It is not necessary here to enter into a discussion of the merits of the system; it is enough to recall the late Emperor's speech in regard to it, in which he declared that he would punish any officer who fought a duel, but would dismiss from the army anyone who refused to do so. The first clause of this apparent paradox restrains the practice from becoming an abuse or a general evil; the second imposes it as a necessity in serious cases.

The penalty consists in a longer or shorter period of arrest, fixed within certain limits, and in case of the death of one of the combatants the survivor is confined in a fortress for three years, provided that the duel has taken place with the consent of the superior officers of the regiment sitting officially as a council of honour, and that the encounter has been conducted in accordance with the requirements of the law. Any informality is most severely visited. The regimental council takes charge of the officer's reputation, and if it declares that there need be no meeting, honour is satisfied. In private life any individual may appeal to the decision of a court of honour chosen by himself and his adversary, and such decisions are considered final. But if any person refuses either to fight or to appeal to such arbitration, he is mercilessly excluded from all polite society wherever the facts are known.

The customs of the country being of this nature, the existence of fighting associations among students can be both explained and defended. That some other nations consider the practice of duelling as altogether barbarous and antiquated, has nothing to do with the case in hand. An individual cannot change the conditions of the society in which he is obliged to live, and must either conform to them or be excluded from intercourse with his fellows. To learn to fight is, in Germany, as necessary as learning to eat decently is in England, and the schools of fighting are the Korps and other University unions.

As a direct consequence, they are also schools of life, and in some degree of etiquette. A man learns there exactly what sort of language is courteous, what words may be spoken without giving offence, and in what an insult really consists. By this means a vast amount of trouble is saved for society, and a uniform standard of behaviour is secured which is universally respected and adhered to by all who call themselves gentlemen. The council of the Korps represents the council of the regiment, or the social court of honour appealed to by civilians. The conversation of the members with each other, though familiar in the extreme, is regulated by rigid rules.

The slightest approach to discourtesy between members of the same Korps must be followed by an instant apology, the refusal of which entails the immediate ejection of the offender with ignominy, and what is more, the announcement of the fact by circular letter within the month to every Korps student in every one of the numerous Universities of the empire. A dishonourable action of any kind is visited in the same way. The publicity of such a scandal is enormous. Seven or eight thousand young men are simultaneously informed that one of their number is disgraced, and at the end of the year all those older men who have been Korps students in their youth, are also informed of the fact. This amounts to warning some thirty or forty thousand gentlemen, chiefly in the higher ranks of society, against an individual, who, in one circumstance or another, is almost certain to be brought into contact with some of them. Such an institution cannot be laughed at, and its censure is no joke.

But even a Korps student's life is not made up merely of fighting and study. There is a very jovial side to it, and if its jollity is sometimes made the subject of reproach this is due to the fact that the few thoroughly lazy students are of necessity the very ones who are most seen. It cannot be denied that beer plays a considerable part in the life of German students. It is also an important element in the existence of the nation. German beer, however, is not English ale, any more than it is to be confounded with the nauseous concoctions sold under its name in other countries.

German beer is protected by law, and unoppressed by taxation. To adulterate it is a crime, an attempt to tax it would bring about a convulsion of the empire. Its use, in quantities that amaze the understanding, does not appear to have made Germans cowards in war, nor laggards in commerce; still less does it seem to have stupefied the national intellect, or dulled the Teutonic keenness in the race of nations. The first military power in the world drinks as much beer as all the rest of the universe together, and probably a little more. The commercial nation that undersells Englishmen in England, Frenchmen in France, Italians in Italy and Turks in Turkey, consumes more malt liquor than they drink of all other liquors.

The intellectual race that has produced Kant, Goethe and Helmholtz, Bismarck, Moltke, Mommsen, and Richard Wagner in a century, swallows Homeric draughts of beer at breakfast, dinner and supper. That other nations do not follow their example, and laugh at their potations is of little consequence. Even if the Germans do not to some extent owe their national characteristics to their national drink, it cannot be asserted with any show of reason that beer has swamped their intelligence, damped their military ardour or drowned their commercial genius. Beer is the natural irrigator of conservative principles and intellectual progress. A little of it is good, much is better, and too much of it can never produce delirium tremens. Can more be said of any potable concoction manufactured by humanity for its daily use?

The Korps student drinks beer, therefore, and as though he felt a sort of religious reverence for the drink of his fathers, he has invented laws and rules for the ceremony, from which no departure is allowable. Every meeting of the Korps begins and ends with a 'Salamander.' At the president's word the glasses or stone jugs are moved rhythmically upon the oaken board. Another word of command, and each student empties his beaker. Then the vessels are rattled on the table, while he slowly counts three, with the precision of a military drum, then struck sharply again three times, so that they touch the table all together, and the meeting is opened or closed, as the case may be.

The same ceremony is performed when the health of any one is drunk by the whole Korps. The principle is that on peaceful occasions the drinking-cup takes the place of the rapier, and is used for saluting and for combat, as the sword is used in the duel. To give as much as is received is the object of both. As much as one student drinks to another's health, so much must the others drink in return. If two fall out in a discussion, the one may challenge the other to a beer duel. The weapons are full glasses, there is an umpire who gives the word, and he who empties his glass the first is the conqueror. The president can order any one to drink a certain quantity *pro poena*, as a penalty for breaking a known rule, and the fellows have the same privilege in regard to the novices.

There is another element, and a very important one, in the conduct of the jovial meetings. Singing is a traditional and indispensable business at every regular *Kneipe*. Every student has a standard song-book at his place, containing both the words and music. As singing at sight is taught in every common school throughout the country, the result is not so cacophonous as might be expected. The voices are young, fresh and manly, the tunes full of life and of an easy nature, the verses simple and often grand, for they are selected from the writings of celebrated poets. The spirit of the poetry is generally patriotic or fraternal, always essentially national.

The whole effect is fine and elevating, and those who have sat as young men at the table of a numerous Korps do not easily forget the sensations evoked by the strains in which they have joined. Song holds a large place in German life, and an essentially good one. As a means of strengthening popular patriotism no one has ever denied its efficacy, and as a mere pastime it is probably the most pacific and harmless that could be named. It may even be believed that the capacity and willingness among young men to amuse themselves with chorus singing indicates to some extent a national love of law and order. Italians are solo-ists, in music and in principles. Germans are born chorus singers, and their great men do not sing themselves, but conduct the singing of others.

The University of which Greif was a student, and which shall be called for convenience Schwarzburg, was one of the old-est in the country. The town in which it was situated possessed in a high degree the associations and the architectural features which throw a mediaeval shadow over many northern cities, causing even the encroaching paint-brush of modern progress to move in old-fashioned lines of subdued colour. In northern lands antiquity is not associated with the presence of dirt, as it is in the south. Nuremberg does not look modern because its streets are clean and there are no beggars, nor does the ancient seat of the Teutonic Knights at Marienburg look like a hotel because its lofty corridors and graceful halls, with their cross vaults springing from central columns, are carefully swept and free from dust.

It would be interesting to examine the causes which produce this odd artistic phenomenon. In Italy the process of cleans-ing is destroying altogether the associations of antiquity and the artistic beauty which once charmed the traveller. Heidelberg, Nuremberg, and most places in Germany seem to have gained rather than lost in outward appearance by the advance of civi-lisation. Possibly, the Germans of today resemble their ancestors of the fourteenth century more closely than a modern Floren-tine resembles Lorenzo De' Medici. Possibly, in Germany such restorations as are necessary are executed with a keener percep-tion of beauty in the model. Possibly, too, German conservatism, Gothic, thoughtful, stern, expresses itself in all it does; even as the Italian's queer love of change and fetish worship of what, in other lands, was called progress thirty years ago, shows itself in all his visible works.

Architecture exhibits a nation's feeling far more exactly than literature or any other branch of art or science. People may, or may not, read the books that fill the market, and nobody cares whether they do or not except the author and the publisher. But people must live in houses of some sort, and, if they are rich enough to choose, they will not live in houses they do not like, nor worship in temples of which the architecture irritates their nerves. Now architects are placed in the same position towards the house builders of the nation, in which authors stand towards the reading public. If people are conservative, and like old-fashioned buildings, the architect must satisfy his customer's love of tradition, just as the professional writer must write what is wanted, or starve. The difference in the result is that houses last some time whereas books do not.

Greif was deeply attached to the University town. He had spent many happy hours within its walls, and had passed through many exciting moments of his young life amidst its high, narrow streets and ancient buildings. Such a place naturally exercised a greater influence over him than over most men of his age. Born and bred in the heart of the Black Forest, brought up in the house that had sheltered his race for centuries, he would have felt uneasy and out of his element if he had been all at once transported to a modern capital. But in Schwarzburg he felt that he was at home. The huge cathedral with its spires and arches and rich fretwork of dark stone, seemed to him the model of what all cathedrals should be.

The swift river that ran between overhanging buildings, and beneath old bridges that were carved with armorial bearings and decorated with the rare ironwork of cunning smiths, famous long ago, bore in its breast the legends of his own forest home, and was impersonated in many a verse he had learned to sing with his comrades. The shady nooks and corners, the turns in the crooked streets, the dark archways of old inns, the swinging signs with their rich deep colour and Gothic characters, the projecting balconies, glazed with round bull's eyes of blown glass set in heavy lead, the marvellously wrought weathercocks of iron and gold on the corners of the houses, every outward detail of the time-honoured and time-mellowed town spoke to his heart in accents he not only understood but loved.

Even the modern note did not jar upon him. There were few officers in the streets, few soldiers in bright uniforms. Occasionally a troop of white *cuirassiers* rode slowly through the main thoroughfare, looking more like mediaeval knights than Prussian soldiers. Their enormous stature, their bronzed faces, their snow-white dress and gleaming corslets, the stately, solemn tramp of their great horses, their straight broad blades without curve or bend erect at their sides, all made them utterly unlike the ordinary soldiery of present times, and rendered their appearance perfectly harmonious with their surroundings. Even the students in their long boots and coloured caps did not look modern, as they strolled along in knots of three and four from the University to the mess at dinner-time, or thronged the pavements of the high street towards evening, when the purple light was on the cathedral spires and the shadows were deepening below.

Greif loved it all, and to some extent his affection was returned. He was certainly the most popular student who had ever trod the stones of Schwarzburg, as he was by nature one of the most thoroughly German. He had his quarrels, no doubt, but the way he settled them only served to increase his reputation. He was pointed out as the man of forty duels, who had never received a serious wound, and it was said to his credit that he never wantonly provoked any man, and that his victories had been chiefly gained over adversaries from neighbouring Universities. He was looked upon as the natural representative of Schwarzburg in all great affairs, and when he presided, in the turn of his Korps, over one of the periodical festivities, his appearance was the occasion for a general ovation.

The feeling that he was to be warmly welcomed was pleasant to Greif as he got out upon the platform and shook hands with a dozen who awaited him, but the remembrance that this was probably his last return as a student among his comrades gave him a passing sensation of sadness. He was approaching the end of a very happy period in his life, and though there was much happiness in the future, he was young enough to regret what he must leave so soon. Few men know what it is to be the central figure at a great University, and those who have been so fortunate know well enough how painful is the leave-taking and how hard the last goodbye to the scene of their triumphs. That moment had not yet come for Greif, but he could not help seeing how very near it was.

The students led him home to his lodgings over the river, and installed themselves as they could, all smoking and talking at once, while he opened his boxes and disposed some of his belongings in their places. They told him all the news, with the vivacity of men who have twenty-four hours the start of a friend. The Rhine Korps had increased its numbers considerably and seemed already inclined to show its teeth to the Westphalia Korps. The Saxon Korps had lost one of their best fighters, who had suddenly gone to another University. Hardly any of the Prussian Korps had arrived, and it was doubtful whether they could renew the lease of their old drinking-hall.

They themselves—their yellow caps showed that they were Swabians—were already on the look-out for new 'foxes' to enlist, and believed that they had secured a couple of excellent novices. The fencing-master of the Prussians had declared his intention of fighting a pitched battle—sabres and no bandages—with the fencing-master of the Rhiners. It was to be hoped that neither would be badly hurt, as they were both good teachers and worth their salaries. There was a new waiting-girl at the Stamm-Kneipe where they dined, and of course all the foxes would fall in love. They, the fellows, would of course not think of such a thing. It would be quite beneath their dignity.

As for the professors, all those who were not favourites grew older and older and duller and duller. One of the oldest and dullest had been married in the summer to a girl of eighteen, a crying shame which ought to be visited by some demonstration. Why should a professor marry? Was not Heine right, and were not some kinds of professors cumberers of the earth, as Achilles called himself when Patroclus had been killed? Horrible creatures all those whom the Swabians disliked! The professor of

Roman law looked more like a disappointed hyena than ever, and as for his colleague, the professor of Greek philosophy, he had begun by looking like Socrates, when he was born, and time had done its work with its usual efficacy. Would not Greif be ready soon? It was supper-time.

Greif was thinking of the vanity of human sentiment. A few hours earlier he had been oppressed by one of the most melancholy moods that had ever afflicted him. Now, as he stood still for a moment, looking through the open window at the stars as they began to shine out above the cathedral spire across the river, he felt as though ten years had passed since he had driven down through the forest. Only the image of Hilda remained, and seemed to drown in light the gloomy forebodings that had so much distressed him. As for Hilda's own warning, it had been nothing but the result of her sorrow at parting. And since parting there must be, he would enjoy to the full what was left of this happy student life, with its changing hours of study and feasting, of poetry, and fighting, and song that almost mingled with the clash of steel.

'Are you ready?' asked the students in chorus.

Greif set his yellow cap upon his close-cut golden hair.

'Yes—come on! *Vivat, floreat, crescat Suabia!* The last semester shall be a merry one!'

And away they went, crowding down the narrow staircase, laughing, jesting, and humming snatches of tunes as they burst out into the quiet shadowy street below.

CHAPTER 7

Greif was not able to throw off the memories of his vacation so easily as he had at first imagined. The busy week that followed his return to Schwarzburg furnished enough excitement to divert his thoughts for a time into a more cheerful channel, and he was further reassured by the fact that his father's letter contained nothing that could alarm him. Everything was going on at Greifenstein as usual. Hilda and her mother had returned to Sigmundskron. The shooting was particularly good. A postscript informed Greif that nothing had been heard from a certain person, who was not named.

The young man thought his father's handwriting was growing larger and more angular than ever, and that instead of becoming less steady with advancing years, the letters looked as though they were cut into the paper with the point of a sharp knife. Some days passed quickly by, and he began to think that he had disturbed himself foolishly, and had suffered his judgment to be unbalanced by the impulsive speeches of Hilda and of his own mother. Then, all at once, as he sat one morning at his accustomed place in one of the lecture-rooms, noting in a blank book the wisdom that fell from the lips of a shrivelled professor, his thoughts wandered and the vision of Hilda rose before his eyes, with the expression she had worn when she had spoken of that terrible catastrophe which was in store for him.

He could not imagine why he should have thought of the matter so suddenly, nor why it seemed so much more important than before. It required a strong effort to concentrate his mind once more upon what he was doing, and when he succeeded, he was aware that the point of the professor's argument had escaped him. Mechanically he looked at his neighbour to see whether he had been making notes. The latter was a man much older than himself, and was busily writing upon loose sheets. He did not look up, but he seemed to understand what Greif wanted, for he handed him, or tossed him, the piece of paper on which he was scribbling, numbered the blank page beneath it, and went on quickly without even turning his eyes. Greif thanked him, and in the next pause of the lecture copied the notes into his own book. At the end of the hour Greif returned the sheet and repeated his thanks. He did not know the man, even by sight, a fact which surprised him, as the stranger was rather a striking personage.

'I am very much obliged,' he said. 'I was absent-minded—thinking of something else.'

'That is always rash,' replied the other. 'I am very glad to have been of service to you.'

Although Greif was not fond of making acquaintances among students who wore no colours, he could not refrain from continuing the conversation. The two were the last to leave the hall and went down the broad staircase together.

'You have not been long in the University,' he observed.

'I have only just arrived. I have migrated from Heidelberg. Permit me to introduce myself,' he added according to German custom. 'My name is Rex.'

'My name is von Greifenstein. Most happy.'

'Most happy.'

Both bowed, stopping for the purpose upon the landing, and then looking into each other's eyes. Rex was a man of rather more than medium height, thin, but broad-shouldered and gracefully built. He might have been of any age, but he looked as though he were about thirty years old. It would not have surprised any one to hear that he was much older, or much younger. Thick brown hair was carefully brushed and smoothed all over his head, and he wore his beard, which was of the same colour, carefully trimmed, full and square. A soft and clear complexion, a little less than fair but very far from dark, showed at first sight that Rex rejoiced in perfect health.

The straight nose was very classic in outline, the brow and forehead evenly developed, the modelling about the eyes and temples very smooth and delicate. But the eyes themselves destroyed at once the harmony of the whole face and gave it a very uncommon expression. This was due entirely to their colour and not at all to their shape. The iris was very large, so that little of the surrounding white was visible, and its hue was that of the palest blue china, while the pupil was so extremely small as to be scarcely noticeable. The apparent absence of that shining black aperture in the centre, made the eyes look like glass marbles, and rendered their glance indescribably stony. Greif almost started when he saw them. 'You preferred Schwarzburg to Heidelberg, then,' he remarked, by way of continuing the conversation.

'For my especial branch I think it is superior.'

'Philosophy?' asked Greif, thinking of the lecture they had

just attended.

'No. That is a pastime with me. I am interested in astronomy and in some branches connected with that science. You have a celebrated specialist here.'

'Yes, old Uncle Sternkitzler,' answered Greif irreverently.

'Exactly,' assented Rex. 'He is a shining light, a star of the first magnitude. If there is anything to discover, he will discover it. If not, he will explain the reason why there is nothing. He is a great man. He knows what nothing is, for there is nothing he does not know. I am delighted with him. You do not care for astronomy, Herr von Greifenstein?'

'I do not know anything about it, and I have no talent for mathematics,' answered Greif. 'You intend to make it a profession, I presume.'

'Yes, as far as it can be called a profession.'

'How far is that, if I may ask?'

'Just as far as it goes after it ceases to be an amusement,' answered Rex.

'That may be very far,' said Greif who was struck by the definition.

'Yes. If you call it a profession, it is one for which a lifetime of study is only an insignificant preparation. If you call it a study and not a profession, you make of it a mere amusement, like philosophy.'

'I do not find that very amusing,' said Greif, with a laugh.

'Nothing is amusing when you are obliged to do it,' answered the other. 'Duty is the hair shirt of the nineteenth century. A man who does his duty is just as uncomfortable while he is doing it as any Trappist who ever buckled on a spiked belt under his gown.'

'But afterwards?'

'Afterwards? What is afterwards? It is nothing to you or me. Afterwards means the time when you and I are buried, and the next generation are writhing in hair shirts of their own making, and prickly girdles which they put on themselves.' Rex laughed oddly.

'I differ from you,' answered Greif.

'You are a Korps student, sir. Does that mean that you wish to quarrel with me?'

'Not unless you choose. I am not in search of a row this morning. I differed from you as to your view of duty. It seems to me contrary to German ideas.'

'Facts are generally contrary to all ideas,' answered Rex.

'Not in Germany—at least so far as duty is concerned. Besides, if science is true, facts must agree with it. Political ethics are a science, and duty is necessary to the system that science has created. What would become of our military supremacy if the belief in duty were suddenly destroyed?'

'I do not know. But I know that it will not make the smallest difference to us, what becomes of it, when we are dead and buried.'

'It would change the condition of our children for the worse.'

'You need not marry. No one obliges you or me to become the fathers of new specimens of our species.'

'And what becomes of love in your system?' inquired Greif, more and more surprised at his acquaintance's extraordinary conversation.

'What becomes of anything when it has ceased to exist?' asked Rex.

'I do not know.'

'There is nothing to know in the case. The motion—you would call it force—the motion continues, but the particular thing in which it was manifested is no longer, and that particular thing never will exist again. Motion is imperishable, because it is immaterial. The innumerable milliards of vortices in which the material of your body moves at such an amazing rate will not stand still when you are dead, nor even when every visible atom of your body has vanished from sight in the course of ages. Every vortex is imperishable, eternal, of infinite duration. The vortex was the cause before the beginning and it will remain itself after the end of all things.'

'The prime cause,' mused Greif. 'And who made the vortex?'

'God,' answered Rex laconically.

'But then,' objected the younger student in some surprise,
'you believe in a future life, in the importance of this life, in duty,
in all the rest of it.'

'I believe in the vortex,' replied the other, 'in its unity, individuality and eternity. Life is a matter of convenience, its importance is a question of opinion, its duties are ultimately considerations of taste. What are opinions, conveniences and tastes,
compared with realities? The vortex is a fact, and it seems to me
that it furnishes enough material for reflexion to satisfy a mind
of ordinary activity.'

'You hold strange views,' said Greif thoughtfully.

'Oh no!' exclaimed Rex, with sudden animation. 'I am not at
all different from any other peaceful student of astronomy, I can
assure you. Neither the vortex nor any other fact ever prevents
any man from doing what is individually agreeable to him, nor
from enjoying everything that comes in his way, or calling it sinful, according to his convictions.'

'And are you a happy man, if the question is not indiscreet?'

'Ah, that is your favourite question among philosophers,'
laughed Rex, 'and it shows what you really think of all your
beliefs about duty and the rest of the virtues. You really care for
nothing but happiness, if the truth be told. All your religions,
your moralities, your laws, your customs, you regard as a means
of obtaining ultimate enjoyment. There is little merit in being
happy with so much artificial assistance. Real originality should
show itself in surpassing your felicity without making use of
your laborious methods in attaining to it. The trouble is that
your political ethics, your recipes for making bliss in wholesale quantities, take no account of exceptional people. But why
should we discuss the matter? What is happiness?

'Millions of volumes have been written about it, and no man
has ever had the courage to own exactly what he believes would
make him happy. You may add your name to the list, Herr von

Greifenstein, if you please, and write the next ponderous work upon the subject. You would not be any happier afterwards and you would be very much older. If you really desire to be happy, I will tell you how it is possible. In the first place, are you happy now?'

Rex fixed his stony stare, that contrasted so strangely with his beautiful face, upon Greif's eyes. He saw there an uncertainty, a vague uneasiness, that answered his question well enough.

'Yes,' answered the younger man in a doubtful tone, 'I suppose I am.'

'I think your happiness is not complete,' said Rex, turning away. 'Perhaps my simple plan may help you. Interrogate yourself. What is it that you want? Find out what that something is—that is all.'

'And then?'

'And then? Why, take it, and be happy,' answered Rex with a careless smile, as though the rule were simple enough.

'That is soon said,' replied Greif in a grave tone. 'I want what no man can give me.'

'Nor woman either?'

'Nor woman either.' 'And something you could not take if it were before you, within reach?'

'No. I want nothing material. I want to know the future.'

'Surely that is not a very hard thing,' answered Rex, looking at his watch.

'It must be dinner-time,' said Greif politely, as he noticed the action. He had no wish to detain his new acquaintance.

'Indeed, it is just noon. I fear I have kept you from some engagement.'

'I assure you, it has given me the greatest pleasure to meet you,' answered Greif, holding out his hand.

'The pleasure has been quite upon my side,' returned Rex, bowing with alacrity.

And so they parted, Rex plunging into a shady side street, while Greif continued his walk towards the dining-place of his Korps, thinking as he went, of the queer person he had just seen for the first time. His name was strange, his conversation was unusual, his eyes were most disagreeable, and yet oddly fascinating. Greif thought about him and was not satisfied with his short interview. The man's remark about the future was either that of a visionary, or of an absent-minded person who did not always know what he was saying. Greif himself could hardly understand how he had been led, in a first meeting with one who was altogether a stranger, to speak so plainly of what disturbed him. It was not his custom to make acquaintances at a venture, or to refer to his own affairs with people he did not know. He reflected, however, that he had not committed himself in any way, while admitting that he might easily have been drawn on to do so if the interview had been prolonged.

At dinner he asked his friends whether any of them knew a student whose name was Rex. No one had heard of him, and on learning that he was a man older than the average, they murmured, and said one to another that Greif was beginning to cross the borders of Philistia. After the meal was over, Greif went to his lodgings and tried to work. The sudden anxiety that had seized him in the morning during the lecture grew stronger in solitude, until it was almost unbearable. He pushed aside his books and wrote to his father, inquiring whether anything had happened, in a way which would certainly have surprised old Greifenstein if he himself had been less nervous about the future than he actually was. It was a relief to have written, and Greif returned to his labours more quietly afterwards.

He did not see Rex again in the lecture-room, though his eye wandered along the rows of heads bent down over busy hands that wrote without ceasing. Rex was not among them. He had said that he considered philosophy an amusement, and he probably came to the hall where it was taught when the fancy seized him to divert himself. But the desire to talk with him again became stronger, until Greif actually determined to go in search of the man.

The sun had gone down, and he stood at his open window as he had done on the evening of his arrival, watching almost unconsciously for the first stars to shine out above the cathedral spire. The air was very quiet, disturbed by no sound but the swirl of the deep river against the stone piers of the bridge far down below the student's window. There was something melancholy in the ceaseless rush of the strong water, which reminded him of the sighing of the trees at home, on that last morning when he had sat with Hilda at the foot of the Hunger-Thurm.

At such a time anything which recalled the circumstances of the vacation necessarily brought with it an increase in his anxiety. Greif thought of the evening that was before him if he joined his comrades at their usual place of meeting, and the prospect was distasteful. He would be glad to escape from the lights and the noise and the drinking and singing, even from his position of importance among his fellows, who made him their oracle upon all University matters. He would prefer to pass an hour or two in quiet conversation, in a quiet room, with Rex the student of astronomy and mathematics. He did not know where he lived, nor whether he would be at home at that hour, but it was easy to satisfy his curiosity upon both points.

He found the address he wanted at the Beadle's office. Rex lived in a dark street near the cathedral. Greif climbed many flights of steps, finding his way by striking one match after another. At the top there was but one door. He knocked twice and waited. There was no answer, and he knocked again. He was sure that he could hear someone moving inside the apartment, but the door remained closed. Annoyed at being kept waiting he pounded loudly with the piece of iron and called on Rex by name. He was rewarded at last by hearing footsteps within.

'Who are you?' asked an angry voice. 'And why are you making such a hideous noise?'

'My name is von Greifenstein,' replied Greif, 'and I want to see Herr Rex.'

He was preparing for a disagreeable encounter with some unknown person, when the door opened quickly and he found himself face to face with Rex himself. His expression was bland in the extreme as he held up the light he carried and greeted his guest.

'I beg your pardon,' he said in tones very unlike those Greif had just heard. 'I had no idea that it was you. Pray come in.'

'I am afraid I am disturbing you,' answered Greif, hesitating as though he had forgotten the tremendous energy he had put into his knocking.

'Not at all, not at all,' repeated Rex, carefully fastening the door when Greif had entered. 'You see I am a newcomer and have no friends here,' he continued apologetically, 'and I did not imagine that you knew my address.'

After passing through a narrow passage, Greif found himself in a large room with three windows. It was evident that Herr Rex lived more luxuriously than most students, for there was no bed in the place, and an open door showed that there was at least one other apartment beyond. A couple of bookcases were well filled with volumes, and there was a great heap of others upon the floor in the corner. Two large easy-chairs stood on opposite sides of the porcelain stove, which at that season was of course not in use. A broad table in the centre was covered with books, many of them new, and papers covered with notes or figures were strewn amongst them in the greatest disorder. Near one of the windows Greif noticed a writing-desk, upon which lay a few drawing and writing materials and a large sheet of paper. It was clear that Rex had been at work here, for a bright lamp stood upon the desk and its strong light fell from beneath the green shade upon the mathematical figure that had absorbed the student's attention.

'It is a very quiet lodging,' remarked Rex, drawing forward one of the arm-chairs and then seating himself in the other. 'It is just what I wanted. I do not like noise when I am reading.'

Greif did not exactly know what to say. To visit a student in his rooms when he had only met him once, was a new experience, and Rex's stony blue eyes seemed to ask the object of his coming. It was evident that Rex only spoke of his habitation in order to break a silence which might have been awkward.

'The fact is,' said Greif, as though answering a direct question,

'I have been thinking of what you said the other day.'

'You do my remarks an honour which I believe they have never received before,' replied Rex, bending his handsome head and smiling in his brown beard.

'Do you remember? I said that I needed only one thing to make me happy. I wanted to know the future. You answered that it must be easy to get my wish. Were you in earnest, or did you speak thoughtlessly? That is what I came to ask you.'

'Indeed?' Rex laughed. 'You said to yourself that your acquaintance was either a fool or an absent-minded person, did you not?'

'Well—' Greif hesitated and smiled. 'Either visionary or absent-minded,' he admitted. 'Yes, I could not explain your remark in any other way.'

'Of course you could not, unless you suspected that I might be a charlatan.'

'That did not occur to me—'

'It might have occurred to you, considering what I had said. It might occur to you now, if I answered your question. But on the other hand it is of no importance whether it does or not. My reply will contribute to your peace of mind by helping you to catalogue a man you do not know among the fools and charlatans of whom you have heard. Would you like to know the future? I can tell it to you, if you please.'

'The vortex, I suppose,' answered Greif rather scornfully.

'Yes. I can tell you the direction of the vortices of which you are composed, for a time, while they are on their way to join other vortices in the dance of death. The vortices do nothing but dance, spin and whirl for ever through life, the farce; through death, the tragedy and through all the eternity of the epilogue. What do you wish to know?'

'You are jesting!' exclaimed Greif moodily. 'I wish you would be in earnest.'

'In earnest!' cried Rex contemptuously. 'What is earnestness?'

He rose and went to the desk upon which the lamp was

burning, opened it and took a fresh sheet of paper from within. Greif watched him with considerable indifference. He had not found what he had sought and he already meditated a retreat. Rex paid no attention to him, but rapidly described a circle upon the paper and divided it into twelve parts with a ruler.

'Do you remember the date of the day we met?' he asked, looking up.

'It was a Monday,' replied Greif, wondering what his companion was doing.

'That will do. I have a calendar,' said Rex.

He consulted an almanac which he drew from his pocket, made a few short calculations, and jotted down certain signs and figures in various parts of the divided circle. When he had finished he looked attentively at what he had done. The whole operation had occupied about a quarter of an hour.

'I do not wonder that you are anxious,' he remarked, as he resumed his seat in the easy-chair, still holding the sheet of paper in his hand.

'What have you discovered?' inquired Greif, with an incredulous smile.

'You are threatened by a great calamity, you and all who belong to you,' replied Rex. 'I suppose you know it, and that is the reason why you want to know the future.'

Greif's cheek turned slowly pale, not at the announcement, but at the thought that this chance student perhaps knew of Rieseneck's existence, and of all that his return might involve.

'Herr Rex,' he said sternly, 'be good enough to tell me what you know of me and my family from other sources than that bit of paper.'

'Not much,' answered the other with a dry laugh. 'I barely knew of your existence until I met you the other day, and I have not mentioned you nor heard your name spoken since.'

'Why then, you can know nothing, and your figures cannot tell you,' said Greif, not yet certain whether to feel relief at the protestation of ignorance, or to doubt its veracity.

'Shall I tell you what I see here?'

'Tell me the nature of the calamity.'

'Its nature, or the cause of it?' inquired Rex, scrutinising the sheet of paper.

'I suppose that they must be closely connected. Let me know the cause first—it will be the surest test.'

Rex laid the paper upon his knee, and folded his hands, looking his guest in the face.

'Herr von Greifenstein, this is a very serious matter,' he said, 'If I tell you what I have just discovered, you will certainly believe that I knew it all before, and that I am acting a comedy. You must either bind yourself to put faith in my innocence, or we must drop this affair and talk of something else.'

Greif was silent for some moments. To refuse was to insult a man of whom he had gratuitously asked a question. To promise with the intention of keeping his word was impossible. He found himself in an awkward dilemma. Rex helped him out of it with his usual skill.

'I will tell you what is passing in your mind, and why you are silent,' he said. 'You feel that you cannot believe me. I do not blame you. You will not give your word in such a case, because you must break it. You are quite right. You are full of curiosity to learn how much I know about you. It is very natural. The wisest thing to be done, is to sacrifice your curiosity and I will tear up this piece of paper.'

'No—wait a moment!' cried Greif anxiously, putting out his hand to prevent the act.

'I do not see any other way out of the difficulty,' observed Rex, leaning back in his chair and looking at the stove. 'You may do this, however. You may think what you please of me, provided you do not express your disbelief. I am the most pacific of men, and I have a strong dislike to fighting at my age. Moreover, you asked me the question which led to all this. Even if I answer it, am I bound to explain the reasons for my reply? I believe the code of honour does not require that, and if there is nothing offensive to you in my predictions, I do not see why we need quarrel after all, nor what it matters how I obtained my information. I will promise, too, not to impart it to anyone else. Of course, the simplest way of ending the matter would be to say no more about it.'

Somehow Rex's words seemed to change the position. Greif was inwardly conscious that he would not leave the house without discovering how much his companion knew, and if this submission to his own curiosity was little flattering to his pride, it was at least certain that he could obtain what he wanted without derogating from his dignity if he would follow the advice Rex gave him.

'The compact is to be this, I understand,' he answered at length. 'You will tell me what you know, and I will express no opinion as to the way in which you arrived at the information. Is that what you desire?'

'It is what I suggest,' answered Rex. 'And I bind myself voluntarily to silence.'

'Very good. Will you continue your predictions? Will you tell me the cause of the danger?'

'You and your family are threatened with great misfortune through the return of an evil person—a relation, I should fancy—who has been absent many years.'

Greif started at the directness of the assertion, and an exclamation of something like anger rose to his lips. But he remembered the compact he had just made.

'Will he return?' he asked in a voice which showed Rex that he was not mistaken.

'Inevitably,' answered the latter. 'Therein consists the peculiarity of your situation. You are at the mercy of the inevitable. You cannot retard by one day the catastrophe, any more than you can prevent one of the planets from returning to a given point in its orbit. He will return—let me see—'

'Can you tell me when?' asked Greif, who for a moment had forgotten his scepticism.

Rex seemed to be making a calculation, and repeating it more than once in order to be sure of its accuracy.

'In three months, more or less. Probably before Christmas.

He is now at a great distance, in the south-west—'

'It is impossible that you should guess so much!' exclaimed Greif, rising in great excitement.

'You were not to express an opinion, I believe,' observed Rex, looking coldly at the younger man.

'Can you describe him?' asked Greif, almost fiercely.

'Oh yes,' replied the other. 'He is elderly, almost old. Perhaps sixty years of age. He is violent, unreliable, generally unfortunate, probably disgraced. That is no doubt the reason why you dread his return—'

'Look here, Herr Rex!' cried Greif, interrupting him violently. 'I do not care a straw for our compact, as you call it—'

'You agreed to it. I did not desire to speak further in the matter.'

'Will you agree to forget that there was any compact?' asked Greif desperately.

'Oh no, certainly not,' answered his tormenter. 'And you will not forget it either. You are a man of your word, Herr von Greifenstein. All I can do is to hold my tongue and tell you nothing more.'

'That need not prevent my quarrelling with you about something else—'

'No, if you find it possible. It is not easy to quarrel with me.'

'But if I were to insult you—'

'You will not do so,' returned Rex very calmly and gravely. 'You are bound not to attack me about my predictions, and so far as any other cause of disagreement is concerned, I think you will find it hard to discover one, for you came here to make a friendly visit, without a thought of quarrelling. I think you must see that.'

Greif walked up and down the room in silence for some minutes. He felt the superiority of Rex's position, and would not stoop to force the situation by any brutal discourtesy. At the same time he was distracted by the idea that Rex had not yet told him half of what he knew.

'You are right,' he said at last. 'I am a fool!'

'No, you are an agglomeration of vortices,' answered Rex with a smile 'Shall I tell you one fact more, one very curious fact?'

'Tell me all!' answered Greif with sudden energy.

'In the nature of things, you should have news of that person today. You have not heard from him before coming here?'

'No, and I think nothing could be more improbable than that I should have news of him at all, beyond what you tell me. Besides, I could prevent the possibility of such a thing.'

'How?' inquired Rex.

'By trespassing upon your hospitality until midnight,' answered Greif with a laugh, in which his natural good temper reappeared once more.

'Will you do so?' asked the student with the greatest readiness. 'Here is a test of my veracity. Whether you stay here, or go home, or wander out alone by the river, you will hear of that individual before midnight.'

'But nobody knows I am here.'

'The stars know,' answered Rex with a smile. 'Will you stay with me, or will you go home? It makes no difference, excepting that by staying you will give me the advantage of your company—'

'What is that?' asked Greif. There was a loud knocking at the outer door.

'Probably news from your uncle,' answered Rex imperturbably. 'Will you open the door? There can be no deception then.'

'Yes. I will open the door.'

A telegraph messenger was outside, and inquired if Herr von Greifenstein were in the lodging.

'How did you know where I was?' asked Greif.

'It was marked urgent and so I inquired at the Poodle's office,' answered the fellow with a grin as he signified the official by the students' slang appellation.

Greif hastened to the inner room and tore open the envelope, his face pale with excitement.

'My father telegraphs—"Your uncle has written his intention to return at once—" Good Heavens!'

He tossed the bit of paper to Rex and fell back in his chair overcome by something very like fear.

Rex glanced at the despatch and then returned to the study of his figure without betraying any surprise.

CHAPTER 8

Greif's first sensation was that of astonishment, almost amounting to stupefaction. Rex could have desired no more striking fulfilment of a prediction than chance had vouchsafed to him in the present instance. For he admitted to himself that fortune had favoured him, even though the arrival of the news within twenty-four hours was not in his belief a mere coincidence. The telegram might have come at any other moment and might have found Greif in any other place. As for Greif, he saw at a glance how impossible it was that Rex should have foreseen the incident, or planned the circumstances in which it occurred. He could not have known that Greif was coming that evening, unless he knew everything, and moreover the despatch was fresh from the office, and twenty minutes had not elapsed between the time of its reception over the wires and of its delivery into Greif's hands.

If the occurrence was strange, its effect upon the young man was at least equally unforeseen. Greif had always despised persons who professed to dabble in the supernatural, and had laughed to scorn all the so-called manifestations of spiritualism, mesmerism, and super-rational force. When he had heard that the great astronomer Zollner had written a book to explain the performances of Slade, the medium, by means of a mathematical theory of a fourth dimension in space, Greif had believed that the scientist was raving mad. Up to the moment when the telegram had arrived, he had been convinced that Rex was a cheat, who had accidentally learned certain facts connected with the Greifensteins and was attempting to play the magician by making an adroit use of what he knew.

When brought suddenly face to face with a phenomenon he

could not explain, Greif's reason ceased altogether to perform its functions. The news he had just received was startling, but the bewilderment caused by its arrival at that precise juncture made even Rieseneck's return seem insignificant, in comparison with Rex's power to foretell the announcement of it.

'I do not understand,' said Greif, staring at his companion.

'Nor I, beyond a certain point,' replied the elder man, looking up from his paper.

'How could you know?'

'I did not, until a few minutes before I told you. Of course you thought I did. It is very natural.'

'It could hardly have been a coincidence,' said Greif, almost to himself.

'Hardly.' Rex smiled.

'And yet,' continued Greif, 'I do not see any way of explaining it all.'

'I could show you, but it would need several years to do so.'

'It is not a personal gift?'

'No, it is a science.'

'Of what kind?'

'It is that part of astronomy in which the public does not believe. Do you understand?'

'Astrology?' inquired Greif with a rather foolish and yet incredulous smile. 'I thought that was considered to be nothing but mediaeval ignorance.'

'It is considered so. Whether it is really nothing better than a superstition you have had an opportunity of judging.'

'But how can you reconcile it with serious science?'

'The vortex reconciles everything—even men who are on the point of quarrelling, when the circumstances are favourable.'

'But if all this is true, there is no reason why you should not know everything—'

'Not everything. There are cases when it is clear from the first that a question cannot be answered. With better tools, a man might do much more. But one may foretell much, if one will take the trouble. Will you hear more of what I have discovered about you?'

Greif hesitated. His strongly rational bent of mind suggested to him that after all there might be some trickery in the prediction so lately fulfilled, though he was unable to detect it. But if Rex foretold the future Greif felt that he must be influenced, and perhaps made very unhappy by the prophecy, which might in the end prove utterly false. It would be more prudent, he thought, to wait and lay a trap for the pretended astrologer, by asking him at another time to answer a different question, of which it should be certain that he had no previous knowledge. The conclusion was quite in accordance with Greif's prudent nature, which instinctively distrusted the evidence of its senses beyond a certain point, and desired to prepare its experiments with true German scepticism, leaving nothing to chance and fortifying the conclusion by the purification of the means.

'Thank you,' he said at last. 'I will not hear any more at present.'

'Which means that you will ask me an unforeseen question one of these days to test my strength,' observed Rex with a smile.

Greif laughed rather nervously, for the remark expressed exactly what was passing in his mind.

'I confess, I meant to do so. How did you know what I was thinking?'

'By experience. Are not the nine-tenths of every human being precisely like the nine-tenths of the next? The difficulties of life are connected with that tenth which is not alike in any two.'

'Your experience must have been very great.'

'It has been just great enough to teach me to recognise the point at which no experience is of any use whatever.'

'And what is that point?'

'Generally the sweetest in life, and the most dangerous.'

'You speak in riddles, Herr Rex.'

'One man's life is another man's riddle, and if he succeeds in guessing its solution he cries out that it is a sham and was not worth guessing at all.'

'I believe you are a man-hater,' said Greif.

'Why should I be? The world gives me all I ask of it, and if that is not much the fault lies in my scanty imagination. The world is a flower-garden. If you like the flowers, pluck them. Happiness consists in knowing what we want, or in imagining that we want something. To take it is an easy matter.'

'Then everybody ought to be happy.'

'Everybody might be—if everybody would take the consequences. That is the stumbling-block—the lack of an ounce of determination and a drachm of courage.'

'Paradoxes!' exclaimed Greif. 'Life is a more serious matter—'

'Than death? Certainly.' Rex laughed.

'I did not say that,' returned Greif gravely. 'Death is the most serious of all earthly matters. No one can laugh at it.'

'Then I am alone in the world. I laugh at it. Serious? Why, it is the affair of a moment compared with a lifetime of enjoyment!'

'And what may come afterwards does not disturb you?'

'Why should it? Is there any sense in being made miserable by the concoctions of other people's hysterical imagination?'

Greif was silent. He was young enough and simple enough to be shocked by Rex's indifference and unbelief, and yet the man exercised an influence over him which he felt and did not resent. Phrases which would have sounded shallow in the mouth of a Korps student, discussing the immortality of the soul over his twentieth measure of beer, produced a very different impression when they fell from the lips of the sober astronomer with the strange eyes. Greif felt uncomfortable, and yet he knew that he would certainly seek the society of Rex again at no distant date. At present all his ideas were unsettled, and after a moment's silence he rose to go.

'Do not forget your telegram,' said Rex, handing it to him.

'Shall you go to the philosophy lecture tomorrow?' asked

Greif as he reached the door.

'Perhaps.'

Rex insisted on showing his guest down the stairs to the outer door, a civility which was almost necessary, considering the darkness of the descent. As Greif went down the narrow street, Rex stood on the threshold, shading the light with his hand and listening to the decreasing echo of the footsteps in the distance. Then he re-entered the house and climbed to his lodging.

'So much for astrology!' he exclaimed, as he sat down opposite the empty chair which Greif had lately occupied. For a long time he did not move, but remained in his place, with half-closed eyes, apparently ruminating upon the past conversation. When he rose at last, he had reached the conclusion that his coming to Schwarzburg was a step upon which he might congratulate himself.

From that day his acquaintance with Greif gradually ripened into an intimacy. Its growth was almost imperceptible at first, but before a month had passed the two met every day. Greif's companions murmured. It was a sad sight in their eyes, and they could not be reconciled to it. But Greif explained that he was thinking seriously of his final degree, and that he must be excused for frequenting the society of a much older man, after having given the Korps the best years of his University life. He even offered to resign his position as first in charge, but the proposition raised a storm of protests and he continued to wear the yellow cap as before.

He wrote to his father frequently, but after the first confirmation of the telegram he got no further news of Rieseneck. He described Rex, and spoke of his growing friendship with the remarkable student, who seemed to know everything, and old Greifenstein was glad to learn that his son's mind was taking a serious direction. He wrote to his mother more than once, in terms more affectionate than he had formerly used, but her answers were short and unsatisfactory, and never evoked in his heart that thrill of pity and love which had so much surprised him in himself during the last weeks at home. He wrote to

Hilda, but her letters in reply had a sadness in them that made him almost fear to break the seal.

It was at such moments that the anxiety for the future came upon him with redoubled force, until he began to believe that the person most directly threatened by that fatal catastrophe which had been foretold must be Hilda herself. He thought more than once of putting the question to Rex directly, to be decided by his mysterious art. It would have been a relief to him if the decision had chanced to be contrary to his own vague forebodings, but on the other hand, it seemed like a profanation of his love to explain the situation to his friend. He never spoke of Hilda, and Rex did not know of her existence.

And yet Rex was constantly at his side, a part of his life, an element in his plans, a contributor to all his thoughts. He would not have admitted that he was under the man's influence, and the student of astronomy would never have claimed any such superiority. It was nevertheless a fact that Greif asked his friend's advice almost daily, and profited greatly thereby, as well as by the inexhaustible fund of information which the mathematician placed at his disposal. Nevertheless Greif did not lay the trap by which he had intended to test Rex's science, or expose his charlatanism, as the result should determine. He could not make up his mind to try the experiment, for he liked Rex more and more, and began to dread lest anything should occur to cause a breach in their friendship.

It chanced that on a certain evening of November Greif and Rex were sitting at a small marble table in the corner of the principal restaurant. They often came to this place to dine, because it was not frequented by the students, and they were more free from interruption than in one of the ordinary beer saloons of the town. They had finished their meal and, the cloth having been removed, were discussing what remained of a bottle of Makgrader wine. Greif was smoking, and Rex, as he talked, made sketches of his companion's head upon the marble table.

A student entered the hall, looked about at its occupants, and presently installed himself in a seat near the two friends, touching his blue cap as he sat down. The pair returned the salutation and continued their conversation. The student was of the Rhine Korps, a tall, saturnine youth, evidently strong and active, but very sallow and lean. Greif knew him by sight. His name was Bauer, and he had of late gained a considerable reputation as a fighter. Rex glanced curiously at him once, and then, as though one look had been enough to fix his mental photograph, did not turn his eyes towards him again.

Bauer ordered a measure of beer, lighted a black cigar and leaned back against the wall, gloomily eyeing the people at more distant tables. He looked like a man in a singularly bad humour, to whom any piece of mischief would be a welcome diversion. Rex abandoned his sketch of Greif's head, looked surreptitiously at his watch and then began to draw circles and figures instead. Presently he slipped his hand into his pocket and drew out the almanac he always carried about him.

'What are you doing?' asked Greif, interrupting himself in the midst of what he had been saying.

'Nothing particular,' answered Rex. 'Go on. I am listening.'

'I was saying,' continued Greif, 'that I preferred my own part of the country, though you may call it less civilised if you please.'

'It is natural,' assented Rex, without looking up from his figure. 'Every man prefers the place where he is born, I suppose, provided his associations with it are agreeable.' Then he unconsciously spoke a few words to himself, unnoticed by Greif.

'Saturn in his fall and term-cadent peregrine.'

'It is not only that,' said Greif. 'Look at the Rhine, how flat and dull and ugly it grows—'

He was suddenly interrupted by the close presence of the other student, who had risen and stood over him, touching his cap and bowing stiffly.

'Excuse me,' he said in a harsh voice, 'my name is Bauer—from Cologne—I must beg you not to insult the Rhine in a public place, nor in my hearing.'

Greif rose to his feet at once, very much astonished that any one should wish to quarrel with him upon such a pretence. Before he could answer, however, Rex anticipated him by addressing the student in a tone that rang through the broad room.

'Hold your tongue, you silly boy!' he said, and for the first time since they had become friends Greif recognised the angry accents he had heard through the door when he had first gone to Rex's lodging.

'*Prosit!*' growled Bauer. 'Who are you, if you please?'

'My name is Rex. My friends the Swabians will manage this affair.'

'I also desire to cross swords with you,' said Greifenstein politely, using a stock phrase.

'*Prosit!*' growled Bauer again. He took the card Rex offered him, and then, with a scarcely perceptible salute, turned on his heel and walked away.

Greif remained standing during some seconds, gazing after the departing student. His face expressed his annoyance at the quarrel, and a shade of anger darkened its usual radiance.

'Sit down,' suggested Rex quietly.

'We must be off at once,' said Greif, mechanically resuming his seat.

'There is to be fighting tomorrow morning, a dozen duels or more, and I will settle with that fellow before breakfast.'

'That is to say, I will,' observed the other, putting his pencil and his almanac into his pocket.

'You?' exclaimed Greif in surprise.

'Why not? I can demand it. I insulted him roundly, before you challenged him.'

'Do you mean to say that you, Rex, a sober old student of Heaven knows how many semesters, want to go out and drum with *schlagers* like one of us?'

'Yes, I do. And I request you as the head of your Korps to arrange the matter for tomorrow morning.'

'You insist? How long is it since you have fenced? I should be sorry for that brown beard of yours, if a deep-*carte* necessitated shaving half of it.' Greif laughed merrily at the idea, and Rex smiled.

'Yes, my friend, I insist. Never mind my beard. That young man will not fight another round for many a long semester after I have done with him.'

'Were you such a famous *schlager* formerly?'

'No. Nothing especial. But I can settle Herr Bauer.'

'I do not know about that,' said Greif shaking his head. 'He is one of the best. He came here expressly to pick a quarrel with me, who am supposed to be the best in the University. He is in search of a reputation. You had better be careful.'

'Never fear. Go and arrange matters. I will stay here till you come back. It is too early to go home yet.'

Greif was amazed at his friend's determination, though he had no choice but to do as he was requested. He walked quickly towards the brewery where he was sure of finding the second in charge of his Korps, and probably a dozen others. At every step the situation seemed more disagreeable, and more wholly unaccountable. He could not imagine why Rex should have cared to mix in the quarrel, and he was annoyed at not being able to settle matters with Bauer at once. His mind was still confused, when he pushed open the door of the room in which his companions were sitting. He was hailed by a chorus of joyful cries.

A couple of novices sprang forward to help him to remove his heavy overcoat. Another hastened to get his favourite drinking-cup filled with beer. The second in charge, a burly fellow with many scars on his face and a hand like a Westphalia ham, made a place for the chief next to his own.

'We have had a row,' Greif remarked when he was seated at the board and had drunk a health to all present.

'Ha, that is a good thing!' laughed the second. 'Tell us all about it.' He drank what remained in his huge measure and handed the mug to a fox to be filled. Then he took a good puff at his pipe and settled himself in an attitude of attention.

'We have had a row at the Palmengarten,' said Greif. 'Rex and I—'

'You have quarrelled with Rex?' interrupted the second. He

and all his companions detested the man because he took Greif away from them. There was a gleam of hope for the chief if he had quarrelled with his Philistine acquaintance, and all present exchanged significant glances.

'No. That is not it. A fellow of the Rhine Korps has quarrelled with both of us. He says his name is Bauer. Rex called him a silly boy and told him to hold his tongue before I could speak.'

'Rex!' exclaimed all the students in chorus.

'Ha, that is a good thing!' laughed the second, blowing the foam from his ale. 'Provided he will fight,' he added before he drank.

'Rex is my friend,' said Greif quietly.

The murmurs subsided as though by magic, and the burly second set down his measure almost untasted.

'I wanted to fight the man first,' continued Greif, 'but Rex objected and appealed to me as the head of a Korps to get the matter settled at once. He wants to fight tomorrow morning with the rest.'

'*Prosit!*' laughed the second. 'We thought he was a Philistine! He must be forty years old! What a sight it will be!' cried a dozen voices.

'As he demands it, we must oblige him,' observed Greif.

'A good thing! A very good thing!' exclaimed the second more solemnly than before. He rarely said much else, and his hand was infinitely more eloquent than his tongue.

'I hope it is,' said Greif. 'This is your affair. You had better go and see the second of the Rhine Korps at once. Rex is waiting for the answer at the Palmengarten. Remember he is determined to fight at once.'

'He shall drum till the hair flies about the place,' answered the second, with an unusual flight of rhetoric, as he slipped on his overcoat and went out.

'You are not going?' asked the students as Greif showed signs of following his brother-officer.

'I cannot leave Rex waiting,' objected Greif.

'Send for him to come here! If he really means to fight, he is not such a Philistine as we thought!' cried two or three.

'If you like, I will send for him,' answered Greif. 'Here, little fox!' he exclaimed, addressing a beardless youth of vast proportions who sat silent at the end of the table. 'Go to the Palmengarten and say that Greifenstein wishes Herr Rex to come here. Introduce yourself properly before speaking to him.'

The huge-limbed boy rose without a word, gravely saluted and left the room. Greif was his idol, the type which he aspired to imitate, and he obeyed him like a lamb.

'So Rex means to fight,' remarked one of the young men, who sat opposite to Greif. 'Was he ever in a Korps?'

'Possibly,' answered the chief.

'"The Pinschgau lads went out to fight,"' hummed the student rather derisively, but he did not proceed further than the first line of the old song. Some of the others laughed, and all smiled at the allusion to the comic battle.

'Look here, my good Korps brothers,' said Greif in his dominating tones, 'I will tell you what it is. Rex means to have it out with Bauer tomorrow morning. If he turns out a coward and backs down the ground before the Rhine fellow, you can make game of him as you please, and you know very well that I shall have nothing more to do with him, and that he will be suspended from all intercourse with the Korps. I have my own ideas about what he will do, though Bauer is a devil at deep-*carte* and has a long arm. Until the question is settled you have no right to laugh at an honourable man who is to be our guest-at-arms, because he is not a Korps student.

'He is our guest as much as the chief of the Heidelberg Saxo-Prussians was when he came over last spring to fight the first in charge of the Franks. Every man who wants to fight deserves respect until he has shown that he is afraid to stand by his words. There—that is all I have to say, and you know I am right. Here is a full measure to the health of all good Swabians, and may the yellow and black *schlager* do good work whether in the hands of guest or fellow. One, two and three! *Suabia Hoch!*'

'*Hoch! Hoch! Hoch!*' roared twenty lusty young voices.

The speech had produced its effect, as Greif's speeches usually did, and every student drained his cup to the toast with a good will.

'But after all,' said the young fellow who had hummed the offensive song, 'your friend has not handled a *schlager* since the days of the flood. It is not likely that he can get the better of such a fellow as Bauer—may the incarnate thunder fly into his body! I can feel that splinter in my jaw to this day!'

'My dear boy,' said Greif, 'one of two things will happen. Either Rex will give Bauer a dose, and in that case you will feel better; or else Bauer will set a deep-*carte* into Rex's jaw, exactly where he hit you, and if that happens you will feel that you are not alone in your misfortunes, which is also a certain satisfaction.'

'You seem remarkably hopeful about Rex,' observed the student. 'Here he comes,' he added as the door opened and Rex appeared attended by the fox.

Every one rose, as usual when a visitor appears under such circumstances. Rex bowed and smiled serenely. He had often been a guest of the Swabians and knew all present. In a few moments he was seated on the chief's right hand. Greif rapped on the table.

'Korps brothers,' he said, 'our friend Rex visits us in a new capacity. He comes not as usual to share the drinking-horn and the yellow-black song-book. He is with us today as a guest-at-arms. Let us drink to his especial welfare.'

'To your especial welfare,' said each student, holding his cup out towards Rex, and then drinking a short draught.

'I revenge myself immediately,' answered Rex, rising as he moved his glass in a circle and glanced round the table. The phrases are consecrated by immemorial usage. He drank, bowed and resumed his seat. He knew well enough that the Swabians did not like him over well, but he was determined that, sooner or later, they should change their minds.

'I congratulate you,' said the same student who had been

talking with Greif, 'upon your quarrel with Bauer. You could not have picked out a man whom I detest more cordially. Observe this slash in my jaw—two bone splinters, an artery and nine stitches. It is a reminiscence, not dear but near.'

'A fine cut,' answered Rex, gravely examining the scar. 'A regular *renommir schmiss*, a gash to boast of. A deep-*carte*, I suppose?'

'Of course,' said the other, with the superiority of a man who knows the exact part of the face exposed to each cut. 'It could not be anything else. He has the most surprising limberness of wrist, and he never hits the bandage by mistake—never! You strike high *tierce* like lightning and your blade is back in guard—oh yes! but before you are there his deep-*carte* sits in the middle of your cheek. Whatever you do, it is the same.'

Everyone was listening, and Greif frowned at the speaker, whose intention was evident. He wanted to frighten Rex by an account of his adversary's prowess. Rex looked grave but did not appear in the least disturbed.

'So?' he ejaculated. 'Really! Well, I can put a silver *thaler* in my cheek and save my teeth, at all events. They are very good.'

A roar of laughter greeted this response.

'But that is contrary to the code,' objected the student, laughing with the rest. He was not an ill-humoured man in reality.

'Yes—I was joking,' said Rex. 'But I once saw a man fight with an iron nose on his face.'

'How was that?' was asked by everyone.

'He was a brave fellow of the right sort,' said Rex, 'but he had a long nose and a short arm. In fact he had formed the habit of parrying with his nose, like a Greek statue—you know, all those they find have had their noses knocked off by Turks. Now the nose is a noble feature, and is of great service to man, when he wants to find out whether he is in Italy or Germany. But as a weapon of defence it leaves much to be desired. The man of whom I am telling you had grown so much used to using it in this way, that whenever he saw anything coming in the shape of a *carte* he thrust it forward as naturally as a pig does when he sees an acorn. After a couple of semesters the *cartes* sat on his nose from bridge to tip, one after the other, like the days of the week in a calendar.

'But when the third semester began, and the *cartes* began to fall too near together, and sometimes two in the same place, the doctors said that the nose was worn-out, though it had once been good. And the man told the second in charge, and the second told the first, and the first laid the matter before the assembled Korps. Thereupon the whole Seniorum Conventus sat in solemn committee upon this war-worn nose, and decided that its owner need fight no more. But he was not only brave; he possessed the invention of Prometheus, combined with the diabolical sense of humour which so much distinguished the late Mephistopheles. He offered to go on fighting if he might be allowed an iron nose. Goetz of Berliehingen, he said, had won battles with an iron hand, and the case was analogous.

'The proposition was put to the vote and carried unanimously amidst thunders of applause. The iron nose was made and fitted to the iron eye-pieces, and my friend appeared on the fighting ground looking like a figure of Kladderadatsch disguised as Arminius. He wore out two iron noses while he remained in the Korps, but the destruction of the enemy's weapons more than counterbalanced this trifling expense. When he left, his armour was attached to a life-sized photograph of his head, which hangs to this day above two crossed rapiers in the Kneipe. That is the history of the man with the iron nose.'

There had been much half-suppressed laughter while Rex was telling his story, and when he had finished, the students roared with delight. Rex had never before given himself so much trouble to amuse them, and the effect of his narrative was immense.

'He talks as if he knew something about it,' said one, nudging his neighbour.

'Perhaps he helped to wear out the nose,' answered the other still laughing.

'A health to you all,' cried Rex, draining his full measure.

'And may none of you parry *carte* with the proboscis,' he added, as he set down the empty cup.

'Ha! That is a good thing!' laughed the voice of the burly second as he entered the room, his face beaming with delight.

'Out with the foxes, there is business here for a few minutes.' The foxes, who were not privileged to hear the deliberations of their elders upon such grave matters, rose together and filed out, carrying their pipes and drinking-cups with them. Then the second sat down in his vacant place.

'Well?' asked Greif. 'Is it all settled.'

'Yes. The cattle wanted to fight you first. I said the Philistine insisted—excuse me, no offence. Good. Now—that was all.'

The second buried his nose in a foaming tankard.

'Is it for tomorrow morning?' asked Rex calmly.

'Palmengarten, back entrance, four sharp.'

'What do you mean?' asked Greif. 'Are we to fight in the Palmengarten, in the restaurant?'

The second nodded, and lighted his pipe.

'Poetic,' he observed. 'Marble floor—fountain playing—palm trees in background.' 'Then we must go there at that hour so as not to be seen?'

'The Poodle thinks it is at Schneckenwinkel, and is going out by the early train to lie in wait,' chuckled the burly student.

'There he will sit all the morning like a sparrow limed on a twig.'

'Have we any other pairs?' asked Greif absently.

'Three others. Two foxes and Hollenstein. He is gone to bed and I am going to send the foxes after him. We can make a night of it, if you like.'

'I will stay with you,' said Rex, who seemed jovially inclined.

Neither Greif nor the second thought it their business to suggest that their combatant had better get some rest before the battle. When two o'clock struck, Rex was teaching them all a new song, which was not in the book, his clear strong voice ringing out steadily and tunefully through the smoky chamber, his smooth complexion neither flushed nor pale from the night's carousal, his stony eyes as colourless and forbidding, as his smile was genial and unaffected.

As they rose to go, he caught sight of a huge silver-mounted horn that hung behind his chair.

'I will drink that out tomorrow night, with your permission,' he said with a light laugh.

'Bravo!' shouted the excited chorus.

'He is a little drunk,' whispered the student whom Bauer had wounded, addressing his neighbour.

'Or a boaster, who will back down the floor,' answered the other shrugging his shoulders.

'I hope you may do it,' said the first speaker aloud and turning to Rex. 'If you do, I will empty it after you to your health, and so will every Swabian here.'

'Ay, that will we!' exclaimed Greif, and the others joined readily in the promise. Seeing how probable it was that by the next evening Rex would be in bed, with a bag of ice on his head, it was not likely that they would be called upon to perform the feat.

'It is a beer-oath then!' said Rex. 'Let us go and fight.'

And they filed out into the narrow street, silently and quietly, in fear of attracting attention to their movements.

CHAPTER 9

The scene presented by the Palmengarten restaurant at four o'clock in the morning was extremely strange. Since Greif and Rex had dined together in the place on the previous evening, the arrangement of the hall had been considerably changed. The palms alone remained in their places around the four sides, and their long spiked leaves and gigantic fans cast fantastic shadows under the brilliant gaslight. The broad marble floor was cleared of furniture and strewn with sawdust, some fifty chairs being arranged at the upper end of the room, around and behind the fountain, whose tiny stream rose high into the air and tinkled as it fell back again into the basin below. A few small tables remained in the corners. The place was lighted by a corona of gas-jets, and was on the whole as bright and roomy a fencing ground as the heart of a Korps student could desire.

The proprietor, who entered with enthusiasm into the scheme, moved about, followed by a confidential waiter in his white apron, examining every detail, adjusting the position of the tables and chairs, turning the principal key of the gas-jets a little so as to obtain the best possible flame, and every now and then running to the door which opened to the outer chambers, as he fancied that he heard someone tapping at the street entrance. The whole effect of the preparations suggested something between a concert and the reception of a deputation, and no one would have suspected that a party of young men were about to engage in a serious tournament amidst the fantastic decorations and the shadows of the beautiful plants, beneath the flood of light that bathed everything in warm lustre.

Presently the expected signal was heard, and the proprietor rushed breathlessly to the outer door. Greif, Rex and their companions entered swiftly and silently, followed by the liveried servant of the Korps who carried an extraordinary collection of bags and bundles, which he dropped upon the floor with a grunt of satisfaction as soon as he was inside. Then he took up his burden again, at the command of the burly second, and carried his traps into the illuminated hall. With the speed of a man accustomed to his work he began to unpack everything, laying out the basket-hilts of the rapiers, adorned with battered colours, side by side, and next to them half a dozen bright blades freshly ground and cleaned, each with its well oiled screw-nut upon the rough end that was to run through the guard, while the small iron wrench was placed in readiness at hand.

Then three leathern jerkins were taken from their sacks and examined to see whether every string and buckle was in order, then the arm and neck bandages, the iron eye-pieces, the gauntlets padded in the wrist, the long gloves and stout caps with leathern visors worn by the seconds, the regulation shirts for the combatants, the bottle of spirits for rubbing their tired arms, a couple of sponges, and a dozen trifles of all sorts—in a word, all the paraphernalia of student warfare.

The next person to appear upon the ground was the surgeon, a young man with a young beard, who had not been many years out of a Korps himself, and who understood by experience the treatment of every scratch and wound that a rapier can inflict. He also carried a bag, though a small one, and began to lay out his instruments in a business-like fashion upon the table reserved for his use. Then there was another summons from the door and the members of the Rhine Korps filed silently in, their dark blue caps contrasting oddly with the brilliant yellow of the Swabians. They saluted gravely and kept together upon the opposite side of the room. Next came the Westphalians, in green caps, and the Saxons with black ones, till nearly a hundred students filled half the available space in the hall. Then the seconds in charge met together in the centre and looked over their lists of duels. There was a moment of total silence in the chamber, until the result was known, for no one could tell exactly which duel would be fought first. Then the four separated again and returned quickly to their comrades.

'We are to let fly first,' said the Swabian second to his chief. 'Now, Hollenstein, old man, jump into your drumming skin!'

'You will be next,' said Greif turning to Rex and speaking in an undertone. 'You had better dress while Hollenstein is out with the Saxon. The affair will not last long, I fancy.'

Hollenstein, a thickset fellow with a baby's complexion, but whose sharp eye showed his temper, went quietly about the operation of dressing, assisted by a couple of foxes, the second in charge and the Korps servant, who was as expert in preparations for duels as an English valet in dressing his master for following the hounds. In ten minutes everything was ready, the seconds on each side drew on their gloves, settled the long visors of their caps well over their eyes, took their blunt rapiers in hand and stepped forward.

The witnesses of each party, also gloved, stood on the left of the combatants, it being their duty to watch the blades, and to see whether either fencer backed down the ground. The umpire took out his pocket-book and pencil and stop-watch, and placed himself where he could look across the fighting. The armed fighters stood up face to face at half the length of the room, a novice supporting the right arm of each high in air.

'*Paukanten parat?* Are the combatants ready?' inquired the umpire, who was the chief of the Westphalians.

'*Parat!* Ready!' was answered from both sides simultaneously.

'Silence!' cried the umpire. 'The duel begins. *Auf die Mensur! Fertig! Los!*'

Hollenstein and his adversary walked forward, accompanied by their seconds. Each struck a formal tierce cut at the other, and a halt was cried. They scarcely retired and the umpire repeated the words 'To the fight! Ready! Go!' and the duel began in earnest. Both were accomplished swordsmen, and the combat promised to be a long one. They exhibited to the admiring spectators every intricacy of *schlager* fencing, in all its wonderful neatness and quickness of cut and parry. From time to time a halt was called, and each man retired to his original place, his right arm being caught and held in air by the 'bearing-fox,' as the novice is called whose business it is to fill the office. The object of this proceeding is to prevent a rush of blood to the arm, which might cause pain and numbness in the member and interfere with the combatant's quickness.

'A couple of good fencers,' remarked Rex as he rose from his chair and went to prepare himself for what was before him.

'You will see what will happen,' answered Greif with a smile of confidence in his comrade.

The 'drumming,' as the students call it, proceeded for some minutes, and nothing was heard in the hall but the sharp whistle and ring of the blades and the sound of shuffling feet upon the sawdust-covered floor. All at once Hollenstein turned his hand completely round upon his wrist in the act of striking what is called a deep-*carte*, remained a moment in this singular position, which seemed to confuse his adversary, and then as the latter was making up his mind what to do, suddenly finished the movement and returned to his guard in time to parry the inevitable tierce. A thin line of scarlet instantly appeared upon the Saxon's face, straight across his left cheek.

'Halt!' cried both seconds at once.

'She sat!' exclaimed the second of the Swabians, throwing down his blunt sword and making for a goblet of beer that was placed in readiness for him, as though he took no further interest in the proceedings. Hollenstein stood as usual with his arm supported by the novice, while the Saxon was examined by the surgeon.

'*Abfuhr!*' said the latter. The word means that the wounded man must be removed.

'Please to declare the *Abfuhr!*' said the Swabian second relinquishing his glass and turning sharply to the umpire.

'Saxonia is led away,' declared the Westphalian chief, making a note of the fact in his pocket-book, and shutting up his watch.

Before he had finished speaking, Hollenstein had given up his sword and was beginning to disarm, while a fox wiped the perspiration from his placid pink face.

'Nicely done, old man,' said Greif, coming up to him.

'I like that way of doing it, do not you?' inquired Hollenstein with a childlike smile. 'I practised all last summer on my father's orderly. You know we always keep fencing things at home.'

'And how did the soldier like it?' asked Greif with a laugh.

'Better than you would,' replied the other laughing, too. 'He is a clever churl and has discovered the answer to the attack. Give me some beer, little fox!'

The novice obeyed, and a Homeric draught interrupted the interview. Greif turned to Rex, upon whose face the iron eyepieces were being adjusted. All the Swabians present were collected around him, excepting the second, who sat in solitary glory by his beer, opposite the Rhine Korps, awaiting events with stolid indifference.

'Take care!' said Greif whispering into the ear of his friend. 'I have never seen you fence, and Bauer's *cartes* are famous.'

'Remember the big horn!' said some of the men around

124

him.

'I will not forget it,' answered Rex smiling, as he opened and shut his hand in the gauntlet, and then held out the palm to be chalked. 'And I hope you will not forget your promises either,' he added.

'Will you not have a glass of brandy?' asked someone with a scarcely perceptible tinge of irony.

'My friend,' replied Rex, turning sharply round in the direction of the speaker's voice, 'exactly fifteen minutes after the word "Go," I will drink a bottle of champagne with you, and I should be greatly obliged if you would direct the waiter to put the wine in ice at once, as it will scarcely be cool in so short a time.'

'Willingly,' said the student with a dry laugh, in which some of the bystanders joined, while all looked curiously at the man who seemed so absolutely sure of success. Greif's face was grave, however, and he himself selected the rapier for Rex's hand. All was ready and the adversaries stood up in their places. Bauer the Rhine Korps man, was an ugly sight. The eye-pieces gave a singularly sinister expression to his sallow face, and his disorderly hair looked like a wig of twisted black wire, while the jerkin he wore seemed almost dropping from his long, sinewy frame. He made his sharp weapon whistle three or four times in the air and tapped his foot impatiently upon the marble floor as though anxious to begin. Greif's heart beat quickly, and he was conscious that he would infinitely rather fight the duel himself.

The umpire began by declaring that the duel was between Herr Bauer of the Rhine Korps and Herr Rex, who fought with Swabian weapons.

'Formerly of the Heidelberg Saxo-Prussians,' said Rex quietly.

Everyone started and looked at him, on hearing the name of the most renowned Korps in Germany.

'With a charge?' inquired the umpire, politely, and holding his pencil ready to enter the fact upon his note-book.

'First,' answered Rex laconically.

The students looked at each other and began to wonder how

it was possible that such an important personage as a former chief of the Heidelberg Saxo-Prussians could have so long concealed his identity. But the umpire did not wait, though he reflected that Rex must have been in activity a very long time ago. Of course, the statement must be true, as any one might verify it instantly by a reference to the registers.

'*Paukanten parat?*' inquired the umpire.

'*Parat!*'

The spectators observed that Bauer's first *tierce* was more than formal, and that if Rex's guard had not been good, it might very well have done some damage. Rex's fencing was altogether different from Hollenstein's. He seemed to possess neither the grace nor the dexterity which distinguished that gentle swordsman, although in figure he was far lighter and more actively made. And yet Bauer could not get at him. He was one of those fencers who seem to work awkwardly, but who sometimes puzzle their adversaries more than any professional master of the art. His movements appeared to be slow and yet they were never behind time, and he had a curious instinct about what was coming. Bauer's famous deep-*cartes* were always met by a cut which at once parried the attack and confused the striker.

Once or twice Rex's long blade shot out above his adversary's head with tremendous force, but Bauer was tall, quick and accomplished, and the attempt did not succeed. Greif began to feel that the match was by no means an uneven one, and he breathed more freely.

'I think you could manage it, if you tried harder,' he whispered to Rex, during a short halt.

'Of course,' answered Rex. 'What do you expect?' Even through the iron eye-pieces Greif could see the colourless, stony stare of his friend's eyes.

Greif would have been more than satisfied if the duel ended without a scratch on either side, and such a result would have more than surprised the spectators of the encounter. Every one present knew by experience that in *schlager* fencing a month's practice is worth all the theory and skill which a man might possess who had not touched a rapier for years. Nevertheless, as the encounter proceeded, and both remained unhurt, Greif regretted that Rex should have boasted that Bauer would be disabled and laid up for a long time. Meanwhile the saturnine Rhine man grew slowly angry, as his arm became wearied by the protracted effort. His wiry locks were matted with perspiration, his shaggy brows knit themselves into an ugly frown, which was made more hideous by the black iron spectacles, he stamped his foot angrily, and made desperate efforts to get at Rex's face with his favourite under-cut.

'I am going to try now,' said Rex during the next halt, and turning his head to Greif.

He went forward again, and every one noticed that his rapier was higher than usual and seemed not to cover him at all. He brandished it in the air in a way that looked utterly foolhardy. Bauer came on furiously, feeling that if he failed now he must be laughed at forever. His long arm turned with the rapidity of lightning, and everyone saw the whistling blade flash towards Rex's unprotected cheek. To the amazement of all present the cut did not take effect. There was a loud clash of steel, accompanied by a harsh, grating noise. With irresistible fury Rex had brought down his weapon, countering in *carte*, parrying with his basket-hilt and then tearing, as it were, the reverse edge of his flexible blade through his enemy's face, from forehead to chin. 'She sat!' exclaimed the Swabian second, mechanically. But instead of dropping his blunt sword and making for his beer, he stood open-mouthed, staring stupidly at the unfortunate Bauer, as though he could not believe his eyes. The surgeon ran forward, looked at the wound and almost immediately nodded to the umpire.

'Rhenania is led away!' said the latter, in the midst of a dead silence.

It would have been contrary to custom and etiquette for the Swabians to manifest any noisy satisfaction at the result of the affair, but as Rex drew back he was surrounded and hemmed in by Greif's comrades, who tore the rapier from his grasp, pressed his gloved hands, untied the strings and loosed the buckles of his jerkin, wiped the slight perspiration from his face, and divested him of all his defensive accoutrements almost before he had breath to speak. A couple of novices rubbed his arm, while twenty young fellows congratulated him in an undertone. The two who were nearest were the student whom Bauer had formerly hurt, and the one with whom Rex had promised to drink the wine. The latter held a glass of champagne to the conqueror's lips.

'Your health,' said Rex as he drank. 'It is not too cold to drink,' he added with a smile when he had tasted the liquid.

'With a little practice, you would have to drink it hot,' laughed the other.

'You must teach me that trick,' said the rosy-cheeked Hollenstein. 'It is the best I ever saw.'

'The Rhine Korps will have to make a contract for buying iron noses wholesale,' remarked someone else, referring to the story Rex had told on the previous evening.

Greif stood nearby, looking on, with undisguised satisfaction, and not yet altogether recovered from his surprise. He could see at a glance that Rex's position with regard to the Korps was wholly changed, and that henceforth his friend was likely to be almost as popular as himself. The fact that Rex had been chief of the Saxo-Prussians was in itself a sufficient recommendation and would long since have inspired them with respect, had Rex chosen to disclose his former dignity. Greif wondered why he had been silent, but, on the whole he was glad that the man should have earned popularity by an exploit rather than upon the strength of his former importance.

For the present, conversation was impossible. A couple of Greif's novices were to go out for the first time, and it was necessary to encourage them and see that everything went well. Swabia was in luck on that day, for the two youths acquitted themselves honourably, each fighting fifteen rounds without being touched, and each inflicting a couple of very small scratches upon their enemies.

'A white day for the Swabians,' said Greif, when he at last sat down to a sausage and a glass of beer for breakfast.

His Korps had nothing more to do with the proceedings, for they had no more duels on the day's list, and as none of them had been hurt, they prepared to watch the subsequent fights over a glass of beer, collecting themselves round Greif, Rex, and the thirsty second. It was by this time about five o'clock in the morning. The gas burned steadily overhead and the meeting of arms proceeded as regularly and quickly as any Roman show of gladiators. From time to time the Korps servants washed the blood-stained marble floor and threw down fresh sawdust for the next encounter. The surgeon and the wounded were kept out of sight behind the plants, and nothing disagreeable met the eye. The gleam and flashing of the steel swords under the yellow light, the gay colours of the caps, the quick movements of combatants and seconds were all pleasant to see against the background of stately exotic plants which made the hall look like a great conservatory.

Greif looked at it all and enjoyed it, almost wishing that this might be the last scene of the kind which he should attend, and that he might always have the impression of it when he thought of his student life, so different from the dismal meetings that sometimes took place in deserted barns, or in outhouses of country inns. In some ways he preferred the Palmengarten as a fighting ground to the forest glades in which the summer duels were sometimes fought. He felt, as he sat there, chief of his Korps, and looked up to by everyone, very much as he fancied a Roman emperor must have felt in his high seat over the arena. A deep sense of satisfaction descended upon his soul. He had the best place, his Korps had been victorious, his best friend had highly distinguished himself, justifying Greif's own opinion of him, and gaining in ten minutes the respect and admiration of all his comrades. Rex watched him in silence, as though trying to guess his thoughts.

'Yes, you are a lucky fellow,' he said at last, hitting the mark as usual. The words chilled Greif, and his expression changed. All at once, in that crowded place of meeting, amidst the satisfaction of victory and the excitement of other struggles, the memory of his home in the dark forest rose before him like a gloomy shadow. His mind went back to that evening when Rex's first prediction had been so suddenly fulfilled, and then, in an instant, it flashed upon him that only last night Rex had been drawing circles and strange figures upon the marble table at the moment when Bauer had approached them. He turned to his friend and spoke in a low voice.

'You knew it by the figure,' he said. 'That is the reason you were so confident.'

'Yes,' answered Rex quietly. 'Of course I did.'

'It is true that you are a first-rate fencer,' remarked Greif doubtfully.

'Nothing extraordinary. The man had not a chance, from the first, especially as we settled the matter so soon after the question was asked.'

'What question?'

'The question I asked when I set up the figure.'

Greif was silent. He could not bring himself to believe in what he regarded as a sham science, and he could not reconcile any belief in such absurdities with the indubitable fact that Rex was a most enlightened man, learned in his own department, cultivated in mind, a scorner of old-fashioned prejudices and ideas, distrustful of all cheap theories and of all scientific men who talked eloquently about the progress of learning. That such a person should put any faith in astrology was a monstrous incongruity. And yet Rex not only trusted in what he pretended to foretell, but was actually willing to risk serious personal injuries on the strength of his divinations. Greif thought of what he had read concerning fanatics and the almost incredible good fortune which sometimes attended them. Then a wild desire overcame him to know what Rex had seen in the figure on that memorable night which had brought the news of Rieseneck's intended return.

'We have not spoken of those things lately,' he said after a long pause. 'Will you tell me what it is that must happen to me, according to your theory?'

'There are some things of which it is best not to talk at all,' Rex answered, looking earnestly at his companion. His hard eyes softened a little.

'Is it as bad as that?' asked Greif with an attempt to laugh.

'It is as bad as that, and as it will all happen through no fault of yours, and since nothing which you, at least, can do, could prevent it, it is better that you should not know.'

'You will not tell me?'

'Not unless you insist upon it, and you will not.'

'Why not? I do insist, as much as one friend can with another.' Greif could not quite submit to Rex's way of saying what he would do, or would not do.

'There are good reasons why you should not,' returned the latter calmly. 'In the first place we are good friends, and if I told you what is before you, it would be impossible not to injure our amicable relations. You feel that, as well as I do. If warning could help you in the least, I would not be silent. If I had any advice to give you, I would offer it, at the risk of offending you. You know that in your heart you would not quite believe me, if I spoke, and that you would always fancy I had some object in view, until all were accomplished. Even then you might never forget the disagreeable association between my personality and your calamities. I prefer to remain where I am in your estimation. Besides, why should I cause you all the pain of anticipation, when it can do no good? After all, nobody is infallible. What if I had made a mistake in my calculations?'

'That is true.' answered Greif, though his tone showed some doubt. Although he really did not believe that calculation or mathematics of any sort had anything to do with Rex's seeming knowledge of future events, the possibility of a mistake seemed small indeed, when Rex himself suggested it.

'I knew you would not insist,' said Rex. 'Indeed it is much better to watch those two fellows drumming on each other's heads, and to drink our early draught in peace without speculating about the future. Look at them! It is nearly a quarter of an hour, and not a scratch yet, though they hit each other with every *tierce*, flat as a soup-plate falling upon a millpond. But it is a pretty sight.'

Greif did not answer. The gladiatorial show had lost its charms for him and his mind brooded gloomily over coming events. The sun was not up, though it was broad dawn when he and his companions went out into the cool, silent streets, realising when they breathed the morning air the closeness of the heated atmosphere they had quitted. They separated by degrees, dropping off, one after the other, as each approached his lodgings, but before going home they all accompanied Rex to the street door of his dwelling.

When Greif was alone he threw open his window to the fresh morning breeze, and sitting down as he was, drank in the air, which to him seemed so delightfully sweet, though it would have chilled a weaker man to the bone. It was all the refreshment he needed, in spite of a sleepless night, spent chiefly in an atmosphere heated by gas and heavy with the fumes of tobacco. The morning, too, was exceptionally clear and beautiful. A scarcely perceptible mist blended the neutral tints of the old town with the faint colours of the sky, which changed by gentle degrees from dark blue to violet, from violet to palest green, then to yellow and then at last to the living blue of day above, while a vast fan of golden light trembled above the spot whence the sun would presently rise. The level rays gilded the slender cathedral spire, and the glass of many a pointed gable-window in the town sent back the flaming reflexion. All above was warm, and all below was cold in the blue shadow that still darkened the flowing river and the narrow streets beyond.

For a time Greif gave himself up to the pleasure of the sight and sensation. His instinctive love of nature was strong enough to absorb his whole being at certain moments, for it was real, and not cultivated, thorough and altogether unconscious of itself. But when the exceptional loveliness of the dawn and sunrise was drowned in the flooding light of an ordinarily fine day, Greif rose from his seat by the window and went about the business of dressing regretfully, as though he wished that the morning might sink back again into the twilight, as quickly as in the far north, when the sun first shows the edge of his disc above the horizon in early spring.

He had no thought of taking any rest, and intended to go to the University as usual, for it was a part of his Teutonic character to take his amusement at the expense of his sleep rather than to the detriment of his work. After such a night an Italian would have gone to bed, a Frenchman would have swallowed a brimming glass of *absinthe* and would have passed the day in visiting his fellow-students, or fellow-artists, an Englishman would have taken a plunge in the icy river and would have gone for a walk in the country. But Greif did none of these things. He drank his coffee and went to his books and his lectures as though nothing unusual had happened.

He did it mechanically and felt himself obliged to do it, as much as any guard-officer in Berlin, who comes home from a ball at dawn, exchanges the inadmissible kid gloves and varnished boots he wears in society for the regulation articles of leather, smoothes his hair with the little brushes he always has in his pocket, draws his sword and marches out with his company of grenadiers to the exercising ground, as merrily and as naturally as though he had spent the night in bed.

Before he left the house again, Greif received a letter from his father. It was some time since the latter had mentioned Riese-neck and Greif did not now expect any news concerning him. He turned pale as he read the contents. It appeared that Riese-neck had landed in Europe and intended to proceed without delay to Berlin, in order to report himself at the Home Office as one who desired to take advantage of the amnesty with the intention of residing in his native country.

'I myself,' wrote Greifenstein, 'have serious doubts in this matter. I cannot believe that your uncle is included in the general pardon for political offenders. He committed a crime against both civil and military law and was condemned by a court-martial. It would have been more respectable to shoot him at once. As this was not done, I have actually been obliged to write to him, now, warning him that in my opinion he is not safe. In the meanwhile, be careful, my dear boy, and keep amongst your own Korps, where you are not likely to have trouble about your infamous relation. He is not worth fighting for, though you would of course be obliged to go out if a stranger made disagreeable remarks.

'Happily, in a little more than a month, you will be at home, where such things cannot occur. Praise be to Heaven, we are very well, though your mother continues to be more silent than usual. Hexerl has got over the distemper very well and is a fine pup. I have decided not to fell the old wood, though it is quite time. What need have I for the money? Let the trees stand till the wind blows them down. Perhaps you will be glad, though you do not often go to that part of the forest. I have sent your rifle to Stuttgardt to be re-sighted as you wished. And so, goodbye.'

Greif put the letter into his pocket and went gloomily on his way to the lecture, reflecting that at that very moment Rieseneck was probably on his way to Berlin.

CHAPTER 10

The snow fell heavily in the Black Forest during the third week of December. It lay in great white drifts against the huge rampart of Greifenstein, blown against the rough masonry by the bitter north wind, until the approach to the main gate was a deep trench dug in the white covering of the earth. The driving blast had driven great patches of flakes against the lofty wall so that they stuck to the stones and looked like broad splashes of white paint. The north sides of the pointed roofs on the towers were white, too, and gleamed in the occasional bursts of sunshine that interrupted the fierce weather. In the forest, the slanting branches of the firs were loaded down with irregular masses of snow, through which the needle foliage looked as black as ink. Not a spot of colour was visible anywhere, for everything was either black or white.

Old Greifenstein was no more afraid of the weather than he was of anything else. Day after day he went out with his gun and his dog, to fight his way for miles through the drifts, up and down hill, over the open moor where the snow was not knee-deep, under the giant trees from which great lumps of it fell now and then upon his fur cap and grizzled hair, down into the dells and gorges where it was nearly up to his neck, and where his sturdy dog struggled wildly through the passage his master had made.

Greifenstein pursued the only amusement of his life in his own solitary fashion, rarely shooting at anything, never missing when he did, killing a buck once or twice in a week and bringing it home on his own shoulders for the use of his household, or lying in wait for six or seven hours at a time to get a shot at a stag; grimly pleased to be always alone, and silently satisfied in the thought that all was his, and his only, to kill or to let live at his *seigneurial* discretion. The keepers knew that he wanted no companions, and they kept out of his way when he was abroad, not dissatisfied perhaps that their tireless master should do most of their work in the bitter weather, leaving them to smoke their pipes in their cottages or to drink their beer and cherry spirits in the inn of the distant village. He left the house in the morning and rarely returned before dusk. It is not strange that his humour should have grown more stern and melancholy under such circumstances.

Greifenstein and his wife seemed to understand each other, however, and though days passed during which they scarcely exchanged a word, neither complained of the other's silence nor felt the slightest desire to do so. From time to time one of the servants declared that he could bear the life no longer, and gave up his large wages and gorgeous apparel to return to the city. He was replaced by another, without any remark. Contrary to German custom, Greifenstein never expected any one to stay long in the house, and merely stipulated that anyone who wished to leave should give warning a fortnight previously.

Neither he nor his wife were yet so old as to tempt servants to stay on for the death, in the hope of picking up something worth having in the general confusion. There was something strange in the way the pair lived, lonely and unloved in their ancient home, amidst a crowd of ever-changing attendants, who succumbed one by one to the awful dreariness of the isolated life, and went away to give place to others, who, in their turn would give it up after six months or a year. And yet neither Greifenstein nor Clara would have changed their existence.

Greifenstein had abandoned the attempt to explain his wife's illness, if she were really ill, but he could not help seeing the alteration that was going on for the worse in her appearance and character, and the sight did not contribute to his peace. He himself looked much the same as ever. After receiving the news that his half-brother intended to return, he stiffened his stiff neck to meet whatever misfortune was in store for him; and when he learned that Rieseneck was in Europe, he only set his teeth a little closer and tramped a little more savagely through the snow-drifts after the game. He knew that he could do nothing to hinder the progress of events, and he knew that if his brother came to Greifenstein, he should need all his strength and energy in dealing with him. There was nothing to do but to wait.

As for Clara's secret, the more he thought about it, the more persuaded he was that it was not connected with Rieseneck, but with some other person. He grew anxious, however, as he watched her, for it was now clear that unless something occurred to revive her vital energy and her spirits, she must soon become an invalid altogether, even if she did not die of her sufferings. More than once, Greifenstein proposed to go away, to travel, to spend the winter in a southern climate, but she refused to leave her home, with a firmness that surprised him. There was Greif, she said, and Greif must be considered. When he was married they might go away and leave the castle to the young couple. Until then she would not move. Greifenstein could not but see the wisdom of this course. Meanwhile he attempted to induce his wife to live more in the open air, to ride, to drive, to do anything. But she confessed that she was too weak to face the inclement weather.

Greifenstein was a kind-hearted man in his own peculiar way, and he began to be sorry for her. She no longer distressed his sense of fitness, as formerly, by her inopportune interruptions, her wild smiles, her hysterical laughter, her pitifully flippant talk. He said to himself that she must be ill indeed, to be so serious and quiet. Perhaps she needed amusement. His ideas of diversion were not of a very gay nature, and since she would neither leave the house nor the country he did not quite see what he could do to amuse her. But the thought that it was necessary for her health grew until he felt that it was his duty to do something. Then he hesitated no longer and made a desperate attempt, involving a considerable sacrifice to his own inclinations. He proposed to read aloud to her out of the best German authors. Even poor Clara, whose sense of humour was almost wholly gone, smiled faintly and opened her faded eyes very wide at the suggestion.

'What an extraordinary idea!' she exclaimed.

The time when Greifenstein made his proposition was the evening, when the two sat in their easy-chairs on each side of the great heraldically carved chimney-piece in the drawing-room. They generally read to themselves, and each had a small table with a shaded lamp and a pile of books.

'My dear,' answered Greifenstein, 'it is not a question of ideas. I have examined the matter and I have come to the conclusion that you must be amused. It is therefore my duty to provide you with amusement. As I cannot sing, nor dance, and as you do not play cards, I cannot think of any more fitting method of diverting you than by reading aloud. German literature offers much variety. You have only to choose the author you prefer, and I will read as much as you like.'

Greifenstein was absolutely in earnest, and delivered his remarks in his usual dry and matter-of-fact way. When he had finished speaking he took up the volumes that were on his table, one after the other, and looked at the titles on the covers, as though already trying to decide upon the one which would best suit his purpose. Clara did not find a ready answer to his arguments, and her smile had disappeared. Her wasted hands lay idly in her lap, and her tired head sank forward upon her breast. She wished it were all over, and that she might fall asleep without the dread of waking. Greifenstein did not notice her.

'What shall it be?' he asked. She raised her face slowly and looked at him.

'Oh, Hugo, I would rather not!' she exclaimed faintly.

Her husband laid down the volume he had last taken up, leaned back in his chair, folded his knotted hands over his knee and looked at her intently.

'Clara,' he said after a few moments, 'what is the matter with you?'

'Nothing, nothing at all!' she answered, with a feeble effort to look cheerful.

'There is no object in telling me that,' returned Greifenstein, still keeping his eyes fixed upon her. 'There is something the matter with you, and it is something serious. I have watched you for a long time. Either you are bodily ill, or else some matter troubles your mind.'

'Oh no! Nothing, I assure you,' she replied in a scarcely audible tone.

'I repeat that it is of no use. I do not wish to question you, my dear,' he continued, almost kindly. 'Whatever your thoughts are, they are your own. But I cannot see you wasting away before my eyes without wishing to help you. It is part of my duty. Now a man is stronger than a woman, and less imaginative. It may be that you are distressing yourself with little reason, and that, if you would confide in me, I might demonstrate to you that you have no cause for repining. Consider well, whether you can tell me your trouble, and give me an answer.'

Clara listened, at first scarcely heeding what he said. Then as she realised the nature of his request and thought of her secret, she fancied that she must go mad. It seemed as though some diabolical power were at hand, forcing her slowly, slowly, against her will, to rise up from her chair, to tell the story, to speak the truth. Her brain reeled. She could hear the fatal words ringing through the room in the familiar tones of her own voice, distinctly, one by one, omitting nothing in the immensity of her self-accusation. She could feel the icy horror creeping through bone and marrow, as the truth tortured her in the utterance of it. She could see Greifenstein's grey face transformed with rage and hatred, she trembled under the inhuman savageness of his fiery eyes, she saw his tall body rise up before her, and his hand raised to strike, and she covered her face to die.

It was only a waking dream. The stillness roused her to life, her hands dropped from her eyes, and she saw her husband sitting quietly in his place and gazing at her with the same kindly, anxious glance as before. She had not spoken, nor uttered any sound, and Greifenstein had not seen the death-pallor under her paint. He had only seen her lift her hands to her face and take them away again almost immediately. In that moment she had suffered the pain of hell, but her secret was still her own. That terrible, unseen power that had pressed her to speak was gone, and no one knew what was in her heart.

'You are certainly very far from well,' said Greifenstein, returning to the attack with characteristic pertinacity. 'Can you not make up your mind to tell me?'

'No!' she cried suddenly in a terrified voice. Then out of sheer fright she made an enormous effort over herself, and laughed aloud. Under the influence of that mortal dread, in the supreme exertion she made to destroy the effect of the monosyllable that had escaped her lips, the laugh sounded natural. It was well done, for it was done for life or death, and if it failed she was betrayed. That single 'No' had been almost enough to ruin all, but her laugh saved her, though she trembled in every weakened joint when its echoes died away among the carved rafters of the great room, and she felt the drops of cold perspiration moving softly over her forehead towards the rouge on her cheeks.

'Ah,' exclaimed Greifenstein, 'that sounds more like yourself. Perhaps we ought to talk more in the evening. It does me good to hear you laugh nowadays. Let us talk, by all means. I am sure all this is only a foolish fit of melancholy, is it not?'

'Oh, no doubt it is. Let us try and talk, if you like.'

'I am too silent a man for you, Clara,' said her husband reflectively. 'It is certainly my duty to make an effort.'

'It is just as much mine,' she answered with an earnestness that attracted his notice. She was thinking that unless she roused herself, the fearful scene that had been enacted in her imagination might someday take place in reality.

'No,' said Greifenstein. 'It is you who are ill, and it is you who must be amused. Now, what do you say to my proposition? Shall I read something to you? Shall it be Goethe, or Schiller, or Heine? You know all the modern writers well enough.' 'Something from Heine then, if you will,' answered Clara. 'You are so kind! Perhaps he will make us laugh.'

'Yes,' echoed her husband. 'Perhaps Heine will make us laugh.'

The ghastly entertainment began, and continued for an hour, but the merriment was not as great as had been anticipated. The writer's marvellous wit was lost upon Greifenstein who, in the conscientiousness of his attempt to read well and expressively, confused his own mind to such an extent as to understand very little of what passed his lips. As for Clara, she closed her eyes and leaned back in her chair, scarcely knowing what her mind was dwelling on, but conscious of an added horror in her miserable life, so great that all before seemed well-nigh insignificant. She tried to listen from time to time, but her husband's voice sounded as though it were far away, reaching her through some muffling medium that intervened between her and him.

The clock of the castle struck ten, and Greifenstein closed the book with a sort of military precision when he reached the end of the sentence he was reading. Clara roused herself to thank him.

'It has been so good of you!' she said. 'I have enjoyed it very much.'

'We will read every evening, until you are better,' answered her husband with great determination. And he kept his word, although his plan for diverting the poor lady was not attended with much success.

Night after night he took his seat by the fire, exactly half an hour after the evening meal was ended. Night after night Clara sat with half-closed eyes, hearing his wooden voice, as in a dream, and wondering how all would end. There was no change in their lives or habits beyond the introduction of what Greifenstein called the amusement of his wife. It was all the same, the monotonous succession of morning and evening, of night and noon and evening again. Possibly the lives of these two persons might have continued to crawl along in the narrow channel they had made for themselves during many years more, if the events which had been so long preparing had been retarded; for Greifenstein was a man of habit in everything, incapable of weariness in the performance of what he considered to be his duty, and Clara's really strong health might have carried her through half a lifetime of exasperating stagnation.

Indeed, if things altered at all after the conversation about her state, the change was for the better. A fictitious calm descended upon the old house, and a certain gentleness found its way into the relations of the couple which was agreeable to both. With Clara this was the result of exhaustion and despair. She felt herself wholly unable to bear any great disaster should it fall upon her, and she was grateful to her husband, and prayed, if she prayed at all, that both might die peacefully during those days. She even had a vague belief that Heaven would not really bring about that hideous catastrophe that haunted her dreams, and that forced her to dream of it when she was waking. Had she not been a faithful wife to the stern, grey man who had sat opposite to her for five and twenty years? Had she not been a fairly good mother to Greif, if not very loving, nor very wise, at least what people call a good mother?

Her conscience told her that, at least, and she felt how great a comfort it was to think that she had not been wholly bad. Moreover, she had been placed in strange circumstances when she had done the deed, whatever it was, and if she had not been as young at that time as she had pretended to be, she had yet not been so old as to understand thoroughly what she was doing. Heaven would surely not be so unkind as to visit upon her now the sins of her youth; now, when a quarter of a century of peaceful married life had intervened between that day and this; now, when Greif himself was grown to a man's estate and was to be married in his turn.

Surely, there was mercy for her. But if there were none, if Heaven were to be more just than kind, what would become of her? The thin blood beat in her hollow temples as she thought of it, and then sank back suddenly to the tired heart whence it had risen. Above all else, the thought of Greif was unbearable. He, too, must know, if anything were known. He, too, would turn upon her, and force her to drain the last dregs of the death-draught. But she still believed and hoped, hoped and believed, that the day would never come.

And yet it was at hand, now, after all those months of agonising fear, just when she deluded herself with the sweet thought that it might never come at all. Greifenstein came home in the dusk one afternoon, and found a letter upon his desk in his own room. He broke the seal and read it while his teeth ground upon each other, and his face turned grey. He did not utter a sound, he did not strike his forehead nor clench his fist, nor fall into a chair. He only stiffened his neck a little and stood silently gazing at the fire. After a moment's reflexion, he tossed the letter into the flames and waited until it was quite burnt. Then he rang the bell.

'Listen, Jacob,' he said to the servant who came, and his voice did not tremble. 'A friend of mine has written to say that he is coming to the forest to shoot. He comes alone, as I go myself. It is bad weather, and he may find his way here at any hour. When he presents himself, bring him immediately to this room and send for me. I will not go far from the castle until he arrives.'

The servant asked the gentleman's name.

'Herr Brandt,' answered Greifenstein without hesitation.

The letter had informed him that Rieseneck's application to

be included in the amnesty had been absolutely refused, and that he had fled a second time under an assumed name. He appealed to his brother to help him over the frontier to Constance, and said that he might arrive at any time after his letter.

When he was alone, Greifenstein sat down to consider the situation, after carefully filling and lighting the pipe his son had brought him at his last visit. He was in the habit of doing this every day when he came home, and it seemed to him that to omit any detail of his ordinary life would be to show an amount of emotion quite unworthy of himself. It was one of those small acts, performed alone, which are the truest indications of a man's character. If he was not able to smoke his pipe as usual, it must be because he was unable to bear calmly what had come upon him, and consequently was not fit to meet his wife at dinner without betraying his anxiety. It was not an act that showed indifference, as many would think. On the contrary, it was the expression of his indomitably conscientious nature. To change one small thing in his demeanour, even when he was alone, would have been to begin badly and at a disadvantage.

He scrupulously put his feet upon the same spot on the fender at which they usually rested when he came home, he sat in his accustomed attitude, and he smoked with his accustomed solemnity. It would be a mistake to exaggerate the importance which Rieseneck's coming had in his eyes, as far as any material consequences to himself were concerned. There was no ruin before him, no inevitable disaster. He dreaded the moral side of the incident, and worst of all the possibility of his being obliged to tell Clara of the existence of his disgraced brother. He knew well enough that the newspapers would contain an account of Rieseneck's attempt, and he feared lest some journalist with a long memory should recall the fact of the relationship.

Like most men who have formerly lived in a capital, he fancied that every one still knew him, and respected him, and he attached immense importance to the mere mention of his name. That he should be called the brother of a disgraced and criminal officer in a journal, seemed to him a terrible calamity, an almost unbearable blow to his pride. He did not guess that he was as really forgotten as though he had been twenty years dead. The days when he had worn a uniform seemed very near to him still, and he could not realise that his own youth could seem so distant to those who had once known him.

His whole nature revolted against the thought of meeting Rieseneck, and though he was not troubled by an active imagination he could not help thinking of the bitter words he would use in the interview. There was nothing cynical in his moral composition. To him, honour was a fact and not a prejudice, a priceless possession of his own, a household idol for which he was at all times ready to sacrifice every other consideration. The existence of his brother was a rent in the wholeness of that fact, a flaw in his title to that possession, a stain upon the divinity of that domestic god. Greifenstein was very unhappy, and his trouble took the form of resentment against the offender, rather than of a mild and harmless self-pity.

He was hindered from forgetting and he would not forgive, for the injury was real, as he saw it. In crowded cities men have other things to do than to trouble their peace concerning ideals. A neighbour, a friend, a relation, falls into overwhelming disgrace—they pause a minute and then pass on, reflecting with all the certainty gained by long experience, that the world will soon forget, and that, after all is said, their brother's infamy is no concern of theirs. But when men who are scrupulously honourable themselves, and who respect their own family traditions of honour more than anything else on earth, are shut off from the world for many years, they cannot look at such matters as city folks do.

The less they have to do the more they think of their household history, and the greater is the pride they feel in reviewing the biography of their race. A sort of medieval twilight descends upon their latter years, and their souls receive the heraldic vision. They brood gloomily over the misdeeds of some long-dead ancestor, and their faces glow when they think of their crusading forefathers. They fight again the battles of long ago, they charge

with Welf or Weiblingen, they follow the Kaiser to his corona-
tion in imperial Rome, they strive through the press of knights,
they perish with Conradin in Naples, they prick hotly after the
standard of the great Rudolf, they kill and riot throughout the
Thirty Years' War, they shed their heart's blood with Frederick,
they fall at Austerlitz, they rise at Leipzig, they are with Blucher
at Waterloo, with 'Unser Fritz' at Koniggratz, with Schmettow's
gallant *cuirassiers* in the deadly ride of Mars la Tour, and they
land themselves each evening before the carved *escutcheon* of the
old chimney-piece at home, the proud descendants of a race of
heroes known to fame.

And yet, though all be true from first to last, fame knows
little of them. Who remembers their names? Their fathers for
ages were gentlemen like themselves, never very great or powerful, sometimes poor, almost insignificant in the great throng of
light-hearted soldiers on whose necks empires have rested, and
by whose hands kingdoms have been overthrown. Probably not
one of all those dead knights ever felt half the pride in himself
that is felt in him by his representative in the nineteenth century,
nor experienced half as much pleasure in gazing at his battered
shield with its half-defaced cognisance, as now brings the blood
to his descendant's cheek as he looks at the carved stone sem-
blance of the original.

In the trained sight of this modern gentleman, the past is
more real than its own reality was long ago; he is more loyal
than the law, more royalist than the king, more protestant than
Luther, more conservative than a Chinese sage. An insinuation
against any member of his race, though he have been dead since
the first Crusade, is a direct insult to himself, to be wiped out
by personal combat. His sleeping passions, if roused, take but
one direction, to fight for something, his king, his religion or
his honour. His memories and his prejudices are complicated,
interwoven and entangled beyond all belief; his character is simple, for his only principle is that those prejudices and traditions
are alike infallible and unassailable, and that no sacrifice must be
spared in defending them. Such is the old-fashioned German

country gentleman, and such was Hugo von Greifenstein.

Rieseneck, a traitor to his country, the betrayer of a military trust, condemned, a fugitive and publicly infamous, was about to enter the sacred place of his brother's idols. For a few hours at least he was to abide under the roof which sheltered such precious memories. His abominable presence was to defile the honourable dwelling of all the Greifensteins. Worse than that, his execrated name was to be coupled with that of Greifenstein himself in the public prints. Matters could not be worse, in the estimation of the iron-grey man who sat solemnly smoking his pipe before the fire, and straining every faculty to maintain his usual composure even in his solitude.

The situation seemed unbearable, and yet it must be borne. Every moment was in all likelihood bringing Rieseneck nearer, every minute might be the last before his coming. There was nothing to be done. Greifenstein had not even the diversion of making preparations for the man's hurried journey, since any show of preparation might be detrimental to the scheme. His plan was to start in the early dawn of the next morning with guns and dogs as though for a shooting expedition, to ride as far as possible, then to leave the horses and to cross the frontier into Switzerland.

Nothing could be easier, and he knew that Rieseneck was aware of the fact from his knowledge of the locality. Moreover it was probable that although the application for pardon had been refused, no attempt would be made to arrest the fugitive. He would be allowed to leave the country unmolested, as it would be considered impolitic to increase the scandal by consigning him again to the fortress whence he had escaped so many years before. Greifenstein had nothing to fear for himself, and he cared nothing what became of his brother, provided that he were not caught. Nevertheless, he suffered extremely while he waited, for he dreaded the meeting, as he could not have dreaded any material danger.

He was making a calculation with the object of fixing some limit of time within which Rieseneck must arrive, and he came to the conclusion that the catastrophe could not be far distant. Rieseneck would probably come to the nearest railway station by train from Stuttgardt, and walk thence to Greifenstein, leaving any luggage he might have with him to be forwarded after he had made good his escape. In that case, if he had started on the day when he wrote, his coming might be only retarded a little by the fact of his being on foot, whereas the lad who brought the post was mounted.

A knock at the door interrupted his reflexions. Something told him that Rieseneck was at hand, but he turned his head with studied calmness so that he could see the servant's face, and held his pipe steadily between his teeth.

'Herr Brandt has arrived,' said the man, quietly, as though nothing unusual were occurring. Greifenstein, even in that moment, had the courage to scrutinise the attendant's features, but their expression betrayed no suspicion.

'Show him in,' returned the master of the house in unshaken tones. He rose slowly to his feet and stood with his back to the fire. The light of the flames was far brighter than that of the solitary lamp that stood upon the desk, and threw the vast black shadow of Greifenstein's gaunt frame against the opposite wall, so that it towered up like a spectre of fate from the floor to the carved brown beams of the ceiling.

The servant threw the door wide open and stood aside, as a tall old man entered the room.

Chapter 11

It is doubtful whether Greifenstein would have recognised his brother, if he had met him under any other circumstances. Forty years had passed since they had met, and both were old men. The difference between their ages was not great, for Greifenstein's father had died within the year of his son's birth, and his mother had married again three years later. In her turn she had died when both were young men, and from that time Greifenstein had seen little of his half-brother, who had been brought up by his own father in a different part of the country. Then young Rieseneck had entered the Prussian service, and a few years later had been ruined by the consequences of his evil.

Greifenstein saw before him a tall man, with abundant white hair and a snowy beard, of bronzed complexion, evidently strong in spite of his years, chiefly remarkable for the heavy black eyebrows that shaded his small grey eyes. The latter were placed too near together, and the eyelids slanted downwards at the outer side, which gave the face an expression of intelligence and great cunning. Deep lines furrowed the high forehead, and descended in broad curves from beneath the eyes till they lost themselves in the beard.

Kuno von Rieseneck was evidently a man of strong feelings and passions, of energetic temperament, clever, unscrupulous, but liable to go astray after strange ideas, and possibly capable of something very like fanaticism. It was indeed not credible that he should have done the deeds which had wrecked his life, out of cold calculation, and yet it was impossible to believe that he could be wholly disinterested in anything he did. The whole effect of his personality was disquieting.

He entered the room with slow steps, keeping his eyes fixed upon his brother. The servant closed the door behind him, and the two men were alone. Rieseneck paused when he reached the middle of the apartment. For a moment his features moved a little uneasily, and then he spoke.

'Hugo, do you know me?' 'Yes,' answered Greifenstein, 'I know you very well.' He kept his hands behind him and did not change his position as he stood before the fire.

'You got my letter?' inquired the fugitive.

'Yes. I will do what you ask of me.'

The answers came in a hard, contemptuous voice, for Greifenstein was almost choking with rage at being thus forced to receive and protect a man whom he both despised and hated. But Rieseneck did not expect any very cordial welcome, and his expression did not vary. 'I thank you,' he answered. 'It is the only favour I ever asked of you, and I give you my word it shall be the last.'

Greifenstein's piercing eyes gleamed dangerously, and for an instant the anger that burned in him glowed visibly in his face.

'Your—' He would have said 'your word,' throwing into the two syllables all the contempt he felt, for one whose word had been so broken. But he checked himself gallantly. In spite of all, Rieseneck was his guest and had come to him for protection, and he would not insult him. 'You shall be safe tomorrow night,' he said, controlling his tongue.

But Rieseneck had heard the first word, and knew what should have followed it. He turned a little pale, bronzed though he was, and he let his hand rest upon the back of a chair beside him.

'I will not trouble you further,' he said. 'If you will show me a place where I can sleep, I will be ready in the morning.'

'No,' answered Greifenstein. 'That will not do. The servants know that a visitor is in the house. They will expect to see you at dinner. Besides, you are probably hungry.'

Perhaps he regretted having shown his brother, even by the suggestion of a phrase, what was really in his heart, and the feeling of the ancient guest-right made him relent a little.

'Sit down,' he added, as Rieseneck seemed to hesitate. 'It will be necessary that you dine with us and meet my wife. We must not excite suspicion.'

'You are married then?' said Rieseneck. It was more like a thoughtful reflexion than a question. Though he had written to his brother more than once, the latter's answers when he vouchsafed any, had been curt and businesslike in the extreme.

'I have been married five and twenty years,' Greifenstein replied. It was strange to be informing his brother of the fact. Rieseneck sat down upon a high chair and rested his elbow upon the table. Neither spoke for a long time, but Greifenstein resumed his seat, relighted his pipe, and placed his feet upon the fender, taking precisely the attitude in which he had been when his brother was announced. The situation was almost intolerable, but his habits helped him to bear it.

'I was also married,' said Rieseneck at last, in a low voice, as though speaking to himself. 'You never saw my wife?' he asked rather suddenly.

'No.'

'She died,' continued the other. 'It was very long ago—more than thirty years.'

'Indeed,' said Greifenstein, as though he cared very little to hear more.

Again there was silence in the room, broken only by the crackling of the fir logs in the fire and by the ticking of the clock in its tall carved case in the corner. A full hour must elapse before the evening meal, and Greifenstein did not know what to do with his unwelcome guest. At last the latter took out a black South American cigar and lit it. For a few moments he smoked thoughtfully, and then, as though the fragrant fumes had the power to unloose his tongue, he again began to talk.

'She died,' he said. 'She ruined me. Yes, did you never hear how it was? And yet I loved her. She would not follow me. Then they sent me some of her hair and the boy. But for her, it might never have happened, and yet I forgive her. You never heard how it all happened?'

'I never inquired,' answered Greifenstein. 'You say she ruined you. How do you mean?'

'She made me do it. She was an enthusiast for liberty and revolution. She filled my mind with ideas of the people's sovereignty. She talked of nothing else. She besought me on her knees to join her party, as she called it. She flattered me with dreams of greatness in a great republic, she illuminated crime in the light of heroism, she pushed me into secret societies, and laughed at me for my want of courage. I loved her, and she made a fool of me, worse than a fool, a traitor, worse than a traitor, a murderer, for she persuaded me to give the arms to the mob, she made me an outlaw, an exile, an object of hatred to my countrymen, a thing loathsome to all who knew me. And yet I loved her, even when it was all over, and I would have given my soul to have her with me.'

Greifenstein's face expressed unutterable contempt for this

man, who in the strength and pride of youth had laid down his honour for a woman's word, not even for her love, since he had possessed that already.

'It seems to me,' he said, 'that there was one very simple remedy for you.'

'A little lead in the right place. I know. And yet I lived, and I live still. Why? I do not know. I believed in the revolution, though she had forced the belief upon me, and I continued to believe in it until long after I went to South America. And when I had ceased to believe in it, no one cared whether I lived or died. Then came this hope, and this blow. I could almost do it now.'

Greifenstein looked at him curiously for a moment, and then rose from his place and went deliberately to a huge, dark piece of furniture that stood between the windows. He brought back a polished mahogany case, unlocked it and set it beside his brother upon the table, under the light of the lamp.

Rieseneck knew what he meant well enough, but he did not wince. On the contrary he opened the case and looked at the beautiful weapon, as it lay all loaded and ready for use in its bed of green baize cloth. Then he laid it on the table again, and pushed it a little away from him.

'Not now,' he said quietly. 'I am in your house. You would have to declare my identity. It would make a scandal. I will not do it.'

'You had better put it into your pocket,' answered Greifenstein grimly, but without a trace of unkindness in his voice. 'You may like to have it about you, you know.'

Rieseneck looked at his brother in silence for a few seconds, and then took the thing once more in his hands.

'Do you mean it as a gift?' he asked. 'You might not care to claim it afterwards.'

'Yes.'

'I thank you.' He took the revolver from the case, examined it attentively and then slipped it into his breast-pocket. 'I thank you,' he repeated. 'I do not possess one.'

Greifenstein wondered whether Rieseneck would have the courage to act upon the suggestion. To him there was nothing horrible in the idea. He was merely offering this despicable creature the means of escape from the world's contempt. He himself, in such a case, would have taken his own life long ago, and he could not understand that any man should hesitate when the proper course lay so very clear before him. He went back to his seat as if nothing unusual had happened. Then, as though to turn the conversation, he began to speak of the plans for the morrow. He did not really believe in his brother's intentions, but as an honourable man, according to his lights, he considered that he had done his duty in giving the weapon.

'We can ride a long distance,' he said, 'and then we can walk. When you are once at the lake, you can find a boat which will take you over. I warn you that it is far.'

'It will be enough if you show me the way,' answered Rieseneck absently. 'You are very kind.'

'It is my interest,' said Greifenstein, unwilling that his feelings should be misinterpreted. Then he relapsed into silence.

Of the two, Rieseneck was the more at his ease. Possibly he did not realise how his brother despised him. Moreover, he had associated during many years with people of many nations, and he did not feel at once that his brother was so very different from these, or so very differently situated towards him. His mind, too, was somewhat unbalanced by the shock he had lately received, and his attention was concentrated upon himself rather than upon the things and persons he saw. During the greater part of his life he had made use of his acute intelligence in his dealings with the world, and under any other circumstances he would in all likelihood have made a determined effort to gain his brother's sympathy.

But in the refusal of his application for a pardon he had believed certain, he had suffered a severe blow. Deep in his tortuous nature there existed at least one sincere and good quality, which was his passionate love for his native country. It had been distorted indeed, through the influence of another strong affection, the love for his wife while she had lived, and, being mis-directed by her agency, the very strength of his patriotism had been the chief cause of his ruin. Now, however, forty years of exile had effaced all belief in parties or in the efficacy of revolu-tionary change, and had left him nothing but the original love of his native land, for itself, as it was, or as it might be, were it empire, kingdom, or republic.

What did it matter, whether Germany were subject to one form of government or to another? Time had softened his ha-treds and had spread its dim mantle over his own disgrace, while it had exalted his beloved nation among all the nations of the earth. Germany's victories, Germany's unity, the glory of her imperial race, the pride of her iron statesmen, the untold pos-sibilities of her future existence, all were his, as they belonged to every born German by right, to share in and to rejoice over with all his heart. For forty years he had dreamed of returning, if it were only to live under an unknown name in some quiet hamlet, if it were merely for the sake of feeling that he was like a nameless drop of the blood that flowed in his country's veins. He asked nothing but the permission to end his life upon the soil whereon he had been born.

Few years remained to him, and he could have done no harm, even had he wished it. His request had been refused, as Greifen-stein had foreseen that it must be, on the ground that he was not a political delinquent, but a military criminal, on the plea that the forgiveness of such a misdeed would be contrary to all prec-edent, and would constitute a very bad example. Those unbend-ing principles by which Germany had risen to her high place would not yield a hair's-breadth for all the supplications of a man who had betrayed his trust, though he were old and broken down, harmless, and even, perhaps, somewhat to be pitied. The law was not made for the young rather than for the aged; it was the same for all, unchangingly just and pitilessly conscientious.

But Rieseneck had suffered in the one tender spot that re-mained in his heart, and the wound had deadened his sensi-bilities in all other respects, while it had slightly disturbed the balance of his faculties. It is hard to believe that he would have spoken of his dead wife as he did, if he had realised exactly what Greifenstein felt towards him. The sufferings of the last week had revived in him the memories of long ago, and he had talked almost against his will of what was in his mind.

He sat silently by the table, and finished his cigar. As he threw away the stump that remained, Greifenstein looked at the clock and laid down his pipe.

'We dine in a quarter of an hour,' he observed, rising to his feet. Rieseneck rose, too, and spread his broad thin hands to the blaze of the fire.

'There is a room here which is conveniently situated for you,' said Greifenstein opening a door, and then striking a match to show the way. He lighted the candles upon the dressing-table and turned to his brother. Rieseneck was looking at him with a singularly disagreeable expression, which Greifenstein could not understand.

The simple action had roused the exile's hatred and jealousy. During the last hour he had thought little of where he was; now he suddenly realised the extent of what he had forfeited. There was nothing especial, in the simply furnished bedroom, to account for his feelings. The thought that hurt him embraced far more than that. He saw his brother rich, honourable, respected, living in his ancestral home, in his own country and possessing a full right to all he enjoyed. He did not know that there were rarely guests in Greifenstein; he only saw how natural it was that they should come, and he hated his brother for his power to live as his fathers had lived before him, and to entertain whom he pleased under his own roof.

He thought bitterly of his own beautiful home in Chili, for his affairs had prospered in his exile, and he had lived in a princely fashion. He had lacked nothing for many a long year, saving only the right to build his home upon an acre of German ground. But that he could not have, and that he envied his brother with all his heart. Greifenstein, however, paid no attention to the angry light in Rieseneck's eyes.

154

'You will find the room convenient,' he said. 'You can lock your door, and if there should be any pursuit and the police should come here you have only to go through that press. There is a door in the back of it. Look.'

He opened the panel and held the light forward into the dark way beyond.

'Where does that lead to?' inquired Rieseneck.

'To a small room in the thickness of the main wall. Thence a winding stair descends to a passage. Follow that and you will come out in the Hunger-Thurm.'

Such devices are common in buildings of the old time in Germany, and Rieseneck manifested no surprise. He only nodded gravely. Greifenstein closed the panel and then left him alone. Rieseneck, however, determined that before going to rest he would follow the passage to the end and ascertain whether it really afforded a means of escape, or whether his brother had contrived a trap for him. In the meanwhile the ordeal of dinner was before him, and it was necessary that he should assume the part of the visitor, lest Greifenstein's wife should suspect anything. He wondered vaguely what sort of woman she was and whether she knew of his existence.

Greifenstein took the precaution of sending word to his wife that there was a visitor in the castle. In her nervous state he feared lest the sudden appearance of a stranger might agitate her, and although he had long abandoned the idea that she knew anything of Rieseneck, his cautious mind admitted the pure possibility of their having been previously acquainted. Even in that extreme case, however, he could not believe a recognition probable, for he himself would certainly not have known Rieseneck, nor admitted that the bearded old man was the person from whom he had parted forty years before. Greifenstein's chief thought was to get the man away and out of the country without any unpleasant incident, and in order to accomplish his purpose he forced himself to behave in his usual manner. After all, twenty-four hours would settle the matter, and the first of the twenty-four was already passed.

When Clara heard that there was to be a guest at dinner, her first sensation was one of extreme terror, but she was reassured by the information her maid gave concerning the general appearance of Herr Brandt. The woman had not seen him, but had of course heard at once a full description of his personality. He was described as a tall old gentleman, exceedingly well dressed, though he had arrived on foot and without luggage. The maid supposed that his effects would follow him, since he had chosen to walk.

Beyond that, Clara could ascertain nothing, but it was clear that she did not consider the details she learned as descriptive of the person whose coming she feared. On the contrary, the prospect of a little change from the usual monotony of the evening had the effect of exhilarating her spirits, and she bestowed even more attention than usual upon the adornment of her thin person. The nature of the woman could not die. Her natural vanity was so extraordinary that it might have been expected to survive death itself. She belonged to that strange class of people who foresee even the effect they will produce when they are dead, who leave elaborate directions for the disposal of their bodies in the most becoming manner, and who build for themselves appropriate tombs while they are alive, decorated in a style agreeable to their tastes.

Clara arrayed herself in all her glory for the feast; she twisted the ringlets of her abundant faded hair, until each covered at least one obnoxious line of forehead and temples; she laid the delicate colour upon her sunken cheeks with amazing precision, and shaded it artistically with the soft hare's foot, till it was blended with the whiteness of the adjacent pearl powder; she touched the colourless eyebrows with the pointed black stick of cosmetic that lay ready to her hand in its small silver case, and made her yellow nails shine with pink paste and doeskin rubbers till they reflected the candlelight like polished horn. With the utmost care she adjusted the rare old lace to hide the sinewy lines of her emaciated throat, and then, observing the effect as her maid held a second mirror beside her face, she hastened to touch the shrivelled lobes of her ears with a delicate rose colour that set off the brilliancy of the single diamonds she wore as earrings.

She opened and shut her eyelids quickly to make her eyes brighter, and held up her hands so that the blood should leave the raised network of the purple veins less swollen and apparent. The patient tire-woman gave one last scrutinising glance and adjusted the rich folds of the silk gown with considerable art, although such taste as she possessed was outraged at the effect of the pale straw colour when worn by such an aged beauty. Another look into the tall mirror, and Clara von Greifenstein was satisfied. She had done what she could do to beautify herself, to revive in her own eyes some faint memory of that prettiness she had once seen reflected in her glass, and she believed that she had not altogether failed.

She even smiled contentedly at her maid, before she left the chamber to go to the drawing-room. It was a satisfaction to show herself to someone, it was a relief from the thoughts that had tormented her so long, it was a respite from her husband's perpetual effort to amuse her by reading aloud. For a few hours at least she was to hear the sound of an unfamiliar voice, to enjoy the refreshing effect of a slight motion in the stagnant pool of worn-out ideas that surrounded her little island of life.

She drew herself up and walked delicately, as she went into the drawing-room. She had judged that her entrance would be effective, and had timed her coming so as to be sure that her husband and Herr Brandt should be there before her. The room looked just as it usually did; it was luxurious, large, warm and softly lighted. Clara almost forgot her age so far as to wish that there had been more lamps, though the shade was undeniably advantageous to her looks. She came forward, and saw that the two men were standing together before the fire.

The door had moved noiselessly on its hinges, but the rustle of the silk gown made Greifenstein and Rieseneck turn their heads simultaneously. Clara's eyes rested on the stranger with some curiosity, and she noticed with satisfaction that his gaze fixed itself upon her own face. He was evidently impressed by her appearance, and her vain old heart fluttered pleasantly.

'Permit me to present Herr Brandt,' said Greifenstein, making a step forward.

Clara inclined her head with an expression that was intended to be affable, and Rieseneck bowed gravely. She sank into a chair and looking up, saw that he was watching her with evident interest. It struck her that he was a very pale man, and though she had at first been pleased by his stare, she began to feel uncomfortable, as it continued.

'You are old friends, I suppose,' she remarked, glancing at her husband with a smile.

Both men bent their heads in assent.

'I had the honour of knowing Herr von Greifenstein when we were both very young,' said Rieseneck after a pause that had threatened to be awkward.

'Indeed? And you have not met for a long time! How very strange! But life is full of such things, you know!' She laughed nervously.

While she was speaking, the intonations of Rieseneck's voice seemed to be still ringing in her ears, and the vibrations touched a chord of her memory very painfully, so that she forgot what she was saying and hid her confusion in a laugh. Greifenstein was staring at the ceiling and did not see his brother start and steady himself against the chimney-piece.

At that moment dinner was announced. Clara rose with an effort from her seat, and stood still. She supposed that Herr Brandt would offer her his arm, but he did not move from his place. Greifenstein said nothing. A violent conflict arose in his mind and made him hesitate. He could not bear the idea of seeing his wife touch even the sleeve of the man he so despised, and yet he dreaded lest any exhibition of his feelings should make Clara suspicious. The last consideration outweighed everything else.

'Will you give my wife your arm?' he said, addressing Rieseneck very coldly.

There was no choice, and the tall old man went to Clara's

side, and led her out of the room, while Greifenstein followed alone. They sat down to the round table, which was laden with heavy plate and curious pieces of old German silver, and was illuminated by a hanging lamp. A hundred persons might have dined in the room, and the shadows made the panelled walls seem even further from the centre than they really were.

Vast trophies of skulls and antlers and boars' heads loomed up in the distance, indistinctly visible through the dim shade, but lighted up occasionally by the sudden flare of the logs from the wide hearth. The flashes of flame made the stags' skulls seem to grin horribly and gleamed strangely upon the white tusks that protruded from the black boars' heads, and reflected a deep red glare from their artificial eyes of coloured glass. The servants stepped noiselessly upon the dark carpet, while the three persons who shared the solemn banquet sat silently in their places, pretending to partake of the food that was placed before them.

The meal was a horrible farce. There was something sombrely contemptible to each one in the idea of being forced into the pretence of eating, for the sake of the hired attendants who carried the dishes. For the first time in his life Greifenstein's hardy nature was disgusted by the sight of food. Rieseneck sat erect in his chair, from time to time swallowing a glass of strong wine, and looking from Clara's face to the fork he held in his hand. She herself exercised a woman's privilege and refused everything, staring consistently at the monumental silver ornament in the midst of the table. When she looked up, Rieseneck's white face scared her. She had no need to see it now, for she knew who he was better than any one, better than Greifenstein himself.

That power whose presence she had once felt, when alone with her husband, was not with her now. A deadly fear overcame every other instinct save that of self-preservation. She struggled to maintain her place at the table, to control the shriek of horror that was on her lips, as she had struggled to produce that feigned laugh ten days ago, with all her might. But the protracted strain was almost more than she could bear, and she felt that her exhausted nerves might leave her helpless at any moment. She had

159

read in books vivid descriptions of the agony of death, but she had never fancied that it could be so horrible as this, so long drawn out, so overwhelmingly bitter.

In truth, a more fearful ordeal could not be imagined, than was imposed by a relentless destiny upon this miserable, painted, curled and jewelled old woman as she sat at the head of her own table. It would have been easier for her, had she known that she was to meet him. It would have been far less hard, if she had lived her life in the whirl of the world, where we are daily forced to look our misdeeds in the face and to meet with smiling indifference those who know our past and have themselves been a part of it. Even a quarter of an hour for preparation would have been better than this gradual recognition, in which each minute made certainty more positive.

There was but one ray of consolation or hope for her, and she tried to make the most of it. He had come because he had failed to obtain his pardon, and his brother was helping him to leave the country quietly. She was as sure of it, as though she had been acquainted with all the details. Tomorrow he would be gone, and once gone he would never return, and her last years would be free from fear. The fact that he came under a false name showed that she was right. In an hour she could excuse herself and go to her room, never to see his face again. Her hands grasped and crushed the damask of the cloth beneath the table, as she tried to steady her nerves by contemplating her near deliverance from torture.

Greifenstein was the bravest of the three,—as he had also the least cause for anxiety. He saw that it was impossible to continue the meal in total silence, and he made a tremendous effort to produce a show of conversation.

'There has been much snow this year, Herr Brandt,' he said, raising his head and addressing his brother. Rieseneck did not understand, but he heard Greifenstein's voice, and slowly turned his ghastly face towards him.

'I beg your pardon,' he said, 'I did not quite hear.'

'There has been much snow this year,' Greifenstein repeated

with forcible distinctness.

'Yes,' replied his brother, 'it seems so.'

'After all, it is nearly Christmas,' said Clara, trembling in every limb at the sound of her own voice.

Only an hour more to bear, and she would be safe for ever. Only another effort and Greifenstein would suspect nothing. Rieseneck looked mechanically at his brother, as though he were trying to find something to say. In reality he was almost insensible, and he hardly knew why he did not fall from his chair.

A servant brought another dish and Clara helped herself unconsciously. The man went on to Rieseneck, and waited patiently until the latter should turn his head and see what was offered to him.

Clara saw an opportunity of speaking again. She could call his attention by addressing him. One, two, three seconds passed, and then she spoke. It would be enough to utter his name, so that he should look round and see the attendant at his elbow. 'Herr Brandt'—the two syllables were short and simple enough.

'Herr von Rieseneck,' she said quietly.

In the extremity of her nervousness, her brain had become suddenly confused and she was lost.

Chapter 12

As the words escaped Clara's lips, Greifenstein started violently and made as though he would rise, laying his hands on the edge of the table and leaning forward towards his wife. The echo of Rieseneck's name had not died away when the unhappy woman realised what she had done. Rieseneck himself turned suddenly towards her and the blood rushed to his pale face. Clara's head fell forward and she covered her eyes with her hands, uttering a short, sharp cry like that of an animal mortally wounded. The servant stood still at Rieseneck's side, staring stupidly from one to the other. Fully ten seconds elapsed before Greifenstein recovered his presence of mind.

'You are ill, Clara,' he said in a choking voice. 'I will take you to your room.'

He did not understand the situation, and he could not guess how his wife had learned that the visitor was not Herr Brandt but Kuno von Rieseneck. But he was horrified by the thought that she should have made the discovery, and his first idea was to get her away as soon as possible. He came to her side, and saw that she was helpless, if not insensible. Then he lifted her from her chair and carried her through the wide door and the small apartment beyond into the drawing-room. Rieseneck followed at a distance.

'You can go,' said Greifenstein to the servant. 'We shall not want any more dinner tonight.'

The man went out and left the three together. Clara lay upon a great divan, her husband standing at her side, and Rieseneck at her feet. Her eyes were open, but they were glassy with terror, though she was quite conscious.

'Clara—are you better?' asked Greifenstein anxiously.

She gasped for breath and seemed unable to speak. Greifenstein looked at his brother. 'I cannot imagine how she knew your name,' he said. 'Did you know her before?'

Rieseneck had turned white again and stood twisting his fingers as though in some terrible distress. Greifenstein had not noticed his manner before, and gazed at him now in considerable surprise. He fancied that Rieseneck feared discovery and danger to himself.

'What is the matter!' he asked impatiently. 'You are safe enough yet—'

While he spoke Clara endeavoured to rise, supporting herself upon one hand, and staring wildly at Rieseneck. The presentiment of a great unknown evil came upon Greifenstein, and he laid his hand heavily upon his brother's arm.

'What is the meaning of this?' he asked sternly. 'Do you know each other?'

The words roused Rieseneck. He drew back from his brother's touch and answered in a broken voice:

'Let me go. Let me leave this house—'

'No!' exclaimed the other firmly. 'You shall not go yet.'

Again he grasped Rieseneck's arm, this time with no intention of relinquishing his hold.

'Let him go, Hugo!' gasped Clara. She struggled to her feet and tried to unloose the iron grip of her husband's fingers, straining her weak hands in the useless attempt. 'Let him go!' she repeated frantically. 'For God's sake let him go!'

'What is he to you?' asked Greifenstein. Then, as though he guessed some fearful answer to his question he repeated it in a fiercer tone. 'What is he to you? And what are you to her?' he cried, facing his brother as he shook him by the arm.

'You have cause to be angry,' said Rieseneck. 'And so have I.' He fixed his eyes on Clara's, and something like a smile flitted over his features.

'Speak!' commanded Greifenstein, to whom the suspense was becoming unbearable.

Clara saw that Rieseneck was about to utter the fatal words, and with a last remnant of energy she made a desperate attempt to cover his mouth with her hand. But she was too late.

'This woman is my wife, not yours!' he cried in ringing tones.

In an instant Greifenstein thrust his brother from him, so that he reeled back against the wall.

'Liar!' he almost yelled.

Clara fell upon the floor between the two men, a shapeless heap of finery. Rieseneck looked his brother in the face and answered the insult calmly. From the moment when he had recognised Clara, he had felt that he must see the whole horror of her fall with his own eyes in order to be avenged for his wrongs.

'I told you my wife was dead,' he said slowly. 'I believed it. She is alive. She has lived to ruin you as she ruined me. Clara von Rieseneck —that is your name—stand upon your feet—lift up your infamous face, and own your lawful husband!'

Even then Clara might have saved herself. One vigorous protest, and Greifenstein would without doubt have slain his brother with his hands. But she had not the strength left to speak the strong lie. She dragged herself to her accuser's feet and threw her arms about his knees.

'Mercy!' she could not utter any other word.

'You see,' said Rieseneck. 'She is alive, she knows me!'

'Mercy!' groaned the wretched creature, fawning upon him with her wasted hands.

'Down, beast!' answered the tall old man with savage contempt. 'There is no mercy for such as you.'

Greifenstein had stood still for some seconds, overcome by the horror of his shame. One glance told him that his brother had spoken the truth. He turned away and stood facing the empty room. His face was convulsed, his teeth ground upon each other, his hands were clenched as in the agony of death. From his straining eyes great tears rolled down his grey cheeks, the first and the last that he ever shed. And yet by that strange instinct of his character which abhorred all manifestation of emotion, he stood erect and motionless, as a soldier on parade. The deathblow had struck him, but he must die on his feet.

Then after a long pause, broken only by Clara's incoherent groans and sobs, he heard Rieseneck's footstep behind him, and then his brother's voice, calling him by his name.

'Hugo—what has this woman deserved?'

'Death,' answered Greifenstein solemnly.

'She helped to ruin me through my faults, she has ruined you through no fault of yours. She must die.'

'She must die,' repeated Greifenstein.

'She has given you a son who is nameless. She cast off the son she bore to me because through me his name was infamous. She must pay the penalty.'

'She must die.'

Greifenstein did not turn round even then. He crossed the room to the chimney-piece and laid his two hands upon it. Still he heard his brother's voice, though the words were no longer addressed to him. 'Clara von Rieseneck, your hour is come.'

'Mercy, *Kuno!* For God's sake—'

'There is no mercy. Confess your crime. The time is short.'

The wretched old woman tried to rise, but Rieseneck's hand

kept her upon her knees.

'You shall do me this justice before you go,' he said. 'Repeat your misdeeds after me. You, Clara Kurtz, were married to me in the year eighteen hundred and forty-seven.'

'Yes—it is true,' answered the poor creature in broken tones.

'Say it! You shall say the words!'

Her teeth chattered. Transfixed by fear, her lips moved mechanically.

'I, Clara Kurtz, was married to you in the year eighteen hundred and forty-seven.'

The woman's incredible vanity survived everything. Her voice sank to a whisper at the two last words of the date, for Greifenstein had never known her real age.

'You caused me to betray the arsenal,' continued Rieseneck inexorably.

'I did.'

'You abandoned me when I was in prison. When I escaped you refused to follow me. You sent me false news of your death, with a lock of your hair and the child.'

Clara repeated each word, like a person hypnotised and subject to the will of another.

'Then you must have changed your name.'

'I changed my name.'

'And you induced Hugo von Greifenstein to marry you, knowing that he was my brother and that I was alive. I had often told you of him.'

Clara made the statement in the words dictated.

'And now you are to die, and may the Lord have mercy upon your sinful soul.'

'And now I am to die. May the Lord have mercy upon my sinful soul.'

Released from the stern command of her judge, Clara uttered a low cry and fell upon her face at his feet.

'You have heard,' said Rieseneck to his brother. 'It is time.'

Greifenstein turned. He saw the tall old man's great figure standing flat against the opposite wall, and he saw the ghastly face, half hidden by the snowy beard. He glanced down, and beheld a mass of straw-coloured silk, crumpled and disordered, and just beyond it a coil of faded hair adorned with jewelled pins that reflected the soft light. He crossed the room, and his features were ashy pale, firmly set and utterly relentless. He had heard her condemnation from her own lips, he thought of his son, nameless through this woman's crime, and his heart was hardened.

'It is time,' he said. 'Have you anything more to say?'

He waited for an answer, but none came. Clara's hour had struck and she knew it. There was deep silence in the room. Then the stillness was broken by a gasp for breath and by a little rustling of the delicate silk. That was all.

When it was done, the two brothers stooped down again and lifted their burden and bore it silently away, till they reached the room in which they had first met. Then Greifenstein made sign that they should go further and they entered the chamber beyond, and upon the bed that was there, they laid down the dead woman, and covered her poor painted face decently with a sheet and went away, closing the door softly behind them.

For a moment they stood looking at each other earnestly. Then Rieseneck took from his pocket his brother's gift and laid it upon the table.

'It is time for us also,' he said.

'Yes. I must write to Greif first.'

Half an hour later the short and terrible tragedy was completed, and of the three persons who had sat together at the table, suffering each in his or her own way as much as each could bear, not one was left alive to tell the tale.

Outside the house of death, the silent, spotless snow gleamed in the light of the waning moon. Not a breath of wind sighed amongst the stately black trees. Only, far below, the tumbling torrent roared through its half-frozen bed, and high above, from the summit of the battlement that had sheltered so many generations of Greifensteins from danger in war, and in peace from the bitter north wind, the great horned owls sent forth their melancholy note, from time to time, and opened wide their cruel hungry eyes, as the dismal sound echoed away among the dark firs.

Then all was confusion in an instant, within and without. Lights flashed out over the snow from the deep, low gateway, voices rang in accents of alarm through the halls and spacious corridors, huge watch-dogs sprang to the length of their rattling chains and bellowed out their deep-mouthed cries, the shrieks of frightened women rose high above the noise and were drowned again by the loud bass voices of excited serving-men. Then there was the clatter of iron shoes upon the stone pavements as the startled horses were led out into the moonlight from their warm dark stalls, the tinkle of curb chains, the wheeze of tightening leather girths, the clicking of curb and snaffle between champing teeth, the purselike chink of spurs on booted heels, the soft dull thud of riders springing into saddles.

The iron-studded gates creaked back upon their huge hinges, as the burly porter, pale with fear, dragged open the heavy oak panels. Lanterns flashed, stable-boys and house servants elbowed each other in the narrow way and flattened themselves against the damp stone walls, as they heard the tramp of the approaching feet. Then four strong horses trotted out, two and two, into the moonlight beyond, each bearing on his back a messenger of the terrible tidings, and all breaking into a brisk gallop as the party disappeared in the mottled black and white distance under the mighty trees.

One rode for Sigmundskron, and one for the nearest surgeon, one for the distant town, and one to bear the ghastly tale to Greif himself, the nameless orphan, who at that moment was marching sword in hand beside the tall standard of his Korps, at the head of a thousand students, in all the magnificence of his fantastic dress, leading the great torchlight procession which closed the academic year, and which crowned with a splendid revelry the last act of his student life. As he strode along, proud, successful, popular, the envy of all his fellows, the idol of his Korps companions, pale-faced servants were laying the body of his father beside his dead mother in the state chamber of Greifenstein, and frightened menials were trembling under the weight of the tall dead man whose snowy beard blew about in such fantastic waves before the draught of every opened door.

As he went up the steps of the festal drinking-hall wherein the last students' feast of the year was to be celebrated, and over which he himself was to preside, three women were met together in distant Sigmundskron, repeating the service for the dead, before the smouldering embers of their poor fire, by the dim light of their one smoking candle. An hour later, as the orchestra thundered out the strains of the soul-stirring *Landesvater*, sustaining but not covering the glorious chorus of a thousand fresh young voices, a grey-haired woman in a dark cloak was riding slowly through the snowy ways of the dismal forest, her horse led carefully by the booted groom who had brought the news.

Her face was paler than ever it was wont to be, but not less brave. Her well-worn mantle was no fit covering against the bitter Christmas air, but her heart was not cold within. She knew that Greif would come in the morning, or at noontime, and cost what it might, she would not let him face his awful sorrow alone, or feel that none but a hired hand had smoothed his dead mother's faded hair, or closed his dead father's staring eyes. She did what she could. She sat as she might upon the man's saddle, and she faced the cruel cold unflinchingly, encouraging the fellow who led her horse with such words and promises as she was able to devise.

But the distance was great, the snow was deep, and the stout Mecklenburger roan had breasted the steep road at a gallop only an hour before. The castle clock was striking half-past four when the strong-hearted Lady of Sigmundskron was lifted from her seat to the pavement within the walls of Greifenstein, half dead with cold, and horrified at the thought of what she had come to see, but calm, determined and full of dignity as only women, and such women, can be, in the presence of a horrible catastrophe. She took what they offered her, a glass of strong wine and a slice of venison, scarcely cold from the ghastly meal that had preceded the tragedy. She did not suffer herself to think whence it came, for she needed strength, not only to do her duty, but to impose order and quiet in the terrified household.

Then she listened to the story and visited the rooms. There were policemen in the house, quiet men in dark uniforms with great yellow beards and grave faces, and there was the surgeon, an insignificant country leech in spectacles, who would have been pompous anywhere else and at any other time, but who looked singularly helpless and subdued. Other officials would doubtless come in the course of the early morning, to report upon what had happened, but now that there was a responsible person present, a relation of the dead and one in authority, no great difficulty could arise.

One thing only Frau von Sigmundskron had not understood, and that involved the understanding of all the rest. She did not know who the stranger was, whose coming seemed to have led to the final catastrophe. She guessed indeed that he must be Rieseneck, but there was no evidence of his identity. It was not until she had been three hours in the house that she extracted from one of the servants an account of what had occurred before the three had so suddenly left the dinner-table. The man remembered having been told that the visitor was Herr Brandt, but his mistress, when he was waiting at the guest's side had certainly called him by another name.

It was 'von Riesen'—and something more. The servant was sure of that, and the baroness was satisfied. She did not care to tell him what the name really was, for she began to see dimly that the triple murder and suicide were in some way the result of the exile's coming. Nothing had been found, not a scrap of writing to give an explanation, not a sign to indicate a clue. The surgeon's evidence was simple. The lady had been strangled, the two gentlemen had shot themselves. Nothing showed that there had been any struggle. Greifenstein and his guest had been found in two chairs, each having in his hand a revolver of which one chamber was empty.

The position of the wounds showed that they had not fired upon each other. While the cause of their action was a total mystery to everyone except Frau von Sigmundskron, the steps of it were singularly clear. It was evident that they had killed Clara deliberately and had then killed themselves. Even the baroness was obliged to admit to herself that the mere fact of the exile returning suddenly was wholly inadequate to account for the three deaths.

She was a brave woman, and though she was profoundly horrified and grieved by what had happened she was conscious that she had not suffered any great personal loss. She had never known Rieseneck, she had never liked Clara, and her friendship for Greifenstein had not been great. Greif himself was safe, the only one of the family for whom she felt any affection, and in whom all her hopes for her daughter's happiness were centred. But for him, she would have refused the occasional hospitality of the castle as she had once refused the tardy assistance of its possessors. It is due to the memory of Greifenstein to repeat here that he never at any time realised the extremity of her need, and that it had been long before he had learned that she was really poor. But the Lady of Sigmundskron did not know this, and she could not comprehend how completely her penury had been hidden from her relations by her own wonderful management and indomitable pride.

At present, her thoughts were absorbed by the necessity of meeting Greif when he arrived, which must be within a few hours, and she sat calmly in her chair under the light of the candles that illuminated the chamber of death, trying vainly to frame some consoling speech which might break the violence of his sorrow. She knew how he had loved his father, and during his last visit she had noticed his increasing affection for his mother. She knew that he was aware of Rieseneck's existence, and she tortured her weary brain in the attempt to find some explanation that would not pain him needlessly, and which might nevertheless seem to account in some measure for the calamity that had overtaken him.

But her trouble was thrown away, and many a cunning lawyer might have laboured in vain to frame out of the facts a consistent narrative. As the morning approached, the intensity of her thoughts was diminished by her bodily fatigue, and she dreamed of other things, wondering somewhat vaguely whether it were right to marry her child to the son of the murderer and suicide whose dead body lay beside that of his victim under the yellow light of the tall candles, to the nephew of the traitor, whose tall figure was stretched upon a couch in the room beyond.

To most women the situation would have been infinitely more painful than it was to Therese von Sigmundskron. She was more like a sister of a religious order than a woman of the world. Years of ascetic practices, of constant self-sacrifice, of unswerving devotion had refined her nature from the fear of death, or the dread of its presence. We ask in vain why an existence of painful labour elevates some characters and debases others, inspires courage in some and in some destroys the power to face the inevitable.

We search our experience and we know that the fact exists, we apply our intelligence to the study of it and we admit that the cause of the fact escapes us. The seekers after explanations are bold with big words which tell us nothing, and call themselves physiological psychologists, or if that definition fails they say that they are psychological physiologists, and establish a difference in meaning between the one title and the other. But all the Greek words they can spell with Latin letters cannot show us what the human heart is, nor make us believe that it is seated in the right or in the left side of the brain, nor yet that it is established in the middle, in the island of Reil; any more than we admit that the human heart has anything to do with the little muscle-pump we carry in our breasts and which sometimes stops pumping just at the wrong moment for our convenience.

'Life is a continuous adjustment of internal relations to external relations,' says the Apostle of the Misunderstanding. 'Adjustment' is good, for it means nothing.' It would have shown better taste, however, to substitute for it a beautiful term of some sort, with a Greek root, a Latin suffix and an English termination, because in that case a large majority of people would never have found out that the whole phrase was blatant nonsense. What are internal relations? Did the chief destroyer of common sense, the chief executioner of good English, mean, perhaps, the relations between that which is within and that which is without? He might have said so. It would not have meant much, but it would undoubtedly have meant something. And if life is this, then death must be the opposite, and death becomes 'a cessation of the adjustment of internal relations to external relations,' and if that is what it means we ought to say so when a man is dead, although nature continues to adjust the internal and the external relations afterwards in a way we do not care to see.

Fortunately for Frau von Sigmundskron, she had not read the works of the Apostle of the Misunderstanding, and was consequently able to bear her situation with some degree of equanimity. But it was a hard one for all that, and she could not help making some very ignorant but sincere reflexions upon that state we call life, and upon that other state which is so near to it. What her thoughts would have been like had she known all that had happened, it is not easy to say. If she had known that she was entitled by the laws of her country to Greifenstein and to all that belonged to the name, as the only living and legitimate heir, she would certainly have looked at the future in another way.

But she had no reason for thinking that all was not Greif's. So far as she knew, she was still the poor widowed gentlewoman she had been twelve hours earlier, struggling against poverty, starving herself for her daughter, looking to herself for courage and support, and to her child's wellbeing as the only source of her own happiness. The same in all respects save one, and that one change brought with it many bitter doubts. So long as Greifenstein and Clara had been alive, Hilda's marriage with Greif had seemed right in her eyes. She regretted Rieseneck's disgrace, as a family disaster, but her conscience was not so sensitive as to look at it in the light of an obstacle to the union.

Now, however, there was that before her—there upon the bed of state in the glare of the lights—which changed everything very much. Between Greif and Hilda lay Greif's murdered mother, and Greif's father dead by his own hand. Therese von Sigmundskron was a Greifenstein at heart, and she would rather face misery and starvation than give her child to one whose name must for ever be branded with such a story. Very soon she felt that it would be impossible, and the prospect of so much suffering for Hilda appalled her. She thought of Greif, too, and she was profoundly grieved for him, for she had already looked upon him as her son.

Of course, for the present, there could be no talking of the matter. If the poor fellow did not go mad with sorrow, he would nevertheless wish to put off his marriage for a year or more. She thought of Hilda's disappointment at the prospect of even retarding the happy day, she thought of the girl's despair when she should know that the day could never come.

Then her resolution almost broke down, and she even argued with herself against it. Greif was innocent. It was no fault of his, he had no share in the fearful doings of last night, he was far away, thinking of Hilda, dreaming that he led her up the aisle of the church, counting the moments until he could come back to her. Why should he suffer the consequences of what others had done? Why should Hilda's young life be wrecked, condemned, perhaps, to perpetual poverty, ruined, most assuredly, by the over-throw of its only happiness? Could they not marry and live here, as Greif's father and mother had lived for years? Could they not be everything to each other, and nothing to the world?

Why had Greifenstein and Rieseneck killed Clara? The question cut short the good baroness's attempt to justify the marriage. It rose suddenly in her mind and covered every other thought with a veil. Since that day when poor Clara had behaved so strangely on hearing of the amnesty, Frau von Sigmundskron had always believed that she knew more of Rieseneck than any-one else supposed. Rieseneck had come, and he had not been in the house three hours when everything was over. What had happened? No one knew.

Those who had known had acted out their own tragedy to the end and were gone with their secret. The authorities had already taken cognisance of their deaths and had drawn up their preliminary report. The three would be buried, perhaps side by side, in the vault of the Greifensteins, and no living person could ever know what had passed during their last moments. The most careful search had brought no trace of writing to the light, excepting a letter addressed to an unknown person, evidently written before the catastrophe, which had been found, directed and stamped for the post, upon the library table. Everything in the house had been found in order, every object in its place. The servants had heard the two shots and had tried to enter the room, but it had been locked within. A lad had climbed along the cornice until he could see through the window, and had come back pale with terror. In the presence of the whole household the door had been forced, and all had seen together the hideous sight. That was all there was to be known.

As the castle clock struck one hour after another, the baroness felt that every minute was carrying the secret further beyond her reach, and yet, as the time passed, the effect of that secret's existence upon her own mind grew more and more clear to herself. She could never give Hilda to Greif. She could never suffer her child to mate with a man whose existence was overshadowed by such a history, innocent though he assuredly was himself.

And yet Greif was coming, and she had ridden all those weary miles through the freezing night in order to meet him at his own gate, in order to comfort him, to give him the help of her presence, the consolation of a friend in his utmost need. Would it console him to know that he must lose the only surviving thing that was dear to him, the hope of Hilda? Her heart beat at the thought of the pain he would suffer, though it had been calm enough in the sight of the great horror.

But she could not yield the point. In spite of her gentle face she had all the unbending qualities of her masterful countrymen, as well as all the pride of the Greifensteins. She could not yield, let the resistance cost what it might.

The late winter's dawn stole through the crevices of the windows, which had been opened more than once during the night.

The contrast of the still grey rays, seen through the flickering light of the candles that filled the place of death, was terribly unpleasant. The baroness rose and fastened the shutters carefully. As she turned back she shuddered for the first time since she had come. The slight exertion had stirred her tired blood and had made her momentarily nervous. The room looked very naturally. The huge carved bed of state with its enormous canopy was where she had always seen it when she had visited the house. The massive furniture was arranged as usual, saving that there were high pedestals placed about the bed to support the heavy candlesticks. Nothing else was changed. But upon that bed lay two straight things, side by side, covered all over with fine linen. The great secret of death was there, and death had taken with him the key-word of a strange mystery.

CHAPTER 13

Rex sat in a careless attitude in a corner of Greif's small room, watching his friend as he arrayed himself in the official dress of a Korps student for the coming festivity. It was to be Greif's last appearance in public as a fellow. Tomorrow there would be a meeting of the Korps and he would resign his functions, and someone else would be elected in his stead. Rex watched him curiously and hummed the first *stanza* of the *Gaudeamus*—

Give our hearts to gladness, then,
While the young life flashes!
When our joyous youth is gone,
When old age's aches are done,
Earth shall have our ashes!

'I wish you would not sing that song!' exclaimed Greif, a little impatiently. 'There will be time enough to exercise your voice upon it when we begin to throw away the torches.'

'It is the only song I ever heard that has any truth in it,' answered Rex.

'You ought to write one about the vortex, and call it the physicist's Lament,' laughed the other.

'The idea is not new. Scheffel made geological jokes in verse

175

and sang them.'

'Go thou and do likewise! But do not make the idea of turning into a philistine more unpleasant than it naturally is.'

'We have all been through it,' said Rex, 'and most of us have survived the change. With insects, the caterpillar turns into the pretty moth. With Korps students, the butterfly becomes sooner or later a crawling, philistine grub. The moral superiority of the worm over the moth is manifest in his works. Have you read your speech over?'

'I know it by heart. Help me with the scarf, will you?' 'Vanity of vanities!' laughed Rex as he began to knot the coloured silk.

Greif's costume is worth a word of description. He wore a close-fitting yellow jacket, heavily trimmed with black, white and yellow frogs and crossed cords, in the hussar fashion, and finished at the neck in the military manner with a stiff high collar. His legs were encased in tight breeches of white leather, and long polished boots with riding flaps were drawn above the knee. The long straight rapier hung in its gleaming sheath by his side, the colours of the Korps being done in velvet upon the basket-hilt. Over his right shoulder he wore a heavy silk scarf of the three colours, which was tied in a big knot near the sword-hilt.

Upon his bright hair a very small round cap, no bigger than a saucer, and richly embroidered with gold, was held in its place by mysterious means, involving the concealment of a piece of elastic beneath his short curls. Upon the table lay a pair of white leather gauntlets. The whole effect was theatrical, but in the surroundings for which the dress was intended, it could not fail to be both striking and harmonious. It displayed to the best advantage the young man's fine proportions and athletic figure, and where there were to be hundreds similarly arrayed, with only a difference of colour to distinguish their even ranks, the result could not differ greatly from a military parade. Indeed the costume is not more gaudy than many modern uniforms and is certainly as tasteful.

'I am sorry it is the last time,' said Greif sadly, as his friend finished the knot. Then he went to the window and looked once more at the dim outline of the cathedral spire and listened to the water rushing through its cold bed in the dusk far below. He knew that he should look out but a few times more. He did not know that this time was the last. Rex was looking for his overcoat, and as he moved about the room he sang softly another *stanza* of the old song—

Short and sweet this life of ours,
Soon its cord must sever!
Death comes quick, nor brooks delay,
Ruthless, he tears us away,
No man spares he ever.

'For heaven's sake, do not sing that song anymore!' cried Greif. 'I am sad enough, as it is, without your cat's music.'

Rex laughed oddly.

'I am as sad as you,' he said, a moment later, with an abrupt change of manner. 'You do not act as though you were,' observed Greif. 'What are you sad about?'

'World-sorrow.'

'Has the vortex fallen ill?' inquired Greif ironically.

'It is likely to, I fear. Come along! It is time to be off. You must not keep everybody waiting.'

Something in the tone of his voice struck Greif and affected him disagreeably. He held up the light to Rex's face, and saw that he was pale, and that his strange eyes looked weary and lifeless.

'What is the matter, Rex?' he asked earnestly. 'Are you in any trouble? Can I do anything for you?'

'Nothing, thank you,' answered the other quietly.

Greif set down the lamp upon the table and seemed to hesitate a moment. Then he turned again and laid his hand upon his friend's arm.

'Rex, do you want money?' asked Greif. 'You know I have plenty.'

In the eyes of a Korps student the want of cash appears to be the only ill to which flesh is heir. Rex smiled rather sadly.

'No, I do not want money. I thank you, all the same.'

'What is it then? In love?'

'In love!' Rex laughed. 'I would tell you that soon enough,' he added carelessly. 'No—it is a more serious matter.'

'If I can be of no use to you—'

'Look here, Greif,' interrupted the other, 'we have grown to be good friends, you and I, during this term. You are going away, and I may never see you again. You may as well know why I fraternised with you so readily. I have had your friendship so far, and if I must lose it, I may as well lose it at once.'

Greif opened his bright eyes and stared at his friend in considerable astonishment. He thought that he knew him well, and he could not imagine what was coming.

'I do not see what could happen to cause that,' he answered.

'Do you remember that evening when you first came to my rooms?'

'Of course.'

'Have I gained any advantage from our acquaintance, excepting your society and that of your Korps? Think well before you answer.'

'Certainly not,' replied Greif. 'I am quite sure that you have not. What a foolish question!'

'It seems so to you, no doubt. But it is far from foolish. You say that you remember that evening well. Then you recollect that I told you I knew nothing of you or your family. I made certain predictions. Well, I made them according to the figure, as you saw by the unexpected arrival of that telegram. But I lied to you about the rest. I knew perfectly well who you were, whence you came, and what your father's half-brother had done.'

Greif had drawn back a little during the first part of this declaration. At the statement that Rex had deceived him he started and drew himself up, his face showing plainly enough that his wrath was not far off.

'And may I ask your reasons for practising this deception upon me?' he inquired coldly.

'There is but one reason, and that is of a somewhat startling nature,' returned Rex, leaning back against the table and resting his two hands upon it. 'You allow that I have got no personal advantage out of your friendship. I desired none. I only wanted to know you.'

'Why?'

'Because I am your cousin. My name is Rieseneck. I am the only son of your father's half-brother.'

Greif's eyes flashed, and the hot blood mounted to his face. The information was surprising enough, and his hatred of his uncle was likely to produce trouble.

'How did you dare to impose upon me in such a way?' he cried angrily.

'No one ever speaks to me of daring,' answered Rex, who seemed quite unmoved. 'I dare do most things, because I have nothing to lose but a little money, my good name of Rex, and my life. As for my not calling myself Rieseneck, I have not imposed upon you any more than upon anyone else, by doing so. My father calls himself Rex, and I have never been known by any other appellation.'

'But you should have told me—'

'Doubtless, and so I have. It is true that I have chosen my own time, and that I have allowed myself the pleasure of knowing you before disclosing my identity. You would have refused to have anything to do with me had you known who I was. After all, you are the only relation I have in the world, and I have asked you for nothing, nor ever shall. I learned that you were a student here, and I came to Schwarzburg expressly to meet you. I noted your usual seat at the lecture where we met, and I put myself next to you with the intention of making your acquaintance. Now I have told you everything. You are at liberty to know me or not, henceforth. You prefer not to know me. Is it so? Well, I have done you no injury. Good-bye. I wish you good luck.'

Thereupon Rex took up his hat and with a slight inclination of the head went towards the door. His stony eyes did not turn to Greif, who might have seen in them a strangely pained expression, which would have surprised him. Greif hesitated between his sincere friendship for Rex and his horror of any one so closely connected with Rieseneck. It was very hard to choose the right course with so little preparation, and he was thrown off his balance by the sudden disclosure. But his natural generosity, combined with an undefinable attraction he felt towards the man, overcame all other considerations.

'Rex!' he called out, as his friend was already passing through the doorway.

Rex stopped and stood still where he was, turning his head so that he could see Greif.

'Stay,' said Greif almost involuntarily. 'We cannot part company in this way.'

'If it must be at all, it were best that it were done quickly,' answered Rex, holding the handle of the door.

'It must not be done,' returned Greif in a decided tone. 'If I am attached to you, it is for what you are, not for what your father was, or is.'

'Think the matter over,' replied the other. 'I will wait, if you please. I deceived you once. It is fair that I should submit to your decision now.'

He closed the door and went to the window, where he stood still, looking out into the dusk, and turning his back upon Greif. The latter paused an instant, and then came forward and laid one hand upon his friend's shoulder. He acted still under the same impulse of generosity which had first prompted him to keep Rex back.

'Rex—it depends upon you. If you will, we shall be friends as ever.'

'I?' exclaimed Rex, turning suddenly. 'With all my heart. Is there anything I desire more?'

'Good—so be it, then!' answered Greif taking his hand boldly.

'So be it!' repeated Rex.

'And now,' said Greif, 'why did you choose this moment to tell me your secret?'

'Do you want to know? There is a reason for that, too, and not a pleasant one.'

'I can hear it.'

'Tonight my father will sleep under your father's house. You will hear the news before morning. Tomorrow I shall leave here to meet him in Switzerland—or not, as the case may be. He has been refused the benefit of the amnesty, but he will be allowed to leave the country quietly. I cannot leave him alone any longer.'

Greif turned a little pale at the intelligence.

'Then this is the danger you foretold,' he said.

'Yes.'

'What will happen at Greifenstein tonight?'

'How can I tell!' exclaimed Rex. 'There may be an angry meeting. There may be worse. Or your father's heart may be softened—'

'You do not know him. Then my uncle has written to you?'

'I received the letter today, before coming here. Do you see that it was better to have this explanation now, rather than to wait for tomorrow?'

'Yes—it was better. Let us go, for the time presses—truly I have no heart for this sport tonight. I wish I were at home.'

'Do not wish,' said Rex gravely. 'You could not help matters.'

Greif extinguished the light and the two men groped their way down the dusky staircase in silence, both feeling that an exceptionally difficult situation had been passed through with singular ease, both recognising that the explanation had been hurried over in a way hardly to be accounted for, except by the theory that neither wished to lose the other's friendship. And yet, both Greif and Rex knew that their decision had been final. The one had nothing more to conceal. The other had nothing left to forgive. Rex, like Rieseneck himself, believed that his mother had died long ago. Greif, like all the rest, was ignorant of his own mother's identity. Sons of one mother they went out of the house side by side, not dreaming that they were anything more than cousins, whose fathers were half-brothers, little guessing that within a few short hours the father of each and the mother of both would be lying stiff and stark in the chambers of lofty Greifenstein.

They reached the great dark buildings of the University, and found themselves in a dense crowd of students of all colours, on the outskirts of a multitude of others who belonged to no associations. Here they parted, for Rex could not walk in the Swabian Korps and must go with the black hats.

'We shall meet in the hall,' said Greif hurriedly. 'Your place is at our table as usual.'

And so they parted. In a few moments, Greif had found his companions by the tall standard whose colours caught a few struggling rays of light from the street-lamps. Everyone was talking, smoking, stamping cold feet upon the stones in the effort to keep warm, cracking jokes, both good and bad, craning necks to see the position of the standards, making agreements for pairing at the *Landesvater*, and generally complaining that the town clocks were all slow that night in Schwarzburg. Occasionally, a roar of laughter arose in the distance, where some unlucky *burgher* had found his way into a group of students and was being made the butt of a good-humoured jest.

And beneath the high, laughing tones, the perpetual hum of a thousand talking voices neither rose nor fell, but droned unceasingly like the long pedal in a fugue, whose full deep note stands still amidst the strife of moving sounds, as the sun stood while the battle was fought out in Ajalon. The very life of the multitude seemed to produce a sound of its own, in the breathing of a thousand pairs of strong young lungs, in the beating of a thousand young, untired hearts, in the pulsation of so much youth brought together to one place. A blind man might have thought himself in the presence of some one monstrous human giant, overflowing with enormous vitality, warming the whole night with his breath, stirring the whole air with each careless movement of his vast body.

There is something mysterious in a crowd, most of all in a

crowd at night. The throng has simultaneous perceptions and movements, a joint sense of power or of fear, a circulation of consciousness as complete as that which exists in the nerves of every individual. Thousands of men, of whom each alone would act differently from his fellows, are all irresistibly impelled to think the same thoughts, to feel the same emotions, to yield to the same influences, or to join in the same work of destruction. But no one of them all can tell why he so feels, thinks and acts; the mystery of the crowd is upon him, and sways him whither it will, powerless, half unconscious, and wholly irresponsible.

The deep cathedral bell tolled the hour of seven. Before the strokes were all counted, the hum of the multitude had swelled to twice its former strength, and everyone felt himself jostled a little by his neighbour. Then came the sharp, clear voices of those who directed the forming of the procession, the shuffling of many feet, and the muffled but irritated movements of those who had to make way. Then rose a sudden flare of light in a corner of the dark mass, followed quickly by another and another, till many hundreds of torches were aflame, sputtering, smoking and sending up tongues of flame into the black air.

Again a word of command, and the even tramp of footsteps began to be heard, a mere patter as of big raindrops upon stones at first, but swelling gradually, and increasing, till the sound roused great echoes from the glowing buildings, while the blazing pitch flared up, brighter and brighter, into a broad sea of flame that flowed away in a narrow stream of fire as the great company filed out of the square into the street beyond. Then, as the place of meeting was emptied, a breeze of cold air rushed into the vacant space; there was hurrying and scurrying of those who remained last, as they ran to take their places, and while a burst of march music was heard in the distance at the head of the column, the last stragglers fell into the file behind, the last torch disappeared into the narrow street, and the broad space that had been so full was left utterly deserted, illuminated only by a dozen dim gaslights in exchange for the lurid glow which a moment earlier had lit up every wall and house from corner stone to pointed gable.

In front of all, marched the Swabians, the high standard waving in front, the burly second of the Korps striding along upon its left with drawn rapier and clattering scabbard, while upon the right Greif walked, an erect and commanding figure, thrown into strong relief by the bright lights behind him. His face was pale, and his teeth were set, for as he led the head of the column he found time to reflect upon what had occurred during the last hour, and time to fear what was yet to happen. Willingly he would have left the rank and hastened to his lodging in time to be ready for the night train.

A few short hours would have brought him to his home to learn the truth, were it good or evil. But the thing was impossible. He was of all others that night the man most watched, most admired, most envied. It was his last torchlight procession, his last turn of presiding at the great festival that was at hand, the last draught of that brilliant student's life he loved was at his lips. He could never again do what he was doing tonight. Tomorrow another would be chosen in his place, and tomorrow he was to join the dull ranks of the outer philistines. The thought brought suddenly a flash of wild recklessness into the gloomy atmosphere of his reflexions, and as he halted the column before the Rector's house and started the ringing cheer for the '*Magnificus*,' his voice rang out with a metallic clearness that surprised himself.

'*Hoch! Hoch! Hoch!*' The vast chorus that followed his lead cheered his heart.

What could Rieseneck do at Greifenstein, after all? There might be a disagreeable scene. Two of them, perhaps. That would be all, and Rieseneck would go away, never to return again. Rex and his predictions? Bah! The man believed in the power of the stars, and Greif, who trod so firmly at the head of a thousand torches, believed in youth, and would not forfeit his last draught of glorious youthfulness for any such nonsense.

On and on the procession marched, halting in the street where some favourite professor lived, in order to give him three thundering cheers, then tramping on to another and another, down the high street, round the cathedral, back at last to the square whence they had started.

Shoulder to shoulder the students ranged themselves against the walls of the houses in serried ranks, drawing back as much as possible, so as to leave a broad space in the middle. There was a pause, and a deep silence for several minutes. Then the trumpets and horns flared out the grand old hymn of student life, the 'Gaudeamus igitur, juvenes dum sumus,' and all those fresh young voices took up the strain with that perfect unison which only Germans know how to give to an improvised chorus—

Gaudeamus igitur, juvenes dum sumus, post jucundam juventutem, post molestam senectutem, nos habebit humus, nos habebit humus.
Ubi sunt, qui ante nos in mundo fuere? Vadite ad superos, transits ad inferos, ubi jam fuere.
Vita nostra brevis est, brevi finietur, venit mors velociter, rapit nos atrociter, nemini parcetur.
Vivant omnes virgines faciles, formosae, vivant et mulieres, vivant et mulieres bonae, laboriosae.
Vivat academia, vivant professores, vivat membrum quodlibet, vivant membra quaelibet, semper sint in flore.

As the last *stanza* was sung, in slow and solemn measure, the students began to throw away their torches. First one alone shot out from the belt of fire that surrounded the square, meteorlike in a wide arch, and fell in the centre of the open space amidst a shower of sparks. A dozen followed almost immediately, then a hundred, and hundreds more, till all the thousand lay together, a burning heap, throwing up clouds of lurid smoke into the night, and illuminating the great buildings with a broad red glare. Greif stood still a moment, watching the bonfire, and then sheathed his rapier and turned away. To him it was a sorrowful sight, this ending of his last torchlight procession. He remembered how, as a young novice, he had stood in the same place, his heart full of a strange enjoyment, and he wished that he could go back to those days and live his life again.

During nearly three years since that time he had been a student; during more than one he had been a soldier, serving his time with the *cuirassiers*, and coming into the town as often as he could to spend an hour with his Korps. It was all over now, never to begin again. Only among those soldiers whom he had learned so easily to love, could he hope to find again something of that good fellowship he had enjoyed with the brethren of the Swabian Korps. Only in larger strife could he henceforth feel that glorious excitement of combat which had grown to be one of his nature's chief cravings. The Korps life had done its work in the direction of his character, developing his latent love of organisation and law, accustoming him to look upon cold steel as the arbiter of right, and upon his country as the strongest among those that draw the sword.

'*Earth shall have our ashes!*' he exclaimed sorrowfully as he turned away, quoting the last words of the song.

'Undoubtedly,' answered a familiar voice beside him. 'Undoubtedly—wherefore the best thing we can do is to make the earth ours without delay.'

Greif laughed, as he recognised Rex. The latter had made his way round, during the throwing of the torches, in order to accompany his friend to the drinking-hall. They moved away together in the great crowd. One ceremony was ended, the next would begin in little more than half an hour, as soon as all the Korps were collected in the hall. This time, however, the company would include the Korps only, with their friends, and such members of other Universities as had come over to Schwarzburg to join in the festivity.

'And now for my last speech,' observed Greif, as they walked. 'I wonder what is happening at home.'

Rex did not make any answer, but Greif saw that he bent his head, and seemed to start nervously. The reply came long afterwards, as they were ascending the steps of the drinking-hall.

'I would rather not know what is happening,' said Rex. 'But I would like to know where you and I shall be, tomorrow at this hour.'

'Probably together, with all good Swabians, at my farewell feast.'

Rex shook his head. There was not time for more, as they were already within the building and Greif was obliged to attend to other matters.

The hall was splendidly decorated. Each of the Korps had a portion of the walls allotted to it, before which its tables were arranged in order. From the rafters to the floor vast draperies of coloured stuffs were hung and festooned so as to show off the insignia of each association to the best advantage, panoplies of swords and helmets, *escutcheons* with broad bands of gold, silver and black, scores of richly mounted drinking-horns, taken from every kind of beast, from the Italian ox, from the Indian buffalo, from the almost extinct ibex, and from the American mountain sheep—gifts from old members of the Korps who had wandered over the world, but had not forgotten their old companions— silver tankards upon brackets, old standards of softened hue projecting out above, or crossed above coats-of-arms, in short, every object of beauty and value which had become the property of the Swabians during the last fifty years. Every other Korps had done the same, till not a foot of the walls was left bare. High above, in a gallery, sat the musicians, who were to accompany the songs with their instruments, during the night.

The students assembled quickly and took their seats. As the clock struck nine, Greif, as president of the presiding Korps, called for silence, and ordered the opening 'Salamander.' Hundreds of glasses rattled upon the oak boards in strict time, and the official *Kneipe* was declared opened. The music burst out gloriously, echoing among the great wooden beams of the high roof, and song upon song rose full and melodious from below. At last Greif rose again to his feet, and all eyes were turned upon him in the dead silence which succeeded the joyous strains. He was very pale, but it was easy to see that his pallor was caused by the emotion of thus taking leave of his old comrades, rather than by any nervousness about his speech.

He spoke long and well, interrupted occasionally by a short

loud burst of applause. It was his especial good fortune to address the assembled Korps for the second time since his name had been inscribed upon the rolls of their beloved *Alma Mater*; his greatest sorrow was caused by the thought that he had thrown his last torch, and must soon drain his last toast as one of their number. Life was divided by a sharp line into two portions, of which the sadder began when rapier and colours were hung up at home to accumulate the dust that falls from philistinism.

Then the head must weary itself with staid matters, and the hand must loosen its hold upon the *schlager* and forget its cunning fence. Happy were those who merely exchanged the whistling blade of the student for the heavy sabre of the soldier, the green forest glade of the *mensur* for larger battlefields and the hope of brighter fame, who, having shed an ounce of blood in defence of their student colours, could look forward to shedding all, to the last drop, for king and country.

Happy were those few to whom the Korps was the beginning of an active life, and not the mere breathing space of liberty and good fellowship between the school bench and the desk. But whatever was to follow, whatever had gone before, none knew so well as they themselves, how sweet was the first taste of freedom, and how swiftly the bright time glided away amidst the music of the rapiers, the clash of beakers, and the song of free German voices.

Greif dwelt upon the importance of the Korps in the life of the University, upon the part played by the University in the life of the whole land, and did not scruple to trace Germany's victories directly to their origin in the daily life of German students, so different from that in other countries. Moreover, in his own opinion, and in that of most of his hearers, Schwarzburg had no rival—certainly none, he added, in the eyes of those who belonged to it. Where, in all Germany, were there such professors, such monuments of learning? What schools had given more famous names to the land, or even so many? As the good mother at home was to each student in that assembly, so was their dear *Alma Mater* to them all. He drank his beaker to all good Korps students, to all the brave colours there assembled, to all the professors, to the University itself,

'*Hoch*, Schwarzburg! *Hoch!*' he cried in ringing tones as he raised his glass high in air.

'*Hoch! Hoch! Hoch!*' shouted hundreds of voices.

'*Ad exercitium Salamandri! Eins! Zwei! Drei!*'

Greif brought his glass down upon the table as he spoke the last words, and the long roll began, like rattling musketry, again and again, to the due number of times.

Greif sat down amidst thunders of applause. As a matter of fact, he had made a speech rather better than the average of such performances, but a cool observer, or one accustomed to such scenes would have known that he could not fail to be loudly applauded. He was the favourite hero of them all. Young, handsome, brave, popular, not lacking the assurance that leads a crowd, it might have been foreseen that his last feast would crown his University triumphs, with a success passing even his own not very modest expectations.

CHAPTER 14

The music rose and swelled and died away. Beneath the brilliant light there was clashing of beakers and joyous drinking of deep toasts in the intervals between the songs. At regular intervals Greif demanded silence and proposed the health of each of the other Korps, one by one, in the order of their precedence for the year. A couple of hours passed in this way, and then the signal was given for the singing of the *Landesvater*, and the instruments struck up the stirring strain. Then at the head of each table rose the two eldest fellows, each with a pointed sword in his hand. In time with the music, they stood and struck their rapiers one against the other, exchanging caps at the last bars, and running the sharp blade through the embroidered velvet, so that the small head covering ran down upon the hilt.

Next, while the others stood upon the floor, the two leaders mounted upon the bench behind each row, on opposite sides of the table, clashing their swords in time, high above the heads of the carousers; and as the verse ended, each snatched the cap from the crown of the man who sat below him and ran it down his blade as he had previously done with his partner's. Reaching in due time the end of the board, the two stood crossing and recrossing their weapons, until all the others in the great hall had done the same and not one head remained covered. With this the first half of the *Landesvater* was ended, and a solemn toast was drunk to the health of the sovereign.

The second part was gone through in a similar manner, the leaders returning along the rows with the same ceremony and restoring to each man his own head covering at the conclusion of each verse. It is a strange old custom of which it is not easy to discover the origin, though the meaning is clear enough. Every man of the assembly pledges his head to live and die for his sovereign prince or king, and in a country where loyalty is a fact, and patriotism a passion, the expression of both by an ancient ceremony is solemnly imposing.

So great is the respect felt for the *Landesvater* and the sincerity of those who take part in it, that even in such a multitude of recklessly gay youths, the strictest sobriety is required of all until it is over, and is exacted under penalties of considerable severity. Once over, the mirth and enjoyment proceed in an increasing ratio, though it is to the credit of the German student that his gaiety on these public occasions never degenerates into unbridled licence, and that while he sings, laughs and jests over his fiftieth glass, he maintains the outward forms of habitual courtesy towards his fellows, together with a sort of manly dignity not unworthy of his stern Gothic forefathers.

The liquor is bland and almost harmless, and the heads are strong, and backed by iron constitutions. The object is not intoxication but jollity, and there is a deliberation in the manner of attaining the end by spending eight or nine hours over it, which effectually prevents such scenes as occur at festive meetings where the time is limited and men make themselves beastly drunk in the attempt to be merry before midnight. There is no closing hour for the German students' carousals. The official part of the affair is declared to be at an end at twelve or one o'clock, but all may stay as long as they please, and many are still in their places when the day dawns.

Greif and Rex sat side by side at the head of the long table. It was long past midnight, but neither felt the need of sleep. Greif dreaded to go home, for he felt that he was taking his last leave of a life he loved. Rex, who was unnaturally calm, even for a man of his solid nerve, sat motionless beside his friend, emptying his huge beaker twice in every hour with unfailing regularity. He talked quietly but constantly, interspersing queer bits of cynicism and odds and ends of uncommon wisdom in his placid conversation. Greif knew by his manner that he was in reality sad and preoccupied, but was grateful for his pleasant talk, which blunted the keen edge of this rupture with first youth's associations.

From time to time Greif wondered rather vaguely whether his relations with Rex would continue in after life, and, if so, whether they would not be affected for the worse by the revelation of Rex's identity. The excitement of the evening had perhaps momentarily expanded his natural generosity too far, and while he was quite aware that he could not now draw back from the friendship with honour, he was by no means sure that he might not afterwards regret his readiness to receive so kindly, as a cousin, him whom he had so much liked before he had been aware of the relationship. As he sat there, conversing with Rex, he attached an amount of importance to the situation which would have amazed him, had he known that of which both were ignorant, namely, that Rex was his half-brother as certainly as Rieseneck was half-brother to old Greifenstein.

The hours wore on till scarcely fifty students remained in the hall, and they of the sturdy kind who make very little noise over their amusements.

'Shall we go home, or stay till morning?' asked Greif at last, hesitating whether to light a fresh cigar or not.

'We might adjourn to your room,' suggested Rex. 'We can finish the night there.'

There was a stir near the door, and Greif looked round, idly at first, to see what was the matter, then with an expression of dismay. A man had entered the hall, a man with a ghastly face, who seemed to be making inquiries of the knot of Korps servants who waited for their tardy masters. Greif's eyes fixed themselves in the anticipation of evil, when he saw that the fellow wore the Greifenstein livery and was one of his father's grooms. What was most strange was that he wore boots and spurs, as if he had ridden hard, though he could only have reached Schwarzburg by the railway.

'Karl!' cried Greif in a tone that made the man start. 'What are you doing here?'

Karl crossed the hall, his face growing paler than ever, and his teeth chattering. He had not had time to recover from the thought of what he had left behind him. His hands trembled violently as they grasped the military cap he held.

'Herr Baron—' he stammered, staring at Greif with wide and frightened eyes. 'Herr Baron—' he began again, trying to frame the words.

'Speak, Karl!' exclaimed Greif making a desperate effort to seem calm, though he instinctively dreaded the words which must fall from the man's lips.

The groom turned appealingly to Rex, who sat motionless in his place, scrutinising the messenger with his stony glance.

'My God!' cried he. 'I cannot tell him! Sir, are you a friend of the Herr Baron?'

Rex nodded, and laying one hand upon Greif's shoulder as though to make him keep his seat, rose and made a sign to the groom to follow him. But Greif would not submit to be treated like a child, and sprang up, seizing the man's arm and drawing him nearer.

'I will hear it myself,' he said firmly. 'Is it my father?' he asked in uncertain tones. Karl nodded gravely.

'I caught the train as I jumped from the saddle,' he answered.

'My mother sent you?' asked Greif anxiously.

The groom shook his head, and his tremor increased, while he stared wildly about as though in search of some escape from his awful mission.

'Speak, man!' cried Greif, mad with anxiety. 'My father is ill—and you are here though my mother did not send you—speak, I say.'

'They are dead,' answered Karl in a low voice.

Greif sank into his seat and covered his face. Suddenly Rex's impenetrable eyes flashed, and he, last of the three, turned white to the lips.

'Is there another gentleman at Greifenstein?' he asked quickly.

'He is also with them, sir.'

'Dead?'

'He shot himself.'

Rex closed his eyes and held the table with his two hands, for he knew who the stranger had been. Seeing that Greif did not move, and supposing that Rex was a mere acquaintance, the man took courage to tell the story, speaking in a low voice to Rex.

'The gentleman arrived before dinner,' he said. 'Their merciful lordships dined together, but the butler said they left the table before it was time. Then they heard firing in the house. We broke the doors and found the Lady Baroness dead, in the room beyond the Herr Baron's study, and in the study the Herr Baron dead with a pistol in his hand, and the other gentleman dead with another pistol in his hand. I saw them. They had shot themselves as they sat in their chairs before the fire, but the fire was nearly gone out, though the lamp was burning. And then we saddled and rode, we four, one for the police, one for the doctor, one for Sigmundskron, and I for the railway, and here I am. You are a good friend of the young Herr, sir?'

'Yes, that I am,' answered Rex, starting as though from sleep.

'Then it would be best, sir, that you should tell me whither I should go, for the young Herr will be worse if he sees me.'

'Ask your way to the Red Eagle Inn,' said Rex, 'and stay there till we send for you.'

He gave the man a handful of loose coin, thoughtful of all contingencies, as he ever was.

'You need not talk about this horrible catastrophe,' he said, as he dismissed the frightened groom.

The latter disappeared as fast as he could, glad to get away from the sight of Greif's misery, and glad to have found someone to help him in telling his fearful tale. When he was gone Rex laid his hand upon Greif's shoulder, and spoke in a tone of quiet authority.

'Come with me,' he said. Greif rose to his feet like a man in a dream, and allowed Rex to put on his topcoat for him, and to lead him out of the almost deserted hall, through the group of servants who loitered at the door and made way respectfully for the pair to pass.

'Whither?' asked Greif as they stood in the cold street.

'To your room,' answered Rex, quietly passing his arm through his friend's and gently urging him to move forward.

Greif did not remember afterwards how he had found his way from the hall to his lodging. Neither he nor Rex spoke during the quarter of an hour they employed in reaching the street door, but Rex's arm was aching with the effort of sustaining and directing his companion. He lit a taper and prepared to help him up the stairs. But the sight of the familiar entrance recalled Greif to himself and dissipated the first stupor of his grief. He ascended the steps firmly, though he went like a man overcome with fatigue, to whom every movement is difficult. Still silent, Rex lit the lamp in the small room, and began to help Greif to take off his mantle. But Greif pushed him aside gently and sat down as he was upon the well-worn chair. Rex went and sat himself down in a corner at some distance and waited. His instinct told him that his friend must have time to recover from the first shock before anything could be done. He shaded his eyes from the light with one hand, and thought of his own sorrow.

The silence was intense. It was as though the spirits of the dead, of the mother of both and of the father of each, were present in the commonplace chamber where sat their two sons, not knowing each other for brothers, though overwhelmed by the same calamity. It seemed as if the murdered woman and her dead murderers were standing silently in the midst of the small room, watching to see what should happen to those they had left behind.

At last Greif raised his white face and looked towards Rex.

'I must go,' he said simply.

'Yes,' answered Rex. 'We must bury our dead.'

Greif looked at him as though asking for an explanation of the words. He had not heard all the groom's story.

'My father is also with them,' said Rex, answering the unspoken question. Greif grasped the table and stared at his companion stupidly for a moment. Then all at once his pale face grew luminous and his eyes glittered.

'Rieseneck?' he cried, in a suffocated tone. 'Your father has slain mine and yet you are here—' He rose from his seat, half mad with horror, as though he would spring upon his friend. But the latter interrupted him, in a tone which enforced attention.

'Your mother is dead—God knows how. Your father and my father shot themselves, sitting in their chairs.'

Again Greif's head sank upon his clasped hands, and again the deadly silence descended upon the chamber.

The long December night was over and it was broad dawn when the two men got out of the express train at the station nearest to Greifenstein. Without a word they entered the carriage that had been waiting for them, and the sturdy horses plunged into the forest, breasting the ascent as only strong animals can on a cold winter's morning. The early light made the great trees look unspeakably gloomy and mournful. There was not a tinge of colour to relieve the dead black shadows, or the icy grey of the driven snow. The tall firs stood solemn and motionless like overgrown cypresses, planted in an endless graveyard, filled with myriads of snow-covered graves, and in the midst Greif and Rex were whirled along over the winding road, pale as dead men themselves as they sat side by side in their dark garments, with set lips and eyes half closed against the freezing wind.

But when the towering wall of Greifenstein came into sight far off above the black tree-tops, Greif started and leaned forward, fixing his eyes upon his home; nor did he change his attitude until the carriage drew up before the deep gateway, and he was aware of a crowd of men and women who stood there awaiting his arrival. Before all the rest, he saw the tall thin figure of Frau von Sigmundskron. Her white hands were clasped together and she was bareheaded. Standing out before the others, in her gown of sober grey, she looked like a mediaeval saint suddenly come down to earth in modern times. As Greif descended she held out her arms to greet him. He realised that she must have journeyed from Sigmundskron in the night in order to be before him.

'I thank you,' he said, kissing her hands.

With an effort of will that would have done credit to his dead father, he entered the castle, bending his head gravely in acknowledgment of the servants' tearful salutations. Though most of them were the merest hirelings in the house, who had lately succeeded others like themselves, yet almost all were in tears. Frau von Sigmundskron looked at Rex in some surprise.

'A friend?' she asked with some hesitation.

'More,' answered Greif. 'Let us go to some place where we can be alone.'

He shivered as he felt that he was under the very roof where those he loved best were lying cold and stark in death, but he set his lips and clenched his fingers, determined to bear all that was in store for him. Frau von Sigmundskron hesitated as they approached the door of the drawing-room, and she looked sideways at Greif.

'Better to my rooms,' he said. And so the three went on through corridors and staircases till they reached the young man's apartments. He closed the door, and glanced at Rex.

'Madam,' said the latter at once, 'I am called Rex, but that is not my name. I am the son of Kuno von Rieseneck. I have Herr von Greifenstein's permission to pay my last duty to my dead father.'

Frau von Sigmundskron raised her gentle eyes in astonishment and looked from one to the other of the two men.

'Rex is my best friend,' said Greif. 'He needed no permission of mine to come here. I will explain all at another time. And now—' his voice broke, and he turned away, but recovered himself almost immediately. 'And now, I beg that you will tell us what you know.'

The good baroness detested weakness in herself and could not bear to see it in others, so that she told her story clearly and concisely, though with much caution and thoughtful tact. While she spoke she watched the two friends, who sat motionless beside her, their hands clasped upon their knees, their heads bent down, their faces white with emotion. The sun was already above the hills, and while she spoke the first rays fell through the ancient casement upon the carpet of the room, casting soft reflexions upon the pallid features of the three persons.

'I will go to them,' said Greif when she had finished, and he rose to his feet. The baroness prepared to show him the way, and Rex would have followed, but she stopped him by a gesture.

'I will come back for you,' she said. 'They are not together.'

She let Greif enter the chamber alone and softly closed the door after him. Then she returned to Rex. He was standing where she had left him.

'I have something to say,' she began, 'and something to give you. This letter is yours. It was found in the room, sealed, directed and stamped, as though it were to be posted, as it would have been had you not come. Nothing has been discovered for Greif, and this must have been written by Herr von Rieseneck. You are older than Greif, though he is brave enough, poor fellow. Here it is. Will you be alone to read it? I will go into the next room until you call me.'

'Madam,' answered Rex, taking the letter, 'I will not trouble you by any exhibition of my feelings, if you will stay here.'

He looked at the superscription, and cut the envelope open neatly with his pocket-knife so as not to break the seal. Frau von Sigmundskron was too well-bred to watch his face while he read the contents. Had she looked, she would have been terrified.

The note was very short, but it contained enough to shake even Rex's calm nature.

My son, when you receive this, I shall be dead. I arrived here this evening and I have discovered that Frau von Greifenstein is your mother, my wife. She made me believe that she was dead and married my brother under a false name. She has atoned for her crimes to her two husbands, who have done justice upon her, and now we also are about to pay the penalty of having executed that justice which is above all laws. At the point of death, I give this secret into your keeping. Your brother is a nameless bastard. Do not ruin him by betraying the shame of your father and of his. You are rich, but were you poor you would have no title to my brother's inheritance. Do not come to this place. They will bury me as decently as I deserve. Farewell. God keep you, and make you happier than I have been.—Your father,

Von Rieseneck.

Schloss Greifenstein, December 20.

As Rex read the words he instinctively turned away. His face was hideously distorted and his stony eyes seemed changed into coals of fire. Every fibre of his strong nature was strained and tortured by the iron grip of his suffering. Every pulse of his body beat with a frantic rage for which no outlet was possible. His eyeballs burned with excruciating pain as he attempted to read again the letter he still held in his hands. He was one of those habitually calm men who become almost insane when they are angry, and in whose placid strength passion of any sort, when roused, finds its most dangerous material. For a full minute he stood speechless, feeling as though his emotion must find some physical expression, lest it should kill him there and then.

He heard a footstep, and then the door opened and closed softly. Looking round, he saw that he was alone; Frau von Sigmundskron had understood from what she could see of his attitude that the letter had brought him news even worse than that of his father's death, and she had felt that to stay any longer would have been to intrude upon a sorrow in which she could have no share.

Seeing that she was gone, Rex abandoned all restraint over himself, and submitted for a time to the overwhelming influences that surrounded him on all sides. His face became livid as he threw himself upon the couch, and his fingers were twisted unnaturally, as though their nerves were irritated by a strong electric current. Lying on his back, he rolled his head from side to side, like a man tortured on the rack, while his reddening eyes kept their sight fixed upon a blank point of the ceiling. The pain in his temples was as that of a red-hot screw boring its way through his brain, and while his white teeth ground audibly upon each other his quick-coming breath blew a scarcely perceptible foam from his strained and parted lips.

Father, mother, honour, were gone at one blow. Not the mother he had learned to dream of as a boy, when some faint memory of her fair face was still with him; not the tender and gentle mother who, if she had lived, would have been dearest on earth to him, and whose untimely death had lent her something heavenly and brightly mysterious; not the mother of whom his father had often told him, who from her place of peace looked down, perhaps, and smiled when he did well, or was pained when he did wrong; not the mother who, in his sleep, seemed to walk beside him when he was a child, robed in white, holding him by the hand and pointing heavenwards, like the picture of the Guardian Angel so common in his native country; not that mother who was to him the embodiment of all that was pure and lovely, and saintly and kind; not that sweet mother who for nearly forty years had held her secret place in the strange labyrinths of the lonely student's heart, to whose angelic figure he had often turned for consolation when weary with the aimlessness of deep study that led to nothing, or when satiated with all the useless, pleasureless pleasure which money could give and which there was no one to forbid.

That dear image was gone, but she was not the mother he had lost. She who had borne him was lying near him now, under that very roof. She had cast him off, him and his father, to spend all those years when he had thought her dead, with another man, worst shame of all, with the brother of her husband. And she had borne another son, she had given a brother to her first-born, whom the world called noble and rich, who in truth was penniless and nameless as any beggar in the street. She had heaped dishonour upon father and son, and she had borne in dishonour a second son and shamed the spotless life of a second father. And this woman, this wretch, this creature for whom no speakable name could be found, was his own mother, and was henceforth to stand in the place of her whose mere memory had been half divine.

Her vile life, forfeited for her crimes as shamefully as though she had died by the defaming hands of the common hangman, her hideous existence was thrust before him in all its abomination, as the source of his own, in the stead of all that had seemed most holy and chaste and worthy of his reverence. Was not her blood in his veins? Must not her evil nature of necessity show itself sooner or later in his own? Better the ounce weight of a finger upon that little bar of steel, to press which was to go beyond the risk of human infamy, beyond the possibility of reproducing in his own life the merest shadow of the sins that had darkened hers to the end. Better to cross at once that bridge whose passage is never choked because all who go over move ever in the same way, and none pause whose path has led them to its hither side. Better to leap at once and take his secret out of human keeping.

He would not have believed the horror if he had learned it from living man. But the message came from those who had sealed its truth with the dark red seal; it came from two men who had not been mistaken, of whom either, suspecting a mistake, would have slain the other for the mere accusation; old men not carried away by a fleeting resemblance, by the breath of a word half understood, by suspicion of a glance only half seen; stern, bold men—too stern to relent, but far too brave to be moved suddenly to senseless wrath against an innocent woman; proud men, both, who would have denied to each other the possibility of their common shame, so long as denial was humanly possible.

There could be no doubt, no shadow of a hope. Greif von Greifenstein was brother to Rex, and both were fatherless and motherless on the same day. Why live on, beneath the weight of memories which no time could efface and no future happiness soften? Had he any obligations to mankind, had he any pride of half-fulfilled hopes, of half-satisfied ambition? What had his life been? A nameless one, though of the two he alone could claim a name, if all were known. What had he done with it? He had attempted to explore the sources of life and the first origin of all those strange states which life brings with it. He had spent years in patient study, and again for months he had experimented upon his own incomprehensible sensations, by alternately procuring himself every pleasure and amusement which money could command, and then seeking the contrast of solitary asceticism.

His iron constitution of body had survived all, but his bright intelligence had wearied of the struggle, bruising its keen edge against the rocky barriers of the eternal and the unknown. Wiser than his fellows, he knew that he was no wiser than before; stronger than they, he knew the weakness of all strength; brave as the bravest, bravery seemed to him but a clumsy exhibition of vanity at best, and altogether contemptible from the moment it began to seek occasions for showing itself. He could have understood playing the coward for sake of examining the sensation, and would have laughed at his own vanity, when it led him to redeem his character the next moment by some act of reckless daring.

What was it all, but an amazing show of puppets, an astounding dance of lay-figures, animated by strings of which the ends opposite from men were lost in infinite distance? To dance, or not to dance, was all the choice men had, and rather than play a part in such a show as fell to his lot, it seemed better to break the strings and let the miserable marionette fall into the black hole behind the stage.

The possibility of adding a fourth link to the chain of death arrested Rex's frenzy. Since it was so easy to die, the escape from an earthly hell was always at hand. If, then, he lived, it must be of his own free will, and it did not beseem a man to do with such an ill grace what he did from his choice. Either he must end the matter decently and quietly at once, or, choosing not to end it, he must gather his strength and resume the direction of his existence. No other conclusion was possible. His secret was his own, and none need know it. All was over, and the disclosure of the truth could not help justice, any more than its concealment could injure any one. On the contrary, to tell what he knew would be to ruin Greif.

At the thought of Greif, Rex grew calm, and sat upright on the couch, supporting himself with his hands and gazing absently at the opposite wall. He had something left to live for, since Greif was his brother— Greif, who was at this very moment weeping over the body of her who was mother to both, looking for the last time upon that face which doubtless recalled to him the same tender memories Rex himself had cherished so long and so faithfully. A strong desire to see her took hold of him. The mistaken veneration of a lifetime was gone in a moment and Rex experienced the necessity of putting in its place the truth, however horrible it might be.

But, unknown to him, a touch of tenderness remained in the bottom of his heart. Sinful, ruined, dead by the hands of the men she had foully wronged, she had nevertheless been his mother. He said to himself that he would see her, in order that the last impression might finally wipe out all those that had been sweet before it; but in spite of every circumstance of shame that had attended her death, and in spite of his own reasoning, what drew him to her was in reality the strength of what he believed to be wholly eradicated and torn from him, the unconscious longing to see once more the face of her who had borne him, and whose image had been with him since he was a little child.

To see her, and then—what then? The future was a blank, of which the monotony was broken only by the figure of Greif. The idea of devoting himself to his brother, and of expending all his strength and intelligence in the attempt to make him outlive the dreadful memory of this day, presented itself to Rex's mind. He smiled faintly, for the thought was unlike most of his thoughts. He did not remember to have ever before entertained a similar project. He had sacrificed his inclinations many times in the pursuit of knowledge, and even occasionally out of good nature, but he had never set himself the task of systematically benefiting another man. And yet, he knew well enough that Greif would need support and help and comfort, and that there would be none at hand to offer all these, save Rex himself.

He rose from his seat and paced the room, his hands behind him, his eyes bent down. His face still bore the marks of his sudden and terrible suffering, but the perfectly balanced powers of his mind were already beginning to assert themselves. The habit of scepticism, that is, of systematic inquiry into all that befell him, was too strong to remain long in abeyance, and the equilibrium of the mental forces, cultivated to excess by his method of study, was too stable in nature to be long disturbed, even by the greatest calamity.

Today he saw the necessity of applying his intelligence to the alleviation of Greif's sorrow and to the preservation of Greif's existence, endangered by such a blow. In a few weeks at the latest, his own sufferings would acquire an objective interest, and would become so many data for study in the great case of all humanity. Rex could never have been a hero. He could never have detached his own individuality from its place in his map of mankind, so as to believe himself different from all other men, as heroes must believe themselves. He felt that the balance lay between his own life and death, and that he could turn the scale at his own choice; he could never have made himself forget life in the hope of victory, nor death in the fear of failure.

Incapable of any transcendental belief whatsoever, his intelligence had deified free-agency, while his unacknowledged suspicion of a directing power asserted itself in his theories concerning nature's fatalism. He supposed that the machinery of the universe produced inevitable phases in the lives of individuals and of nations; he knew that in all that had happened to him he had been free to exercise his choice between two alternatives. Such a choice was now before him, and for the first time in his life he determined to devote himself to the welfare of another.

Chapter 15

An hour later Rex was supporting Greif as he returned from the state bedchamber to his own room. Strong and determined to be calm as the young man was, the sight had been too much for him, and it was clear that unless he could obtain sleep his nerves must break down under the strain they suffered. He reeled in his walk like a man half asleep, his bright eyes were glassy and fixed, his relaxed fingers were incapable of grasping Rex's arm, and the latter held him upright upon his feet and almost carried him along the dim corridors.

Rex also had seen, but when he had once been face to face with that which had irresistibly drawn him to the room, he had felt no desire to look again. The drawn, white features of the dead lady recalled nothing to his mind out of the sweetness of the past, while their fixed expression of pain intensified the horror of the present until it grew unbearable. He had stayed long in the other chamber, where his father lay, and as he gazed upon the stern dark face his wrath rose, swelling tumultuously in his breast, as the tide of the sea, ebbing away as he thought of what was beyond and as he realised that all vengeance had been accomplished, and all justice done, so that no one remained alive against whom he could feel anger, no one upon whom his hand could fall. They had taken the law into their own hands and had executed its extreme sentence upon her who had wronged them, and they had expiated their deed in their own bodies. Never was tragedy so swift, so desperate and so complete.

And now the morning sun was high in the heavens, mocking the solemn darkness of men's hearts with his fierce brightness, shining upon the ancient walls of Greifenstein as coldly and clearly through the keen winter air as he had shone yesterday and as he would shine tomorrow. From eave and stringcourse and dripstone of the old castle the melting patches of dazzling snow sent down mimic showers of diamond drops, and the moisture thawed from them made dark stains upon the grey masonry. A redbreast skipped about the furrows made in the white carpet by the carriage wheels, paused, turned his tiny impertinent head, and glanced up at the ramparts with a squint, as though to tell the time of day by the sun and the shadows of the projecting eaves.

From the paved court of the stables, where all had been hurry and confusion on the previous night, came the occasional noise of an impatient hoof stamping upon the stones, the even sound of brushes on smooth coats as the men leisurely groomed the horses, the tinkling of curb-chains polished and rubbed together by idle lads who were in no hurry, and occasionally the echo of a voice, instantly subdued to an undertone as the speaker remembered that this day was not to be like other days. At the door of the servants' hall the two comfortable policemen in their dark uniforms and shining buttons sunned their fair beards as they smoked their morning pipes, exchanging a remark in a low voice about once in five minutes, and never without previously looking round to see whether any one was listening to them, but chiefly occupied in watching an underkeeper who was feeding the big hounds in a sunny corner of the inner court.

Nature, in her pitiless irony, seemed more than usually mirthful on that clear morning. It was such a day as old Greifenstein who lay upstairs, dead beside his dead wife, would have chosen to tramp far into the forest, with his gun on his shoulder and his dogs at his heels. It was such a day as would have made poor Clara's lot seem easier, softening her tortured conscience in a thaw of passing satisfaction, pleasant while it lasted, transitory as the gleam of light and warmth in the dismal winter of the Black Forest.

The forest itself alone was unchanged. The trees looked blacker than ever against the blue sky and under the violent light. Around the vast amphitheatre of the hills they stood motionless in their even rows, like a great assembly of dark-robed judges, judging the dead who lay in their midst, inquisitors whom no brightness could brighten, and in whose sombre countenances no smile was reflected from the glorious sky and dazzling light. Silent, grand, funereal, they stood in their places as they had stood a hundred years ago, before those lives began which had now suddenly gone out, as they would stand when those other lives were extinguished which now were young.

Neither Greif nor Rex were seen again that day. In the course of time the representatives of the law arrived, did their office, and were regaled with a collation by the butler, during which they sat upon the chairs which last night had been occupied by those whose end they had come to ascertain. The case was very plain and their duties were simple. They went away and took the two policemen with them. Frau von Sigmundskron moved noiselessly about the house, giving the necessary directions when there were any to be given, occasionally sitting down in a quiet corner to read a few pages of a devotional book she had found.

More than once she went to the different rooms where Greif and Rex had withdrawn, to see whether she could be of any use. Greif was always in the same place, leaning back in a great easy-chair, pale and exhausted with grief, but evidently master of himself. At last she found him asleep, and she drew a long breath of relief, for she knew that the chief danger was past. When she went to Rex she found him reading, and he did not relinquish his occupation during the whole day, so far as she could ascertain. Whether he understood what he read, or not, was more than she could determine. The volume contained a part of Goethe's works, and when she glanced at the page she saw that the student had selected the second part of Wilhelm

Meister for his reading. He always looked up quietly when she entered, thanked her, and said that he needed nothing.

Frau von Sigmundskron could not rest. The sense of responsibility which she felt might alone have sufficed to sustain her energy, but her mind was disturbed by a matter even weightier in her eyes. The tremendous difficulties of the future presented themselves very clearly to her mental view, and she knew that before long they would not be mere shadows of things to come, but actual problems with which she must grapple, and upon the solution of which she must concentrate all her strength. Tomorrow, or the next day at the latest, the earth would close for ever over what remained of those poor beings whose departure from life had saddened her own and made it seem so hard to understand.

But when the three were buried, she could no longer remain at Greifenstein. There would be no reason for prolonging her stay, even had she wished to do so, and indeed her wishes would lead her homewards as soon as her duties were all fulfilled. She had never before been separated even for a day from her child, and though she was strong and sensible in mind and knew that Hilda was safe with old Berbel, she was conscious that it was painful to be away from her. She would therefore return to Sigmundskron. From that moment her trouble would begin. It was not conceivable that Greif should go away without seeing Hilda, and yet there were many reasons why it would be better that the two should not meet.

She had foreseen the struggle during the hours of the night, but it had not then appeared so formidable as now. She had then thought more of Greif, and it had not seemed impossible to tell him frankly what she felt. As she reflected upon what must be done, she saw that Hilda was the principal figure in the situation, and she realised that Hilda's happiness was infinitely more dear to her than anything else in the world. She hesitated, and for some time she told herself that the marriage must take place, come what might.

To her, all that had happened since the previous evening was shrouded in an impenetrable mystery. Her imagination failed utterly to account for the desperate doings of which the horrible result was before her. She could have understood that the two brothers might have quarrelled on meeting after so many years, and that in a moment of reckless anger they should have shot each other. Clara might have perished in the struggle, while endeavouring to part them. But there was a dreadful appearance of deliberate intention in the whole tragedy which made such a hypothesis untenable.

That Clara had been intentionally murdered, she could not doubt. Greifenstein might have slain her in a fit of passion and might have taken his own life afterwards, but this could not account for Rieseneck's suicide. She could have believed that for some unknown reason Rieseneck had killed his brother and Clara, and after disposing their bodies as they were found, had shot himself. But the examination proved the contrary. It was plainly evident that both men had died in their chairs by the weapons found in their own hands. Rieseneck had written to his son, but Greifenstein had not, or, at least, if he had written anything it had not been discovered. Rex alone could know the secret, therefore, if it had been revealed at all. She was ignorant that in Germany, when a suicide has been committed, the law has a right to see whatever letters were last written by the deceased.

The stamped letter, addressed to Rex, had attracted her attention, and she had taken it from the table with the intention of posting it the next day, not meaning to conceal it, but, on the contrary, to send it without delay to its destination. The legal gentlemen, courteous to the good lady, had not pressed her with any questions, taking it for granted that if she had found any letter or any clue to an explanation she would naturally offer it at once. And so it chanced that Rex alone could know the truth if anyone knew it. That he had been terribly moved by what he had read, she had seen for herself, but whether the letter had contained a full explanation of the circumstances, it was not possible to judge. If so, it was more than probable, she thought, that Rex would show it to Greif in due time, and that when the first shock was over the contents would be communicated to herself.

The question was whether this would happen before Greif saw Hilda. In spite of her natural repugnance to such a plan, she almost resolved to ask Rex directly whether what he had received threw any light upon the situation. If she could know why those three persons were dead she could better guide her course in the future.

If Greifenstein had been a murderer, as well as a suicide, his son could not have Hilda for his wife. It was Greif's misfortune, and the baroness gave him all the pity she could spare from her own child, but the point could not be yielded. She closed her eyes and tried to think it over. She thought of Hilda, married and leaving Sigmundskron to live under the very roof where such deeds had been done, and the mere idea was painful and repugnant. Greif was wholly innocent of all that had happened, but the stain was upon his name, and the blood of his father was in his veins.

Hilda's children would be the grandchildren of a murderer. Old Greifenstein had not ended his days in a shameful prison, merely because he had found courage to take his own life quickly. But if he had done the deed he was a common murderer, and the moral result was the same, whether he were alive or dead; the indelible disgrace rested upon his son, and would brand the lives of his son's sons after him. Hilda loved Greif, and Greif loved Hilda, but that was no argument. Better that Hilda should drag out a solitary and childless existence than be happy under such a name; far better that Greif should submit to half a century of lonely and loveless years, than get children whose names should perpetuate the remembrance of a monstrous crime.

Hilda would suffer, but suffering was the lot of mankind. The baroness wondered sadly whether her daughter's disappointment could possibly equal what she herself had borne on that day when her gallant soldier-husband had been shot down in battle. Could Hilda's sorrow be like her own? Even if it were,

Hilda must bear it rather than take such a name—unless, indeed, old Greifenstein had been innocent of his wife's death. No one could know that except Rex, and would he answer her question? In her horror of the whole situation she wished that she might go back to Sigmundskron and end her life in barely decent poverty with Hilda, and never again think of the marriage. But her rigid sense of duty reproached her for such a thought, which made her feel as though she were trying to lay down the responsibility that had fallen to her lot. Her untiring conscience took up the burden again, to bear it as it might.

Rex must answer her, and upon his answer would depend everything. It was not an easy matter to question him, however, and for the present it was wholly impossible. She must meet Hilda while she herself was yet undecided, so that it seemed simplest to be roughly frank with the girl, to tell her plainly what had happened, what was known and the extent of what no one knew, showing her clearly that if old Greifenstein should turn out to have been guilty, she must give up all thought of Greif and submit to her poor lot with the best grace she could.

Greif would go away and travel, perhaps for several years. He would find interests at last, which might help him to forget his darkened youth. Hilda and her mother would live as they could, and when the mother died Sigmundskron must go to the hammer. At all events it was not encumbered with debts, and its sale would leave the child a pittance to save her from starvation; possibly she would have more than before, but Frau von Sigmundskron could not judge of that. Possibly, too, Hilda's sixty-four quarterings would help her to gain admittance as a lady-canoness in one of those semi-religious foundations, reserved exclusively for the old nobility, of which several exist in Germany.

The short winter's day was over when Frau von Sigmundskron reached this stage in her meditations. Lights were brought to the room where she was, and a servant came to ask her what she would eat. She scarcely knew what she answered, but she remembered that some hours had passed since she had been to see Greif or Rex and she roused herself to go upon the errand of inquiry. In the corridor she was met by another person who came to ask about the dispositions for the morrow, an ominous creature in black, the sight of whom recalled at once the hideous realities of the day, from which her mind had wandered in her anxiety for Hilda's welfare. She gave the necessary directions and continued upon her way.

'Come in,' said Greif's voice as she knocked cautiously at the door.

As soon as she entered she saw that his state had been improved by the rest he had taken. His eyes were quiet, his colour pale but natural, his manner mournfully calm. In the morning she had feared he might fall into a delirious fever.

Frau von Sigmundskron came and stood beside him. He was comforted by her presence, though he had not always been sure that he liked her. At present, he knew what good cause he had to be grateful to her for what she had done, and he felt that she was his only relation in the world, the only woman alive who could in any way take the place of what he had lost. If he had not been very fond of her before, it was because he had not understood her, and because in his eyes her personality was entirely eclipsed by Hilda's. He put out his hand and took hers, and pressed it gently.

'You are very good,' he said. 'I am glad you have come.'

She sat down beside his easy-chair and gazed into the fire. There was no light in the room save that of the pine logs, blazing in the great chimney. Her reflexions of ten minutes earlier seemed very far away, for the sight of him and the sound of his voice had suddenly recalled those hopes for Hilda from which she had got so much happiness.

'You have slept,' she said. 'I am glad, for you needed rest.'

She did not know what to say, and there was a pause before she spoke again, during which Greif did not move. Unconsciously he had taken the manner of one ill, and lay back in his seat, his eyes half closed, his hands resting upon the arms of the chair, making no effort and only hoping that none would be required of him.

'Dear Greif,' said the baroness at last, 'you will go away, will you not?'

He started a little and his expression changed, as though the question pained him.

'Yes,' he answered. 'I will go away—when it is over.'

'Shall it be tomorrow, then?' asked Frau von Sigmundskron very softly.

'Yes. Tomorrow morning. I would it were tonight. And then—' he stopped and passed his hand wearily across his forehead, letting it drop nerveless by his side almost immediately.

'And then?'

'Then I must see Hilda before I go.' His eyelids quivered, and his lips shut themselves closely.

'Yes,' answered the baroness in a tone of hesitation.

'Yes, I must see Hilda,' Greif repeated. 'And when I am gone—then—then—'

This time Frau von Sigmundskron said nothing, for she saw that he was suffering, though she dared not guess what was passing in his mind. He seemed to be trying to speak.

'When I am gone—' he began, but the words died on his lips. 'Do not talk of this now, dear Greif.'

He roused himself and sat straight in his chair. There was something of his father's look in his face, and his companion noticed that his fingers were strained as he grasped the carved wood in the effort to steady himself.

'I must say it now,' he answered firmly. 'Tomorrow I shall not be able to talk much, and it may happen that we shall never have another opportunity.'

'Never?'

'Perhaps never. It is to be goodbye. You must find another husband for Hilda, for I may not come back. That is what I wanted to say.'

The baroness turned a startled look upon him and leant forwards toward him from her seat. She had not expected such a turn in the drama.

'You do not suppose that I, an honourable man, would expect you to give your daughter to the son of a murderer?'

The question was put so sharply and concisely that Frau von Sigmundskron was taken unawares. The thought had been painful enough when it had passed unspoken through the confusion of her reflexions, but Greif's statement gave it a new and horrible vividness. With a single sharp sob, she hid her face in her hands, and Greif saw that they trembled. His own heart was beating violently, for he had nerved himself to make the effort, but he had not anticipated the reaction that followed closely upon it. He felt as though, in pronouncing the detested word, he had struck his father's dead face with his hand.

'God knows how I loved him,' he said, under his breath. 'But he did the deed.'

Frau von Sigmundskron did not distinguish the words he spoke, but she felt that she must say something. Her hands dropped from her strained and tearless eyes and fell upon her knees.

'Oh, Greif! Greif!' she almost moaned, as she stared at the blazing logs.

'That is what it comes to in the end,' he answered, summoning all his courage. 'I cannot marry Hilda. It was bad enough to be half disgraced by my father's brother—you were kind enough to set that aside. It is worse now, for the stain is on the name itself. I cannot give it to Hilda. Would you have her called Greifenstein?'

The baroness could not speak. Half an hour earlier she would not have dared to hope that Greif would himself renounce her daughter, but it was different now. She could not look upon his agonised face, and listen to the tones that came from his tortured heart, as he gave up all he held dear for the sake of acting honourably, she could not see his suffering and hear his words, and yet brutally admit that he was right, and that his sacrifice was a necessity. And yet her own conscience told her that her first thought must be for her own child, and not for him. She stared at the fire and answered nothing.

'Would you have her write her name "Hilda von Greifenstein"?' he asked, forcing the words sternly from his lips. 'Would you have her angel purity darkened with the blood that is on my house?'

'But you, Greif—what will become of you?'

'It matters little enough, so that I do no harm to those I love,' he answered.

'It does matter,' said the baroness gently. 'It is not right or just that an innocent man should suffer for the deeds of others.'

'It is right that he should suffer anything, rather than injure those who are not only innocent but free from inherited reproach.'

There was a sudden energy in his manner which surprised his companion. His white face was illuminated by a sort of radiance from within, his voice was full and firm, the glance of his eyes piercing and determined.

'It is right,' he continued, 'and I will do it, come what may. Indeed I must, for in spite of your kind heart and words you would not give her to me. But even if you would, I would not take her, I would not make her the mother of more Greifensteins. Ay—you look at me—I love her too much. That is the reason. If I loved her less—oh, then, I would take her. I would take my beautiful Hilda for my own sake, and in her love I would try and forget the horrors of my younger years. I would forget, for my own sake, that my father was a murderer and a suicide, my father's brother a shameful traitor, myself a man clothed in the infamy of others, until the world can hardly distinguish between my innocence and their guilt.

'I could live with Hilda, somewhere in this lonely forest, and with her I might bury memory and talk lightly of love beside its very grave. And Hilda would be willing, too, and if I did not love her as I do, I would take her—whether you would let her go or not—no, forgive me—I should not speak so to you, who are the best of women—but you would consent, for you are so kind. But the thing is impossible. She would remember, and I should remember also, when our sons grew up and had to meet the world with the brand of our name upon their faces. Look at Rex. He is my best friend. Yesterday I learnt that he is my cousin. Even he has hidden his father's deeds under a common, meaningless name.

'How much more should I hide my head! How much less right have I, than he had yesterday, to make an innocent girl, or any woman, the wife of a Greifenstein! No—go to Hilda, tell her the truth, let me see her once, and I will rid you of myself when I have said goodbye. You are her mother, and you alone can tell her all— all except the last word, and when I have spoken that word, I will go away, Rex and I together, and you will not hear of me anymore.'

Greif ceased speaking. He had risen from his chair to pace the room while he spoke and he now stood with folded arms before the baroness, his eyes fixed on hers as though waiting for her answer. He was very young, and it was perhaps the first time in his life that he had spoken out before any one. He was too much excited to think whether his speech would sound theatrical and exaggerated or not. He meant every word of what he had said, and that was enough for him. He meant to do what was right and honourable, and that is enough for any man.

Frau von Sigmundskron's gentle eyes fell before his fixed gaze. Feeling as she did, and remembering what she had felt when she had come to him, she was ashamed to meet his earnest glance. There were few better women in the world, few whose goodness showed itself so clearly both in deeds and intentions, and yet she was conscious, rightly or wrongly, that Greif was outdoing her in generosity. To her the words he had spoken had a ring of heroism in them, and he himself seemed to grow in dignity and strength as he stood before her. She hesitated, the speech came to her lips, failed, took courage and came again. Once more she raised her head and looked into his eyes.

'Greif—you are a brave man, and you will understand me,' she said. 'When I came here, I felt all that you have said. I felt it in the long night, before you were in the house. I meant to tell you what you have told me, as kindly as I could, not now, but later. It would have been hard, for I am more than fond of you.'

'It would have been your duty, and it would have been right,' answered Greif calmly.

The baroness laid her hand upon his folded arms.

'It would not have been right, Greif,' she said in a low voice that trembled a little. 'It might have seemed so, for I did not know you as I know you now. You have done all that a man can do, more, perhaps, than almost any man would have done. I did not wrong you in what I felt, nor in what I meant to say, but I could never say it now. Take Hilda, and call yourself as you will, for you are worthy of her and neither you nor she will ever regret it.'

Greif looked at her for a moment, and then knelt beside her and kissed her hands.

'You will,' she said, and there were tears in her eyes.

'I cannot,' he answered, in heartbroken accents. Then, rising, he stood and leaned against the chimney-piece and bowed his head against the carved wood.

He could not feel as she did, and his nature was incapable of such a sudden revulsion as had taken place in her heart. He knew how bravely generous she had been, but her kindness changed nothing in the situation, beyond awakening in him a sense of heartfelt gratitude for which he had expected no such cause as she had given. The fear of doing an injury to Hilda was still foremost in his mind. He had said that even if her mother would consent, he would not take her, and what he felt when that consent was so unexpectedly thrust upon him was a measure of his earnestness.

'Nothing is spared me,' he said, almost under his breath. 'Not even your generosity!'

His action was to depend wholly upon his own free will, and he knew that it would have been far easier to renounce his love if Hilda's mother had helped him with her opposition. There she sat, offering him what he must not take, thrusting upon him that which his whole nature craved, and which his honour alone bid him refuse. Her sweet voice sounded like the soft music of temptation.

'Do not say so, Greif,' she said. 'Remember that you are wholly innocent, and that Hilda loves you with all her heart and soul. Why must you force yourself to do what will make her and me so unspeakably wretched? After all—I take the most worldly argument—it is for her and for me to decide. You have concealed nothing, and I know all, and if I say that your goodness and your heroism outweigh the rest, should you not be satisfied? And besides, you are young. You do not know how very quickly the world forgets.

'A score of years hence, who will remember the evil deeds of last night? They were not even done in a city, those who did them had hardly any acquaintances, and perhaps no friends. You yourself are not old enough to be known to many, and you can live here until your children are grown up. It seems to me that I was wrong even to have thought of separating you two, wholly wrong and mistaken and that I ought to ask your forgiveness for my intention.' Thus she pleaded the cause of his own heart, giving many and good reasons why he should yield, while he stood struggling with himself and wishing that he could stop his ears against her persuasion. To him the horror was more vivid than to her, and she could not understand his dread of associating Hilda with the curse that had fallen upon his house.

'I cannot,' he said firmly, when she had ceased speaking.

She rose and stood beside him.

'Think of it, Greif,' she answered. 'You must not break her heart for a scruple of honour.'

Then she went out softly, wondering at herself, but sure that she had done the best.

CHAPTER 16

Frau von Sigmundskron was too conscientious a person to omit a mental review of what had passed. She knew, indeed, that she had acted kindly and generously, if not wisely, and she believed that in some cases kindness might be better than wisdom. She was struck by one point in Greif's language. He assumed as a certainty that old Greifenstein had killed Clara, whereas the baroness had been inclined to attribute the crime to Rieseneck alone. At first she did not understand Greif's readiness to believe that this evil deed had been his father's, but presently, as she thought over the whole matter, it struck her that she had no reason for acquitting the one rather than the other, so far as evidence was concerned, but that she had wished Greif's father innocent for Greif's own sake. The good lady was much disturbed on finding that her wishes had been strong enough to bias her mental view without her knowledge, and she grew more and more satisfied with the course she had pursued after Greif had spoken. She saw clearly, now, that Greif was indispensable to her for Hilda's happiness, and she comprehended that he was worthy of the girl.

In the wicked world which surrounded the Black Forest on all sides, persons would have been found malicious enough to suspect that Greif really wished to be free from his engagement with Hilda. He himself, had he been less excited, would have hesitated before speaking as he had done, lest such a motive should be attributed to him. He would have acted and talked with more diplomacy and less outward energy, though with the same inward conviction, and it is by no means impossible that Frau von Sigmundskron's first intention might in such a case have remained unchanged, and that she would have gently acquiesced in Greif's proposal to give up the marriage. But there was no guile in the baroness, and but little in Greif himself.

He had been carried away in his speech by the sincerity of what he felt, the more easily because his whole nature was unstrung by grief; and Hilda's mother had seen in him only the hero, ready to sacrifice everything for her he loved, and woman-like, she had felt irresistibly impelled to reward him on the spot by a generous sacrifice of those convictions which his real or fancied eloquence had already destroyed. So simple was she, that it did not strike her that Greif's own position was changed, that he was all at once his own master, possessed of a large fortune and perhaps of tastes which he had concealed during his father's life. If the aforesaid wicked world had been acquainted with the circumstances, it would assuredly have taken this view into consideration.

But that portion of mankind in which are included so many of our acquaintance, but in whose numbers we ourselves are never found, were very far from Greifenstein, and the Lady of Sigmundskron knew little of their modes of thought. She saw that Greif was honest and she sought no malicious explanation of his intentions. On the contrary, the longer she reflected upon the interview, the more she admired him, and strange to say, the nearer she came to accepting his opinion of his father's guilt.

She had meant to see Rex, and she had not been altogether decided to wait and allow the natural course of events to bring her the information she desired about his letter. She remembered with some surprise that her decision in the matter of the marriage was to have depended upon the knowledge of old Greifenstein's culpability or innocence which she had hoped to gain from Rex. It was evident that her mind was tired, and she resolved at last to rest. It was her duty, however, to see Rex before sleeping, if only to inquire about his state. She would certainly not ask him any questions.

She found him reading still, or pretending to read, by the light of a shaded student's lamp. Upon another table there was a tray with a couple of covered dishes upon it. His older and tougher nature showed itself there, she thought, for he must have given the order himself. He rose politely as she entered, and offered her a chair. His manner contrasted so strongly with Greif's, as to make her wonder whether he were in reality much affected or not.

'I will not stay,' she said. 'I only came to see how you were, and whether I could do anything for you.'

'You are very kind. I have all I need, and more. Have you seen Greif?'

'Yes. He has slept and I think he is safe. At first I feared lest his mind should be affected. He is younger than you, Herr von— Herr Rex— and perhaps he is more sensitive.'

'Perhaps,' replied Rex thoughtfully. 'Would he care to see me?'

'I have no doubt—that is—he may possibly be tired—' she hesitated.

Rex's stony eyes examined her face attentively.

'You have had an interview with him,' he said in a tone of conviction, 'and you have talked about this dreadful matter. I have a communication to make to you, Frau von Sigmundskron. It will not take long.'

The baroness started and looked at him earnestly.

'What is it? she asked.

'You gave me a letter this morning. I will tell you frankly that you ought to have given it to the representatives of the law, for in such cases the law has a right to all letters of the deceased and can even cause them to be intercepted in the post-office.'

'I did not know,' she replied, in some perturbation.

'I did, but as no one asked me for the letter, I did not offer it. I cannot tell you all it contained, nor shall I tell Greif. But this I will tell you. My father arrived here last night, and almost immediately afterwards he and Herr von Greifenstein, jointly, killed Frau von Greifenstein, and then committed suicide.'

'Is there no doubt!' asked the baroness nervously. She turned white at the thought of the scene his words recalled.

'The last confessions of men about to die are generally trustworthy,' remarked Rex rather drily.

'Of course—of course.' She wondered what other communication the letter had contained. 'Exactly, and you may rely upon the exactness of what I tell you. My poor father had no reason for deceiving me, nor was he a man to deceive any one. He had been a fanatic and an enthusiast in his youth, and if his fanaticism led him too far, he paid the penalty in forty years of exile.'

'But what could have induced him—or Greifenstein—'

'Madam,' said Rex courteously, but firmly, 'I regret my inability to answer your question. It must be supposed that two such men had some cause for acting as they did, which seemed to them sufficient.'

220

'Forgive me!' exclaimed the baroness. 'I did not mean to ask you. I thank you for having told me what you have. Am I to tell Greif? I think—indeed I know that what he believes coincides with your account.'

'Then you had better say nothing. I could not show him the letter, and if he knew that there was one, he might naturally enough reproach me with a want of confidence in him. I should be sorry to be placed in such a position, at such a time.'

For a few moments neither spoke. The baroness was formulating another question, which must be put to her companion.

'Herr Rex,' she said at last, 'it is necessary that the last act of this tragedy should be completed tomorrow. You have a voice in the matter—' she hesitated.

'Whatever you do will be well done,' answered Rex. He seemed to think the question over quickly. 'If you have any objections to his resting here,' he said presently, 'I will take him away. Do not let any feeling of delicacy prevent you from being frank.'

'Let them lie together,' replied Frau von Sigmundskron. 'It would be Greif's wish. You are very thoughtful, Herr Rex, but you must not think that any such unkind feeling can exist any longer now. Though there is no real tie of blood, you are one of us. You and Greif should be as brothers.'

A momentary light flashed in Rex's impenetrable eyes.

'I will be a brother to him, if he will let me,' he answered steadily. 'I thank you very much for what you have done and for what you say.'

Frau von Sigmundskron bade him good-night and went away. She was a woman, and her curiosity was strong, though her conscience was stronger. She felt that she was in the presence of some extraordinary mystery, and that Rex himself was a somewhat mysterious personage. His eyes haunted her and disturbed her peace, and yet she could not deny that she was attracted by him. His quiet dignity pleased her, as well as the tone of his voice. She liked his face and its expression, and her deep-rooted prejudices of caste were satisfied, for she recognised in him a man essentially of her own class. There was something very manly, too, about his bearing, which could not fail to impress a womanly woman, no matter of what age. But his eyes followed her and seemed to stare stonily at her out of the dark corners of the room. She was too much exhausted, however, to resist very long the oppression of sleep that came over her, and she was far too tired to dream, or at least to be conscious of dreaming.

With the following morning came the last trial of her strength, and those who saw her wondered how a thin, pale woman, whose hair was already white could show such constant energy, forethought and endurance. She had led a hard life, however, harder than any one there suspected, and she could have borne even more than was thrust upon her, without flinching or bending under the burden. On foot she walked in the mournful procession through the snow and the bitter wind, leaning but lightly on Greif's arm, and sometimes feeling that she was helping him rather than accepting his assistance. It was nearly a quarter of a mile from the castle to the spot where the burial-place of the Greifensteins was built in the depth of the forest, and the road was bad in many parts, though an attempt had been made to clear it, and the footsteps of those who bore the dead smoothed the path for the living who came after.

At last it was over. The last short prayer was said. The great stone slab, green with the mould of centuries, was raised by twenty strong arms and was made to slide back into its place above the yawning steps that led down into the earth, the heavy doors of the mausoleum swung slowly upon their hinges, the huge, rusty lock was secured and the unwieldy key was solemnly placed in the hands of the new master of Greifenstein. With slow steps, two and two together, all went back through the dim shadows of the trees, while the icy wind whistled and roared upon them from every giant stem, and the trodden snow creaked beneath their feet. Two and two they re-entered the low gateway of the castle, till the iron-studded oak clanged behind the last pair, sending rolling echoes along the dark, vaulted way.

An hour later Greif and Rex sat together in sad silence before the big blazing logs in Greif's room, faintly conscious of the comforting warmth, looking at each other from time to time without speaking, each absorbed by the pain of his own thoughts. It seemed as though several hours had passed in this way when Greif at last broke the silence.

'I will ride to Sigmundskron tomorrow,' he said, 'and then we will go away.'

Rex looked at him, nodded gravely and answered nothing.

'We must go together, Rex,' said Greif after another long pause. 'Will you come?'

'I will go with you wherever you will. If we part it shall not be my fault.'

'Thank you.'

The great logs crackled and blazed, sending up leaping flames and showers of sparks into the wide chimney and reflecting a warm red glare which contrasted oddly with the cold and sunless light of the winter's afternoon. The sound and the sight of the fire supplied the place of conversation and animated the stillness.

'Rex, did you know that I was to have been married next month?' Greif asked the question suddenly, as though he had come to an unexpected decision.

'I thought it possible that you would marry soon,' answered his companion.

'I was to have been married to my cousin Hilda in January. How far away that seems!'

'The daughter of Frau von Sigmundskron?'

'Yes. We have been engaged for years.'

'And you are going to Sigmundskron to see her—to tell her—'

'That it is all over.' Greif completed the sentence.

Rex rested his elbows on his knees and leaned forward, staring at the fire. He knew what Greif meant without any further explanation, and he realised how much more his cousin would stand in need of comfort than before. But his active and farsighted intelligence did not accept the necessity of breaking off the marriage. He approved of Greif's wish to do so, and admired his courage, but at the same time he saw the utter desolation and gloominess of the life in store for him if he persisted in his intention. He held his peace, however.

'You see that I could not do otherwise,' Greif said at last. Still Rex answered nothing, and stared persistently into the flames, though his cousin was looking at him.

'Would you,' continued Greif, 'if you were in my place, have the courage to offer such a name as mine to an innocent girl?'

'You are as innocent as she,' observed Rex.

'Personally, but that is not the question. Would you bring her here to live in this house, to be a part of all the evil that has befallen me and mine?'

'You can live where you please,' said Rex philosophically.

'And besides, by a very simple process of law you can call yourself by another name. Do away with the name and live in another place, and you are simply Greif and she is simply Hilda. There could be no question of doing her an injury. Names are foolish distinctions at best, and when there is anything wrong with them it is foolish not to get rid of them at once. Do you think that I would not marry as plain Herr Rex, though I am in reality the high and well-born Horst von Rieseneck? I have but to make application for a legal change, pay the costs and the thing is done.'

'Outwardly, it is true. But the fact would remain. You are Rieseneck and I am Greifenstein, for all our lives, and our children will be Rieseneck and Greifensteins after us, if we marry. I would not lay such a curse upon any woman, much less upon one I love.'

'A curse is a purely conventional term, having no real meaning in life,' replied Rex. 'The reality is you yourself, your love and her love, whether you be the Emperor or Herr Schmidt. At least that is all the reality which can ever affect either of you, so far as marriage is concerned. I do not say that your name, or mine, would not be a disadvantage if we were ambitious men and if we wanted to be statesmen or officers. But I do assert that no sensible person will blame you or me for marrying happily if we have the opportunity, merely because our fathers did evil in their day.'

Greif listened attentively, but shook his head.

'It is strange that you should not think as I do about this,' he answered. 'We think alike about most things. But you need not try to persuade me against my will. I will not yield.'

'Will you take my advice about a smaller matter?'

'If I can.'

'Then listen to me. Do not be hasty. If you must see Fraulein von Sigmundskron tomorrow, do not let your parting be final. You may regret it all your life.'

'What would my regret be, compared with hers, if in the course of time she realised that she had done wrong in taking my name?'

'Are there any men of her family alive?' asked Rex. 'Is there any other branch?'

'No—if there were, they would never allow the marriage, even if I wished it.'

'I did not ask for that reason. If she is alone in the world, take her name. Call yourself Greif von Sigmundskron, and revive an ancient race without letting your own die out.'

Greif was silent. It had not struck him that such an arrangement might be possible, but he saw at a glance that Rex had dealt a telling blow against his resolution. To have married Hilda as Greifenstein would have always remained out of the question, to have chosen a common and meaningless appellation would have seemed an insult to her, but the idea suggested by Rex was alluring in the extreme. He knew how bitterly both Hilda and her mother regretted the extinction of their family and how gladly they would welcome such a proposal. By one stroke of the pen Greifenstein and its memories would be detached from his future life, and there would be something in their place, a name to make honourable, a home in which to plant new associations—above all there would be the love, the pride, the happiness of Hilda herself.

He felt that his determination was weakened, and he made a final effort not to yield, scarcely knowing why he resisted any longer, since the possibilities of the future had grown so suddenly bright. Rex saw at a glance that he had made a deep impression upon his cousin, and wisely left the remedy he had administered to take its effect gradually. He knew human nature too well to fear that Greif could ever shut his eyes to the prospect unveiled to him. Time must pass, and in passing must heal the gaping wound that was yet fresh. Every month would take the ghastly tragedy further away and bring more clearly to Greif's mind the hope of happiness.

As for the rest, it was buried in Rex's heart and no power would ever draw from him the secret of his brother's birth. Rightly or wrongly, he swore to hold his tongue. He did not know to whom the great Greifenstein property would go if he told the world that Greif was a nameless orphan with no more claim to his father's wealth than Rex himself. It seemed strange to be suggesting to Greif the means of discarding a name that never was his, but which must in all probability belong to someone who coveted it in spite of the associations it would soon have for all who heard the tale.

Rex sat in silence thinking over the almost endless intricacies of the situation, and wondering what would have happened if that letter had fallen into the hands of the law, and what would have become of Greif. He would have been absolutely penniless. Not even his mother's heritage, if there were any, would have belonged to him, for Rex could have claimed it as his own. He looked at the handsome face of his cousin, and tried to imagine what its expression would have been, if all things had taken place legally, and if Greif had received only what was his due. The sensation of preserving so much to any one by merely keeping silence was strange to Rex. He did not know whether he himself might not be considered a party in a fraud if the matter were tried before a tribunal, though he had not spoken one untrue word in the whole affair.

Verily, silence was gold. To Greif, Rex's silence was almost equivalent to life itself. One word could deprive him of everything, of Greifenstein, of his name, of every item and miserable object he possessed, as well as of the broad lands and the accumulated money. He would lose all, but in whose favour? Rex did not know. Perhaps the lawful heir of Greifenstein was a poor officer of foot in a third-rate garrison town, eking out his pay with the remains of a meagre inheritance, desperately poor, and as desperately honourable. Possibly there was a connexion with some great and powerful family, into his full hands everything would go, if the truth were known.

Possibly—Rex stopped short in his train of thought, astonished that he should not have sooner hit upon the fact—possibly Frau von Sigmundskron and her daughter were the only living relations. It seemed almost certain that this must be the case, when he thought about it. And if so—if he held his peace, and if Greif persisted in not marrying Hilda—why then he, Rex, was keeping that gentle, half-saintly old lady out of her rights. The new confusion caused by the idea was so great that even Rex's tough brain was disturbed. His instinct told him that the Sigmundskrons were poor—perhaps they were in real want. If he said nothing, if Greif persisted, if in later years Greif married another wife, as was most likely and possible, what sufferings might the man who had brought this about be responsible for! And yet, what a prospect, if he should take his letter from his pocket-book and hand it to Greif, as they sat side by side in the quiet room before the open fire! He had meant to burn the scrap of paper.

It would be easy to toss it into the flames before Greif's eyes. But if ever all those things should happen of which he had been thinking, what proof would remain that the baroness or her daughter had a right to what was theirs even now? If ever that time came, Greif would not believe a spoken word. Would it not have been best, after all, to give the writing to the men of the law, requesting their discretion? No, for all this might be spared, if only Greif married Hilda. Until he had realised what issues were at stake, Rex had been satisfied with the suggestion he had made to Greif, believing that it would ultimately bear fruit in the desired result.

Now, however, it seemed insufficient and wholly inadequate to the importance of the case. Greif must marry Hilda, and the letter must not be destroyed, for it might prove a valuable instrument with which to hasten or direct the march of events. After all—were the Sigmundskrons the only relations?

The idea that they were the only heirs-at-law had presented itself so forcibly that the sudden doubt concerning the fact made Rex desperate. There was no difficulty, however, in ascertaining the truth from Greif himself and without rousing his suspicions. It was even natural that Rex should ask the question, considering what had gone before.

'Have you no other relations, besides the Sigmundskrons, Greif?' he asked.

'None but you yourself.'

'I am not counted, as the connexion is in the female line,' said Rex calmly. 'I mean, if you were to die, the Sigmundskrons would be the heirs, unless you married and had children, would they not?'

'Yes—I suppose they would. I had not thought of it.'

'It seems to me that this constitutes an additional argument in favour of the plan I suggested.'

Greif did not answer at once, for he felt the weight of Rex's words, though he did not understand the whole intention of his cousin.

'I cannot argue with you now,' he said at last, as though wishing to be left to his thoughts.

Rex was too wise to be annoyed, for he saw that Greif's refusal to discuss the matter any further was the result of his inclination to yield, rather than of a hardening determination. The only point immediately important to Rex was that the marriage should not be broken off abruptly at once. He did not know what Hilda's nature might be, and this was an uncertain element in his calculations. It was certainly most probable that if she loved Greif sincerely she would not part with him easily, nor suffer him to sacrifice himself without making a desperate effort to hold him back. On the other hand, and for all Rex knew, Hilda might be a foolishly sentimental, half-frivolous nonentity, who would take offence at the first word which spoke of parting and consider herself insulted by Greif's chivalrous determination. She might be a suspicious girl, who would immediately be attacked with jealousy and would imagine that Greif loved another and wished to be free from herself.

On the whole, Rex, in his worldly wisdom, thought it improbable that Hilda would turn out to be sincere, simple and loving, whereas for her own interest it was important that she should possess these qualifications. Lastly, Rex reflected that Hilda might very well be a selfish, reticent, scheming young woman, who would know how to manage Greif as though he were a child. He almost wished that she might have enough worldly guile to cling to Greif for his fortune as well as for his love— anything, rather than that the marriage should be broken off.

If that disaster occurred, if by Greif's impatient desire to be generous to the extreme limit of what honour could demand, or by Hilda von Sigmundskron's possible lack of affection or of wisdom, the two were to be permanently separated, Rex confessed that he should not know what to do. His own position would in that case be very far from enviable, for he would certainly have been a party in a fraud, of which the practical result had been that the Sigmundskrons were kept out of their property. The moral point presented to his conscience was an extremely delicate one to decide. His nature, as well as his education, impelled him to tell the truth regardless of all consequences, for its own sake; but the question arose, whether he was bound to tell what he knew, when no one asked him for the information.

When the consequences might be so tremendous, and when the least effect that could be anticipated must be the immediate ruin of his brother, he believed that he should be justified in his silence, provided that those who would legitimately profit by the secret he withheld should receive all the advantages to which they were entitled. It seemed to him a case in which his conscience must gamble upon the probabilities. If it turned out well, he might congratulate himself upon having produced much happiness; if he lost the game, he must endure the humiliation of being obliged to communicate the truth to both parties.

It would have been far easier, if he had been called upon to induce Greif to make an apparent sacrifice for the sake of a good he could not understand. The young man's noble disposition was more easily led in the direction of chivalrous self-renunciation, than towards an end involving personal advantage. Indeed Greif would almost invariably have chosen to give rather than to receive. The present difficulty consisted in making him take Hilda, in order that he might unconsciously give her what was hers.

At first Rex had considered only Greif's happiness; now, he must think before all things of Hilda's fortune. He knew Greif well enough to be sure that if the marriage were broken off, he would certainly bestow a considerable portion upon the Sigmundskrons if they were really poor, but this could not be enough. Either Hilda must have all that was hers, by marrying Greif, or Rex must tell the story and precipitate the catastrophe. The only condition of his concealing what he knew, was that every one except himself should gain by his reticence. If this could not be accomplished justice must be done in spite of the consequences.

Though Rex's blood was German, his character had suffered a certain modification by the manner of his bringing up. His mode of thought certainly differed from Greif's to an extent which could not be accounted for upon the ground of temperament alone. Brave, manly and sufficiently generous though he was, Rex undeniably had a preference for accomplishing his ends mysteriously and by diplomatic means, a characteristic more southern than northern, and assuredly not German. He was a man well able to sustain whatever part he chose to play, and it was at least to his credit that he never employed his remarkable powers of concealment to a bad purpose.

In his place, Greif would have told everything, and would

then have offered everything he possessed to compensate the mischief done by the truth; he would not have been able to hide what he knew for a week, in such a case, for his extreme love of frankness would have tortured him until it was out, but if there were no justice to be accomplished, he could have held his peace as well as another. Rex saw far and clearly before him. His sceptical mind could not accept the conventional traditions of truthfulness at any price, of honourable sentiment exaggerated to Quixotism. He felt the necessity of weighing results before acting, rather than of following moral precepts and letting the results take care of themselves.

To him ultimate good was everything, and religious morality was an empty bubble, unless it could be made to contribute directly and clearly to a good result. With Greif's more simple and straightforward nature, truthfulness, and such virtues as go with it, were invested with all the superior importance which religion gives to each present act of life, and so far as the future was concerned, a semi-conscious faith in the efficacy of principle supplied the place of Rex's well thought-out combinations and philosophical disquisitions about relative right and wrong.

CHAPTER 17

The effect of what Rex had said was to hasten Greif's action. After listening to his cousin's arguments, he felt that what was to be done must be done quickly, lest his courage should fail him. If he had been left to himself he would never have doubted his own strength, and would very possibly have waited a day or two before going to Sigmundskron to bid Hilda farewell. Now, however, he felt that to hesitate or delay would be fatal, and he resolved to lose no time in carrying out his intentions. In order to isolate himself more completely from all outward influences he would have sent Frau von Sigmundskron back alone and would have followed her a few hours later; but his sense of common decency, as well as his profound gratitude, forbade such a course. He could not by any means avoid the long drive in her company, and he tried to harden his heart as he submitted to his destiny.

It was certain that, unless she had changed her mind, she would talk of the matter of his visit, and would repeat in his unwilling ear all those arguments which appealed to his heart so strongly, and which so grievously shook his chivalrous resolution.

During the long night that succeeded the day of the funeral ceremony, the sorrow of the parting which was before him assumed such proportions as made the past seem less horrible, and the change from one kind of suffering to another afforded his exhausted nature a relief of which he was not conscious, but which was nevertheless very real. He himself could not understand how it had been possible for him to discuss with Rex matters so closely connected with his future happiness, scarcely an hour after the heavy gates of the mausoleum had closed upon the father he had so deeply loved, and upon the mother he so tenderly regretted. For he did mourn for her sincerely, in spite of his earlier indifference. He was yet too near the catastrophe to attempt to explain it, but in the confusion of his grief her words came vividly to his mind.

He recalled the expression of her face when she had implored him not to forsake her, whatever happened, and he knew that in some way she must, even then, have had a forewarning of her end. He remembered many strange incongruities in her manner, which he had once disliked intensely, but which now pointed to the existence of a secret in her quiet life, and which, having seemed contemptible when she had been alive, took a tragic importance now that she was gone. He recalled very clearly that morning when he had felt a thrill of pitying tenderness for the lonely woman, and when she had responded so suddenly and passionately to his simple words. He had never loved her, and had perhaps had little cause for any affection, but the suddenness and the horror of her death strengthened in him every kind memory, and overshadowed by its dark presence whatever in her life had lacked dignity and worth.

As for his father, he had felt for him a passionate devotion of which he dared not think now. And yet he had been able to talk with Rex, if not freely, at least with a complete command of his faculties. He would have reproached himself with heartlessness, but when his thoughts dwelt upon those he had lost, he knew that the self-accusation was unmerited. Not comprehending what passed in his own mind, and finding himself face to face with a problem that seemed to involve his own life or death, it is not altogether surprising that he should have persisted in undergoing a self-imposed suffering which he almost unconsciously regarded as a test of heroism.

But as he did his best to fortify himself in his intention another power stood before him, not a gloomy presence of evil, not a sorrowful but relentless fate, not a thing in itself terrible, grand or heroic, and yet stronger and more real than any of those other shadows which surrounded his life. He had not known that it was with him in such a shape, he had not realised what it would be to face that which has conquered all men sooner or later. The love of Hilda, which had softened all his youth, but which in its unopposed calm had seemed so gentle and tender that by an effort of his strong will he might put it off if he would, the quiet spirit of calm which had been with him so long, purifying his thoughts, simplifying his hopes for the future, encouraging him ever in each present day, the love of untarnished youth for spotless maidenhood rose up like the dawn upon a traveller in a strange land, shedding its universal light upon the secret places of his soul.

It was a wonderful revelation of beauty appearing in the midst of his sorrow, contrasting the magnificence of its splendour with the darkness in which he would have hidden himself. He groaned as he lay alone in his solitary chamber, and the passionate tears burst from his eyes. He had met at last that which must vanquish all his resolutions, and turn all his desperate efforts into vanity. That sudden flash of radiance in the midst of his grief was but a dark shadow compared with the light of Hilda's face. If the mere thought of her made all resistance seem impossible, would he be able to go to her tomorrow and tell her that they must part? But it was not a mere thought, as he called it. He had thought of her for years, but never in this way; she had dwelt in his heart a long time but he had never felt anything like this. It was true that he had never resisted her presence before.

Could that be the reason? Could it be that love was a companion for the weakest of mankind, if kindly entertained, and yet, if resisted, the master of the very strongest? Greif in his pride of youth believed himself as strong as any, and the sensation of being thus utterly overpowered was crushing and humiliating. He would not yield, but he well knew that he was conquered beforehand, and must be led away captive in the end.

He sat up and tried to reason with himself. It was but an illusion after all, and it was just such an illusion as should strengthen his purpose. If Hilda were indeed, as she doubtless was, this exquisitely lovely creature, could anything be more contemptible than to give her a name which must be a reproach, a position in which her beautiful life must be made half shameful by the memory of hideous crimes?

Momentarily satisfied with himself, he once more laid his head upon the pillow, but he had hardly closed his eyes when Rex's suggestion flashed through his brain, and Hilda's clear voice seemed to cry 'Sigmundskron!' in his ears. The thought of bearing another name, of being no longer Greifenstein, of being the father of a new race in a new home, presented itself to him in all its attractions. After all, said Rex to his conscience, you are wholly innocent, and it is only the sound of the name to which you object or which you fear for her. Take hers and be happy under it, since you would be miserable under your own.

After all, one is as good as another, and it would be better to be plain Herr Rex than to throw over the joy of a lifetime for the sake of three syllables that have a disagreeable ring. Names are nonsense and a man's reputation is his own, not to be made or marred by his father's evil deeds. The Sigmundskrons know all, and it is for them to judge, not for you. If they will make you one of them, what right have you to make them unhappy for the sake of your own prejudices?

Greif was very young to cope with such difficulties, when even love itself was against him. Though Rex said little, that little was eloquent and full of practical sense, like many of Rex's sayings. Greif shed bitter tears and ground his teeth and wrung his hands.

'Hilda! Hilda!' he cried aloud in his solitude, 'what would you have me do, if you knew all, if you knew me, if you knew my heart!'

When a man appeals against his love to the woman who loves him, his resolutions are at their last gasp for existence. Hilda answered his heart before the spoken words were out of his mouth.

'Love me, dear—that is all I ask!' It was as though her voice mingling with his own sounded aloud in the lonely room, and Greif started up, his eyes wide open, his breath caught upon his lips.

It was the merest illusion, but its vividness showed him the power of what produced it. He was struggling bravely for an idea, trying to do what seemed knightly, and noble, and high, and vanquished though he was, he would fight to the very end.

The cold, bright morning rose over the sombre trees and suddenly entered his chamber like the broad reflexion of polished steel, a chilly glare of snow and cloudless sky seen through a window high above the earth in midwinter. Greif awoke from the broken slumber that had come to him at last, and looked anxiously about him. Somehow the sweet vision that had so much disturbed him, when he could see nothing real but the glow of the dying embers on the hearth, was dissipated and gone under the cruelty of the icy daylight.

With a heavy heart he rose and looked out upon the forest. From the place where he stood he could see the tall trees that surrounded the burial-ground of his race, and his eyes grew dark and gloomy as he thought of those who lay there. He was sadder and stronger than he had been a few hours ago. He would sit beside the baroness during the long drive to Sigmundskron, and what she might say would make no impression upon him, no more than the ringing of the horses' bells made upon the frozen snow. He would meet Hilda in the well-remembered sitting-room, and Hilda's mother would leave them alone. It would be cold there, for there was never much fire. She would perhaps be pale—a little pale, and her eyes would be cast down. She would sit upon one side of the stone chimney-piece, and he would stand upon the other. There would be a moment's pause, and then he would tell her everything. It could not last long, and when it was over he would have conquered in the struggle.

He would drive back alone in the late afternoon through the dismal forest. Tomorrow he would leave Greifenstein and go to his lawyer in the city. Half of his fortune should be Hilda's, and she should restore Sigmundskron and marry whomsoever she would. Then he would be free, and he would go away with Rex to some distant country, not to return for half a lifetime, if he ever returned at all.

The plan was simple, comprehensive and satisfactory. Nothing remained but to put it into immediate execution. He had given the necessary orders on the previous night and, as soon as Frau von Sigmundskron was ready, they would start upon their drive. He finished dressing and went in search of Rex. The latter looked even more pale and disturbed than Greif himself, though with characteristic determination he was attempting to eat his breakfast.

'I am going to Sigmundskron,' said Greif entering the room. 'Will you wait for me here? Tomorrow we will go away, or tonight, if you like.'

'I will wait willingly. Where should I go?' Rex rose, pushing the silver salver away from him.

'Very good. I shall be back at dusk. Goodbye.' Greif held out his hand in evident anxiety to get away, for he did not want to hear any more of his cousin's plausible reasoning, and dreaded lest Rex should broach the subject of his errand. But the latter detained him in spite of himself.

'Do nothing rash or hasty, Greif,' he said earnestly. 'A life's happiness is easily thrown away, and hardly found again when you have parted with it—and more than half of life's happiness is the love of woman. Good-bye.'

Greif made his escape as quickly as he could, but Rex had found time and words to touch the strongest cord in his heart. As he descended the stairs he felt again something of the influence that had visited him in the night, and he wished that he had not gone to Rex's room before leaving the house.

The sight of Frau von Sigmundskron, wrapped in her dark mantle for the journey, recalled him to himself. Her kind eyes looked at him almost lovingly from beneath the hood that covered her white hair, as he bent and kissed her hand. Neither spoke as they gained the court and got into the carriage, but while Greif was wrapping her in the heavy furs and arranging a cushion behind her, he felt that she meant to do all she could to dissuade him from his intention on the way, and he knew that the real struggle was yet to come. Then Rex appeared again, bareheaded, to bid farewell to the baroness and to say a few words of heartfelt thanks. He alone knew how much both he and Greif owed to her discretion; far more than she dreamed of, as she answered him and gave him her hand.

The horses plunged forward, their hoofs clashing noisily upon the pavement of the court; out of the bright light the carriage disappeared into the darkness of the gateway and as quickly rolled out again upon the dazzling snow beyond. After that there would be snow and trees and rocks, and rocks and trees and snow, until the grey towers of Sigmundskron loomed up above the tops of the firs.

Greif leaned back in silence, as they spun over the white road. Every moment now was a moment gained, provided that nothing were said to weaken his purpose. He braced himself in his seat, with his feet and his back, as though he expected the carriage to upset, and closed his lips tightly as if to meet a physical accident.

Frau von Sigmundskron glanced at him once or twice and noticed his expression, and his resolution to look straight before him. Had she possessed Rex's penetration, she would have guessed what was passing in his mind. As it was, she vaguely suspected that he had not altogether given up his plan, and the thought made her uneasy. She could see the clearly cut outline of his handsome face without turning her head. He had put on a fur coat, and she thought that fur was singularly becoming to fair men who had good complexions—a frivolous observation, apparently, but in reality not so worthless as it appeared. She was thinking of the impression Greif would make upon Hilda, and wondering whether the girl would find him greatly changed or not. She was woman enough to suppose that much would depend upon the first moments of the meeting which was about to take place, and upon the look Greif should first see in Hilda's eyes.

If he found her sad, pale, ready to pity him, his nature would be hardened, partly because he hated to be pitied by any one, partly because that same irritation would help him to execute his purpose. But if, on the contrary, Hilda met him with an ill-concealed joy, if there were light in her bright eyes and colour in her cheeks, if her voice spoke sympathy in his sorrows while her face told him of her gladness in the meeting, then things might turn out very differently. After all, thought Frau von Sigmundskron, Greif was only a man, and could not be expected to act altogether wisely unless a woman helped him.

She had certainly not always held such beliefs, but in latter years they had grown upon her. Sigmundskron was a women's establishment and naturally independent. The baroness had grown to think that, after all, women, when thrown entirely upon their own resources, can manage better than men. She was sure that no three men could have lived so decently and fairly well upon as little as sufficed for herself, Hilda and Berbel. It is true that the distance from such daily forethought and hourly prudence as she needed in her life, to such wisdom as Rex, for instance, possessed so abundantly, was considerable; but the baroness looked upon that as an insignificant argument, if indeed it presented itself to her mind at all. She thought little of Greif's determination to persist, if only Hilda could seem more glad to see him, than sympathising in his misfortunes.

With a woman's wholesale faith in woman, she believed utterly in the power of one of Hilda's glances to keep Greif at Sigmundskron for ever. Especially good women believe in all other women, more than those who are neither notably good nor notably bad. A man's faith in his fellows bears little or no relation to his own moral character, the best men being often the most distrustful, and not always the most agreeable companions. But the better a woman is, the more she believes all other women to be both good and wise, a phenomenon not hitherto explained, though very frequently observed.

The baroness held views of this sort concerning Hilda and old Berbel. It was characteristic of her that, as soon as her generosity had got the better of her hesitation in regard to the marriage, she began to consider Greif in the light of a well-beloved adversary, whom the feminine powers of Sigmundskron must vanquish for his own good. It was characteristic, too, that in all her uncertainty she had never considered for a moment the great worldly advantages to be gained or lost.

'We might have sent word that we were coming,' she said, when they had driven more than a mile without speaking. 'Hilda would have come to meet us on the road.'

'It is better so,' answered Greif mournfully.

'I do not see why—it would have given the child such pleasure,' remarked his companion, glancing at his face to see whether his expression would change or not.

'Would it, do you think?' asked Greif in an indifferent tone, though a very slight colour rose in his pale face.

'Indeed it would. It is wrong in you to doubt it. Poor Hilda! She has not too many pleasures of any sort, and meeting you is one of the greatest.'

The blush in Greif's cheek deepened. Again he set his feet firmly before him and braced himself in his seat as though to resist a shock. He hated himself for betraying his feeling in his face, and wished it were night. The baroness continued to speak in gentle tones, determined to obtain an answer from him, and if possible to make him engage in argument, for she believed that if he argued he was lost.

'Yes,' she said. 'It is a lonely life she leads up there. I am too old to be a real companion, and there is only old Berbel besides. It is pathetic to see her begin to count the days as soon as you are gone, and to watch her face as it gradually turns less grave when more than half the score is marked away.'

'Does she do that?' asked Greif, conscious that he was growing crimson.

'Always. She used to do it, when she was a mere child, and you were only an overgrown boy. It seems to me that she always loved you, long before—long ago, I mean.'

Greif sighed, and looked away. The half-boyish blush faded slowly from his cheeks and left his face paler than before. The good lady saw the change with regret, and wondered whether the slip of the tongue she had made in her last sentence could have anything to do with it. But she did not despair, though she allowed a few moments to pass in silence. To her surprise it was Greif who renewed the conversation, and in a manner she had not in the least expected.

'I have always loved Hilda,' he said, avoiding her eyes resolutely. 'Ever since I first remember your bringing her to Greifenstein. We were very small, and it must have been in the spring, for we picked mayflowers and found strawberries in the woods.'

'She was not more than six years old then,' observed Frau von Sigmundskron.

'And I was eleven, I think,' replied Greif, forgetting his effort to be silent in the childish reminiscence. 'Was that the first time you came?'

'I believe so. It was four years after we came to live in Sigmundskron.'

'Why did you not come sooner?' Greif asked. It seemed to him that it would be wise to keep the conversation upon the doings of twelve years ago. Another mile of the road was passed, and he was still unshaken.

'There were many reasons,' answered the baroness. 'We had not always been on the best of terms, perhaps because we had scarcely ever met, and I did not care to seem to be forcing my acquaintance upon my relations, so I stayed away for a while. After all, what really brought us together more than anything else, was the fondness of you two children for each other, which showed itself from the first. They brought you to see Hilda, and then we went to your house again—and so —gradually—'

'I remember that Hilda wore a blue frock the first time she came,' remarked Greif quickly, with an attempt to check the baroness's advance towards present times. The intention was so evident that she could not help smiling a little under her hood, and reflecting with some satisfaction that upon this subject, at least, she was more than a match for him.

'Perhaps she did,' she answered. 'I remember that she once had a blue frock.'

The triviality of what they were saying to each other struck Greif all at once, as compared with the horror of what they had left behind them at Greifenstein. It was but the third day since that fearful catastrophe had darkened his life, and he was exchanging remarks about the clothes Hilda had worn when she was a child. He thought he must be shamefully heartless, unless he were going mad, which, considering his words, seemed probable to himself. He leaned back again, and stared absently at the moving landscape. It seemed to him that his father's spirit was gliding along, high in the black trees beside the road, like mighty Wodin in the northern forests, watching the son he had left behind and listening to the foolish words that fell from his lips. The baroness attributed the sudden chill of his manner, and the gloomy look on his face to another cause.

'That was very long ago,' she said, taking advantage of his silence. 'Since then, Hilda has grown up, and you have become a man, and the love that began when you were children has—'

'I cannot marry her!' exclaimed Greif, so sharply and suddenly that his companion started and looked anxiously into his face.

'Then you will kill her,' answered Frau von Sigmundskron, after a short and painful pause. She, too, was roused to abandon the harmless attempt at diplomacy which had failed, and to speak out what was in her heart.

She was indignant with Greif, and she forgot altogether that she had at first felt precisely as he did himself in regard to the marriage. As the trees flew past and every effort of the strong horses brought her nearer to her home, she knew Hilda was first, and the instinct to defend her child from pain and sorrow gradually began to dominate her. Mild and gentle as she was, she was ready to attack Greif and to force him to marry her daughter whether he would or not. She grew nervous, for the coming meeting between the two might decide their fate, and every moment lost might be the most important. Greif did not reply at once to what she had said, but a shiver passed through his limbs and he drew the furs more closely about him.

'You are wrong,' he said at last. 'Hilda will forget me in time and will marry a better man and a happier one. I did not mean to tell you— I may as well—I shall make arrangements to give her half of what I have in the world. She will be an heiress then, and can marry well.'

Frau von Sigmundskron did not understand him. To her, the speech seemed cynical and brutal, an insult to Hilda's love, a slight upon her own poverty. The gentle lady's pale and delicate face flushed suddenly with righteous anger and her small hands were clenched tightly beneath the furs. There was a bright light in her soft blue eyes as she answered him.

'Hilda will neither accept your fortune, nor forget you— though it would be better, perhaps, if you could pass out of her memory.'

Greif could not see her face which was hidden by the hood she wore, without leaning forward, but her words and her tone surprised him. He had been very far from supposing that he should offend her by making such a proposal or by hinting that Hilda might marry happily at some future time. The emotion he had felt had probably made his voice sound harshly, and after all, he had perhaps shown little delicacy in speaking of the money, but he was quite unprepared for his companion's freezing answer. With Greif, however, it was impossible that any misunderstanding should last long, for he was too honest and frank to submit to being misunderstood himself.

'I do not know what you thought that I meant,' he said, turning towards her. 'But you would not be angry if I had explained myself better.'

Frau von Sigmundskron gave him no assistance, but sat quite still in her seat. In her view he had spoken lightly of her child's love and had proposed to set matters right by giving her some of his money. She was angry, and she believed that she had a right to be.

'I love Hilda,' continued Greif, and his voice trembled a little. If there were a phrase which he had not meant to pronounce, or to think of during the day, it was that. He found himself in a position which obliged him to affirm the strength of his love, and the mere sound of the words disturbed him so that he stopped short, to collect his thoughts.

'You do not act as though you loved her,' said Frau von Sigmundskron coldly. Two days earlier it had seemed to her that in renouncing Hilda he was giving proof of a heroic devotion, and yet she was not really an inconsistent woman.

'I mean to,' answered Greif rather hotly. 'If I refuse to marry her, it is because I love her too much to do her such an irreparable injury. I do not see how I could love her more. As for the rest, it has nothing to do with my love or hers. You are the only heir to Greifenstein after me, and when I die it will in any case be all yours, or Hilda's. I can do nothing with so much, and you may as well have the benefit of what will be yours someday— perhaps very soon. Is that unreasonable? Does that offend you? If it does, let us say no more about it, and forgive me for having said as much.'

'It would be better not to speak of the fortune,' said the baroness, beginning to relent.

'And you understand me—about Hilda?'

'I cannot say that I do,' replied Frau von Sigmundskron with all the obstinacy of a good woman thoroughly roused in what she believes to be a good cause. 'You love her, and yet you are willing to make her miserably unhappy. The two facts do not agree.'

Greif suppressed a groan and looked at the trees before he answered. If she would only have left him alone, it would have been so much easier to do what he knew was right.

'It is perhaps better that she should be unhappy for a time, now, while she is young, than regret her name when she has taken mine.' His own words had a sententious sound in his ear and he felt that they were utterly inadequate, but he was fighting against heavy odds and did not know what to say.

'I tell you that the child would die of a broken heart!' exclaimed the baroness with the greatest conviction. 'You say you love her, but you do not know her as I do. I suppose you will allow that it would be better that she should have moments of regret in a lifetime of happiness, than that she should die.'

She was certainly using strong language, but the time was passing rapidly and in the distance she could distinguish already the grey towers of Sigmundskron crowning the beetling crag. She was to be pardoned if she seemed to exaggerate Hilda's danger, but she believed every word she spoke, and she was growing more and more nervous at every turn of the road.

'If I believed that, if I even thought that were better for Hilda's happiness—'

Greif left the sentence unfinished, for he felt that he was on the edge of the precipice, though he was still inwardly convinced that he was right and that she was wrong. The baroness thought the day was almost won. All her anger melted away in the prospect of success and she talked much and earnestly, dilating upon the situation and using every argument of persuasion which she could devise. But Greif said little, and though he was careful not to offend her afresh, he did not again come so near to committing himself, as he had done once.

'And for that matter,' said the baroness, as the carriage swung round the curve and began the last ascent that ended at the castle gate, 'for that matter, you can call yourself Sigmundskron instead of Greifenstein.'

Greif moved uneasily in his furs. It seemed as though everything were conspiring against him.

CHAPTER 18

Hilda's quick eyes had discerned the carriage when it was still far down upon the road, a mere moving speck in the distance. She had thought it probable that her mother would return on that day, and she knew that she would be driven over from Greifenstein. Moreover, it was very likely that Greif would accompany her, and from the moment when she first saw the vehicle, she watched it and followed it along the winding road until she could clearly see that a man was seated beside her mother. Then the look of anxiety disappeared all at once from her fair face, and was followed by an expression of satisfied happiness which would have been good to see if anyone had been there to watch her.

She was standing upon a high part of the half-ruined building, on the northern side, and a person looking up from the road below could have seen her tall figure in strong relief against the pale winter sky. She had dressed herself all in black, but a wide mantle of coarse grey woollen stuff, gathered into a hood at the top and drawn tightly round her against the biting wind, concealed all her figure, leaving only her face visible. Rough and poor as the material was, it became her well, better perhaps than the richest furs could have done. Its folds fell gracefully to her feet as she held the cloak closely about her, and the unbroken neutral tint showed her height more plainly, and set off the marvellous beauty of her skin with a better contrast than any brighter colour.

Sigmundskron had been very desolate and lonely during the last two days, since Hilda's mother had ridden away through the bitter night to do her duty in the house of death. Of course both Hilda and the faithful Berbel had their occupations as usual, and talked over them when they were together, but the time had passed slowly and heavily. Hilda could form no clear conception of what had taken place, from the confused account of the groom who had brought the news. The idea that her uncle Greifenstein and her aunt Clara were both dead, as well as another unknown gentleman who had been with them, was very dreadful; but Hilda knew so little of death, that the story seemed melancholy and weird to her imagination rather than ghastly and vivid with realised horror.

By no effort of her mind could she fancy how the three looked, for she had never seen anyone dead in her whole life. She had read of violent deeds in history, but they seemed more like ugly fairy stories than realities, and the tragedy of Greifenstein struck her in a very similar light. It was as though some strange evil genius had passed through the forest, scarce twenty miles from her home, destroying all that he found in his way. They were gone, suddenly, like the light of a candle extinguished, and she should never see them again. They had crossed the boundary into the wonderful land beyond, and perhaps from where they were now they could see her dreaming about them, and asking herself what that great change meant which only takes place once for each man and each woman in the world.

Perhaps—Hilda trembled at the heresy, but let her thoughts run on nevertheless, because after all it was only her imagination that was talking—perhaps that was the end, and there was nothing beyond it. It would be infinitely horrible to be put out of existence altogether, without hope of any life at all afterwards. That might be what was meant by hell, and outer darkness, but upon this point Hilda was not decided. She made up her mind, however, after a little more reflexion, that the Greifensteins could not possibly have been bad enough to deserve to be put out entirely, though she frankly owned to herself that she had never liked her aunt Clara. She was sorry for her now, at all events, and she wished that she had at least made an effort to be more fond of her.

Hilda tried to decide what she should say to Greif when she met him. She never doubted that he would come to Sigmundskron, and in her ignorance of formalities she almost dared to hope that he would stay with her mother for a time. He would certainly not care to remain in Greifenstein for the present. If indeed he should wish to spend a few days with his relations, Hilda foresaw many and great difficulties, but she was surprised that such important household questions as those of bed and board for a possible guest should seem so insignificant when that guest was to be Greif himself.

The real trouble lay in deciding what she should say. It was clear that she could not help looking pleased when he arrived, though it would be her duty to look somewhat sad and sorrowful. Of course she felt for him and he knew it, but he would perhaps expect her to show it very clearly in the first minute and would be hurt if she even smiled. It was not easy not to smile when she saw Greif after a long separation. Perhaps the best way to look very mournful would be to think that he could not marry her for a long time, now, on account of the mourning. But then, Greif had finished his studies and would henceforth be always at home, which in Hilda's opinion would be almost the same thing as being married, provided she could see him all the time.

Then she thought of that strange warning she had given him when they last parted. She had not understood why she spoke, and yet, she had not been able to keep silence. Surely this could not be what was meant. Besides, it was superstitious to believe in such things, and she had been thoughtless in yielding to the impulse. Greif was safe, at all events, and she supposed that everybody's parents must die some day, though not necessarily in such a strange way. Her own father had been killed, too, before she could know him—if she had known him, she would have loved him, as Greif had loved the old gentleman who was now dead.

Hilda became aware that her reflexions were growing more and more heartless and that they did not help her at all, especially as she could not communicate them to Berbel. She resolved not to reflect any more for the present, and applied herself diligently to her household occupations until the morning on which she expected her mother to return. And now she was not to be alone any longer, for the carriage was advancing up the hill and she could plainly see Greif sitting beside the baroness in the big carriage. She knew his fur cap, for it was the same he had worn last year. She gazed a few moments longer at the pair, regretting that she must be thought heartless if she waved her handkerchief as a signal of welcome, and then she swiftly descended the broken steps that led down into the house, closing as well as she could the crazy door of the turret, to keep out at least a little of the strong north wind.

'Berbel! Berbel! Mamma is coming with Herr Greif!' she cried, before she was really within hearing of the room where Berbel was at work.

Her clear voice rang through the stone passages before her as she ran on, repeating the news until Berbel answered her at last.

'Is there anything for dinner?' asked Hilda breathlessly, as she stood in the doorway.

The grey-haired woman looked up from her sewing, over her horn-rimmed glasses. She had a hard, good face, with rough brows, sharp eyes and a large mole upon her chin. She was spotlessly clean, and everything about her was supernaturally neat.

She was broad-shouldered, rather bony than otherwise, and she moved as though nothing were any trouble which merely required exertion.

'There are potatoes,' she answered laconically, but a strangely genial, half comical little smile was twitching at the corners of her solid mouth.

'Nothing else? Oh, Berbel, there must be something else!' Hilda's voice was full of a sudden distress, and her face exhibited considerable dismay.

'I shall find something,' replied the other. 'Better see first whether they are hungry. Poor Herr Greif will not eat much—'

'No—but only potatoes, Berbel!'

'Potato dumplings are good things,' observed the woman.

'And fried potatoes with a stewed hare are better,' she added after a pause.

'Is there a hare, then? Oh, Berbel, you dear old thing, how could you frighten me in that way! Where did you get it? We have not had one for ever so long!'

'Wastei,' answered Berbel. Being interpreted, the name signifies Sebastian.

'And Wastei must have got it by poaching——?' Hilda's face fell.

'No——the forester has given him a licence this year, and I mended his breeches. There you have the whole history.'

Hilda's spirits revived immediately and she broke into a merry laugh, just as the sound of the horses' bells was heard jingling in the castle-yard below the window. She ran down the stairs to meet her mother and Greif. The story of the hare and Wastei's breeches had almost chased away her good intentions to look appropriately sad. The hideous tragedy of the Greifensteins was very far from her simple young life.

The great carriage swung round and drew up before the door of the hall, and Hilda was already standing upon the low steps. She had thrown back her hood when she had descended from the battlements, and had not replaced it. Her glorious hair looked like bright gold against the darkness of the hall behind her, and as the cloak fell from her on each side, the black of her dress suddenly threw out by contrast the brilliancy of her face. In another moment her mother and she were clasped in each other's arms, while Greif stood beside them on the steps.

He closed his eyes for an instant, just as hers were turning toward him. This was the woman he had come to renounce, this was she whose love he could put away at a moment's notice for the sake of an idea— his heart beat violently and then stood still, so that he turned very pale. Her hand was already in his, and he scarcely dared to look at her.

'Greif—are you ill?' she asked anxiously.

He had not seen her smile. He had escaped that, he thought. But as he looked up he saw what was harder to bear than any look of joy at his coming. She, who never used to change colour, was pale to the lips, and in her eyes was a look of terror for him which betrayed all her love, and devotion and power of suffering for him, in the flash of an instant. She had indeed been terrified, for he had turned ashy white as he closed his eyes, and his figure had swayed a little unsteadily as though he had been about to fall.

'Are you ill, Greif?' she repeated, unconsciously drawing him nearer to her.

'It is nothing. My head turned for a moment,' he said.

Hilda was not satisfied, but she saw that whatever had been the matter, he had recovered himself for the present, at least, and she supposed that he was exhausted with the fatigue and grief which had filled the last days. She became silent and preoccupied, as they all entered the hall together and ascended the steps to the sunny sitting-room over the court. Then Frau von Sigmundskron left her alone with Greif, on pretence of taking off her mantle and smoothing her hair, but as she went away she gave him a look which signified that she would not disturb them for some time.

There was the great stone chimney-piece, just as Greif had seen it in his vision of the meeting, and Hilda sat down beside it, as he had fancied that she would. But the room was not cold, as he had anticipated, for the fire was clear and big, and the sun streamed brightly in through the southern window. He had imagined the place chill and dreary, for he knew that he should need the impression of dreariness to help him. Instead, it was warm and sunny, and though Hilda was still a little pale, her pallor did not produce the effect he had expected. He tried to begin, for in spite of all, his resolution was still unbroken, but the words stuck in his throat.

'Greif,' said Hilda, looking up suddenly into his face. 'I do not know how to tell you—I am so sorry, so sorry for you, dear. I have not the words, but it is all in my heart. You understand, do you not?'

She had risen, seeing that he was still standing, and she came to him, and clasped both her hands upon his shoulder and looked up into his eyes. It would have been easier if she had begun in any other way than that. With her touch upon him, her eyes on his, her breath and soft voice so near, he could not play coldness. But he was strong still.

His arms went round her swiftly and pressed her to him, and he kissed her as he had never kissed her before, three times in quick succession. Then he gently led her back to her chair and returned to his own place, standing as he had meant to do, to give himself more courage. She submitted wonderingly, without understanding why he made her sit down, and for a few seconds neither spoke. At last he turned away from her and began to talk, looking at the window to avoid her eyes.

'Hilda, a very terrible thing has happened, and I must explain it to you, in order that you may comprehend what I must do. Will you promise me to listen patiently and to forgive me beforehand for all I am going to say?'

'Yes,' answered the young girl rather faintly. The strong presentiment of evil had come upon her again, as it had come that day when he was leaving Greifenstein. She bent her head and covered her eyes with her hand, as though not to see the blow that was to descend, though she must feel its weight. It was all instinctive, for not the faintest thought of what he was going to say could ever have suggested itself to her mind.

'Yes,' said Greif, 'it is very terrible. But I have come here to say it and I must say it all. You know what has happened. My poor mother is dead, and those who murdered her, have killed themselves—my father and his half-brother. You did not know that I had an uncle?'

Hilda shook her head, looking up for a moment.

'He was a bad man, too,' continued Greif. 'He had been an officer and had betrayed his trust in the times of revolution, was sentenced and imprisoned; he escaped from the fortress, made his way to South America, and lived there for forty years in exile, until the amnesty was proclaimed. He was not Greifenstein, he was Rieseneck, half-brother to my father by the mother's side and younger than he. That was bad enough, however. It was the reason why my father lived here in the forest so quietly. He was afraid that people would remember he was Rieseneck's brother. You see, the affair made a great noise at the time. Your mother knows all about it. Well, it was hard enough, as I say, to have such a disgrace in the family. We did not know that Rieseneck had a son—I found that my best friend—his name is Rex—is he.'

'How strange!' exclaimed Hilda. 'Why is his name Rex?'

'It is not, exactly. He and his father called themselves so in order not to be identified. It was almost necessary for them—as it may be for me now.'

'For you ?' asked Hilda in the utmost astonishment. 'You would change your name—why?'

Greif stared at her. She seemed not to understand at all, and yet he had gone into Rieseneck's story merely to make his own seem more terrible by comparison.

'You must know that, in the world, such calamities as have befallen me leave a mark, a stain even upon the innocent,' said Greif. 'The world looks askance at the sons of murderers.'

'And are you afraid of the world, Greif?' asked Hilda. 'That is not like you. For the Rienesecks, well, I understand—he was disgraced, condemned, imprisoned. But you! It is like a dreadful story of the dark ages, but there is no shame in it, nothing to be ashamed of. It is terrible, awful, appalling, but you can hold your head as high as anyone. Do you suppose it is the first tragedy that ever occurred in your family or in mine? Did not old Sigmund strangle his own brother with his hands, here in this house, seven hundred years ago, and am I ashamed to call him my forefather?'

'That is very different from what has happened to me,' answered Greif. 'You cannot understand, but the world judges according to its light. If I, the son of a man who murdered his wife and killed himself, were to present myself to any man of my own rank and ask him for his daughter in marriage I should receive a refusal, and perhaps an indignant one. I am not considered a fit person to marry an innocent girl of my class, I am stamped with a stained name, branded with the sign of others' crimes, ruined before my life is begun, cut off from happiness, from ambition, from you—O Hilda! that is what I came to tell you—I have spoken very badly—it is best to say it clearly.

'My beloved, this has taken you from me, and me from you, and has cast me adrift from all that remained, from the greatest and best of all. If I could dare to marry you now, to give you my miserable name, to take you to the home that is darkened by so many deaths—I should be the last and lowest of men! It is of no use, for I feel it—the only honourable thing left for me to do, in so much dishonour, is to leave you forever and at once. If I were willing still to make you my wife you ought to despise me, and trample the memory of my love under foot as a vile thing. O Hilda, Hilda! it is death to me, but it is best for you.'

The blow had fallen, and Hilda sat quite still in her place, covering her eyes with one hand, as she had done at first. All through his long preamble, she had felt that there was something dreadful to come, and now it had come indeed, in the shape she least expected, in the shape which of all others she would most have feared. She did not move, but the soft, fresh colour faded from her face, till it was whiter than the white hand she held before it. Greif looked at her, and his head swam. He thought neither of her suffering nor of his own, as the words came fast and incoherent from his pale lips. He went on, insisting, repeating, lamenting with the vehemence of a passionate man who has overcome all that is gentlest in himself and takes a savage delight in rending his own wounds.

'It is done, and you know, now,' he cried bitterly. 'I have fought against myself, against every one, to do this thing—do you think it is easy to give up such a love as you have been to me? And yet, I would not take you, no, not if you pursued me across the world—what right have I to you? The right of loving better than anything God has made was ever loved before? It is gone, that right, gone with my name, gone with all I once was, buried with my father and my mother in the old place beyond Greifenstein. Right? I have no rights any longer—neither to love, nor to hate, nor to be happy in the thought of love, nor of

Hilda. And yet, in all the years to come, you will be with me. I cannot give up the right to remember you, and to think of your dear eyes.

'Ah, if it were but my own fault, how easy it would be to bear! I wish I had wronged you—you would thrust me from you—it would help me—at least, if I had done you harm, I could die for it, and that would be so easy and simple, and would end all so well. I wish I had done some hideous, nameless deed with my own hands, that I might be driven out by men, and forced to leave you by others stronger than I! Anything, anything, anything but this!'

He bent his head against the cold stones of the high chimney-piece, and beat his brow against the hewn carvings of it, closing his eyelids over his dry and smarting eyes, wishing that every moment might be the last of his wretched existence, and at the same time miserably conscious that his strength would outlast all his sufferings. He had meant to be so calm and gentle, he had planned how he would gradually explain all to Hilda and break the shock for her, he had thought that when it was over, he could firmly say one solemn good-bye, and go back to his home alone. He had not known what love could do, nor how he should be tortured and wounded and bruised in the conflict.

But yet he was strong and victorious. His dignity and self-respect had been sorely shaken in the fight, and he had not found the calm and tactful speeches he had planned before; but in spite of every one, and chiefly in spite of his own heart, he had bravely done what he had come to do. The victory was more agonising than any defeat could have been, but it was victory, notwithstanding.

Manlike, in his utmost distress, he had forgotten Hilda's self in the overwhelming thoughts of her that rushed through his confused brain. Her hands had fallen upon her knee and she sat like a statue in the deep old chair, whiter than any marble, her colourless lips parted, her wonderful eyes fixed upon him in a glassy stare. Even her hair seemed to have lost its golden sheen, as though it were suddenly dead or turning into stone. And yet she was not unconscious. A very strong and perfect organisation rarely breaks down under the first shock it receives, no matter how violent. Hilda was not only conscious, she was even able to speak.

'Greif!' She spoke his name clearly, in a low voice.

He started, for he had almost forgotten her presence. He lifted his haggard face and turned towards her, supporting himself with one hand on the chimney-piece.

'Do you mean all you have said?' she asked very slowly, as though each word cost her an effort.

'I mean it all, Hilda,' he answered, his tones still trembling with the violence of the storm that had passed through him.

'You mean that because your father did this deed, you are ashamed to marry me?'

'More than ashamed—'

'And you will go away and leave me forever, for the sake of this idea alone?'

'Ah, Hilda—you have not understood—'

'I have understood all, because I love you, and now I know that you love me with all your heart—'

'Oh, thank you, my beloved! God bless you for seeing the truth—'

'Do not thank me—'

She caught her breath, then with a swift movement she was on her feet, standing beside him. The glassy stare was gone from her eyes, and they shone with a blue light like fire. Her strong white hands suddenly laid hold of his wrists and held him firmly.

'Do not thank me, Greif—or thank me, if you will—as you please. I will not let you go.'

There was a power in her tone which struck him with amazement, a concentrated, unrelenting, almost furious energy that startled him. He had expected tears, protestations, laments; he had thought that she might faint away, that the sight of her sufferings would treble his own. But he had not expected the short sharp outburst of a passion as strong as his, or stronger, he had not foreseen or guessed that this simple girl, brought up so far from the world, would take him by the hands and hold him, and tell him that she would not let him go, with an accent of determination that might have staggered the strongest man.

'You will not?' he exclaimed, aghast at the prospect of a battle worse than the first.

'No,' she answered, still grasping his wrists and gazing into his face with her fiery eyes. 'I will not, and I know that I am strong. I feel it.'

During nearly a minute neither spoke, but Hilda's hold did not relax for a second, and her lids did not once veil the intensity of her look. Even if Greif had possessed a wider experience of women than he had, it would not have helped him much. He was utterly at a loss. His manly nature would have provided him with weapons to rid himself of a woman of coarser instincts, even if he had loved her to distraction, provided he had felt that he must part from her. He would have felt that he could dominate a baser affection and force it down to his will, by sheer strength of purpose, no matter at what cost; but he was met here by something he had never understood, and he did not know what to do. The childlike innocence of Hilda's maiden love gave an extraordinary character to her passion.

The absence of anything like the common expressions of love made the transcendent power of what moved her stand out in magnificent grandeur. Never in his life had he dreamt that her quiet and undemonstrative affection was capable of anything but a calm and beautiful development. He had not guessed the existence of such resistless force as blazed from her eyes, he had believed her only capable of receiving, he had not imagined that she was strong enough to take boldly what was refused her. The radiance of a spotless soul, burning in the white-heat of a passion as pure as itself, dazzled and awed him. As he looked, he felt as though he were held in the grasp of a splendid, wrathful angel, who disputed the possession of him, not with himself, but with the opposing powers of evil.

It is amazing that in such a case he should still have found strength and courage to resist this last great trial of his sincerity. Most men would have yielded and would have accepted their fate. But though Greif was young, and not very wise, he had stern and obstinate blood in his veins, and he was acting under the strongest conviction that had ever possessed him. Knowing her only as he had known her before, the fair and innocent idol of his boyish heart, he had felt that he could never allow her to take his darkened name. In the beginning his intention had been very honourable, in his struggle with himself it had grown high and chivalrous, but in the face of such opposition as he met from her mother and now from herself, it had assumed proportions that bordered upon the grotesque.

And yet as he looked now upon her noble face, illuminated and radiant with a beauty almost too pure for him to understand, he felt even more than before that such a creature could never be allowed to ally herself with one whose name was a reproach among men. He did not know how to oppose her, but he knew that she must be opposed, at any cost, for her own sake.

His eyes fell before her gaze, and his hands trembled nervously in her grasp, so that she began to think that he was yielding, whereas he was in reality making a supreme effort to concentrate his courage and to keep the mastery of himself. While he seemed to be sinking to her will, he was gathering his strength, saying in his heart that if he lost this battle he should never hold up his head again.

The sun streamed broadly through the diamond panes of the casement upon the patched and faded carpet, creeping slowly along his accustomed path in which the hours were marked, as on a dial, by threadbare seams and the leaves and flowers of a half-obliterated design. In the huge chimney the logs burned steadily with a low, roaring sound, and the shabby furniture of the place seemed to doze lazily in the warmth, as old men do whose strength is far spent. And in the midst of the common-place scene a drama was being enacted, less horrible in outward appearance than the tragedy of Greifenstein, but scarcely less fearful to the two young hearts that beat so fiercely and full of life.

The sunlight moved but a very little, as far as would show the passing of a minute, perhaps, and then Greif looked up once more and again met the gaze of Hilda's eyes.

CHAPTER 19

'Hilda, I will die for you, but I cannot marry you.' Greif spoke quietly, but with the utmost decision.

'I have said that I will not let you go,' she answered, 'and I will not. You are my life, and I will not die—I should if you left me.'

'You will forget me,' he said.

'Forget you!' Her voice rang through the room. She dropped his hands with a passionate gesture and turned away from him, making one or two steps towards the window. Then she came back and stood before him.

'Forget you!' she exclaimed again. 'You do not know what you are saying. You do not know me, if you can say it. Do you think, because I am a girl, that I am weak? I tell you I am stronger than you, and I tell you that you are mad. Do you think that if I would have shed the last drop of my blood to save you from pain yesterday, I love you less today? I love you a thousand times more for what you would do, but you shall not do it. I love you as no woman can love, who has not lived long life. And you say that you can go away, and that I shall forget you! As I am a Christian woman, if I forget you, may God forget me, now and in the hour of death! I could not if I would. And you say that you will leave me—for what? Because your father has done a terrible deed, and has taken his own life.

'For a name—for nothing else! What is a name to me, compared with you yourself? I love you so, that if you had yourself done the most monstrous crime, I would not leave you, not if we were to die a shameful death together. And you would leave me, for my own good! For my advantage—oh, I would not have heaven itself without you. Forget! What would there be left to remember, if you were taken? The emptiness of the place where you were, the wide emptiness that all heaven could never fill!

258

Your name—do you love it better than me? But I know that you love me, though you are mad. Then put your name away, cast it from you to whomsoever will have it.

'Do you think that Hilda von Sigmundskron cares for names, or wants new ones? Am I a peasant's child, to sigh for a coronet and to give you up because you have put it off? Be what you will, you are only Greif to me, and Greif, only, means more to me than heaven or earth and all that are in them. You shake your head—what would you say? That it is not true? My love needs no oaths to bind it, nor to prove it. You can see it in my face, for I know that it is there. Yes—you cannot meet my eyes—honest as you are, and good, and noble, and true-hearted as any man that ever drew breath. Do you know why? You dare not—you who dare anything else. I love you the more for having dared this—but you shall not do it. I will not let you go, I will not, never, never!'

Greif had turned his head away and stood leaning against the chimney almost in the same attitude he had taken from the first. She had spoken quickly and passionately and he had not been able to answer anything she said, for she did not pause, replying herself to the questions she asked and giving him no time to oppose her.

'I was wrong,' he said, half bitterly, half tenderly. 'You will not forget me any more than I can forget you. It will make it harder to say goodbye.'

'It shall never be said, until one of us two is dying, Greif.'

'We cannot change our fate, though we love ever so dearly,' he answered. 'Think, Hilda, if you took me as I am, what you might suffer in after years, what our children would surely suffer when they went out into the world, and the world began to whisper that they were the grandsons of that Greifenstein—'

'What is the world to us, dear? And as for our sons, if God sends us any, I know that if they grow up to be brave gentlemen, loyal and true, the world will leave them in peace.'

'The world is a hard place—'

'Then why have anything to do with it? I have been happy,

here in the forest, for so many years—could you not be happy here with me?'

'I should still be my father's son—I should still be Greifenstein.'

'Would I have you anything else?'

'Hilda, it is impossible!' cried Greif with suddenly renewed energy. 'I have said all. Must I say it again?' 'If you were to say it a thousand times, it would not make it more true. But I will listen to all you tell me, if you like.'

With a calmness that showed how certain she felt of her victory, Hilda resumed her seat at the opposite side of the fireplace, folded her hands together, and leaning her head against the back of the easy-chair, watched him with half-closed eyes. She was not tired, and would very probably be able to sustain the contest longer than he. After the first shock of the announcement was over, under which she had suffered more in one moment than would have sufficed to fill a week with agonising pain, the strong impulse to hold him had come upon her and her elastic strength had been roused to its fullest energy. But the memory of that one moment of agony was enough to make her guess what she would feel if he left her.

Arguments repeated a second time rarely seem so forcible as when they are first heard. Painfully and conscientiously Greif recapitulated his reasons, trying to speak coldly and concisely, exerting himself to the utmost and summoning all the skill he could command in order to state his case convincingly. Hilda could not have put the idea that possessed him to a more cruel test than this. It began to dawn even upon himself that he was in pursuit of a chimera, and the necessity for the enormous self-sacrifice, upon which he insisted, was breaking down in the face of such a determined opposition on the part of those who were more interested than himself.

Doggedly and persistently he continued, nevertheless, fighting his love as though it had been a devil, thrusting Hilda's from his thoughts as though it had been an evil temptation, savagely determined not to part with his belief in what he took for his duty. It was a strange sight, and would have afforded material for reflexion to an older and wiser person than Hilda.

'That is all I have to say,' he concluded. 'It seems to me that I cannot say it more clearly. You know what it costs me to repeat it all.'

An expression of intense pain passed over his face, and he turned away in order to hide it from Hilda. He was hardly able to make his strained lips pronounce the last words.

'I am not convinced,' said Hilda after a moment's pause. 'No eloquence in the world would convince me that you and I should sacrifice our lives for an idea, merely to save ourselves from the possibility of a few ill-natured remarks hereafter. That is all it comes to in the end. I will tell you the history of this idea.'

She seemed calmer than ever, but the light had not faded from her eyes, and Greif felt that she was ready to spring upon him in an instant, to grasp his hands in hers and to say again that she would not let him go. He glanced nervously towards her, and the look of suffering returned to his face.

'The history is this,' she said. 'When the dreadful thing happened, you thought of me. Then it seemed to you that you should free me from our engagement. That seemed hard to you, because you love me so much—it was so hard that it took all your strength to make the resolution. You have spoken to my mother and to me. Now, I ask you whether my mother, at least, is not old enough to judge what is right? Did she agree with you, and tell you that you should give me up?'

'No—she did all she could to persuade me—'

'Of course,' interrupted Hilda. 'Of course she did. Now shall I tell you why you will not allow yourself to be persuaded, and why you insist on ruining your life as well as mine?'

She rose again, gently this time, and came and stood beside him. He turned his head away as though it hurt him, and as she spoke she could see only his short, bright curling hair.

'You will not be persuaded, because it was so hard for you to make the resolution at first, that you believe it must be right in spite of every other right, and you would sacrifice yourself and me for an idea which is strong only because it hurt you to accept it at first. Everything you have done and said is brave, noble, generous—but you have gone too far—you have lost sight of the true truth in pursuing a truth that was true yesterday. It never was your duty to do more than offer to set me free. And as for the name, Greif dear,—I have heard that such things are done—would you, if it pleases you—that is, if it would help you to forget—would you take mine, darling, instead of letting me take yours? Perhaps it would make it easier—you are only Greif to me, but perhaps if you could be Greif Sigmundskron to yourself, and live here, and never go to Greifenstein nor think of it again—perhaps, my beloved, I could help you to forget it all, to the very name that pains you so.'

She laid her hand upon his shoulder and pressed her cheek softly against his curls as she spoke the last words, though she could not see his face. The accents were so low and tender that her voice sounded like soft music breathed into his ear.

'No—no! I must never do it!' he tried to say, but the words were very indistinct.

Hilda felt him move nervously, and she saw that he was grasping the chimney-piece with both hands as though to support himself by it. In another moment his broad shoulders seemed to heave and then shrink together. He staggered and almost fell to the ground, though Hilda did her best to hold him. With a great effort he gained the chair in which she had sat and fell back in it. His eyes were closed and the lids were blue, while his tightly compressed lips moved as though he were biting them.

Hilda knelt beside him and took his cold hands. The colour was all gone from her face, for she was terribly frightened.

'Greif, Greif!' she cried in anguish. 'What is it, my beloved? Speak, darling—do not look like that!'

'I am in great pain,' he answered, not opening his eyes, but faintly trying to press her fingers.

She saw that he was ill, and that his suffering had nothing to do with his previous emotion. She opened the door quickly and called for help. Her mother's room was very near and Frau von Sigmundskron appeared immediately.

'Greif is ill—dying perhaps!' exclaimed Hilda dragging her into the little sitting-room to the young man's side.

The baroness leaned over him anxiously, and at the touch of a strange hand his purple lids opened slowly and he looked up into her face.

'It is in my head—in the back,' he succeeded in saying.

Greif had fallen in harness, fighting his battle with the morbid energy of a man already ill. To the very end he had held his position, resisting even that last tender appeal Hilda had made to him, but the strain upon his nerves had been too great. He was strong, indeed, but he was young and not yet toughened into that strange material of which men of the world are made. The loss of sleep, the deadly impression made upon him by the death of his father and mother, the terrible struggle he had sustained with himself, all had combined together to bring about the crisis. At first it was but a shooting pain in the head, so sharp as to make his features contract. Then it came again and again, till it left him no breathing space, and he sank down overcome by physical torture, but firm in his intention as he had been in the beginning. It was all over, and he would not argue his case again for many a long day.

'Take me home—I am very ill,' he gasped, as the baroness tried to feel his pulse.

But she shook her head, for it seemed to her that it was too late.

'You must stay here until you are better,' she answered softly. 'The jolting of the carriage would hurt you.'

He closed his eyes again, unable to speak, far less to discuss the matter. The mother and daughter whispered together and then both left the room, casting a last anxious glance at Greif as he lay almost unconscious with pain.

Great was the consternation of Berbel when she heard that the young lord of Greifenstein had suddenly fallen ill in the house, but she was not a woman to waste words when time pressed. There was but one thing to be done. Greif must have Hilda's room and Hilda must take up her quarters with her mother. His carriage must fetch the physician from the nearest town, and bring such things as might be necessary. To Berbel's mind everything seemed already organised, and before anyone had time to make a remark she had set about arranging matters to her own satisfaction. There was only one difficulty in the way, and that was Greif himself, who, in spite of his acute suffering had not the slightest intention of submitting to an illness at Sigmundskron.

In the first moment the pain had altogether overcome him, but he gradually became so much accustomed to it as to be able to think more connectedly. The idea of remaining where he was seemed intolerable. To be taken care of by Frau von Sigmundskron, to be under the same roof with Hilda, would be to give up the contest for which he had sacrificed so much. He did not understand that his mind would act very differently when he had recovered, and that much which seemed disagreeable at present, might be attractive then.

He rose to his feet without assistance, and he saw that he was alone. Hilda had gone in one direction and her mother in another in search of something to alleviate his suffering. To get out of the house was the work of a moment. In the court there was the groom who had driven him, still rubbing down his horses and setting things to rights before going inside to warm himself. The man was the same who had brought Greif the news at Schwarzburg, a devoted fellow, born and bred on the estate, unlike the house servants who had been changed so often.

'Karl,' said Greif, going up to him, 'you must harness and drive me back to Greifenstein at once. I am sorry for you, but I am too ill to stay here. I will walk down the road—come after me as soon as you can.'

There was nothing to be done but to obey the simple order. Karl looked surprised but lost no time, especially as Greif was already going out of the gate. In a trice the collars were on the horses again, the traces hitched, the reins unwound, and Karl was seated upon the box. He was glad for himself, though he thought it a very long pull for the horses. The road went downhill over most of the way, however, and Karl reflected that when his master was once in the carriage behind him, he could drive as slowly as he pleased. Just as he was ready, Frau von Sigmundskron and Hilda appeared upon the threshold of the hall, both looking pale and anxious. They had found Greif gone from the sitting-room and had at first imagined that he had lost his way in the house; but Hilda's quick ears caught the sounds that came from the court and she knew that the groom was putting the horses in.

'What is that?' asked Hilda, addressing the groom. 'Why have you harnessed again?'

'The merciful lord has ordered it,' returned Karl, lifting his military cap with one hand while he held the reins with the other. 'The merciful lord has walked down the road, and I am to overtake him.'

Therewith Karl turned his pair neatly and the horses trotted slowly towards the gate.

'Stop, stop!' cried Hilda, running down the steps and following him, while her mother came after her more slowly.

Karl drew up and looked back.

'Herr von Greifenstein is very ill,' the girl said. 'He will never be able to drive alone so far—indeed he ought to stay here and you should go for the doctor.'

She was so much confused that she hardly knew what to say, when her mother joined her, calmer and more sensible.

'You say that he went out of the gate. How long ago?' inquired the elder lady.

'It may be five minutes.'

'Did he say anything besides ordering the carriage?'

'He said he was ill and must go home at once, and that he was sorry for me.'

Frau von Sigmundskron hesitated. It was clear that Greif had not been so ill as she had at first supposed, or he could not have walked out alone, ordered the carriage and gone on without support. Karl interrupted her meditations.

'Merciful ladyships forgive me,' he observed, 'but if he walks farther he will be more ill.' He gathered the reins and prepared to move on.

'Go, Karl,' said the baroness, and in a moment he was gone.

'Mother—you ought to have gone, too—' Hilda began, looking into her face with an expression of mingled anxiety and disappointment.

'I do not see how I could, my child,' answered the baroness. 'If Greif was strong enough to go it was best that he should do so. It would be hard for us to take care of him. He has his cousin at Greifenstein, and they can send for me if he is worse. Besides—' She hesitated and stopped.

'What?' asked Hilda anxiously.

'He showed good sense, since he was able to go. It is not the custom in the world for young men to make long visits in such cases.'

'The world, the world!' exclaimed Hilda wearily. 'I have heard so much of the world this morning. Mother—He will not send for you. We shall not know how he is—'

'I will take care that we may know,' answered the baroness quietly. 'He is young and very strong. Perhaps it is only fatigue after all, and we shall hear that he is well tomorrow.'

Hilda's instinct told her to slip from her mother's side, to pass the gate and run down by the short and steep descent to the foot of the hill. The road made a wide sweep before passing this point and she would have been certain to reach it long before the carriage. But she knew that such wildness could produce no good result. She would stand there waiting for the carriage, it would come, Greif would tell Karl to stop, and then—what could happen? There would be a sort of momentary renewal of the scene which had ended a quarter of an hour ago, with the unpleasant addition of the driver as a witness. She could not get in and drive with him, and so the situation would have to end abruptly, perhaps in another attack of that pain which had so suddenly prostrated Greif.

It was very hard that he should have escaped in this way, and nothing but his suffering could excuse his conduct; but to have him return now would be almost worse. After all, Hilda was woman enough to know that she had got the best of the argument at the last, and that Greif's abrupt departure looked very much like a precipitate flight. She knew also that he loved her, and that it would be impossible for him to leave the country without seeing her again. No woman would believe the man she loves capable of that. It was therefore madness to think of intercepting him upon the road, in order to exchange another word.

With hands loosely joined together and hanging down, Hilda stood gazing at the vacant gateway. The happiness she had anticipated an hour earlier, when she had descried the distant carriage that brought Greif to her, had been strangely interrupted, and yet she was not altogether unhappy now, though she was very sad and silent. For all the world she would not have unlived that hour, nor unsaid the words that had passed her lips. The time had been very short, and yet it had sufficed to show her what Greif's love for her really was, and what he was willing to suffer for her sake. She had, too, the satisfaction of feeling that this suffering had not been brought upon him by herself, and that she had used all her strength to relieve him of it.

He had indeed refused to give up the burden to the very end, but Hilda did not believe that he would bear it many days longer after what she had said. Her youth and strength refused to accept such an evil destiny, and her keen feminine perception told her that more than half of his obstinacy had been morbid and unnatural, and would disappear with the change wrought in him by rest and quiet. Her anxiety now was for him, and did not concern herself any longer. She knew nothing of illness save as a sort of vague misfortune, a state of undefined pain during which people stayed in bed and were visited by physicians. Never during her lifetime had any one of the three women who composed the little household been ailing even for a day, and though Hilda had sometimes been told, when she was visiting at

Greifenstein, that Clara was not well enough to appear, she had only fancied how the poor lady would look when she was not painted and her hair was all out of curl.

That did not help her to realise what an illness meant. She could only recall the look on Greif's face when he had reeled to the chair and then thrown his head back, while his closed lids turned purple. For a long time that was the only picture evoked in her mind when sickness was spoken of.

Frau von Sigmundskron looked at her daughter, without understanding her thoughts. She guessed what the nature of the interview had probably been, but she had no means of knowing how it had ended. Nevertheless she was willing to wait until Hilda chose to speak, and she knew that she would not wait long. Presently she passed her arm through her daughter's and led her gently back towards the house. The latter made no resistance, but walked quietly beside her across the sunny court. When they reached the door of the hall Hilda turned and looked again towards the gate.

'I wonder how it will be when he comes in by that way again!' she said.

Then she went in with her mother and entered the sitting-room, and sat down in her old place, in the chair into which Greif had fallen. She was left alone for a few minutes, while Frau von Sigmundskron went to tell Berbel that Greif was gone after all, and that there was no need to upset all the household arrangements.

The fire was still burning brightly, though one of the logs had fallen into two pieces, making a great cave of coals and flames in the midst. The slow sun had not crept as far as the next thread-bare seam upon the faded carpet. The room was the same as it had been a quarter of an hour earlier. Hilda thought of all that had happened while that log was being burned through, and while the bright sunlight had moved across that narrow space. She spread her white hands to the blaze, and looked at the red glare between her fingers.

She was not altogether as calm as she looked, but she was certainly far less moved than might have been expected. There was a solidity about her nerves that would have driven to despair the morbid worshippers of the decadent school of romance, a natural force which made it very hard to understand her. Womanly she undoubtedly was, but of that type in woman which is rarely seen in cities and not often in the country.

There is a hopefulness inherent in perfect physical organisations that have never been strained by unnatural means, which makes them seem hard and unfeeling to weaker natures. They have a way of sitting still without betraying their thoughts, when they are not called upon to act, which produces the impression that they feel nothing, and care for nothing but themselves. It is only in great moments that they are seen at their best, and that their overpowering strength in action excites wonder. They show none of those constant changes that belong to very nervous people, and make them interesting as studies of sensibility.

Their faces do not reflect the light and shade of every passing circumstance, their voices are not full of quickly contrasted intonations which tell more than words themselves, they do not blush and turn pale at every suggestion of happiness or unhappiness to themselves, everyday speeches do not raise in their minds quick trains of association, linked and running on like an ascending scale in music, to culminate in a little moment of emotion, in a little flutter of the heart, half pleasant, half painful.

Their strong pulses beat quietly, in an unvarying rhythm, the full and even flow of blood maintains a soft colour in their fresh faces; when they are tired they sleep, when they are awake they are rarely tired; what they could do yesterday, they can do as well today, and they feel that they will be able to do the same tomorrow. They never feel those sharp thrusts close to the heart that tell us how quickly one thrust a little sharper than the others would end all. They do not lie awake in the hours of the night counting the blows of the cruel little hammer that beats its prison to pieces at last and is broken in the ruin of the breast that confined it.

And the world counts it all to them for dullness and lack

of delicate feeling, with little discernment and less justice, until the day when it sees them roused by such passions as alone can rouse them, or suffering such deadly pain as only the strongest can live to suffer.

The baroness came back in a few minutes and stood beside Hilda, laying her hand upon her daughter's forehead, and bending down.

'What did he say to you, child?' she asked.

'He said that he would not marry me because it would be a shame that I should be called Greifenstein after what has happened.'

'That was what he told me,' replied her mother, leaving her and taking up a piece of needlework that lay on the table. She could not be idle. 'That was what he told me,' she repeated thoughtfully. 'And I answered that he was mistaken.'

'He said you had done your best to persuade him,' said Hilda, and then relapsed into silence.

'Do you know what I did?' she asked presently.

'I suppose you told him that you did not care for such things as names.'

'Yes—I said that. But I took his hands, and I told him that I would not let him go. I think I was very angry at something, but not at him.'

Frau von Sigmundskron laid her work upon her knees and looked at the young girl attentively for some seconds.

'Was I wrong?' Hilda asked, turning round as she felt her mother's gaze upon her.

'No. I do not see that it was wrong, but I think I should have acted differently. I think I would have tried to make him see—well, I never was like you.'

'I am sorry—I would do anything to be like you, mother dear.'

'You need not be sorry, child. You are like someone I loved better than myself—you remind me of your father. And what did Greif say to that?'

'He refused to the very last—then he had that pain in his

head and I thought he was going to die. You know the rest. O mother, what will become of him, and when shall we see him again?'

'I do not know when we shall see him, dear, but I do not think he will be very ill. When a man has the strength to do what he has just done, and go away on foot, as he went, he is not in a dangerous state.'

Frau von Sigmundskron resumed her needlework and did not speak again for a long time. She had found time to think, and Greif's conduct was strange in her eyes.

CHAPTER 20

Karl overtook Greif before the latter had walked half a mile. The rapid decision, the brisk walk and the biting air had contributed to alleviate the intolerable pain to which he had momentarily succumbed, and as he lay back among the furs he began to fancy that he should not be ill after all, and to regret the scarcely decent haste he had employed in making his escape. But when he tried to think over what had happened he found that his brain was confused and his memories indistinct. Of one thing only he was quite sure, that he had accomplished his intention and had renounced Hilda forever.

With the emotion caused by the thought the pain seized him again and he lay almost unconscious in his seat while Karl guided the horses carefully along the steep road. Before many miles were passed, Greif was aware of nothing but the indistinct shapes of trees and rocks that slipped in and out through the field of his aching vision. Everything else was a blank, and the least attempt at thought became agonising. At one time he could not remember whether he was going towards his home or away from it; at another, he was convinced that someone was in the carriage with him, either his father or Frau von Sigmundskron, and he tried vaguely to reconcile the fact of their presence with his inability to see their shapes.

At last he knew that he was being lifted from the carriage, and he made an effort to straighten himself and to walk upright.

But strong arms were round him and bore him through bright halls where the low sun shot in level rays through stained windows, and along broad dim corridors that seemed as though they would never end, until at last he was laid upon a bed in a warm room. There, all at once, as in a dream, he recognised Rex, who was standing beside him and holding his hand.

'I must be ill, after all,' he said faintly.

'Very,' answered Rex. 'Do you know me? Can you tell me what has happened to you?'

Greif stared at him for a few seconds and then answered with an effort.

'I have done it,' he said, and closed his eyes.

After that, he was conscious of nothing more, neither of daylight nor of darkness, neither of solitude nor of the presence of Rex and of those who helped him in his incessant care. A day passed, and another, one physician came, then two, and then a great authority was summoned and installed himself in the castle, and visited the sick man six times during the day, and feasted royally in the meanwhile, after the manner of great authorities, who have an amazing discernment in regard to the good things of this life, as well as an astonishing capacity for enjoying them.

All manner of things were done to Greif of which he never knew anything. He had ice upon his head and burning leaves of mustard on his feet, he was fed with strange mixtures of wine and soup, of raw meat and preserves, all of which he swallowed unconsciously without getting any better. Still he tossed and raved, and moaned and laughed, and cried like a child and howled like a madman.

The great authority shook his head and pensively drank the old burgundy that was set before him, partaking of a delicate slice of game between one sip and another, and thoughtfully cropping the heads of the forced asparagus when he was tired of the venison. For a long time he and Rex said little to each other at their meals, and the physician was inclined to suppose that his companion was a man of merely ordinary intelligence. One day, however, as Greif grew no better, Rex determined to startle the good man, by ascertaining what he knew.

In order to lead the conversation he threw out a careless remark about an unsettled question which he knew to be agitating the scientific world, and concerning which it was certain that the great doctor would have a firm opinion of his own. To the astonishment of the latter, Rex disputed the point, at first as though he cared little, but gradually and with matchless skill disclosing to his adversary a completeness of information and a keenness of judgment which fairly took away his breath.

'You almost convince me,' said the physician, who had quite forgotten to help himself a second time to green peas, though they were the first he had seen that year. 'Upon my word, Herr Rex, you almost convince me. And yet you are a very young man.'

'How old do you think I am?' inquired Rex with a faint smile.

The doctor examined his face attentively and then looked long at his hands. He became so much interested that he rose from his seat and came and scrutinised Rex's features as though he were studying the points of an animal.

'I am amazed,' he said, as he sat down again and adjusted his napkin upon his knees. 'I do not see anything to prove that you are more than two or three and thirty.'

'I was forty years old on my last birthday—and I was still a student at Schwarzburg,' replied Rex quietly.

'You have a very fine action of the heart,' observed the doctor, 'I would not have thought it, but your age heals the wound in my vanity.'

Now it is a very singular fact that from that hour the great physician should have paid more attention to Greif and less to the venison and asparagus, but it is certainly true that his manner changed, as well as his conversation, and that he bestowed more care upon his patient than he had ever given to any sick man since he had become celebrated. Ever afterwards, he told his learned acquaintances that the only man he had ever met who gave promise of greatness was a quiet person who lived in the Black Forest.

Rex had satisfied himself, however, that the doctor knew a great deal, though he had not a high opinion of medical science in general, and almost said so. Greif, nevertheless, continued to be very ill indeed, and his state seemed to go from bad to worse. Rex was anxious, and watched him and nursed him with unfailing care. He knew well enough what Grief had meant by the few words he had spoken after he was brought home, and he knew all that his cousin's action involved. His reflexions were not pleasant.

It seemed to him as though fate were about to solve the difficulty by cutting all the knots at once. If this terrible fever made an end of Greif, there would be an end also of the house of Greifenstein by the extinction of the last male descendant. Greif, the penniless and nameless orphan, would lie beside his father as Greif von Greifenstein, and the fortune would go in the ordinary course of the law to the Sigmundskrons, to whom it really belonged. But if Greif recovered and persisted in refusing to marry Hilda, the greatest injustice would be done to the widow and her daughter. Rex's views of right would not be satisfied if the Sigmundskrons received only a part of the fortune which was legitimately theirs, and Rex thought with horror of the moment when he might be obliged to go to Greif and disclose the truth.

He was a man of very strong principles, which were detached from any sort of moral belief, but it seemed as though his intelligence were conscious of its failing, in spite of all his reasoning, and were always trying to supply the lacuna by binding itself to its own rules, to which its faith had been transferred. He knew perfectly well that if Greif could not be persuaded that he was acting foolishly it would be necessary to reveal the secret. Rather than that Greif himself should be made to suffer what such a revelation implied, it would be almost better that he should die in his unconscious delirium.

Human life, in Rex's opinion, was not worth much, unless it afforded a fair share of happiness, and he knew well enough that

Greif could never recover from such a blow. The loss of fortune would be nothing in comparison with the loss of name, and with the dishonour to his dead mother's memory. Rex knew what that meant, though even he had not been made to bear all that was in store for Greif in such a case.

In the dim room he looked at his brother's face. He had grown so much accustomed to the droning sound of his ceaseless ravings, as hardly to notice it when he was in the room, though it pursued him whenever he was alone. He watched Greif's pale features, and wondered what the result would be. If Greif died, the lonely man had nothing left to live for. Greif had come into his life, just when he was beginning to feel with advancing years that neither fortune nor science can fill the place of the human affections. As for the love of woman, Rex had never understood what it meant. He had entangled himself in more than one affair of little importance, partly from curiosity, partly out of vanity, but in his experience he had never found a companion in any woman, nor had he ever known one whom he would not have left at a moment's notice for the sake of any one out of half a dozen occupations and amusements which pleased him better than lovemaking.

To this singular absence of emotions he perhaps owed his youthful looks, at an age when many men are growing grey and most show signs of stress of weather. He had never cared for his father's society, first, because he had lacked all the early associations of childhood on which alone such affection is often based, and, secondly, because he had differed from him in all his ideas and tastes as soon as he had been able to think for himself. Their relations had always been amicable, for Rex was not a man, even when young, to quarrel easily over small matters, and old Rieseneck had sent him at an early age to Germany, supplying him very bountifully with money, in the belief that he ought to atone in every way for the injury done to his son by his own disgrace.

Beyond a regular correspondence, which had never savoured much of ardent affection, there had been nothing to unite the two during many years past. Then Rex had taken the trouble to find out his cousin, had liked him more and more, and had at last learned that he was not his cousin but his brother. Now, as he saw him lying there between life and death, he admitted to himself that he loved him, and that he took the trouble to remain alive merely for his sake. But for Greif, that fatal letter would have been enough to make him give it up.

In truth, the life which Rex had condescended to leave in himself did not promise well. The physician did his best, which was as good as any man's when he chose that it should be, but Greif was daily losing strength, and the inflammation of the brain showed no signs of disappearing. It is probable that if he had been thrown with any other companion than Rex, the great doctor would have shaken his head and would have announced that there was very little hope. But Rex acted upon him as a stimulant, and his impenetrable, stony eyes made the physician feel as though his whole reputation were at stake. The latter even went to the length of sitting up all night when the patient was at his worst, a thing he had not done for many a long year, and probably never did again during his comfortable existence.

Greif was going to die. The doctor had very little doubt of it. In all his experience he had never known such an obstinate case of meningitis in a man so young and so strong. The grey morning dawned and found him and Rex standing upon each side of the bed that looked unnaturally white in the gloom. Still, Greif was alive, though his moaning had grown very faint, and his strength was almost gone. Rex held his breath every now and then, as the sound ceased, fearing lest every moment should be the last.

The doctor tried to make out the time without carrying his watch to the night-light, failed and returned it to his pocket with a half-suppressed sigh. He had done all that he could, and yet Rex's stony eyes were fixed on him in the early twilight, and his reputation was at stake. He knew that the thread might break at any moment, but he believed that if Greif lived until sunrise he would live until noon, and die about three o'clock in the day.

'Herr Rex,' he said quietly, 'I think you had better send for Frau von Sigmundskron, if she would wish to see him. You told me he had no other relation near.'

Rex's head fell forward upon his breast as though he had received a blow, though he had known all through the night that this morning might be the last, and the doctor had told him nothing unexpected. A moment later he left the room quietly. He was met by a servant before he had gone far.

'Tell Karl to put in the Trachener stallions and drive to Sigmundskron as fast as they can go. He must bring back the baroness before noon. Your master is dying.'

He would have turned away, but the man detained him with a question he did not hear at first.

'What did you say?' he asked.

'A messenger has just come from Sigmundskron to inquire,' the servant said.

'I will see him. Give the order to Karl quickly,' said Rex.

In the hall a queer-looking man was brought to him. He was one of those thin, wiry, dark and straight-haired men of the Forest who seem to belong to a race not German, whatever it may be. He wore patched leather breeches, from the side pocket of which protruded the horn handle of his long knife. His legs were bare, his shirt open at the neck, his waistcoat with silver buttons was flung carelessly over one shoulder, and a small fur cap was thrust back from his forehead, upon which a few drops of perspiration were visible. His small and piercing eyes met Rex's boldly.

'The baroness sent me to know how the young gentleman was,' he said, speaking in the Swabian dialect.

'Herr von Greifenstein is dying,' answered Rex gravely.

'Then I had better go and tell her so,' said the man, calmly, though his face fell at the bad news. He was already turning away when Rex stopped him.

'Have you come on foot?' he asked, looking curiously at a fellow who could run over from Sigmundskron and go back almost without taking breath.

'Of course,' was the answer.

'Then you can go home in the carriage. I have just ordered it. Give him something to eat quickly,' he added, turning to the servant, 'before Karl is ready.'

'I shall be there before your carriage,' observed the man carelessly. 'Especially if you will give me a drink of cherry spirits.'

'Before the carriage?'

'Not if I stay here,' said the other. 'But I can beat your horses by half an hour at least.'

'What is your name?' asked Rex while the servant was gone for the drink.

'Wastei.'

'Sebastian, I suppose?'

The man shrugged his shoulders, as though to say that he did not care for such a civilised appellation. Rex took out his purse and gave him a gold piece, a generosity elicited by his admiration for the fellow's powers.

'Take that, Wastei, and here is your liquor.'

Wastei nodded carelessly, slipped the money into his waistcoat pocket, drank a quarter of the bottle of cherry spirits at a draught, and touching his cap was out of the door before Rex could speak again.

'Did you ever see that fellow before?' Rex asked of the servant.

'No, sir,' the man answered rather stiffly. 'I am not from these parts.'

Rex returned to Greif's room with a heavy heart, and found the physician standing where he had left him, waiting for the sunrise. They both sat down in silence, watching the face of the dying man, and listening to his breathing. There was nothing to be done, save to try and make him swallow some nourishment once in a quarter of an hour.

The dawn brightened slowly, until a soft pink light was reflected from the snow outside upon the ceiling of the room. It was mid-winter still and the nights were long and the days short, the sun rising almost as late as possible and setting suddenly again when the day seemed only half over. When at last the level eastern rays shot into the chamber, Rex and the doctor rose and looked at their patient. He was breathing still, very faintly, and apparently without pain.

'There is a possibility still,' said Rex in a low voice.

The physician glanced at him, and suppressed a professional shrug of the shoulders.

'We shall see what happens at noon,' he answered, but the tone of his voice was sceptical.

To tell the truth he believed that there was no longer any hope whatever, and so far as any such chance was concerned he would almost have risked going home at once. Nevertheless he determined to stay to the very last, partly because his reputation was at stake, partly out of curiosity to watch Rex at the supreme moment. He suspected that the latter was in some way profoundly interested in the question of Greif's life, though he found it quite impossible to make sure whether his anxiety proceeded from affection or from some more selfish motive. For the present, however, he left Rex to himself and went to his own room to rest an hour or two.

The time passed very slowly. Rex's nerves were as firm as the rest of his singularly well-knit constitution, and he was never weary of fulfilling the mechanical duties of a nurse, which he had refused to relinquish, during twelve hours at least of each day, though he was obliged to give his place to an assistant during the remainder of the time.

In order not to be idle as he sat beside the bed, Rex drew figures and made calculations in his pocket-book. He seemed to derive considerable satisfaction from his occupation, for he looked more hopefully at Greif each time he raised his head, though the latter's condition showed no apparent change. His consolation was in reality only transitory, for when the clock at last struck twelve and he laid his work definitely aside, it seemed to him that he had been dreaming and that the case was more desperate than ever. The physician returned and stood beside him, but he looked at Rex more often than at Greif. At last he laid his hand upon the younger man's arm and led him away from the bedside, towards the open window.

'Herr Rex, I would say a word to you. I firmly believe that your cousin will die in a few minutes.' He spoke in a whisper, and Rex bent his head, for he thought his companion was right.

'I have a theory,' continued the doctor, 'that people who are dying are far more conscious of what passes around them than is commonly supposed. It may be true or it may not. Let us at all events be careful of what we say to each other.'

Rex nodded gravely, and they returned to the side of the dying man. It was just mid-day, and Greif was lying on his back, with his eyes open. The physician bent down and laid his ear to the heart. When he raised his head again, he looked about the room, somewhat nervously avoiding Rex's eyes. All at once his attention was arrested by the sound of running feet outside, and he glanced quickly at his companion, who had also heard the noise.

It was the supreme moment, for Greif's consciousness had returned. As often happens at the moment of death a violent physical struggle began. The light returned to his eyes, and the strength to his limbs. He raised himself upon his hands, and sat up, while the doctor supported him with one arm, and with a quick movement put brandy to his lips. It was the work of an instant, and it all happened while Rex was crossing the room. Suddenly, as the doctor watched him, his eyes fixed themselves. In the next instant, he thought, their light would break; and the body he supported would collapse and fall back for ever. It was the last gasp. Then a ringing voice broke the silence, just as Rex had his hand upon the latch. 'I will, I tell you—he is mine!'

The door was flung wide open, and a woman entered the room. Rex had a strange impression of golden hair and gleaming eyes passing him like a flash, like the leap of a lioness springing to defend her young.

The doctor looked up in astonishment. Before he could help

himself he was thrust ruthlessly aside, and Greif was in other arms than his. Hilda bent down as she held him. The fixed stare changed, while the doctor was craning his neck to see what would happen, but the light did not go out, nor did the pupils turn white and dead.

'Hilda! Hilda! Hilda!' His voice was faint but clear. One moment longer he gazed into her face and then sank quietly back upon her arm, with a smile upon his parted lips, his fingers seeking her hand until they lay quite still in hers. He was so quiet that Hilda was terrified. With a low and piteous moan she sank upon her knees beside the bed. It was a cry like nothing those present had ever heard. The physician understood, and bent down to her.

'I think we had better be very quiet,' he said. 'You will frighten him.'

Hilda stared wildly into his face, and saw there an expression that transfixed her with astonishment. Slowly, as though not daring to face the sight, she turned her eyes towards Greif. There was a faint colour in his sunken cheeks, and he was breathing regularly. Hilda pressed her hands to her breast with all her might to smother the cry of joy that almost broke her heart.

The baroness was standing at the foot of the bed with Rex, unconscious of the tears that streamed from her eyes, her hands clasped before her as though in prayer. She looked like the figure of a sainted woman of old. As for Rex himself, he was trembling a little and was conscious that if he had attempted to speak he would not have heard his own voice. But otherwise his outward demeanour betrayed nothing of what was passing within him. He knew as well as the physician that Greif had survived the most dangerous moment and that he would in all probability recover, and he knew that if Hilda's sudden entrance had not given a new impulse to the ebbing life, all would have been over by that time. For a few seconds he was scarcely conscious, though he looked calmer and colder than the doctor himself. He saw nothing but Greif, and his impression of Hilda's appearance was no clearer than it had been when she had rushed past him at the door with a gleam like a meteor.

Half an hour later, Greif was asleep. If all went well he might remain in this state for any length of time from twelve to twenty-four hours. Hilda had been prevailed upon to leave the room with her mother. The assistant took his place by the bedside, and Rex was with the doctor in the adjoining apartment.

'Science is a very pretty plaything,' said the great authority, stroking his grey beard thoughtfully. 'You know so much, Herr Rex, that you and I can afford to look at each other like the augurs and laugh, for we certainly know nothing at all. I would have wagered my reputation against a hospital assistant's pay, that our friend had not sixty seconds of life in him, when that young lady appeared, like a fiery whirlwind, and caught him back to earth in the nick of time.'

'Science unfortunately does not dispose of such young ladies,' answered Rex with a smile. 'They are not in the pharmacopoeia.'

'She is the most extraordinary one I ever saw,' observed the doctor. 'There is a vitality in her presence that affected me like electricity in a water bath. She has eyes like Sigmund the Volsung—perhaps he was her ancestor, since her name is Sigmundskron.'

'He is said to have been,' laughed Rex.

'I can quite believe it. Now I assure you that I thought it was all over. His heart has been very badly strained, and recently, and such a case of meningitis I have rarely seen. Of course he had the advantage of careful treatment; but you may treat and treat as you like, if the heart is weak and nervous and strained, it may stop while the rest of the body has strength enough left to go on for weeks. I suppose they are engaged to be married?'

'Of course.'

'Did you hear her cry out that she would come in? Her mother's excellent propriety would have kept her out. But the young lady knew better than any of us how to save his life.'

Rex did not answer at once, and when he did, he turned the subject. Soon afterwards he went away, for he felt that he must be alone in order to think over what had happened and to regain his natural equanimity.

He had not the slightest doubt but that Greif would now recover quickly, and it seemed very probable that in that case he would no longer hesitate to marry Hilda. At the thought of her, Rex experienced a disagreeable sensation which even he could not understand at first. Hitherto, his chief preoccupation had been the marriage, and scarcely an hour had passed, so long as he had hoped that Greif would live, in which he had not contrasted the happiness in store for his brother, if he took Hilda, with the misery he would have to encounter if he persisted in his quixotic determination.

And now that Rex had seen this girl, of whom he had heard and thought so much during the last ten days, he wished it were possible that Greif might remain Greif without her love. The thought was so selfish and seemed so unworthy in his own eyes that Rex concentrated his mind in an attempt to explain it.

In the first place, he felt a curious disappointment in the midst of his rejoicing over Greif's improvement. He himself had been untiring, faithful, by day and night, in watching over and taking care of the only human being he loved in the world. He wanted no man's gratitude, but he had longed earnestly for the satisfaction of saving Greif himself, of feeling that his first attempt at living for another, instead of for his own individual advantage, had been crowned with success. He had spared no fatigue, and he had suffered every varying torture of anxiety and doubtful hope to the end.

And yet, when the end was reached, Greif was dying. Neither Rex's care nor Rex's devotion could have kept him from slipping over the boundary. Then the door had opened, a woman had entered, and Greif had revived at the very moment of extinction. A bright-haired girl, with gleaming eyes, had done in one second what neither the physician's science nor Rex's loving watchfulness could have hoped to do. To a man who has cared little for women and has thought much of himself, it is humiliating to see a girl accomplish by her mere presence what all his intelligence and energy and forethought have failed to bring about.

Then again, Rex saw that in the future there was nothing for Greif but Hilda. Rex might be swept out of existence, but so long as Hilda remained, Greif would merely feel a passing regret for the man he believed to be his cousin, a regret which Hilda's love would help him to outlive in a few weeks, or months, at the most. He hated himself for his selfishness, and realised that a new phase of his life had begun that day.

The impulses and impressions that beset him were only transitory and not likely to affect his conduct. His fondness for Greif was such that he would certainly rejoice honestly over his marriage and feel the most genuine hopes for his happiness. The only trace the passing hour would leave with him would be an unexpressed antipathy for Hilda. He knew, or he thought that he knew, how easily his systematic habits of thought could conquer such a tendency and reason it away into emptiness, and he went downstairs to make the acquaintance of his brother's future wife with the fullest determination to like her for Greif's sake, and never again to submit to a frame of mind which was contemptible if it was not utterly base. Could anything be more inconsistent than to let his joy at the prospect of his brother's recovery be clouded, because the result was not wholly due to himself? Could anything be more absurdly foolish than to conceive a dislike for a woman whom Greif must marry to be saved from ruin and shame?

Chapter 21

Greif recovered quickly. In due time the celebrated physician departed in great peace, hoping that chance might soon send such another case into his way. Greif and Rex lived together in Greifenstein, and Hilda and her mother were at Sigmundskron. But the distance between the two places had grown very short of late, and scarcely a day passed on which Hilda and Greif did not meet.

He was not quite as strong yet as he had been before his illness, but the time was not far distant when he would be able again to get into the saddle and make short work of the twenty miles that separated him from Hilda. There had never been so many horses in the Greifenstein stables as now, for the work was hard and continuous and the roads bad. To make matters easier, Greif had sent a strong pair to Sigmundskron, so that the two ladies might drive over whenever they were inclined to do so.

On a sunny day in April the two men were walking together in the garden, backwards and forwards from the parapet that followed the edge of the precipice to the porch of the house. Greif rested his hand on Rex's arm, more out of habit now than because he needed support, and as they paced the smooth path the two talked in a desultory way upon whatever was uppermost in their thoughts.

'It seems as though my illness had lasted a year,' Greif said. 'I have even got so far that I do not care to leave this place, after all.'

'Why should you?' Rex asked.

'It would be natural,' answered Greif rather gravely. 'I should have expected to prefer any spot of the world to this.'

'Man is the world, and all that therein is, and the earth he stands on, is no more to him than the clothes he wears. If a thought is in your heart, can you get rid of it by changing your coat? And besides, in the long run a man prefers his own coat and his own patch of earth—both are sure to fit him better than those of other people.'

'I think you are right. Rex, did I act like a madman before I was taken ill?' He asked the question rather suddenly. Hitherto Rex had avoided mentioning what was past as well as he could.

'Yes—you were quite mad,' he answered. 'You fought windmills. That is always a bad sign.'

'It is fortunate that I broke down just then. Suppose that I had held out long enough to go away and that I had fallen ill in some distant place, and that Hilda had not come—I should not have had much chance.'

'No. I was very jealous of her, I remember.'

'Why?'

'Because she saved you, and I could not,' answered Rex. 'Because it is disagreeable for a selfish man to feel that a woman's eyes are better than his skill or strength.'

Greif looked at his companion as though he did not quite understand, but the smile upon the latter's face made matters somewhat clearer. He would not have liked to think that Rex was quite in earnest.

'But for you,' he answered, 'I should have died long before Hilda came.'

'Not at all. If you had shown signs of giving up the ghost earlier, I would have sent sooner. But it was a narrow escape. Another minute would have done it, as I have often told you.'

'Do you know that I have not yet spoken to them about the marriage?'

'Then there is no need of saying anything. They understand as well as you. You need only fix the wedding-day.'

'Not yet,' answered Greif. 'It is too soon.'

'Is it ever too soon to be happy?'

'Sometimes—but I will go to Sigmundskron tomorrow and talk about it.'

'In that case you will be married in three months,' observed Rex with a laugh.

'Not so soon—we must let the year pass first. It would not be decent.'

'Decency is that mode of demeanour in ourselves which satisfies the traditional likes or dislikes of others. There is nothing else in it.'

'If you are going to begin a discussion about comparative right, I will say nothing more. I have lost my taste for argument, and I never had much skill in it.'

'We will not discuss the matter,' replied Rex. 'You will be married in August.'

'I think not.'

'We shall see.'

'Will you go with me tomorrow?' asked Greif, relinquishing the contest.

'You had better go alone, and I shall be best here, with my books. You will not need me to help you to settle matters.'

'Why do you so rarely go with me?'

'Why should I?'

'To keep me company. It is a long drive.'

'The entertainment, so far as I am concerned, is not of a wildly exciting character, when you are talking to Fraulein von Sigmundskron, and her mother is doing needlework, and I am thrown upon my own resources. Whereas if I stay at home and read, I have the pleasure of hearing your very good description of all that I should have been entitled to see and hear had I been present myself. The description occupies five minutes; the expedition takes a whole day. I will stay at home, thank you.'

'But it gives them pleasure to see you,' objected Greif.

'Does your cousin regret my absence from the sitting-room when she is walking with you upon the sunny side of the ramparts?'

'How did you know that we walked there?' asked Greif with a laugh.

'On the same principle which teaches me that a dog will walk on the sunny side of the street—because you would not be likely to walk in the shade at this time of year. Did you say that Fraulein von Sigmundskron regretted my absence on such occasions?'

'She always asks after you when you do not come. Why do you call her by such long names? "Cousin Hilda" is quite enough.'

'It is not a cousinship she could be very proud of. I prefer not to force it upon her. She could not call me "Cousin Horst."'

'She will have as much cause to be proud of your cousinship as of having me for a husband,' said Greif, stopping in his walk and looking at Rex. 'Whatever you say of yourself applies equally well to me in this matter.'

Rex said nothing, but he thought of all the truth there was

in the words which Greif did not know, and never must know. He had not told all his reasons for not going to Sigmundskron, either, and if he had told them, they might not have been altogether pleasing to Greif. He was ashamed of them, even before himself, and thought of them as little as possible. Hilda's presence affected him unpleasantly. What he felt, when he was with her, strongly resembled an unconquerable dislike, which was at the same time wholly inexplicable to himself. He could appreciate her beauty only when he was at a distance from her, and then the memory of it attracted rather than repelled him.

When she spoke, he had an instinctive longing to give her a sharp answer, which was smothered in a phrase of meaningless politeness; but he afterwards took delight in fancying what her expression would have been if he had really said what had suggested itself to him. He could not explain the intense antagonism he sometimes felt against her by any theory or experience of psychology with which he was acquainted. Her look annoyed him, her slightest gesture irritated him, the sound of her voice distressed his ear. Even her grace of motion jarred upon him, and he wished she could be clumsy and slow instead of swift and sure. He had disliked women before, but never in the peculiar way he disliked Hilda. Everything she did looked wrong, though he knew it was right; every word she uttered sounded false to him, though he was well aware that she was one of the most truthful and true-hearted persons he had ever known.

He supposed that what he felt had taken its origin in a ridiculous jealousy, on that day when her appearance had revived Greif at the last moment, and he recurred to the scene constantly and tried to magnify his first impression in order to make his present state of mind seem a little more reasonable. He only half succeeded, however, though he kept what he thought to be his own folly clearly before him at their next meeting and forced his manner and his voice to obey his common sense.

The result of all this was that Rex was once more growing dissatisfied with his life. Had he felt sure of Greif's future he would have gone away and would not have returned until a long lapse of time, and a constant change of scene, had obliterated what was so disagreeable to himself. His prudence warned him, however, that he should stay until all was settled, and Greif was married to Hilda. After that, it mattered little what became of him. He reflected with satisfaction that he was over forty years of age, and that, even if he chose to live out his life, he was not likely to survive his brother. Whether he should not one day find himself so weary of it all as to anticipate his end by a score of years, was a point about which he thought much.

Such tragedies as had darkened Greifenstein rarely take place where there is not a fatal tendency to suicide in the blood. Death had never seemed horrible to Rex in any shape; on the contrary, he took pleasure in speculating upon its possibilities and in dreaming of the sensations which the supreme moment would evoke. To a mind altogether destitute of any transcendental belief whatsoever, death appears to be merely the end of life, to be made as little disagreeable as possible and encountered with such equanimity as a philosopher can command.

To such men as Rex, the idea that there is any obligation to live if one prefers to die, does not present itself, and when they inherit from their fathers an indifference to life, the danger that they may part with it too readily is seldom far distant. The thought of Greif had prevented Rex from stepping over the limit, and his affection for him would probably have kept off such gloomy thoughts altogether for a long time, if Greif had depended upon his companionship. But as Greif recovered and this dependence grew less and less a matter of necessity Rex grew weary again. If he had not felt as he did in regard to Hilda, the two would have been more together than they actually were, and Greif would not so often have driven twice in a day alone over the twenty miles that separated his house from Sigmundskron.

Rex saw this, and saw that Hilda was taking his place, and he became disgusted with himself and the existence he was leading. Nevertheless, his naturally firm character made his outward demeanour even and unchangeable. He was determined that if he must be ridiculous in his own eyes, he would not appear to be so in the eyes of others. For the present he could not leave Greifenstein, for he could be of use to Greif, who would sooner or later be obliged to put his affairs in order, and examine the papers left by his father. Rex feared indeed, lest among these should be discovered some letter from the dead man, explaining to his son what had been so clearly told to Rex himself.

A superficial search had discovered nothing, but he reflected that at such a moment a man might well put what he had written in a place where he was in the habit of concealing precious documents, instead of laying it upon the table. Rex was determined to have the chief hand in the examination of what was found, and to abstract and destroy unopened anything which looked like a letter to Greif. He cared little for any justification in pursuing such a course; from what he had learned of old Greifenstein he believed that he would have been capable of telling the plain truth to his son and of enjoining upon him to give up his name, and to hand over his whole fortune to the Sigmundskrons.

He had been a stern man with fearfully rigid traditions of honour, incapable, Rex thought, of allowing Greif to practise an unconscious deception, willing that he should come to a miserable end rather than seem, even for a moment, to be what he was not. It was almost inconceivable to Rex that he should have died without writing a few words to his son, and if he had done so, Rex had little doubt as to what the letter would contain. Should it be found, he intended to do his utmost to destroy it, unknown to Greif, and in the meanwhile, he did all in his power to hasten the marriage and to put off the evil day when the papers must be examined.

The lives of the two were made somewhat irregular by Greif's constant visits to Sigmundskron, and occasionally by the coming of the baroness and Hilda. The good lady thought that there was little dignity in bringing her daughter to Greifenstein, but she was quite unable to oppose Hilda's determination. So long as Greif had been only in the convalescent stage it had seemed proper enough that the baroness should occasionally come in person to make inquiries, the more so as Greif had placed a pair of horses at her disposal for this very purpose as soon as he could give an order of any sort.

Now that he was perfectly well, however, she felt that in spite of the relationship it was strangely contrary to custom for two ladies to visit a young man who lived alone. She would not have been a German of her class if she had not felt this, but she would not have been herself if she had allowed a scruple of etiquette to stand in the way of Hilda's happiness.

There was still an element of uncertainty in the situation which caused her some anxious moments. Since his recovery Greif had never approached the question of marriage. It was indeed early yet, but the opportunities had already been numerous, and he had not taken advantage of any. The only point which favoured the impression that he had changed his mind, was his frank and easy manner together with his evident desire to see as much of Hilda as possible. But he had not spoken. The baroness was keen enough to fancy that he was prevented from referring to the subject by the painful reminiscence of his last interview at Sigmundskron, and by a natural feeling of shame at the thought of retracting what he had once taken such infinite pains to say. She was determined that the matter should be put upon a sound basis as soon as possible, and she promised herself to lead the conversation to the marriage whenever she had a chance.

Unfortunately for her intentions the chance did not present itself, for Greif spent the time of his visits with Hilda, and talked as little as possible to her mother. The latter could almost have found courage to come alone to Greifenstein, but Hilda would not have allowed her to do so, for she would not have been willing to miss an opportunity of a meeting. In this way matters had continued for some time after Greif had been well enough to decide finally upon his own future as well as upon Hilda's, until he himself felt that he must soon speak his mind, or be very much ashamed of himself for his hesitation.

Of all concerned, Hilda was the one whose character had changed the most since the events of the winter. It seemed as though she had never before realised what she was, nor what she was able to accomplish in the world. From the day of Greif's refusal to marry her at Sigmundskron she had developed suddenly, from a simple girl into a strong and dominant woman. After Greif had left her on that day she had still felt as certain of marrying him as though they were already going to the altar.

When she had known that he was really ill she had felt an inward conviction that he would recover quickly. When she had found him dying she had known that she could save his life. She had acquired a sense of certainty which nothing could disturb, and which had developed simultaneously with a moral energy no one had before suspected that she possessed. If there had ever been any resistance on either side the baroness would not have felt as though her daughter had suddenly taken the mastery over her, but there had been none.

Never, in their peaceful lives, had they experienced opposite desires or incompatible impulses. It had never seemed as though Hilda were submitting to her mother, even when she was a child, because their wishes appeared to be always exactly the same, so that Hilda would have done of her own freewill, and if left to herself, precisely what her mother desired her to do. The consequence was that since Hilda had found that she had a will of her own, she had imposed it upon her mother with the greatest ease; for the latter was so much taken by surprise at Hilda's initiative, as to take refuge in believing that the girl must really want what she herself wanted, and that it was only the appearance which made the result look different.

It was only a half belief, after all, for she could not help seeing that circumstances had singularly developed the girl's character, and that they had been of a nature to do so, exceptional, startling and trying in every way. Frau von Sigmundskron liked to fancy that she could still control every impulse Hilda showed, as well as formerly, but she could not help being proud of her daughter's strength, for Hilda was like her father, a man who, with the sweetest temper imaginable, had dared anything that a man may dare.

Greif carried out his intention of going to Sigmundskron on the day after his conversation with Rex. During the drive he thought of what was before him, as he had thought three months earlier, when the prospect had been very different.

At present he felt that it would be impossible to delay his retractation any longer. So far as his happiness was concerned, the situation might last until the eve of the wedding-day, but there were other considerations to be thought of, which he could not disregard. Hilda and he understood each other without words, but Hilda's mother could not be expected to understand without a formal explanation. She had a right to it. Greif's last act before his illness had been to refuse the marriage; the baroness was entitled not only to know from his own lips that he had changed his mind, but also to be consulted in the matter, as a question of courtesy.

Greif did not know exactly how to manage it. To his mind there would be something inexpressibly ridiculous in asking an interview with Frau von Sigmundskron, for the purpose of formally requesting, a second time, the honour of her daughter's hand. And yet he assuredly could not go to her and say bluntly that he had changed his mind and intended to take Hilda after all. Anything between the two must necessarily take the shape of an apology of some sort and of a retractation, though Greif felt that he had done nothing needing an apology. He could not ask the baroness's forgiveness for having been stubbornly determined to sacrifice his whole life rather than injure her daughter by giving her his name. It was true that he now saw the matter differently, perceiving that he had done all that a man of the most quixotic chivalry could do to prove the case against himself, and that his judges refused wholly to be convinced.

He did not regret what he had done, though he was willing to believe that he had gone too far in the right direction. He had offended no one, for his whole conduct had been guided by the consideration of others. He had therefore nothing to be forgiven him, and no shadow of a reason for putting himself in the position of a penitent. To say that he had been mistaken, and to try and shift the responsibility of his action upon his illness, was not to his taste either. He had not refused to marry Hilda because he had been ill at the time, but because he had been convinced that he ought to do so.

At present he was grateful both to her and to her mother for their readiness to oppose his self-sacrifice. That at least he could say; but after that it would be necessary in common courtesy to put to the baroness the question old Greifenstein had asked long ago, in other words, to renew the formal proposition of marriage. As a man of honour it was indispensable that he should clearly define his position without further delay, and he could see no other way of defining it, satisfactory to himself and to the exigencies of his courteous rule of life.

There was still another matter to be decided, and which did not tend to make the coming interview seem easier. The origin of the whole difficulty had not been removed, and although Greif had made up his mind to submit to the happiness which was thrust upon him, he still felt that to marry Hilda under his own name would be out of the question. He was even more sure of this than before, for he had learned during his convalescence that the tragedy of Greifenstein had been described in every paper of the empire, and he knew that it must be the common topic of conversation. His old comrades at Schwarzburg had read the story and had written, some offering condolences, some refusing to believe the tale at all.

The professors of the University whose lectures Greif had chiefly attended, had written in various manners, and the *Magnificus* himself had deigned to offer his sympathy in a singularly human manner. Most of these communications had been answered by Rex, who explained that Greif had been seriously ill, and Greif himself replied to the more important ones. The horror of the story was known through the length and breadth of the land, and wherever Greif might go for years to come, his name would instantly recall the terrible details of the triple crime.

All the arguments Greif had formerly used with so much force remained unshaken, and he felt that there could be but one way of placing himself and Hilda beyond their reach. Had Hilda never existed, he would have determined to live in retirement, and to allow his race to be extinguished in his own person, rather than perpetuate the memory of such deeds. As it was, he had given up the thought, for the love of her, and he knew that there was happiness in store for him. In order to accept it, however, he must be no longer Greifenstein.

It was strange that each of the three in turn, Rex, the baroness, and lastly, Hilda herself, should have suggested the advisability of his taking the name of Sigmundskron in place of his own. Clearly, it was the only course open to him, but it was a curious coincidence that they should all have had the same thought. On the whole he was ready to follow their advice, but as he drew near to his destination he realised that it must be the first point settled. He did not exactly know how to formulate his request, for he had never known anybody who had asked another for his name. He almost wished that Hilda could manage it for him, which was a proof that he had not yet altogether recovered his strength.

He was glad that Rex had not come, after all. It was one of those errands which he preferred to accomplish alone. Moreover, for some reason which he could not guess, Rex seemed to avoid the Sigmundskrons as much as he could. That he should never remain long in conversation with Hilda, Greif thought natural; his cousin's action might proceed from delicacy, of a curiously unusual kind, or it might be the result of Rex's constant wish to leave the two together as much as possible. In either case it was not altogether surprising. But Greif often wished that Rex would take the trouble to talk to the baroness, so that she might not be left so much alone.

It would have completed the party and made everyone feel more easy; after all, Rex was a man forty years of age, and might reasonably be expected to devote his attention with a good grace to a lady who was not much older than himself, though her white hair contrasted oddly with his uncommonly youthful appearance. But Rex hardly ever failed to find some excuse for staying at home when Greif went to Sigmundskron, and when the ladies came to Greifenstein he generally made his appearance as late as possible. Nevertheless Greif believed that his cousin did not dislike the Sigmundskrons, and it was certain that both mother and daughter thought extremely well of him. Greif could not explain Rex's coldness, and was obliged to ascribe it to some uncommon bias of a remarkable character which he had never wholly understood.

Being full of such thoughts, the time that had elapsed, between the present day and the memorable visit three months earlier, seemed to Greif to have dropped away with all it had contained. He felt as though he had refused the marriage but yesterday and were going to take back his refusal today. Only the weather had changed between then and now. On that morning the ground had been covered with snow, and a bitter wind that cut like a knife had been blowing across the road. It was even yet not spring, but the snow was all gone, and the frost was thawing out of the ground under the warm sun. In a few days the white thorn would begin to bud, and fresh green violet leaves would come out along the borders of the woods. A few birds were already circling in the air above the fir-tops as though expecting to find the flies there already. The warmth and the moisture of everything brought out the sweet smell of the forest and blew it into Greif's face at every turn of the drive.

For the twentieth time since he had been well enough to go out, he watched the sturdy horses' backs as they drew the light carriage up the last steep ascent. For the twentieth time he looked up as he reached the point whence the lower battlements of the half-ruined castle were visible. As often happened, he descried Hilda's tall figure against the sky, and then immediately the gleam of something white, waved high to welcome him. He wondered how she always knew when he was coming.

But Hilda had found that when he came he naturally started

always at the same hour, so that every morning she went up, and stood on the rampart for twenty minutes, scanning every bit of the winding road that was in sight. At the end of that time, if she had not seen the carriage, she knew that he was not coming, and descended again into the interior, her face less bright and her eyes less glad than when she had gone up the steps.

There she was today, in her accustomed place, and a moment later the sun caught the white handkerchief she waved. As he flourished his in return, Greif wondered how he could ever have come over that same road with the fixed purpose of bidding farewell for ever to her who awaited him, and he was amazed at his own courage in having executed his intention, for he felt that he could not do as much now. But there was little time left him for reflexion. Five minutes later the carriage rattled through the gate into the wide paved court, swung round upon its wheels and stopped before the hall door. Out of the dim shadow Hilda came quickly forward and took his hands, and they were together once more, as they had been so often during the last month and a half.

'I have not come to see you,' said Greif, with a laugh that only half concealed his embarrassment. 'I have to request the honour of an interview with your mother today.'

Hilda looked at him a moment and then laughed, too.

'Has it come to this, Greif!' she exclaimed.

'It has come to this,' he answered, his mirth subsiding at the prospect of what was before him.

'And what are you going to say?' she asked. 'That you have changed your mind? That you yield to pressure? That you are the lawful prey of one Hilda von Sigmundskron and cannot escape your fate? Or that you were very ill and never meant it, and are very sorry, and will never do so again? Why did you not bring Rex to talk to me while you are explaining everything to my mother?'

'Rex would not come today. He sends his homage—'

'He always does—I believe you invent it—the message I mean. Rex hates me, Greif. Do you know why? Because he is

297

jealous. He thinks you do not care for his society any longer—'

'That is absurd—you must not say such foolish things!'

They reached the door of the sitting-room as he spoke. Greif entered and found himself with the baroness. Hilda closed the door when he had gone in and went away, leaving the two together.

CHAPTER 22

Frau von Sigmundskron was somewhat surprised when she saw Greif enter the room without Hilda. Greif went up to her with the determination of a man who means to lose no time in getting through an unpleasant business.

'Aunt Therese,' he said—he called his father's cousin 'aunt,' after the German manner—'I told Hilda that I wanted to speak with you alone —do you mind?'

'On the contrary,' answered the baroness. 'Sit down. I will work while you talk. It will help me to understand you.'

'The matter is very simple,' said Greif, seating himself. 'I want to ask whether you are still of the same opinion in regard to my marriage with Hilda, as before I was taken ill.'

'Of course I am—' She looked up, in some surprise.

'Because I am not,' said Greif, delighted with himself at having found a way to make his aunt state her case first.

'Not of my opinion, or not of your own former opinion?' she inquired, rather puzzled.

'I mean to say that I now once more ask for Hilda's hand—'

Frau von Sigmundskron laughed, and laid down her work, to look at his face. She had not expected that he would express himself in such a way. Then all at once she saw that he had meant to act in the most loyal manner possible, and she grew grave, being pleased with him as she almost always was.

'Do you think you need my consent again, Greif? You have it, with all my heart. You need hardly have asked it, for you knew the answer too well.'

'It is this,' said Greif, coming to the point. 'In the first place, I knew very well what you would say, though I thank you all the same; but it was necessary to come to a clear understanding, because there is another point to be settled upon which much must depend. What I said three months ago holds good today. As Greifenstein I cannot marry Hilda. As Greif, I cannot any longer forego the happiness you and she have pressed upon me. But I must have another name—'

'Is it really necessary?' asked the baroness gravely.

'It seems so to me. The papers have been full of our story, and I have received many letters of condolence, and some full of curiosity. It is a tale which no one will forget for many years. Few people could help associating disgrace with so much crime. I wish to marry Hilda under a name by which we may become known if we choose to go into the world hereafter, and which may be free from all disagreeable associations. You yourself suggested that I should take yours, she has suggested it and so has Rex. If you consent, it seems best that it should be so.'

'Sigmundskron—' She pronounced the syllables slowly, almost lovingly, and her eyes were fixed on Greif with a look he did not understand.

He could not know all that the name meant to her. She had married the last man who had borne it by his own right, the gallant young soldier, who was to restore the fallen fortunes of his race, in the only way in which they had ever been restored before, by the faithful service of his country. She remembered how firmly she had believed that he was to be great and famous, how confidently she had hoped to bear him strong, bright-eyed sons worthy of him and like him, who should in their turn do great deeds, of which he should live to be proud. The dream had vanished. Brave Sigmundskron had been shot down like many another, a mere lieutenant, with all his hopes and grand visions of the future, and his wife had been left alone with a widow's pension and her little child.

A girl, too—it had seemed as though nothing were to be spared her. If she had had a boy to bring up, another Sigmundskron to grow to better fortunes than his father, and perhaps to realise all his father had dreamed of for himself, it would have been easier then—but a girl! The name was ended, never to be spoken again, as it had been so many times, in the roll-calls of honour. She had brought him home and laid him beside his fathers, and she herself had broken the shield upon his tomb with her own hands, for he was the last of his race. In him ended the line of ancient Sigmund, as it had begun, in the strife and fury of battle. It had been a glorious line, take it all in all; though its last warrior had been but a poor lieutenant, he had been worthy of his fathers and had died the worthy death. If only Hilda could have been a man!

And now, after so many years, one stood before her, who craved the right to bear that spotless name, though he had not one drop of old Sigmund's blood in his veins. She had even offered it to him herself— she wondered how she could have had the courage. What sort of a man was this, who would call himself Sigmundskron, like her dead soldier, and be Sigmundskron in all men's eyes, and marry Hilda and be the father of many Sigmundskrons to come? She looked at Greif long and wondered what he would turn out to be.

That he was honourable and true hearted, she knew; that he was brave she had reason to believe; that he loved her daughter well, she knew also. But it was hard. Why did he want the name of her beloved dead? Because his own was stained—not by his fault—but it was darkened and made a reproach. Ay, it is easy for a man with a bad name to desire a good one; it is natural; if he be innocent, it is very pardonable. Greif had a right to ask for it, but would she give it? Would she suffer that which had been so long glorious in itself, that which was made sacred by the shedding of good blood in good cause, that which recalled all she had once worshipped—would she suffer that to be made a mere cloak for the evil deeds of Rieseneck and Greifenstein, murderers and suicides? It was hard to do it.

And yet she was willing, nay, even glad, that this man should marry her only child, the only daughter of her husband. She loved him in a way, for he was to be her son, the only son she could ever have. Ah, that was it. Greif was to be her son. She gazed into his face and wondered whether, if she had searched the world, she could have found one goodlier and stronger and truer to be a match for her own child, whether if she ever dreamed of what might have been, she saw in her fancy a son more worthy than this.

And, after all, he did not ask the boon for his own advantage. He had bravely struggled to give up Hilda rather than let her risk the smallest worldly disadvantage or reproach through him. He asked for this for Hilda's sake, not for his own, and would it not be a thousand times better that Hilda, and Hilda's children, should still be Sigmundskron than wear a name black with ill-shed blood? Since she was to have a son given her would she not rather have him Sigmundskron than Greifenstein? Could he ever be a true son to her so long as he was called after those who had treated herself coldly and heartlessly during so many years, and who themselves had come to such an evil end?

She looked at him once more. Then she put out her hands and took his and drew him close to her so that she could see into his eyes. When she saw what was in them she was glad.

'Will you be a son to me, Greif von Greifenstein?' she asked solemnly.

'I will indeed, so help me God, and you shall be my mother,' he answered.

'Then you shall be Sigmundskron,' she said. 'You are brave— be as brave as old Sigmund. You are true—be as true as he. You are faithful —be faithful to death, as he was, who was the last of Sigmund's sons.'

The white-haired lady rose as she spoke, and drawing him still nearer to her, kissed his smooth young forehead, with the pale lips that had touched no man's face since her dead husband had gone from her to his death.

'Go and tell Hilda that you will be Sigmundskron to her in deed, and in heart, as well as in name,' she said.

As she left the room, erect and with firm step, he saw the bright tears burst from her eyes, and roll down her pallid cheeks, though she would not bend her head nor heed them.

For many minutes he stood where she had left him, his hand resting upon the edge of the table, his look fixed upon the door, absently and seeing nothing.

'That is what it is to have a spotless name,' he said, almost aloud.

He went out softly as though from a hallowed place, and closed the door noiselessly behind him. His small anticipations of what that scene would be like, full of many words and attempts at tactful speech, seemed infinitely pitiful and contemptible now, beside the dignity, the kindness, the noble pride and the grand simplicity of the woman who had given him her name. He walked slowly, and his head was bent in thought as he threaded the well-known passages and stairways to the old rampart where he knew that Hilda was waiting for him.

She was sitting upon one of the stone projections, hatless in the April sun, her beautiful figure thrown into bold lines and curves as she looked down upon the road, sitting, but half turned upon her seat. She heard the crazy door of the turret creak and rattle, and she moved so that she could see Greif.

'It has not lasted long,' she said, with a smile. 'Why do you look so grave?' she asked quickly as she noticed his face, 'Has anything happened?'

He sat down beside her and took her hand.

'Do you know what your mother told me to say to you?' he asked.

She shook her head expectantly, and her expression grew bright again.

'She told me to tell you that I would be Sigmundskron to you in deed, and in heart, as well as in name—can I say more?'

'But one thing more,' she answered, as her arms went round him. 'But one thing more—that you will be Greif, my Greif, the Greif I love, always and always, whether in my name or yours, until the end!'

As his own thoughts had dwindled before Frau von Sigmundskron's earnest dignity, so that in turn grew dim and far away in the presence of Hilda's love. All had been right in their own way, but Hilda's speech was the best, and there was the most humanity in it, after all.

A long time they sat side by side in the sunlight, talking of each other and of themselves as lovers will, and must, if they would talk at all. As they were about to go down, Hilda stopped, just at the entrance of the turret, and swung the broken door gently on its creaking hinges.

'You must not let your cousin hate me, Greif,' she said, as though the thought troubled the cloudless joy of the future. 'It would not be right. We must all be one, now and when we two are married. He saved your life by his care—why should he dislike me?'

'He does not, dearest—you are mistaken,' protested Greif, who was much embarrassed by the question. Hilda faced him at once, laying her hand upon his arm.

'He does, and you must see it. Why does he never come here? Why is he so cold when we go to Greifenstein? I do not care a straw for his like or dislike, except because he is your cousin, and because I think we should all live harmoniously together. The strange thing is that he would give his life for you, and I am sure he is honest, though I cannot see into his eyes as I can into yours. What is the reason? You must know.'

'I do not. I can see that he is very reserved with you and does not like to come here. I asked him only yesterday why he always stayed behind.'

'And what did he say?' asked Hilda eagerly.

'Nothing to the point. He said he could not be of any use if he did come—which, after all, is absolutely true.'

'You must find out. He dislikes me now, when we are married it will be worse, a year hence he will detest me altogether and tell you so, perhaps.'

'Do you think he would tell me?' asked Greif with a quiet smile, that did not agree with the sudden glittering of his eyes.

'No,' laughed Hilda. 'That is an exaggeration. But he will make us both feel it.'

'In that case we will not ask him to stay with us,' answered

Greif, half carelessly, half in anger at Rex's imaginary future rudeness.

He saw that Hilda was annoyed by his cousin's conduct, for it was the second time she had spoken of it during the visit, and he determined that he would put the matter very plainly to Rex as soon as he reached Greifenstein, the more so as he himself had noticed it and had already asked Rex for an explanation.

Hilda's face grew grave. She knew how devoted Rex was to Greif, and she felt as though her future husband were to lose his best friend for a meaningless whim of the latter, in which she was involved against her will.

'That must never be,' she answered. 'Next to me, no one loves you as Rex does. I would not have you quarrel for all the world—and it is mere jealousy, Greif, I know—'

'Then he must be a very contemptible character,' said Greif indignantly.

'Because he is so much attached to you that it pains him to see his place taken by another, even by woman? No, sweetheart. That is not contemptible. But you must change it. Tell him to be reasonable—'

'Could I say that you are offended with him?' asked Greif. 'Can I go to Rex and tell him that he must not only be civil but must be a friend to you?'

'You are jesting,' she answered. 'But it is just what I would do in earnest—what I will do, if you will let me. He would understand that. I would say to him, Herr Rex, you are Greif's only relation besides ourselves. It is absolutely necessary for his happiness that we should be on good terms, you and I. Is it my fault? He would answer that it was not, for he is honest. Then it is yours, I would say, and the sooner you turn yourself into a friend of mine, the better it will be for Greif, who is the only person you care for in the world. Is not that common sense?'

'Do you mean to say that?' asked Greif rather anxiously.

'If you will let me, I will,' answered Hilda, returning to her occupation and swinging the old door slowly between her two hands.

'If I will let you!' repeated Greif. 'Do you think I would try to prevent you from saying what you please, darling——'

'You ought to, if you think it would be a mistake—at least, after we are married.'

'I am not sure that I could,' he answered with a laugh.

'No one else could,' said Hilda, looking up at him with flashing eyes. 'If I meant to do a thing, I would do it, of course. Did I not say that I would not let you go?'

'Indeed you did. And you kept your word.'

'And I love you—you know it?'

'It is all I know, or care to know.'

'Well, I will tell you something more. Because I love you, I want to do what you like, and not what I like, and I always will, so long as you love me.'

Greif drew her to him and held her close, and whispered a tender word into her ear.

'But you must understand,' she said. 'It is not because you are to be my husband, that I mean to submit to you. I do not submit at all, and never shall. I am just as strong as you are, and you could not make me yield a hair's-breadth. But I will always do everything you wish me to do, because I love you, and because you love me, not for any other reason. Do you understand?'

'I would not have it otherwise, my darling—and I will do the same——'

'You cannot quite—you cannot feel as I do, Greif. Perhaps, some day— when you and I are old, Greif—then you will love me as I love you now, but then, you see, I shall have learnt how to love you more, and you will still be hindmost in love's race— for women are made to love and men to fight, in this world, and though I could fight not badly, if need were, for you, yet I know better how to do the sweeter thing, than you can ever know. Do you not believe me?'

'Since you would have me——'

'You do not—but you will, some day,' she answered, shaking her beautiful head a little, and tapping the door with her fingers. 'And now, dear,' she added, laying her hand in his and beginning to walk up and down the old battlement, 'and now, shall I tell Rex, or will you?'

'I will tell him,' said Greif firmly.

'Then promise me not to be angry, Greif. I could do it so well—but it is better so. Promise me that you will say it in such a way as shall make you feel afterwards that you have done the best—even long afterwards; in such a way as to show him how you value his friendship. He saved your life, by his care—'

'And you called me back from death with your eyes—'

'Do not think of my eyes, when you are talking to him,' interrupted Hilda gravely. 'Think of all he has done for you, and of what such a noble friendship deserves in return. Think that he is a lonely man, and not so young as you, and that he needs a little affection very much. Think that all I want is that we may be able to live happily together, you and I, and he, when he cares to be with us. But do not think of me —or if you do, think that if you and Rex were parted I should not forgive myself. Do I not owe him your life, as you do? If you had died, because he was not there to tend you—I cannot speak of it—but you owe him much, for it is your life, and I more, for I owe him our two lives together. Will you tell him that?'

'I will try—he will not understand it all.'

'Then, if he has not understood, if you cannot make him see it, then it will be my turn. But you can, Greif dear, I know you can. And it is not a small matter either, though it may seem so now. It is not a small matter to part with such a man as that, nor is it an insignificant evil, that I should have his dislike at the very beginning, before we are married. You must do your best, you must do all you can, and you will succeed—and by and by we will work together. Greif—' she stopped suddenly and looked at him.

'What is it, dear?' he asked.

'Greif, do you think I have any other reason for wanting Rex to like me? Do you think I am a vain woman?'

Greif stared at her a moment and then laughed aloud.

'Why do you laugh?' she asked, quietly. 'Perhaps I am right.

I have read of girls who were so vain that they wanted every man they saw to like them—and I have never seen any man—young, I mean, but you, until I saw Rex—and so I thought—perhaps—'

She did not finish the sentence, but stood looking at him with an expression of serious doubt upon her lovely face that made Greif laugh again.

'Because if that were it,' she said gravely, 'Rex might go, and I should be glad of it—'

'Hilda! How can you have such ideas!' cried Greif at last. Her innocence was so astounding that he could not find words to answer her at once.

'There might be just a possibility—'

'That you, in your heart of hearts, are not satisfied with me alone, but want to make a conquest of Rex besides! Poor Rex! How he would laugh at the idea—Hilda, you must not think such things!'

'Is it wrong?' she asked, turning her clear eyes upon him.

'Wrong? No. It is not wrong to anyone but yourself, and it is really very wrong to believe that you could be capable of a contemptible, silly vanity like that.'

'You do not think I should be—what do they call it—a co-quette—if you took me into the world?'

'You? Never!' And Greif laughed again, as he well might.

In a woman differently brought up it would have been impossible not to suppose that such words were spoken out of sheer affectation, but Greif knew too well how Hilda had lived, to suspect such a thing. Her innocence was such that she did not understand the commonest feelings of women in the world, not even the most harmless.

'I hope not,' she said. 'I do not mean to be bad, though I believe it is very easy, and one does not always know it, when one is.'

'I should think one would know it oneself sooner than anyone else,' answered Greif. 'But if I find out that you are bad, Hilda, I promise to tell you so.'

'Seriously?'

'I do not run any risk. What children we are, Hilda! And how pleasant it is to be children together, on a day like this, in a year like this, with such a creature as you, sweetheart!'

'We cannot always be children,' she answered. 'Will it be very different then, I wonder? Will there be any change, except the good change of loving more than now?'

'I do not see why there should be. Even if that never came, would it not be enough, as it is?'

'Love must grow, Greif. I feel that. A love that does not grow is already beginning to die.'

'Who told you so many things of love, Hilda?'

'Who told me?' she repeated, as the quick fire flashed in her eyes. 'Do I need to be told, to know? Ah, Greif, if you felt what I feel—here—' she pressed her hand to her side, 'you would understand that I need no telling, nor ever shall. You are there, dear, there in the midst of my heart, more really even than you are before my eyes.'

'You are more eloquent than I, sweetheart,' said Greif. 'You leave me nothing to say, except always to repeat what you have said.'

'If I said little—' She stopped and laughed.

'It is not words only, nor the tones of them that make things true. If I had the skill I could say better what would please you to hear, but having none, I make your speeches my own, to be enough for both of us.'

'Do you never feel as though you must speak, or your heart would burst?'

'No—I wish I could, for then the words would come. I think that the more I feel the less I am able to say.'

'You talked very badly when you were trying to persuade me that we ought not to marry,' said Hilda, with a side glance at his happy face.

'And you talked well—too well—'

'Which of us two felt the more, I wonder?'

'What I felt was almost too much. I came near never speaking again. I do not know how I got home that day.'

'And I—do you know? When you were gone, I did not shed a tear, I did not try to run after you, though I thought of it. I went quietly into the house and sat down and told my mother what I had said. Was it heartless, do you think? Was it because I felt nothing? It is true, I did not believe you were really ill, since you had the strength to go away on foot.'

'What was it then?' Greif looked wonderingly into her face.

'It was victory, and I knew it. For one moment I was frightened, and then I saw it all. I saw you come back, as you have come today, to say what you have said. I felt as though my hand were still on your shoulder, as though you could not escape me, do what you might. I never doubted, until that dreadful day when Wastei came over and told my mother that you were very ill. He did not say you were dying, but he told us that your carriage was on the way to fetch us, and that they were sending relays of horses along the road so that we should lose no time—and she would have left me behind.

'But I knew the truth. I knew that if I could see you, you were saved; and then, when I pushed my mother aside and went in, it seemed too late. If I could die at all, being so strong, I should have died in that moment, when your head fell back upon my arm and your eyes closed—and then, a minute later, they told me you were saved, for when I knew you were still alive I knew you would be well again—and then—and then—oh, Greif!'

The tears that pain or sorrow could not have wrung from her, broke forth abundantly in the memory of that overwhelming joy. If Hilda had not been Hilda, the only woman of her kind, Greif would have kissed the tears away as they started from her eyes. But being Hilda, he could not. It was over in a minute, but he had become a little pale and his arm trembled under the light pressure of hers. She brushed the drops away, and saw his altered face.

'What is the matter, dear?' she asked. 'It is only happiness—they do not hurt.'

'Sometimes you are so beautiful that I do not dare to touch

you,' he said softly.

She turned her golden head quickly with a bright smile, and a crystal drop that lingered on her lashes fell upon her soft cheek. It was as though his words had been the breath of the south wind gently shaking the last drop of a summer shower from the petals of a perfect rose.

'How shall I not be vain, if you say such things!' she exclaimed.

'How can I see you so, and not say them?' he asked.

'It is time to go down,' she said. 'We meant to go, when I began to speak of Rex, ever so long ago.'

'I had forgotten Rex.'

'Do not forget him. He is a good friend.'

So at last they descended the broken stair and disappeared into the house. When Greif was ready to go, and the carriage was before the door, Frau von Sigmundskron led him away from Hilda.

'Let it be done soon,' she said, earnestly.

'The marriage?' asked Greif in surprise.

'No—the name. Let it be changed as soon as the lawyers can do it.'

'I will see to it at once,' he answered, wondering at her haste.

She saw the look of inquiry in his eyes and paused a moment, holding his hand in hers.

'I have lived long without a son—give me one—and Sigmundskron has had no lord these eighteen years.'

'I will not lose a day,' he said. 'And once more—I thank you with all my heart.'

He kissed her thin hand, and turned away to bid farewell to Hilda. A moment later the light carriage was whirling out through the castle gate. The two ladies watched until it was out of sight.

'God bless you,' said the mother solemnly, as though she were speaking to Greif. 'God bless you and bring you back to be a son to me—no more Greifenstein, but Sigmundskron, you, and yours for ever, and ever! God bless you!'

Hilda looked at her mother intently. She did not know all that the words meant to the quiet, white-haired woman beside her. She could not know how often in those long years Therese von Sigmundskron had wished that, instead of a daughter, a son had been given to her, to bear the name and wear the sword of her dead husband; she could not know of all the tears her mother had shed in bitter self-reproach at her own ingratitude in thinking such a thought.

'You do not understand, child,' she said, taking her daughter by the hand. 'Come with me.'

She led her to her own room. Upon a piece of black stuff on the wall, were hung two swords, one a sabre, and one a rapier in a three-cornered case, and above them a leathern helmet with a gilded spike. Beneath these weapons was a heavy old carved chest. With Hilda's help she lifted the lid. Within were uniforms and military trappings of all sorts, and in one corner, folded together, a roll of faded bunting. This she took out and unwrapped, and spread it wide upon the floor.

It was torn and patched and faded, for it was the old flag that used to wave upon the dilapidated keep of the castle. On an azure field three golden crowns were set corner wise, two above and one below. Hilda looked at the banner curiously, and then at her mother.

'We must make a new one, Hilda,' she said. 'And Wastei must pick out a tall, straight sapling from the forest—for Sigmundskron has a lord again, and the old flag must float on the wind when he comes to his home.'

Chapter 23

Rex had not been wrong when he predicted that Hilda and Greif would be married in the summer. It had certainly been the intention of the latter to allow the whole year to pass after the winter's tragedy, before tasting the happiness that was before him, but even if his own courage had been equal to the trial of waiting, other circumstances would have determined him to hasten the day. Perhaps the most impatient of all was Frau von Sigmundskron herself, and indeed the oldest are often those most anxious to precipitate events, as though they feared lest death should overtake them before everything is accomplished. The good baroness was by no means old, but she was in haste to see the fulfilment of her hopes. Hilda, who was already supremely happy, would have waited, if Greif had desired it, and she at first approved of his intention to let the proper time of mourning elapse. But Greif yielded without much opposition to the wishes of Frau von Sigmundskron, who, strange to say, was seconded by Rex.

'It seems very wrong to do it,' said Greif to the latter, as they sat one evening together in the arbour of the garden, listening with pleasure to the sound of the cool torrent tumbling along far below. It was late in July.

'There is nothing wrong in that which makes all happy,' answered Rex, taking his cigar from his mouth.

'But there is a decency which is apart from right and wrong,' objected Greif, for the hundredth time.

'Then keep it apart. Besides, decency can be divided under two kinds. The one does not concern us, for it is purely esthetic. As for the other sort, it means that tactful respect for tolerably sensible traditions, by which society expresses its wish to continue to exist in social bonds. It is founded on the necessity which exists, where many live together, of not hurting the feelings of our neighbours. If you can show me that you are offending any one's sensibilities by getting married now instead of five or six months hence, I will give up the contest and go to bed, for it is late. If you cannot, and if you persist, I am ready to argue with you all night.'

And so Greif suffered himself to be persuaded, and the wedding day was fixed in the end of August, and everything was got ready.

Long before this, Rex and Greif had done all that there was to be done in regard to the succession, and had sorted and arranged such papers as had to be examined. But though Greif had willingly left the bulk of the work to his cousin, and though the latter had searched everything far more thoroughly than Greif guessed, not a scrap of writing had been discovered which could be taken for a message from the dead man to his son. Rex wondered what had become of the letter, until at last he began to suspect that it had never been written. At first this appeared to be a wild and inexplicable supposition, but the more he thought of it, the more certain it grew, in his opinion, that Greifenstein had died without leaving a word of farewell to Greif.

The letter Rex himself had received afforded a key to the situation. Old Greifenstein's character had been stern, resolute, moral, unbending. Rex felt certain that if he had written to Greif at all, the letter would have contained a solemn injunction, commanding him to take the consequences of his mother's crimes, to give over the whole fortune and estate to the Sigmundskrons, as lawful heirs thereto, and, after confessing frankly that he was nameless and penniless, to bear his poverty and shame like a brave man, because they were inevitable in the course of divine justice. He would probably have recommended him to enlist as a private soldier, and trust to his education and to his own strength of determination for advancement.

The stiff-necked old gentleman would in all human probability have expressed himself in this manner, and Rex knew Greif well enough to know the son would have fulfilled the father's injunctions and carried out his orders to the letter, no matter at what cost.

On the other hand it was possible that the grim nobleman might have relented at the last minute. He might even have torn up the letter after writing it, and burned the shreds in the library fire. If he did not write at all, it was clear that matters were likely to remain in their existing condition so far as Greif was concerned. He could not foresee that the circumstances of his death would make Greif go to such lengths as to break off the marriage. He would have guessed with a show of probability that Frau von Sigmundskron would not refuse Greif and his fortune for her daughter, on account of the evil associations created in the name of Greifenstein by the triple tragedy. He would have said to himself that he was not obliged to speak, since the money, the only thing which could be contested would, after all, go to the Sigmundskrons; and in that case he would have considered it justifiable to take his secret with him to the grave.

There was only one objection to this attractive theory, and that lay in the letter Rex himself had received. If Greifenstein had determined that his own son was never to have any key to the mystery, he would never have allowed his brother to write down the details for Rex, even with an injunction to secrecy. And he had been a man capable, especially at such a time, of enforcing his will upon Rieseneck. Unfortunately it was impossible to know which of the two men had died first, and here a third possibility presented itself which Rex could not afford to ignore, though it contained a considerable element of improbability.

It was conceivable that Greifenstein should have been the first to die. In that case Rieseneck, who must have felt that he had ruined Greif by his revelations, might have burned his brother's letter, before pulling the trigger. It would have seemed more natural in that case that he should have also destroyed his own, but it might be that he had warned Rex for a good reason. Without such a warning, and if he had been a less devoted friend of Greif's, Rex might perhaps have instituted inquiries into his father's death which would have caused trouble, and which might even, by some wholly unforeseen accident, have revealed the whole truth to Greif himself.

No one could tell what witnesses were still alive to swear to the identity of her who had been the wife of both. There must necessarily have been foul play in procuring the false papers upon which she had contracted her second marriage, and she assuredly could not have forged them alone. It was highly probable that some former associate of hers in the revolutionary times had remained unnoticed in a government office after the troubles were over, and had helped her to free herself from Rieseneck, who had been the instrument of the revolutionary powers, by procuring for her a set of false papers accurate enough to defy detection.

Such things might well have happened at such an unquiet season. It would have sufficed that such a person should communicate what he knew, cleverly shielding himself at the same time, in order to reveal the whole story; and if no one had been warned of the danger, while Rex himself was using all the power of the law to account for his father's death, the result might have been fatal to Greif.

Nevertheless, Rex clung to the theory that Greifenstein had never written at all, and he met such difficulties as the theory presented, by supposing that he had not been aware that Rieseneck was writing to Rex. In any case, nothing had been found after the most exhaustive search, and Rex was beginning to believe, willingly enough, that nothing would ever be discovered. To avoid all risks, however, he did his utmost to hasten the marriage, feeling that after that event there would be less to fear from a disclosure of the truth.

Meanwhile Greif had obeyed the wishes of Frau von Sigmundskron and had taken immediate steps to change his name. In Germany the matter is an easy one, as it is managed chiefly through the Heralds' Office. Nothing is required beyond the formal and legal consent of all persons bearing the name which the petitioner desires to assume. When this is given, the necessary formalities are easily fulfilled, and a patent is placed in the hands of the person who has applied. After that, it is no longer in the power of the family who have given their consent to withdraw the name, under any circumstances whatsoever. In Greif's case, everything was done very easily.

The Heralds' Office was well aware that the male line of the Sigmundskrons was extinct, and that the family was only represented by Hilda and her mother, the necessary documents were forwarded, signed and attested by the two ladies in the presence of the proper persons, and returned. A month later Greif received his patent, sealed and signed by the sovereign, setting forth that he, Greif von Greifenstein, only son of Hugo, deceased, was authorised and entitled to be called henceforth Greif von Greifenstein and Sigmundskron, that he was at liberty to use either or both names and to bear arms, three crowns proper, or, in field azure, either quartered with those of Greifenstein or separately, as good should seem in his own eyes.

And at mid-day on a certain day in June, the wood-cutters in the forest had looked towards the towers of Sigmundskron as they sat in the shade to eat their noon-tide meal, and they had seen a great standard rising slowly to the peak of a lofty staff, and catching the breeze and floating out bravely, displaying three golden crowns upon its azure breadth.

'What is it?' asked one, a young fellow of twenty years.

'It is the flag of the Sigmundskrons,' answered a grey-haired, beetle-browed man, pausing with a mouthful of cheese stuck on the end of his murderous knife. 'I have not seen that these twenty years, since the poor baron was killed in the war. There must be a new lord in Sigmundskron. We will ask tonight in the village.'

And as they talked, the banner, hoisted by Wastei's wiry arms, reached the very top of the staff, and remained there, waving majestically, where many a one like it had waved during eight hundred years and more. At that moment Greif, in his carriage, was coming up the last ascent. He saw the lordly standard, changed colour a little and then rose in the light vehicle and uncovered his head. He felt as though all the dead Sigmundskrons who lay side by side in the castle chapel had risen from their tombs to greet the new possessor of their name. He could not do less than rise himself, and salute their flag, though it was now to be his own. His young heart, full of knightly traditions and aspirations, felt something which a man of a younger race could not feel. It represented much to him, which is lost in the glare of modern life.

It was easy for him to fancy the old Sigmundskrons in their gleaming mail, high on their armoured horses, riding out in a close squadron from their castle gate with their standard in their midst, some to die in defending it, and some of them to bear home its tattered glories in victory. It was an easy matter for him to identify himself with them and to feel that henceforth he also had a part in their history. And there was more, too, in the sight of the gleaming colours and dancing waves of the tall banner. It was to him the signal of a new life's starting-point, the emblem of a new name. Yesterday he had been burdened with the remembrance of blood shed in evil wise, today he began his existence with a fair scroll before him on which no shameful thing was written. As he stood bareheaded in his carriage, he was as it were saluting this new life before him, as well as doing homage to the memory of the dead Sigmundskrons.

So Greif was no longer Greifenstein now, and he informed the few persons whom he wished should know the fact. And the time passed quickly on to the wedding-day. In the meanwhile, between April and August, Rex and Hilda met more often than before, and to all appearances they met on the best of terms, to the no small satisfaction of Greif himself.

'Rex,' he had said one day, 'Hilda is to be my wife, and it is necessary that you should like her. You cannot have any good reason to the contrary, and yet you act as though she were positively repulsive to you.'

Thereupon Rex's stony eyes had expressed something as nearly like astonishment as they were capable of showing, for he was surprised at being found out, almost for the first time in his life, and he perceived that Greif had not found him out alone.

'I am sorry that she should think me capable of disliking her,' Rex answered. 'My position, indeed, is so different from what you both suppose it to be, that I would make any sacrifice rather than see this marriage broken off.'

Greif looked at him a moment, not quite understanding, for it was impossible that he should appreciate all that Rex meant by the words. He was pleased, nevertheless.

'I wish you would go and tell that to Hilda,' he said in answer.

'I will,' said Rex, and he did so on the first occasion that offered.

He and Greif went over to Sigmundskron together. Indeed, Rex went for the express purpose of making his speech to Hilda, and Greif occupied the attention of the baroness for a while in order that the two might talk undisturbed.

'So you have come at last,' said Hilda. 'It is long since we have seen you.'

'Yes, and I have come for an especial purpose,' answered Rex. 'It appears that, in the inscrutable ways of fate, I have passed for an ill-mannered barbarian in your eyes, and so I have come to show myself and to tell you what I think on certain points.'

'You talk very mysteriously,' said Hilda.

'The prologue of a tale should always be mysterious. It is only the epilogue that must needs be clear. The story may be between the two. The matter of all three is very simple, because it concerns you and me. To be plain, Fraulein, I have come to justify myself in your eyes, to make an apology, a declaration and a treaty, all at once.'

'A treaty, at least, must have two sides,' observed Hilda, for she knew now what he was going to say.

'So does an apology,' answered Rex with a laugh. 'To be brief, I apologise to you for having ever so acted as to make you imagine that I was ill disposed towards you; I hereby declare that, far from being an enemy of yours, I would make any personal sacrifice rather than see your marriage hindered; and I propose that we agree henceforth not to imagine any more such things.'

Hilda was satisfied, for she saw that Greif had put the matter plainly. She hesitated a moment.

'What is your first name, Herr Rex?' she asked.

'Horst,' he answered, in some surprise.

'Very well. I agree to all you say. We will be good friends, and you shall be Cousin Horst to me, and I will be Cousin Hilda to you.'

'Thank you,' said Rex.

He wondered why he had ever disliked her, and he even asked himself whether the antipathy he had felt had been real or imaginary. From that time, however, his manner changed and

Greif had no further cause of complaint.

The weeks sped on quickly, and the wedding-day came at last. Everything was done very quietly indeed, as was natural and right, considering that the year of mourning had not yet expired. Only when all was over, Greif made a great feast for all the men of the Greifenstein estates, and another in the court of Sigmundskron for the people of the tiny village.

And it was to Sigmundskron that Hilda and Greif went first, while Rex and the baroness remained together at Greifenstein. There was as yet no outward change in Hilda's home, though a few rooms had been furnished for the newly-married pair. But the old sitting-room was left as it was for the present, and there Greif and Hilda dined together on the first evening, while the peasants were feasting beneath the window, in the August moonlight.

Many a long year had passed in melancholy silence since such merriment had been heard within those grey walls, and the people felt instinctively that a new era had begun for them, that there would be life in the old place again, and that the young lord would build up Sigmundskron to be what it had been before. Though not a foot of land remained to the name outside the ramparts, the feudal tradition had not disappeared. Old men were alive whose fathers had told them of the good old Sigmundskrons, how they had been brave in war and kind in peace, and generous till all was gone, and the voices of these drowned the ill-natured remarks of the few who said that the baroness was a miser and had hoarded her gold these twenty years in the deep vault under the haunted north-west tower, upon the brink of the precipice.

Moreover, as is the nature of peasants, the sight of the feast warmed their hearts towards those who gave it, even before the great joints of meat were cut, or the first cask of beer broached. They had never seen such a banquet before. The long tables went all the way round the great courtyard, and not only had each table a fair white cloth, but there was also a fork at every place, and a stone drinking-jug. And in the midst of the open space stood a row of jolly-looking barrels and casks, there was beer and wine, white Schlossberger and red Affenthaler, but the national cherry spirits were conspicuous by their absence, for Greif knew the fierce Black Foresters well.

Their iron heads could stand unlimited draughts of any drink except alcohol, as the event proved, for though they drank deep, and were merry to their heart's content they filed through the gate soberly enough before the clock struck midnight. But before that there was speech-making, and singing, and dancing of reels under the moonlight that mingled softly with the rays of countless paper lanterns. The latter were marvellous in the eyes of the foresters, though some of those who had served in the army said they had seen the like in Stuttgardt, on the King's birthday, when the Thiergarten was illuminated.

Meanwhile Greif and Hilda sat together by the open window high above the court and looked down upon the merry-making peasants, or talked together. All at once a tremendous voice thundered up from below, imposing silence on the assembly. It was so loud and deep and sonorous that Greif turned his head quickly to see if possible, by the uncertain light, the individual who was capable of making such an enormous noise.

'It is the mayor of Sigmundsdorf,' said Hilda, laughing. 'He has the loudest voice in the world. The people say that when he shouts at Berneck, the fishermen can hear him at Haigerloch in Hohenzollern.'

'I should think they might,' answered Greif.

'And now, gentlemen,' roared the mayor from below, as he addressed the rustics, 'it is our duty to thank the good givers, and to drink to their never-to-be-clouded conjugal happiness. From where I stand, gentlemen, I can see the golden moonlight shining upon the silvery hair—'

The mayor interrupted himself with a ponderous cough.

'The silvery moonlight shines upon the golden hair of the high and well-born Fraulein Hilda—I would say, of the high and well-born Frau von Sigmundskron, junior—'

Greif, listening above, drew in his head to suppress a convulsion of laughter, but the crowd applauded the figure of speech, and the mayor bellowed on.

'—and also upon that of her high and well-born consort and husband, the lord of Sigmundskron.'

The name burst from his lips like a clap of thunder, and Greif grew grave, for it meant something to him.

'And though I could say much more,' continued the mayor, 'I will not, for silence is gold, as the burgomaster of Kalw says. And so, gentlemen, we wish them happiness, a hundred years of life, and a son as handsome as themselves for every tower there is on Sigmundskron. Sigmundskron *hoch!*'

The mayor had seemed to be exerting his full powers during the whole speech, but an unparalleled experience in making noise had taught him the art of reserving a final explosion in the depths of his huge chest, which he knew could never fail to thrill his audience with wonder and delight. His last cheer broke out like the salute of a broadside of cannon, striking the old walls like a battering-ram, till the panes rattled, echoing up to tower and turret, and then reverberating and rolling away among the distant trees, as though it were in haste to fulfil its mission and tell the whole wide forest that Sigmundskron had a lord again, and that Hilda was married to her true love at last.

'Sigmundskron *hoch!*' yelled the peasants in a wild attempt to rival their leader, which not even their numbers could help them to do.

Then Greif took a tall glass from the table and gave it to Hilda, and took another for himself, and the two stood up in the opening of the Gothic window, the moonlight falling upon their happy faces and upon the slender goblets in their hands. Another shout went up from below, and then all was still.

'It is we who have to thank you,' said Greif, in clear, ringing tones. 'It is we who come to ask your help to make Sigmundskron what it was in the old days. May you all live to sup with us each year as tonight, for another fifty years! We thank you for your good wishes, and we drink to you all—to our good friend the mayor of Sigmundsdorf and to all the rest. Hoch, Sigmundsdorf! *Hoch*, the brave foresters! Hoch, the Black Forest we all love! *Hoch*, the dear Swabian land!'

Hilda's silver voice rang high in the last cheer, and then the two touched their glasses with their lips, while all the people shouted with joy below and the mayor's earth-shaking roars of delight made the great owls in the tower shrink into their holes and blink with wonder.

It was a glorious night, and for many a year the people of Sigmundsdorf will remember the look that was on those two beautiful young faces that looked down upon them from the high, arched window, and all agreed that the mayor of Sigmundsdorf had never made such a noble speech as on that occasion, or shown the superiority of his voice over all other voices with such brilliant success.

So Hilda and Greif were married, and none but Rex knew what a mortal danger had hung over their happiness until that day. When all was done and ended, Rex drew a long breath and sat down alone to think over the peril from which Greif had escaped. By this time he was fully persuaded that the latter would never be disturbed by the discovery of a letter left by his father, and he had entirely adopted the theory that no such letter had ever existed. It was a comforting belief, and seemed reasonable enough, so that he classified it amongst his convictions and tormented himself no more.

He could not help reflecting, however, upon the complications that might arise if such a document should after all find its way into Greif's hands, and as he thought over the various turns affairs might take he trembled at the responsibility he had assumed. There were delicate points of law involved, concerning which he himself was uncertain.

In the first place, as Greifenstein, Greif was not married at all. His birth was illegitimate, and if he had been married under the name he supposed to be his, the union was not valid. For the law only acknowledges such marriages as take place under the true and lawful names of both parties. If one or the other, though wholly innocent and ignorant of any mistake, turns out to have been married under a wrong appellation, the office is void and of no effect. The question was, whether Greif, as Sigmundskron, was legally Hilda's husband. Rex was inclined to believe that he was.

The Heralds' Office might withdraw from him the name and arms of Greifenstein, but Rex did not believe that they could interdict Greif from using those of Sigmundskron, since the Sigmundskrons had themselves conferred them upon him, in his own person, whatever he was before. In that case Greif was really and truly Sigmundskron, and he was not really anything else, except a nameless orphan. And, if so, the marriage was valid after all. It was a fortunate coincidence which had given a name to a man who really had none at all.

Of course, if no one but Rex were ever to know the secret, there was no danger in store for the young couple. But if any untoward accident should reveal it, or if any other individual were already in possession of it, their case might be bad indeed. Rex could not think of it without experiencing a very unpleasant sensation. He remembered how old Greifenstein had lived during five and twenty years in ignorance of his own shame, and how it had found him out at last. It would be horrible indeed if such a catastrophe should fall upon Greif and Hilda. But it would be better, in the extreme case, that Greif should learn the truth first.

If Frau von Sigmundskron should be the first to find it out, it was impossible to foretell what might happen. She would find it hard to believe that Greif had not known it when he married her daughter; she would remember how he had done his best to refuse Hilda, and she would ascribe that to his knowledge that he was illegitimate; his change of name would look like a piece of deliberate scheming to supply himself with what he most lacked, a name. She would misunderstand all his actions and misconstrue all his intentions; he would appear to her in the light of a clever actor who had made the emotions he really felt serve the greater ends he had so carefully concealed.

Rex thought of her behaviour with regard to the name, and

he understood the immense value she put upon it; he saw how she had persuaded herself that in Greif her husband's race was to be revived again, and he could guess what she would feel when she discovered that she had conferred what she held most holy on earth, not upon an unfortunate nobleman, but upon a murderer's bastard, who had cleverly robbed her of what she could no longer take back.

Rex thought of the strange fatality which pursued himself and his brother. He himself had been the chief cause of the present situation, both by his silence concerning the secret and by his constant efforts to promote the marriage. If he had possessed old Greifenstein's character, he would have acted very differently. He would have told Greif the truth brutally in order to prevent even the distant possibility of such mischief as might now arise. And yet Rex's conscience did not reproach him. He asked himself whether he could possibly have dealt such a blow upon any human being, especially upon one who had suffered, like Greif, almost all that a man can suffer and live. He wondered whether he were amenable to the law for his silence, though he really cared very little about the legality or illegality of his actions in the present case. He felt that both he and his brother were men beyond the pale of common laws, pursued by an evil destiny that did not quite leave them even in their happiness.

He went back to his own father's story from its first beginning, and beyond that to the untimely death of the father of old Greifenstein, which had led to the second marriage of the latter's mother, and so to the birth of Rieseneck with all his woes and miserable deeds; then to the early quarrels of the two half-brothers, to their separation, to the singular state of things in which Greifenstein hardly knew of his brother's marriage and never saw the face of his brother's wife; then onward to Rieseneck's surrender of the arsenal guard, to his imprisonment, escape and exile, followed by his wife's unlawful marriage to the brother of her living husband, then to the evil fatality which had sent a child in this false union to inherit so much shame and horror, to be saved from it, so far at least, by his unknown brother, appearing as his cousin, Rex, the traitor's son. In such a train of destiny, what might not be yet in store for Horst von Rieseneck and for his brother Greif von Sigmundskron?

Rex almost smiled as he gave to each, in his imagination, the only name that was lawfully his—he smiled at the ingenuity of fate in finding so much mischief to do.

Chapter 24

Rex was mistaken in his opinion concerning the letter. Before he died old Greifenstein had actually written it, as he had intended to do, and had directed it to his son. It is not yet time to explain what became of it, but in order to make this history more clear, it is as well to state at once that it was not destroyed, but was actually in existence at the time of Greif's marriage to Hilda.

It is necessary, however, to consider the development of Rex's character during the year which followed the wedding, in order to understand the events which afterwards occurred. It had been his intention to undertake a journey to South America, when all was settled, in order to wind up his father's affairs, and ascertain the extent of the fortune he inherited. He was well aware that he was very rich, but as this was nothing new to him, and as he had always had whatever he wished, he was in no hurry to find out the exact amount of his income. The property was well administered, too, and there was no danger of loss, as Rieseneck had taken pains to provide against every contingency before making his last voyage to Europe. Rex was personally acquainted with the persons to whom his father had confided the management of his wealth, and so soon as they were informed of the latter's death, they took all the legal steps necessary to secure the inheritance, and remitted large sums of money to the heir at regular intervals and with scrupulous exactness.

At first his situation seemed rather a strange one, and he did not exactly know what to do. Immediately after the marriage he found himself at Greifenstein alone with Hilda's mother, who submitted to the arrangement readily enough. It was natural, she said, that the young people should wish to be left to themselves for some time. They had declared that when they were ready for society they would drive over from Sigmundskron, and bring back the baroness and Rex. These two, being both exceedingly methodical persons, agreed very well, and they found plenty to talk about in the possibilities of the future.

Rex was utterly indifferent to solitude or company, but since the baroness was to be his companion, he took some trouble to make himself agreeable. She, on her part, knew well enough that the days when she could be constantly with Hilda were over, and she was glad that her son-in-law had such a man as Rex for his cousin. For Rex was far too tactful to parade his philosophic views in the presence of a lady whose practical religion he admired and respected, so that the only point upon which the two could have differed seriously was carefully avoided. An odd sort of intimacy sprang up between them, which neither had anticipated.

Frau von Sigmundskron was surprised to find in Rex so much ready sympathy with her ideas, for her German soul would have been naturally inclined to find fault with a man who had been brought up in South America, and whose father could not have been supposed capable of teaching him much sound morality. Nor would it have seemed likely that her somewhat narrow, though elevated view of things in general would find a ready appreciation in one whose great breadth of understanding had made him familiar with all manner of heretically modern notions. She did not comprehend his nature, but she was satisfied in his society.

There are, perhaps, no persons more agreeable to live with than those few who have become conservative through excessive and constant change. They bring back with them to the land of stabilities an intimate practical knowledge of what instability really means, which distinguishes them from people who have lived within the shadow of their own steeple through a lifetime of dogged tradition-worship. Rex had tried everything that the world can give, except fame, which was beyond his reach, and, at forty years of age, he had a decided preference for old-fashioned people. His placid disposition liked their quiet ways and abhorred all sorts of trivial excitement; he was a man who was intimately conscious of the inanity of most forms of amusement, and of the emptiness of most kinds of sensations.

The cold, still depths of his heart could not be warmed to a pleasurable heat by the small emotions which the world covets, and so eagerly pursues. He sometimes wondered what would happen if he were really roused. He had not often been angry in his life, but he had noticed, with his habit of self-observation, that his anger seldom failed to produce tangible results, even when it was half assumed. It was natural to suppose that if he should ever be goaded to madness, he might turn out to be a very dangerous animal, but such a case appeared to him extremely improbable, because he could scarcely conceive of anything which could affect his temper for more than a few minutes. It is certainly true that persons who do not indulge their passions are less exposed to be assailed by them at every turn, though the capacity for passion itself in extreme cases increases in an opposite ratio.

Rex and Frau von Sigmundskron became intimate, therefore, and grew more fond of each other's company than they had expected to be. But they were not left long to their solitary state in Greifenstein. At the end of a week, Greif and Hilda appeared, more radiant in their new happiness than before. They proposed that Rex and the baroness should come over to Sigmundskron for a month, after which they announced their intention of travelling for some time.

Hilda had given Rex her hand, which according to German custom she could not do before she was married. He had almost dreaded to touch it when he saw it before him, so strong was still the first impression he had taken so much pains to conquer. Strangely enough, this was the last time he ever felt a return of his old antipathy. It seemed as though the contact of Hilda's gloved fingers had wrought a change in him. He looked up and saw a smile upon her face.

'Do you hate me still?' she asked.

'No.' he answered, and there was no mistaking his tone.

He did not hate her any more, it was true, but he felt unaccountably embarrassed by her presence. He was silent, preoccupied, strangely dull and unresponsive. 'Why do you never talk before Hilda?' asked Greif, in his straightforward way, when they had all been a week at Sigmundskron together.

'Men are often silent before nature's greatest works,' said Rex quietly, and without looking at Hilda as he spoke.

'Do you hear that enormous compliment?' asked Greif, addressing her.

'I do not understand it,' answered Hilda, with a laugh. 'I believe he hates me still!'

'No,' he answered gravely, 'you are quite mistaken, and I was not thinking of making compliments.'

'But it is true, since Greif has spoken of it,' Hilda said. 'You do not talk when I am present, though both Greif and my mother say that no one talks better. What does it mean, when a man is silent, Greif?'

'It generally means that he is in love.'

'With me?' Hilda laughed gaily at the thought, which conveyed no more idea of possibility to her than it did to Greif, or even, at that moment, to Rex himself.

'I should be, if I were Greif,' Rex answered, pretending to laugh a little.

He thought of what had been said, when he was alone, and there seemed nothing laughable in it. On the contrary, he was angry with Greif for suggesting a thought which had certainly not occurred to him before. He knew well enough, now that he considered the matter, that there was no inherent reason in the nature of things why he might not fall in love with Hilda, and it struck him rather forcibly that he occasionally acted as though he were in that condition, or at least as he might have done, had he been in love at twenty. But he was twice that age, and there was an evident discrepancy between his behaviour and his reasoning, which rendered the supposition utterly absurd. He did not believe that a man could be in love in the smallest degree without being aware of it, and he felt that if he were aware that he loved his brother's wife, he should forthwith leave the country for ever.

Moreover, until very lately he had believed that he positively disliked Hilda, and it would be strange indeed if a strong antipathy had thus suddenly developed into a sentiment capable of suggesting Greif's careless remark. Rex promised himself that when they met that evening at dinner his behaviour should be very different. It was true that he had not thought much about the matter, until Hilda had asked the cause of his silence. He was in the habit of holding his tongue when he had nothing to say, unlike many younger men. He was also aware that he admired Hilda's beauty, as he had always done, even when he had most disliked her personality.

The flash of her eyes and hair as she had rushed to the bed where Greif was almost dying, had produced a permanent impression upon Rex, much at variance with what he had felt towards herself, as distinguished from her outward appearance. He had next attributed his antipathy to jealousy of her; he wondered, now, how he could have made such a blunder. He had nothing but gratitude for her now, for the share she had taken in saving his brother's life, nothing but gratitude and a certain brotherly affection, as undefined as his dislike had been before.

Rex thought he was losing the use of his faculties, or falling into a premature dotage since he could waste so much thought over such an insignificant point, and he made up his mind, after all, not to attempt any determined change in his conduct, but to talk or hold his peace as the spirit moved him. The result was that he talked exceptionally well, very much to his own surprise. Before many days were passed he found that he had so completely altered his behaviour, that he was now generally silent when Hilda was not present, whereas her coming was the signal for him to exhibit an almost unnatural brilliancy.

'I amuse them,' he said to himself, with some satisfaction. 'They are pleased, and that is enough.'

Hilda and Greif carried out their intention of travelling during the autumn. To Greif it seemed impossible that Hilda should any longer remain in total ignorance of the outer world. They would go away, in the first place, for three months, and they would all be back together for an old-fashioned Christmas in Sigmundskron. Their absence would give time for a few of the more essential repairs to be made in the castle, before undertaking the extensive restorations that were necessary. Frau von Sigmundskron had said that she would stay behind and superintend as well as she could.

'And what will you do, Rex?' asked Greif.

'I will help Aunt Therese,' answered the other.

'Why do you not go somewhere and amuse yourself?'

'That is easier said than done. My amusement will consist in counting the days until you come back. We shall both do that.'

'Why not go and stay at Greifenstein as you both did before? It is more comfortable.'

'I prefer this. There is a better view. I think I will buy the top of the hill over there, and lay the foundation of an observatory. It will be an occupation, and they send me so much money that I do not know what to do with it.'

'I hope you are not going to build a house to live in,' said Greif, suddenly. 'Remember that your home is here.'

'Thank you,' answered Rex.

The words were pleasant to him, for in the last month he had begun to feel an attachment for Sigmundskron which he had never felt for any place before. The mere idea of leaving it was painful to him, and if he must be parted for a time from Greif and Hilda—he coupled their names in his thoughts, and rather obstinately, too—he knew that the time would pass more quickly in the old castle than anywhere else. At forty years of age, the idea of beginning again the wandering life he had led so long, rambling from one country and capital to another, now spending a year at a University and then six months in Paris, or a winter in St. Petersburg, never settled, never at home, though at home everywhere—the mere thought was painfully repugnant.

To live with Greif and Hilda in their ancient home, to build at last the noble observatory of which he had often idly dreamed, and to spend the best years of life that remained to him in peaceful study among those he loved, was a prospect infinitely attracting, and apparently most easy of realisation.

When Hilda and Greif were gone, Rex discovered that they were really the central figures in his visions of future happiness. The emptiness they left behind was indescribably dreary. He wondered why he had not experienced the same sensation when he and the baroness had stayed at Greifenstein after the wedding. He had not missed the two so painfully then; indeed he had enjoyed the baroness's society very much, and would not then have been altogether sorry to have been left with her for a longer time. But the month they had spent at Sigmundskron had produced a great change, it seemed.

Before that, he had assuredly not been in the habit of thinking so much about Greif and Hilda, nor, in Greifenstein, had he expected to meet them at every turn, in every dusky corner, when he walked through the house alone, as was the case now. It was quite certain that they had not formerly haunted his dreams; whereas now he could not close his eyes without seeing Hilda's face, and Greif's beside it.

Though their absence was more than disagreeable to Rex, he was, on the whole, rather pleased than otherwise when he discovered how much he regretted their presence. Until lately he had never missed anybody, nor cared whether he were alone or in company. He could not have looked forward with so much satisfaction to passing the rest of his life with Greif and Hilda if he had not cared for their society. The prospect would have been repugnant instead of attractive in that case, and he would have preferred to build a house of his own. He was delighted at the glimpse of the future afforded him during the past month, and he was satisfied with the position he was to occupy in the house. He was old enough to love Greif and Hilda in a somewhat fatherly way, though he looked so young.

After all, a man of forty could be father to a girl of nineteen, and it was a pleasant privilege to call her cousin Hilda, and to treat her as a sort of niece. Rex supposed that before long his brown hair and beard would begin to turn grey. He looked forward to feeling himself older and wiser than Hilda and Greif, as indeed he might, and he intended to take great interest in the education of their children, who would look up to him as to something between a grandfather and an uncle in ten or fifteen years' time. It would be very delightful to teach Hilda's children—and Greif's, and there was nothing to hinder Rex from building his observatory if he pleased.

Of one thing he grew very certain, namely, that life without Greif or Hilda would be intolerable. Fortunately he found sympathy in this thought on the part of Frau von Sigmundskron, who missed the two as much as Rex, though perhaps in a very different way. They talked of nothing but what should be done when the pair came back at Christmas, unless the post had brought one of those short, businesslike efforts of affection which happy couples send to their parents during the first months of wedded bliss.

On those occasions the two sat together discussing the letter as long as there remained in it a word to talk about. Rex would then launch out into vivid descriptions of the town or country whence the news came, supplying every deficiency in the correspondence out of the inexhaustible stores of his memory, telling his companion all that Hilda and Greif must have seen and done, even though they had forgotten to give a full account of their proceedings. The baroness enjoyed these conversations quite as much as though she had received longer letters, but Rex was conscious of an odd impulse to fill up by an effort of his imagination the numerous *lacunae* in the sequence of news. He was aware that his disappointment when no letter came was greater than he had expected, and that it increased until he felt a positive, painful anxiety at the hour when the mail came in.

But though the days sometimes dragged wearily along, they were over at last, and Hilda and Greif came back. They received a great ovation on their return, and the Christmas that followed was a merry one, but no one was so glad to welcome the two home again as Rex. His face was so much changed by his delight that Greif hardly recognised him for the man he had left behind three months ago. As had sometimes happened, though very rarely, his eyes had lost their stony impenetrability for a few moments; the pupils dilated and were full of light; and there was an extraordinary brilliancy about Rex's usually unruffled features, which surprised Hilda herself.

Rex looked at her, too, and he saw that a transformation had taken place. He could not tell whether he preferred the girlish simplicity of three months ago, or the fuller beauty of today. The dress made a difference, also, for though simple still, and severe, what Hilda wore was the work of more skilful hands than her own or old Berbel's. There was the difference between unintentional simplicity, and the simplicity of a refined taste, as in Hilda's self Rex would soon discover the change from the girl to the woman.

Rex did not conceal his gladness, and it was in itself a source of pleasure to the two who had come back. During the first few days there was endless festivity and endless talk about all they had seen and done. There was much to say on both sides, and small time to say it, for it was the Christmas season, and the Sigmundskrons were determined to make it a happy one for all their people. But when Twelfth Night was gone by, and quietness descended upon the four occupants of the castle, they found that they had succeeded in telling each other much more than they supposed, in the intervals between Christmas trees, and dinners for the peasantry, and all the pleasant noise and excitement of the Yuletide.

Very soon their lives dropped into peaceful channels again, and upon the tidal wave of merriment succeeded the calm flow of an untroubled existence. There was no end to the work to be done upon the castle, and Greif entered upon it with boundless enthusiasm, while Rex helped him at every turn with his extraordinary knowledge of all matters in which exactness was required. Hilda marvelled at his amazing versatility and at the apparent depth of his information upon so many matters. No question came amiss to him connected with the restoration, from the customs and mode of life of the mediaeval Germans to the calculation of a Gothic arch or a winding staircase.

'You seem to know everything,' said Hilda one day, unable to conceal her admiration.

'It is a matter of habit,' Rex answered vaguely, whereat she laughed, scarcely knowing why.

'I mean,' said Rex, explaining himself, 'that you are in the habit of supposing that a man only understands his own profession, whereas if he really does understand it, he ought not to find any difficulty in acquiring the rudiments of any other which does not need special gifts. Everything which depends upon mathematics is more or less connected in a mathematical mind.'

'That sounds very reasonable. I wish I had a mathematical mind.'

'You have what is better,' answered Rex, looking at her.

'What is that?'

'Many things. Ask Greif.'

His tone had changed, and he spoke so seriously that she was surprised, for she did not in the least comprehend his mood. It was strange to himself, and he afterwards wondered whether his own words had any sense in them, unwilling to allow that he had spoken out of the fullness of an admiration he had no right to express. He did not say, even to himself, that she was the most beautiful woman, the best, the kindest he had ever known, but at the thought of what he would have said in his own heart, had all restraint been removed, he felt a shock, such as a man feels who strikes his hand against some unexpected sharp object in the dark, and draws back, groping his way carefully lest he should hurt himself again.

Certain it was that his admiration of Hilda threatened to pass the bounds by which admiration of any sort is separated from the stronger feelings that lie beyond it. But as he perceived this in the course of time, he explained it away by telling himself that it was natural and harmless. Loving his brother as he did, it would have been strange if he had not felt something like devotion for the woman who had saved his brother's life. It would have been astonishing if he had not felt a most sincere affection for her, if he had not been willing to sacrifice anything for her.

It was an odd sort of devotion at first, for it grew up like a tender plant surrounded on all sides by sharp pricks, straight in self-defence, and sensitive by avoiding all contact with things hurtful. Rex became conscious of its growth, and was surprised to find anything so delicate and beautiful in his own heart, where such beauties had never grown, or had budded only to wither prematurely, leaving the ground more dry and arid and unpromising than before. It was as though a soft light had dawned in his soul and was gradually brightening into day. From having distrusted himself a little at first, he put an unbounded faith in his own heart since he saw what it contained. He would even talk to Greif by the hour together of Hilda's perfections, vying with her husband in discovering new things to praise, and utterly happy in the freedom of speaking about her which he thus enjoyed.

He fancied that he looked upon her almost as though she had been his daughter, and he imagined that he understood stories he had read, and cases he had known in his own experience, where such pure affections were concerned. He, who was far from imaginative by nature, made romances in the air, in which he fancied that he had once been married to a woman he had loved to distraction—a woman not unlike Hilda, perhaps—and that Hilda herself was the daughter of that union, all there was left to remind him of her who was dead. There was something oddly fantastic in the thought, which satisfied him for a time, and made his life seem full of a love, tender, regretful, expressing itself in a boundless devotion to the one object which recalled it.

And the dead woman grew in his fancy, until she became very lifelike. He could remember how he had closed her darkened eyes, and smoothed her yellow hair, how he had buried her on a dark winter's day, among the fir trees, and how through long years he had mourned for her, while Hilda was a little child at his knee. It was all fancy, but it was very vivid. Then he could go back still farther, he could recall the sound of her voice, for Hilda's own reminded him of it, and out of the misty echoes of past time he could reconstruct conversations, phrases of love, words full of meaning.

He remembered their first meeting, in an ancient castle in a distant land—he had been a guest in her father's house—so long ago. He remembered how they had ridden together so often through a dim forest, and how the echo of the horses' hoofs amongst the ringing trees had broken upon the silvery music of her voice. It all came back to him, the scene, the colour of the shadows; the snort of the horses, the curves of her figure as she sat so straight in the saddle, the silences that said more than words.

Then the scene changed, and they were upon a moonlit lawn in summer. He was standing still, and she was coming towards him through the misty light. His heart beat fast. Slender and tall as a fair spirit she advanced. Her two hands were held out before her, and found his. Face to face they stood in silence, their gaze meeting; was it to be, or not? Then, in that wonderful moment, he felt his own hard eyes soften and saw the warm light in hers. Not a word was spoken, as his arms went round her—then they turned and walked together upon the dark, dewless grass, beneath the summer moon.

And again, he was with her upon a balcony at night. In the warm dusk he could see the whiteness of her face, and the outline of her figure. She had said something, and he had felt the hot blood surging to his forehead, and falling again, as by its own weight, upon his heart. All at once he had answered her with such words as he had not guessed a man could speak, for they had broken forth in a passionate eloquence, unrestrained and fresh with young life, as words first spoken can be. He could not always remember them now; the heartfelt ring of them waked him from his sleep, sometimes; and again, in the midst of the occupations of the day, the stirring echo of their music filled the room in a moment and was gone before he could seize it, or was blown into his ear by the clear breeze that swept the valley.

The dead woman was alive—the woman who had never lived save in his brain—and Hilda was growing to be like her. Rex watched them both, her whom he saw with open eyes, and her who was present with him the instant his eyes were closed. No daughter was ever so exact an image of the mother who had borne her; line for line, the features grew to be the same, shade for shade the colour of the one became the colour of the other, coil for coil the yellow hair of both was wound alike upon the noble head.

And the love of this dead woman, who had never breathed, but whom he had buried with such bitter tears and such heart-broken grief, filled his whole being and twined itself through all the mazes of his complex nature, till no action of his life was independent of it, and no thought free from its all-dominating influence.

In the first beginnings of this creation of his fancy he had found such peace and such sweet melancholy satisfaction that he had encouraged its growth and had tried to persuade himself of its reality. And the reality had come, so far as it can come to anything wholly built up in the imagination. It had also brought with it its consequences, unless it could be said to be a consequence in itself. Rex's devotion to Hilda increased with every day, as she seemed to him to be more and more like the woman he had loved, the mother he had imagined for her in place of her own. For it was out of Hilda herself that his love for a shadow had grown to be what it was, and the shadow itself was but the reflection of Hilda's present brightness upon the misty emptiness of his own past life.

Rex was very happy. The dreams that filled the hours did not hinder his actions; on the contrary, the latter seemed to be supplied at last with the purpose they had lacked during forty years, the purpose to honour the love that was in him, and to please Hilda, the outcome of that love. All that he did seemed to acquire directness and perfection of detail, all that he said was dignified by a tender thought for this child of an adored vision, until those who lived with him were amazed at his wisdom and kindness, and wondered whether the world had ever held his like before.

The busy months went by and the summer was at hand. Much had been done to Sigmundskron, but there was work for years to come, before it should be what Greif dreamed of. But one day in June the work ceased suddenly, and all was hushed and still. The servants trod noiselessly and spoke in whispers, and Rex found himself left to his own devices with no companion but the dear idol of his fancy. The whole household life seemed suspended.

It was the silence of a great happiness. On that fair June morning Hilda had borne her husband an heir to Sigmundskron.

Chapter 25

Berbel, transformed into the housekeeper of Sigmundskron, was busy with the preparations for the christening. A year of uninterrupted prosperity had made her a trifle more sleek than before, and though she still affected a Spartan simplicity of dress, her frock was made of better materials than formerly, and her cap was adorned with black ribbands of real silk.

The day was warm, and Berbel came out into the court to breathe the air. As she stood at the door trying to remember whether she had forgotten anything, a man entered the gate and strode across the pavement. It was Wastei, and he carried in his hand a magnificent string of trout, threaded by the gills upon a willow withe. He bore his burden very carefully, and it was clear that he had gone home to dress himself after catching the trout and before coming to the castle, for he was splendidly arrayed in a pair of new leather breeches and he wore a velvet coat, the like of which had not been seen in Sigmundsdorf within the memory of man, for, like Berbel's ribbands, it was of real silk. Berbel eyed him curiously. She had an odd liking for the fellow.

'God greet you, Frau Berbel,' said Wastei with far more politeness than he vouchsafed to most people, high or low. 'I have brought these fish for the christening feast, and I have seen worse.'

Berbel took the willow wand from his hand, tried the weight, counted the trout with a housewife's eye, tried the weight again, and then nodded approvingly.

'They are good fish,' she said, looking them over once more.

Wastei drew a bright red handkerchief from his pocket, and carefully wiped his sinewy brown hands. Then without further ceremony he sat down upon the stone curb at the corner of the steps, as though he had done his business and meant to rest himself without paying any more attention to Berbel. She liked him for his independence and taciturnity. Moreover, in the old days of starving poverty, Wastei had done her many a good service she had never been able to reward, and had brought many a plump hare and many a brace of quails to the empty larder, swearing that he had come by them honestly, and offering to exchange them for a little mending to his tattered clothes.

Berbel used to suspect that Wastei knew more of the nakedness of the land than he admitted, and that he risked more than one dangerous bit of poaching out of secret pity for the poor ladies who were known to buy so little food in the village. They were better off now, both she and Wastei, but as she looked at the broad expanse of black velvet that covered his square, flat back, she remembered the days when he had come ragged to the back door to throw down a good meal of game upon the kitchen table, going off the next minute with nothing but a bit of black bread in prospect for his supper.

'I will take them to the baron myself,' said Berbel.

Wastei looked up as though he had supposed she was already gone in.

'Thank you, Frau Berbel,' he answered.

Five minutes later she returned, carrying a black bottle, a glass and something small shut in the palm of her hand.

'The baron thanks you and sends you this,' she said, holding out a gold piece. 'And I have brought you this,' she added, filling the glass, 'because I know you like it.'

'Luck!' ejaculated Wastei, slipping the twenty-*mark* piece into the pocket of his waistcoat, and watching the white liquor as it rose nearer to the brim.

He took the glass, twisted it in his fingers, held it to the sun, and then looked again at Berbel.

'God greet,' he said, and tossed off the liquor in a trice. 'Luck!' he exclaimed again, as he smacked his lips.

'Why do you say luck, in that way?' asked the good woman.

'I will tell you, Frau Berbel,' answered Wastei, lowering his tone. 'It is the new coat that brought me luck today.'

'It is a good coat,' observed Berbel, in her usual manner.

'Well, I came by it through a gold piece and a drink of that same good stuff.'

'Cheap. It is a good coat.'

'Do you remember, after the devil had flown away with the old wolf of Greifenstein—'

'Hush, for mercy's sake!' exclaimed Berbel. 'You must not talk like that—'

'He was a wolf. I believe he would have torn a poor free-shot like me to pieces if he could. I had him after me once, and I remember his eyes. If he had been ten years younger and if I had not dropped through a hole I knew of so that he thought I had fallen over the Falcon Stone beyond Zavelstein, he would have caught me. He looked for my body two days with his keepers. Well, the devil got him, as you know, for he killed himself. And after that the young lord was ill and you sent me off at night for news, because Fraulein Hilda could not sleep. Well, you remember how I brought back the bad news, and a gold piece Herr Rex had given me, and which I supposed must be for your ladies because they had not many at that time, though I thought it queer. Good, and the baroness said it must be for me—you remember all that?'

'Very well,' replied Berbel, suppressing a smile by force of habit.

'So I took the gold piece, but I would not use it nor change it, for I said it was the price of bad news, though I owed the host at the Ox three *marks* and a half at the time. I took my gold piece and I put it in a safe place, where nobody would have thought of looking for it.'

'Where was that?' asked Berbel, as he paused.

'Well, if you want to know, I will tell you. There is a place in the forest, called Waldeck, where there is a ruined castle, and before the gate there are three trees and a stump of an old tree farther on—it is all thick and full of brushwood and pines and birches, so that my three trees look very much like the others, but when you have found them, you must take a straight line from the right hand one to the stump—you will find it if you look, and then go on past the stump about a hundred ells, always straight, and then you will come to a flat stone; and the stone is loose so that it turns round easily, if you are strong enough to move it, and underneath it there is a deep hole. I put my gold piece at the bottom of this hole and set a heavy stone upon it, and then I got out and drew the big stone into its place, and went away. I did not think that anyone would be likely to look for a twenty *mark*-piece just in that spot.'

'Improbable,' assented Berbel, her massive mouth twitching with amusement.

'Very. And I said to myself, Wastei, you're a brave fellow, and you shall starve to death rather than use the gold which is the price of bad news; but if the son of the old wolf gets well, and marries Frau Berbel's young lady, and if the good God sends them a boy, then, Wastei, you shall go and get the gold piece and spend it at the christening. You see Herr Rex had given me a drink with the money, just as you did, so that there was a chance of its turning out well after all, and I knew that—because if there had been no chance, why then, money is money, after all.'

'And so now you have bought a coat with it?'

'And what a coat! The Jew had had it in his shop for six months, but nobody could buy it because it was so dear.'

'The Jew?' inquired Berbel, looking sharply at Wastei.

'Yes—and do you know what I think, Frau Berbel?' Wastei lowered his voice to a whisper.

'What?'

'I believe it is the coat the old wolf died in, and that is the reason it brings me luck.'

'What makes you think that?' inquired his companion, knitting her rough brows.

'There is a spot on the collar—here.' Wastei moved closer to her and presented himself sideways to Berbel pointing out the place with his finger. 'The Jew said it was from a rusty nail, or that it might be an ink-spot—but he is only a Jew. That is not rust, nor ink, Frau Berbel. That is the old wolf's last blood—on the right side, just under the ear. He would have shot me for a poacher, if he could, Frau Berbel. Well, I have got his coat, with his own mark on it.'

Berbel shuddered slightly, strong though she was. She liked Wastei, but she had often guessed that there was a latent ferocity in him which would come out some day.

'And how could the coat have come to the Jew's shop?' she asked, after a pause.

'You know they had a houseful of servants, all thieves from the city, and they were always getting new ones, instead of keeping honest folk from the estate. The young lord sent them all away and took his own people, God bless him. But on the night when they all died, the servants were alone in the house, before your lady got over there, and when she did, she could not do everything. I have heard that they buried them all in fine clothes. Well, in the confusion, you may be sure that one of the servants stole the coat with the blood on it, and as he expected to stay in the house, and could not have worn it himself, he took it to the Jew and sold it for what he could get. You see it looks likely, because the Jew would have waited at least a year before trying to sell it, for fear of being caught.'

'That is true,' said Berbel thoughtfully.

'I would not have told the story to anyone else,' observed Wastei. 'But as you know everything, you may as well know this too.'

'What? Is there anything more?'

'Nothing particular,' answered Wastei. 'Except that there was a hole in the pocket,' he added carelessly. 'You see it was not quite new, or I could not have got it for twenty *marks*.'

'So there was a hole in the pocket,' said Berbel. 'Do you want me to mend it for you?'

'No. I think I will leave it, for luck. Besides it is convenient, if I should want to let anything slip through, between the velvet and the lining.'

'That is true,' observed Berbel, watching him intently.

'A thing might lie a long time between the velvet and the lining of a coat in a Jew's shop,' remarked Wastei presently.

'Very long.'

'Long enough for people not to want it, when it is found.'

'It depends on what it is.'

'A ticket for a lottery, for instance, would not be of much use after a year or two.'

'Not much, as you say,' assented Berbel, keeping her eye upon him.

'Or an old letter, either,' said Wastei with perfect indifference.

'That depends on the person to whom it is addressed.'

'A live son is better than a dead father. A message from the dead wolf would not make the christening of his grandson any merrier, would it, Frau Berbel?'

'Better leave dead people alone,' she answered, thoughtfully rubbing the mole on her chin.

'In God's peace,' said Wastei, lifting his small hat from his head. 'Or wherever else they may be,' he added, putting it on again.

There was a pause, during which Berbel reflected upon the situation, and Wastei leaned back against the grey wall, watching a hawk that was circling above the distant crags.

'What will you do with it?' asked Berbel, at last.

'Burn it, or give it to you—whichever you like.'

'You have not read it?'

'It is not the sign-board of an inn—if it were, I could. Besides, it is sealed. There is writing on the back, and I think there is a capital G among the letters. You see there was more than the spot on the collar to tell me whose the coat was.'

343

'It is true that the baron always expected to find a letter from his father,' said Berbel. 'It looks probable, this story of yours.'

'Do you want the paper?'

'Yes. I will keep it in a safe place. In ten years, when there is no more sorrow about the old people, the baron may like to know that his father thought of him.'

'Better burn it,' suggested Wastei, pulling out a match-box, and fumbling in his unfamiliar pockets for the letter.

'I am not sure of that,' said Berbel, who knew that if she insisted, he would destroy it in spite of her. 'After all, Wastei, it is neither yours nor mine.'

'I bought it with the coat. I can burn it if I like,' said Wastei, striking a match and watching the white flame in the sunshine.

'Of course you can, if you like,' replied Berbel unmoved.

'Well, if you want it, there it is,' he said, throwing away the match and handing her the letter. 'Do not spoil the christening with it, Frau Berbel.'

She took the envelope with a great show of indifference and looked attentively at the superscription.

'Is it what I thought?' inquired Wastei.

'To my son Greif. That is what is written on it.'

'It is like the old wolf's manner,' said the other. 'He might have said Greifenstein at least. But I suppose the devil was in a hurry and could not wait for him to write it out. I am sure I would not have waited so long. God greet you, Frau Berbel.'

Wastei nodded and strode across the sunny court, well satisfied with himself. He had planned the whole meeting, with the useless craftiness of a born woodman. Several days had elapsed since he had bought the coat and found the letter in the lining. In spite of his pretended ignorance he could read well enough to make out the address, and he had come to the conclusion that Berbel was the person to be trusted. He would not for the world have destroyed the precious missive, but he was equally determined neither to keep it himself nor to mar the joy of the Sigmundskrons' festivities by putting it into Greif's own hands.

He had known Berbel for many years and he was sure of

her discretion. She would keep it until the proper moment was come, and would give it to the right person in the end. But he had not been able to resist the temptation of making a profound mystery of the matter and he prided himself upon the effective way in which he had executed his scheme. Three words would have sufficed, but he had passed more than half an hour very agreeably in Berbel's company. And Berbel, little guessing the tremendous import of what she held in her hand, had been interested by the long story. It did not enter her mind that the letter could be anything but a word of affectionate farewell, at the time Wastei gave it into her keeping.

Intelligent and keen as she was, for a woman of her class, it nevertheless did not occur to her that she was putting into her pocket the key to the mystery of eighteen months ago. The baroness had never spoken to her familiarly about the tragedy, and she took it for granted that the catastrophe was fully understood by the survivors, though they chose to keep its cause a secret among themselves. Hilda had indeed told her that poor Greif had received no message from his father, but as the baroness had never mentioned the letter to Rex, she supposed that both were in the same position.

Berbel carried the paper to her own room and put it into a strong wooden box with her own most sacred belongings, the few relics of her husband which she possessed, a dozen letters written to her during the war, an old button from his uniform, a faded bit of ribband which had carried the medal for the war of 1866, and which she had once replaced with a new one, a pair of his old soldier's gloves and a lock of his hair. It was all she had left of him, for he had fallen among hundreds and had been buried in the common trench. She envied her mistress nothing in the world except the two swords and the leathern helmet that had been Sigmundskron's—poor woman!

Her husband had fought as bravely and had fallen on the same honourable field as his master, but she had nothing of his, but a little hair, a bit of ribband, a tarnished button and a pair of worn-out gloves. The rough-browed, hard-faced woman kissed each of her poor relics in turn before she closed the box, and the tears were in her eyes as she hid the key away.

She had not decided what to do with the letter, but on the whole it seemed wiser not to deliver it on that day. Indeed it would be almost impossible to do so, for any one not absolutely tactless and careless of others' feelings. Berbel was by no means sure, however, whether she should be justified in keeping it more than a few days. After all, it might possibly contain some message, or some especial injunction which Greif ought to receive at once. To keep such a document concealed for any length of time would have been wholly unjustifiable.

On the other hand Berbel was not sure how such a disclosure might affect Greif. So far as she knew, his illness had been caused by the shock of his father's and mother's deaths, and it could not be foreseen whether a circumstance which must remind him so vividly of that catastrophe might not cause a return of the malady which had attacked his brain. Berbel wished she could consult someone and get good advice in the matter. The wisest person in the house was Rex, but for many reasons she would not go to him. It was not unnatural that, in her position, she should distrust Rex to a certain extent. In the first place he was the only member of the household with whom she had not been acquainted for years, and he was consequently the stranger in the establishment.

Then, too, though he was so exceedingly clever, she could not grow accustomed to his eyes, and their expressionless stare haunted her when she was alone. Berbel did not believe that a man who looked almost blind and nevertheless saw so much better than other people could be really good and honest, since his appearance itself was a deception. How could a man have eyes with no pupils in them, and yet be able to tell a swift from a swallow as well as Wastei himself and at as great a distance? There was evidently something wrong about Rex, and Berbel preferred to trust any other member of the household.

For the rest, there was the baroness and there was Hilda. Either of them would give her good advice without doubt, but it was necessary to choose between them. Berbel was inclined to select Hilda, for she felt more at her ease with her than with Frau von Sigmundskron herself. Moreover it was natural to imagine that Hilda would understand Greif better than anyone else, now that they had been married during nearly a year. On the other hand the baroness was older and wiser, though not so wise as Rex.

The balance lay between the sympathy Berbel felt for the one, and the unbounded respect she felt for the other. She had taken care of Hilda from a child, and the girl had grown up feeling that Berbel was more a friend than a servant, as indeed she was; whereas the baroness, though sincerely attached to the good creature to whom she owed so much, and although overflowing with kindness towards her, could not get rid of the idea of all distinctions so far as to talk intimately with her upon family matters. This consideration, of which Berbel was well aware, ultimately turned the scale, and she determined to go to Hilda with the letter, while regretting that a lingering distrust of Rex's character prevented her from appealing to his fabulous wisdom.

The christening was a very grand ceremony, in the eyes of the village folk, and everything was done in the most approved fashion. It not being the custom in Germany to baptize children as soon as they are born, and as the anniversary of the wedding was not far distant, it was agreed to choose that day for giving a name to the heir of Sigmundskron.

'Call him Greif,' said the baroness, 'after his father.'

'Call him Kraft, for his grandfather,' said Berbel to Hilda, when they were alone.

'He has bright eyes,' said Greif. 'He shall be Sigmund.' And Sigmund he was called. Rex said nothing at first and could not be induced to give any opinion in the matter, though he strongly supported Greif's suggestion after it was once made.

Rex was thinking and his thoughts were very much confused. He would have greatly preferred to spend the festal day in solitude, but this was not possible, and he did his best to join in the rejoicings with a glad face. His efforts were successful, and he made a speech at the family dinner, half jesting, half in earnest, as he proposed Hilda's health, and the child's.

'I am much more accustomed to speaking in public than you would imagine,' he said, 'for I have often made long speeches among students, of which the beginning was beer, the middle beer and the end more beer. For that matter, Greif has done the same, and I have been among those who applauded his eloquence. This, however, is a very different affair —as you will no doubt perceive. For, instead of students, I have two noble dames and a philistine for my audience, and instead of beer and Alma Mater, I have for a subject the beauty, the virtues and the deeds of Sigmund von Sigmundskron and of his own especial alma mater, his dear mother.

'I must trust to her, in the unavoidable absence of Baron Sigmund, due to a tendency to sleep, superinduced by baptism and other things, to convey to him the substance of my words. Nearly a thousand years ago, if there be any truth in history, Sigmund the Bright-eyed came hither with his men and built this hall, in which we are now to drink the health of another bright-eyed Sigmund. In this very place, perhaps upon this very spot, he feasted and wassailed with his warriors, and drained his horn to the future glories of his name.

'His grand old spirit is with us tonight, rejoicing as we rejoice, quaffing the brown *Walhalla*-brew while we sip the nectar of the Rhine Nixies. For many a long year he has sat gloomy and mournful and full of sadness before his untasted horn, watching with his wonderful eyes the single silken thread that bore all the fate of his race, hoping and not daring to hope, fearing and refusing to fear—he who dared all things and feared nothing.'

Rex paused a moment and his colour changed a little. There was a ring of deepest emotion in his voice when he continued.

'The thread has not been broken,' he said. 'The strain was fearful and the danger greater than can be told. One of the silken strands parted, the other has borne the weight that was meant for both. One of the two beings, in whom ran that good and true blood, was taken—in glory; the other is left—to be, in peace, the mother of many a brave Sigmund yet unborn, the mother, first, of him to whom we have given today the spotless name his fathers bore.'

He paused again and lifted high the great beaker of old Rhine wine.

'She—our dear Hilda, can neither guess nor know the love we bear her,' he said, and suddenly the fire that was so rarely seen flashed in his eyes. 'But she shall know it and feel it, one day, in the love we shall bear her son. Drink, all of you the best health the world holds! Drink to Hilda and to Sigmund the younger, drink to the great spirit of the first Sigmund, and to all his glorious line forever! Drink to the hope that, as a thousand years ago he drank to Hilda, so we may be draining this health to a son of Hilda's who may sit here a thousand years from today! To Hilda! To Sigmund! *Hoch*, Sigmundskron, *Hoch!*'

The four voices rang together, even the baroness joining in the cheer. Rex and Greif drained their glasses to the last drop, and each tapped the rim upon his nail; then, with one accord, as though to carry out the ancient custom to its barbaric completeness, both dashed their beakers against the opposite wall, so that they were shivered into a thousand splinters. It is a strange old manner, and the purpose of it is that a glass honoured by a noble and solemn health, may never be defiled by ordinary use again.

Rex sat down in his place and did not speak for some time. He was overcome by an emotion altogether beyond his own comprehension. Unconsciously, in proposing the health, he had identified himself altogether with the race of which he spoke, and for the first time in his life had lost himself in the excitement of the moment. He tried to recall what he had said, but his heart was beating so fast that he could hardly think. He had not meant to say much, he had assuredly not prepared the little speech, and he had most certainly not expected to be carried away by his own words.

Hitherto, when he had been obliged to speak of anything with a certain degree of feeling, out of regard for others, he had been conscious of coldly picking and choosing his expressions to suit the sentiment he was supposed to entertain. He had thought he could do the same now; he had begun with a trivial jest about student life; he had been enticed into a bit of rhetoric about old Sigmund; he had forgotten himself altogether when he spoke of Hilda; and he had ended in a sort of burst of enthusiasm that would have done credit to a hot-headed boy of twenty. He was altogether unconscious as to whether his hearers had been pleased or not.

The baroness, whose feeling about Sigmundskron almost amounted to a religious fervour, sat quite still for a few seconds, and then dried her eyes cautiously as though she were afraid of being noticed. Hilda looked at Rex, wondering what the real nature of the strange man might be, pleased by what he had said and yet surprised that he should have said so much. Rex met her fixed gaze and turned his head away instantly. Greif took a fresh glass. 'Your health, my dear Rex,' he said. He always called him Rex from old habit.

'Your health, dear cousin Horst!' exclaimed Hilda.

Rex started, and took the beaker nearest to him.

'I drink to Hilda's mother,' he said in an odd voice. He looked towards Frau von Sigmundskron, but in her place there seemed to sit another woman, one so like Hilda's self that no human eye could have detected a point in which the one did not resemble the other. He raised the glass to his lips. It was empty, and his lips met only the air.

'Fill before drinking!' laughed Greif.

Rex's hand trembled, as he set down the goblet. The mistake was rectified in an instant and Rex drank the baroness's health. This time as he looked at her, he saw her white hair and delicate thin face in all their reality. The shadow was gone. He had pledged its emptiness in an empty glass.

That night his light burned late, and the owls, if they had looked, might have seen his shadow pass and repass many hundreds of times behind the curtain of the open window. Hour after hour he paced his lonely room, asking himself the meaning of what was happening in his brain. It seemed to him that he was suffering from an extraordinary hallucination, which he had indulged until it had taken possession of his whole being.

Again and again he went back to the first beginnings of his fancy, recalling the time when he had begun to construct out of nothing a love for himself in the past, imagining for Hilda an imaginary mother, who should have been his own imaginary wife. He cursed the puerility of the thought, and yet returned to it again and again in search of the sweet, sad peace he had so often found in his fancied memories.

But that was gone. The scenes he had created grew dull and lost their colour, he forgot the very points which had most pleased him once. And yet he was conscious of acute suffering. It was but a few hours since he had lifted that empty goblet to his lips, and had seen distinctly before him the shadow he loved so well. How was it possible? There was a chair—he had lifted his hand thus—and she had been there. Suddenly his arm was arrested in the very act of the gesture, he grew icy cold, and his stony eyes set themselves in a horrified stare. A cry of despair burst from his lips.

'Great God in Heaven—I love Hilda!'

That was all, and there was silence in the lonely chamber for many hours.

Chapter 26

Day had dawned when Rex staggered to his feet, scarcely conscious of where he was, nor of what had happened, knowing only that he had spent many hours in utmost agony. The sight of the familiar objects in the room recalled the whole train of thought which had preceded the shock he had received. Slowly and painfully he began to walk up and down as he had done during the night. It was not possible for his strong nature to remain for any great length of time in a state of stupor, nor was there any danger of his being again affected as he had been at first. After a little while he grew calm and collected, and he re-alised that something must be done immediately.

He had found the key to all his vain imaginings, to all his varied moods, to the strange disturbance of his faculties in Hilda's presence. He loved his brother's wife, and he knew it. He sought for a remedy, as though he had been assailed by the plague.

There was a medicine close by, in the drawer of his desk, which would cure love or anything else. He knew that. It would be the affair of a moment, the pulling of a trigger, an explosion he should scarcely hear, and there would be no more Rex. The temptation was strong, and moreover there was a tendency in his nature towards suicide which he knew was inherited. It would be a fitting end to the useless life he had led, the son of such a father and of such a mother. No one would guess why he was dead, and it would be soon done. Then indeed there would be no trace left of the old times before the tragedy of Greifenstein. It would be the last page in the history, as he himself was the last survivor, except Greif, and Greif had a right to be happy.

A right—and why? What had Greif done to deserve Hilda more than Rex? He was younger, handsomer, and more fortunate. That was the point. Greif's luck had saved him, and what was life to him was death to Rex. It was pure good fortune. There had not been a struggle or the least desire for one. Rex himself had done everything in his power to push on the marriage, and could blame no one for the result. Greif was happy and Rex was broken-hearted. If Greif had refused to marry Hilda, Rex might perhaps have won her, supplying by his own wealth the fortune which should have been hers through Greif's ruin.

Luck indeed! There was Greif, nameless and penniless in reality, but unconscious of the awful misfortunes he had escaped, delivered from the borrowed name that was stained, and invested with one more noble and spotless than the other had ever been, lord of Sigmundskron, husband of Hilda, father of a new race. What more could the heart of man desire? That was what Greif appeared to be, and was, so far as he himself was aware. And this—Rex drew from a secret place his father's last letter—this was the real Greif whom none knew but Rex.

He read the words carefully many times. Then he leaned back

in his chair and gazed long through the open window at the distant forest. At last he rose and lit a candle. It might be best that he should die now, but if so, this secret must die with him. He had only preserved the writing in case Greif refused to marry Hilda, and now they were not only married, but there was an heir born to them. He held the letter in the midst of the flame, and then the envelope till both were consumed to ashes, and the summer breeze that blew into the room wafted the black remains, light as threads of gossamer, from the table to the floor, and away into dark corners to crumble into dust.

No one could ever guess the secret now, thought Rex, not dreaming that by a strange train of circumstances another letter had been stored away beneath the same roof but yesterday in the safe keeping of honest Berbel. Greif was safe, thought Rex, as he laid his hand upon the drawer again, to take the other thing from its place. He, Rex, would leave no tell-tale letters behind. It should be sharp, short, complete and decisive. There would be some regrets for the lonely man who was gone, and they would never dream how he had purchased their security with his life. He laid the weapon upon the table before him.

Their security? Surely, that was but a theatrical phrase, with no meaning, spoken to make his miserable death seem grand, or at least worthy. Security implied danger, and what danger could his wretched life bring to Hilda or her husband? The thought that Hilda could ever love him was monstrous, the suggestion that he could ever speak loving words to her he loved, since he knew who she was, stung him like a blow on the mouth. That splendid angel could no more stoop from her superb purity, than he, Rex, could have flung a handful of mud in her divine face—no more than he could have entertained for one horrible instant the thought of sullying what God had made so white. He had a bitter scorn of that word security, so soon as it had flashed unspoken through his mind; he cursed his own soul for the contemptible thought. And in his self-abasement, he was heroic, unconsciously, as heroes are. He was to die, but it was for honour's sake, and not for any foul wrong done to man or woman.

He could say that, with a clear conscience. From the moment when he had felt the truth, and had known that he loved his brother's wife, he had been tortured almost past endurance. Not one sweet thought of Hilda had entered his heart, there was nothing there but the stabbing pain of his own folly, and the scaring consciousness that his folly had ended in the most appalling of all truths. There was nothing in his mind but a relentless hatred of himself, a stunning and sudden comprehension of what he had allowed himself to dream.

Even, if there had been no other reason, he deserved to die, he judged himself worthy of death. It was for honour's sake— how could he live and face them all, knowing what he was, even if they did not know? There must be an end, and there could be but one end to his sufferings. He put out his hand and drew the weapon into his grasp.

What was honour, that he should die for it? He had believed in very little beyond himself during forty years, but he believed in honour and had been reckoned a most honourable man among those who had known him. He had risked his life for it many a time, but now, for its sake, he was to take his own life without risk, deliberately, as he would have shot a wild beast, as he would have crushed a poisonous reptile under his heel. What was this thing? Was it a fact, a shadow, an idea, a breath, a god or a devil? What was it, for which such deeds had been done, for which old Greifenstein and Rieseneck had slain his mother and laid down their lives in such stern haste?

A man might well ask what he was to die for, thought Rex. Why did it seem base in him to live, even though every moment of his existence were to be spent in rooting out what he so hated, in burning out what had defiled his soul; and why did it seem noble and brave to die? To die was easy as drawing a breath, to live was a hard and fearful thing. Yet honour said, Die and be satisfied that you are doing right. Did honour always command what was easiest for a man to do? Again, what was it? He had but a few moments left to live, and in a lifetime he had served honour scrupulously.

What if it were but a myth, but a legend of fools, a destroy-ing idol worshipped by brave and brainless visionaries, who had more courage than intelligence, more desire to do right than discernment to sift right from wrong? Pity that so many daring, honest men should have been spitted on rapiers, cloven with sabres, riddled with bullet-holes, for the sake of a vain breath, emptier than the glass he had raised to his lips last night! And yet—he might search, and deny, and argue, and scoff—honour remained a fact. No, not a fact, a law. A law having rules, and conditions and penalties and rewards all defined in the human heart, all equally beyond the range of the human intelligence. His brain could not imagine a question in which honour was concerned, to which his heart did not give the right answer instantaneously, quicker than the brain itself could have solved the problem.

And what the heart told him was right, indubitably and in-disputably right. Then he was to die for something he felt but could not understand, for the decision of some power within him, wiser and swifter and surer than the cool head to which he had trusted so long. To call that power the heart was nonsense, as absurd as to call it a function of the brain. It was distinct from both, it had a being of its own, independent, dominating, tre-mendous in its effects. In danger the head said, stop; the heart said, go on. And honour, then, was the spontaneous reasoning of this superior power, whatever it might be.

But, if it reasoned, so unfailingly and so surely about some things, why had it nothing to say about others? Why could this faultless judge decide of nothing save right and wrong? From habit, doubtless, because we refer no other questions to him. No, for when we ask a question of ourselves, or when one is asked of us by another, we do not always know beforehand which part of ourselves will answer. Mystery of mysteries, to be solved only by assuming that man has an immortal soul. Idle waste of time, thought Rex, looking at the cartridge in his revolver and then slowly setting back the hammer. An idle waste of time, to think of such matters.

Honour or no honour, heart or no heart, the mysterious power within him bade him die. Die, then, and be done with it. He held the weapon in his hand, ready to do the deed. One second, and all would be over. At one end of that polished dark blue barrel was life, with all its dishonour, with all its sufferings, with all the monstrous blackness of evil it held, the life of an honest man who loved his brother's wife in spite of himself, and loathed the thought.

At the other end was death, swift, sharp, sure, the answer to all questions, the solution of all ills, the medicine for all earthly woe. Rex laid the revolver down, and drew back a little from the table. Was it possible that he was killing himself merely to escape suffering, to rid himself of pain, to desist from a contest too bitter for his endurance? If that were it, Rex was a miserable coward, and not the honourable man he had thought himself. With the instinct that prompts many men to do the same at such moments, he rose from his chair and went to the mirror. He started when he saw himself in it.

It was as though the marvellous look of youth that had clung to him so long, had fallen from his face, and left an old man's features behind. His skin was livid, his eyes were sunken, the flesh was drawn and white about his nostrils and brows and temples. His hair and beard, matted with cold sweat, hung in wild disorder about his head and face. It was strange that the bright summer's morning should even seem to change their colour— or was it a defect in the glass? He looked nearer, and he scarcely dared to believe his eyes. There were grey hairs, whole locks of grey, in the soft brown masses. He had heard of such quick changes but had never believed them real. He gazed in silence at the reflexion of himself for some minutes.

'I am an old man,' he said softly, and turned away, forgetting what he had come to see—whether he were a coward or not.

He went back to the table and sat down, supporting his head in his two hands. He realised what he had suffered, and the question returned to his agonised brain. Was he killing himself to escape torture, or out of his love of honour? He wondered bitterly whether any pain could be worse in the future than what he had borne during this night, and during the hours since the dawn had broken in upon him. It seemed impossible. Then on a sudden, the bright image of Hilda burst upon his sight as he pressed his closed lids with the palms of his hands. Hilda was there before him in all her splendour, he could see every line of her face, every shade of its glorious colouring, every twist of her yellow hair.

The light streamed upon him from the whole vision, and he was looking into the bright depths of her eyes. It was exquisite delight, and yet he felt overwhelmed with shame that he should dare to look and love. It was like him to fight to the utmost. With a supreme effort he opened his eyes, and suffered himself to be dazzled by the violent daylight. The vision was gone, but he understood what he must bear, without a sign of pain, if he were to look upon the reality. And yet he knew his own strength. Face to face with Hilda he could have forced his stony eyes to dullness and his features to an indifferent calm. He could do that and not fail. The clear memory of her he had received in that moment told him how much he was able to resist, but showed him also what that resistance would cost; above all it had exhibited to him in all beauty and clearness of detail that upon which he was never to look again.

The pain had been sharp and quick, and was scarcely distinguished from the momentary, involuntary happiness. But he could bear it, and worse. It was not to escape it that he had determined to end his life. Nor would he do the fatal deed if he were sure that he were impelled to it merely in the hope of escaping a little suffering, or much. Whatever his faults might be, he was brave still; braver now, perhaps, than he had ever been. There had been a time when all human action, or inaction, had seemed to him so indifferent in itself and in its consequences, that he had almost scoffed at the idea of contrasting courage with cowardice. But he had not then been put to the test as he was now.

It was not the fear of what he must bear that drove him from existence. He was sure of that. He resolutely set himself to think of what life would be in the future, if he chose it, and if he stayed where he was. It was clear that he could live, if he pleased, and meet Hilda, and Greif, and Hilda's mother, and keep a calm face and a steady voice when he was with them. If it were a question of courage, that would be the least courageous course. It would be easier to suffer anything than to put himself beyond the possibility of ever seeing Hilda again. He owned, in bitter self-contempt, that this was absolutely true.

The sting of death was there, in the choice of total extinction, in the act of leaving all that he loved, as well as in the extermination of that self which held the power to love. But for one thought, life would still be sweet. All the torment of an existence made dreadful by the hopelessness of an unquenchable passion would be nothing, as compared with the hourly joy of seeing Hilda and of hearing her voice. That would compensate for all things, no matter how horrible, except one; but that one outweighed the rest. The certainty that his whole life hereafter must be one long act of treachery to Greif must overbalance everything else.

That was the point of honour he had sought to explain. He thought he had been mistaken, and that his self-hatred and self-contempt had really but little to do with his decision. It was neither for his own sake, nor for Hilda's that he must leave the world so suddenly, but for Greif's. Greif was his trusted friend, Greif was his cousin, Greif was his brother. To feel what he felt for that brother's wife was treachery, no matter how he should hide his feelings or fight against them. The time would assuredly come when he must hate this man, as he now loved him, and his jealousy would take some active shape, and do Greif some real injury.

At any cost, such a catastrophe must be warded off. To leave the two in their happiness and to go away, plunging again into the old existence he hated, would be of no avail. Rex knew human nature well, and was wise enough to include himself in what he knew. He was sure that, sooner or later, his resolution to keep away from Sigmundskron would break down, as much through the insistence of Greif and Hilda, as on account of his own inclinations. Here, too, the humanity of the man showed itself, as well as the weakest points in his self-knowledge and reasoning.

Rex might and could have left Sigmundskron then, and his courage would assuredly have kept him away longer than he suspected, even long enough, perhaps, to cool the heat of his passion and make his return both possible and safe. Had he been called upon to decide the case for another he would in all probability have advised such a course, for he would then have taken into consideration the value of life as a factor in the question. But, for his own part, he held his existence as of little worth, and it would not have needed half of what he now suffered to prompt him to part with it.

At any time during the last ten years, a severe shock to his feelings, or a fit of unconquerable melancholy, would have been enough to suggest to him the advisability of making a precipitate exit from the stage on which he found himself. Death had long possessed attractions for him, and it was long since life had offered him anything for the enjoyment of which he would have taken the trouble to undergo any annoyance whatsoever. Life seemed to him such a very trivial matter that he felt no hesitation in abandoning it, and he only put off the doing so for a few minutes now, out of curiosity to understand more fully the motives of his action.

It was so very simple to pull the trigger of a pistol, and so very complicated to begin a new existence, just when he had believed that his wanderings were over. The future was inexpressibly dismal, lonely and painful, and death was such a natural and easy escape from it. These reflexions were assuredly present, unknown to himself, in the midst of the many thoughts that crowded his brain in that supreme hour, and they must have influenced him in forming his ultimate decision, though he did not guess that they were at work. He saw only the alternative possibilities of an ignoble life or of an honourable death, and he chose the more pleasant, the easier, the quicker. In the twinkling of an eye it would be done, and here would be no more Rex.

Those left behind would think kindly of him; they would suppose he had been mad, and in due time they would congratulate themselves that he had not lived to be a burthen to them. Rex had not any great belief in human sympathy, nor in the regret people felt for the dead. The fact that he could not place credence in the existence of a future life could be traced to his indifference about the present, and in its turn made him sceptical concerning the beliefs of others. Protestations of friendship or affection could mean but little to a man who had scarcely ever expressed either, except from a desire not to seem brutal or unfeeling.

It was true that he was profoundly attached to Greif, but his instinct told him that his attachment was only half reciprocated. He loved Hilda in a way of his own, as men have seldom loved, but he knew that Hilda's thoughts of him did not go farther than a vague half-friendly, half-cousinly regard. It was not likely that he should expect of either a passionate grief over his end, or any exaggerated mourning for his death. The idea that the fact of the suicide, independently of his own personality, would add a deeper shadow to the memories of Greifenstein troubled him very little. He had seen how Greif had forgotten the horror of the tragedy in his love of Hilda, and since Hilda would still be at hand, she would help him to forget this also.

With the coolness of a man of his age, he calculated the extent of Greif's possible distress and reckoned it insignificant. With the generosity of his exceptional nature, he admitted that his fondness for his brother did not depend upon any principle of reciprocity. If he had chosen, eighteen months earlier, to remain alive instead of following the example of his unhappy father, it had been for Greif's sake that he had lived, though Greif had never known it; if now, knowing the thing that was in his heart, he chose to die, it was for Greif's sake still.

He was glad that he was not doing such a deed merely to escape suffering himself. The thought would have stayed his hand, preserving him to undergo the most terrible ordeal he could imagine; whereas, in its absence he could spare himself that, at least, without a pang, while ridding Greif of the presence of a traitor.

The word was too strong, but Rex could not see that it was so. It seemed to him that by all the wild indulgence of his imagination he had fostered that growth of which he had so suddenly been made aware. He could no longer separate the intention from the fact, and he believed himself guilty of both alike, though he was in reality but the victim of circumstances and the sport of a cruel destiny. Everything combined to bring about the unavoidable result, the fatal tendency to suicide that existed in his blood, the excessive emotion of a heart unused to feel, the despair of an absolutely hopeless love, the horror of a self that seemed all at once blackened by the most hideous treachery, even the constitutional fearlessness of a man to whom the moment of death offered no terrors; everything was present which could drive Rex over the brink, and everything was absent which might have held him back.

He rose once more from his chair and made a few steps in the room, with downcast eyes and folded arms. Methodical and rational to the end, he collected his thoughts for the last time and reviewed the result of his melancholy reflexions, forcing himself to state the facts with the utmost plainness and conciseness, as though he were summing up the case before the jury of his faculties, upon whom depended the final verdict. Too wise to die in vain, too brave to die for a selfish motive, too noble to be influenced by any fear of death itself, he was determined that the deed should be done calmly, in the fullest consciousness of its importance to himself and others, to the fullest satisfaction of his own enlightened reasoning.

That his present condition was wholly intolerable, he refused to believe, for he would not admit that there could be anything too hard for him to endure if his own inclinations were alone considered. It was possible that his strength might break down if he were exposed to such an ordeal as life with Hilda and his brother during many years; but he should certainly be aware, in such a case, of the failing of his powers, and he would be able to keep his own secret until the end, or, if not, to do a year hence what he meant to do now. He was far too old, and far too wise, to take his life from romantic and scarcely defined motives, seeking nothing but relief from a half hysteric pain, asking of death nothing but the forgetfulness of life and love.

One watching him might have seen as much, from his face and manner. Being about to die, he looked more like a strong man humiliated by the shame of his own deeds than like a boy in a fit of despair. The look of compact strength that belonged to him was not gone, and his step was firm and even. His face was haggard, pale and drawn, but its expression was calm and determined, full of the dignity of a man superior to all hasty impulses, and very far removed from the influence of all base motives. And his outward appearance represented very truly the moral position he had taken and held with such tenacity.

A wise man might have differed from him, but could not have despised him; a religious person would have been sorry for him, but could not have condemned his profound determination to do what was just according to his light, in perfect sacrifice of himself, to the atonement for an involuntary wrong; a weak man would have envied his strength, a strong man might well have admired his calm power of reasoning in the face of death, and a man of heart would have felt for him.

He stood still before the table and looked out through the open window into the bright summer air. Presently he spoke to himself in a low, distinct voice.

'It is best,' he said decisively. 'I, Horst von Rieseneck, stand here to die, because I love my brother's wife. I die of my own free will. I die because I will not live and feel such a thing in my heart, because I will not be dishonoured in my own estimation. I obey no man, I fear no man, I am influenced by no man. It is my own decision, and I have a right to it. It is my own life and I have a right to take it. It is my own love and I have a right to kill it. I do not die to escape suffering, but the inward conviction of dishonour, which no honest man is called upon to bear. I die in the full possession of all my senses and faculties, and if any of them were disturbed I would wait, in order to judge more calmly. That is all I have to say, I believe.'

It was the last satisfaction Rex could give himself in the world he was about to leave. His intelligence demanded of him that his end should be calm, determined and yet unprejudiced, and that to the very last he should remain open to the conviction of error should any sufficient reason or reasons occur to him within a reasonable time. But no reason why he should hold his hand presented itself, and he was aware that he had reached the supreme moment. He was glad that he had not done in haste what he was now going to do upon mature consideration, for he had always loved to be justified in his actions. But since the result of so much thought had only strengthened his first intention, there was no object in delaying the end any longer.

Having made up his mind definitely, he crossed the room and unlocked the door, reflecting that, since he was to be found dead in a few minutes, there was no use in making a mystery of the fact nor in obliging people to break the door. Keen, cool and practical to the end, the action was characteristic of him. He came back to the table a last time and took the revolver in his hand. He examined the lock, raised the weapon steadily and planted the cold muzzle firmly against his temple. Then he turned his eyes towards the open window and pulled the trigger.

The hammer fell with an inoffensive snap, and Rex frowned. But he had not the slightest intention of relinquishing his purpose. With incredible coolness, he went to a corner of the room and took a box of perfectly fresh cartridges from the drawer where he kept his ammunition; after carefully removing the charges from the revolver, he reloaded the chambers, one by one, raised the hammer and resumed his position. Some moments elapsed before he again lifted the weapon to his head. The incident had shaken his nerves, and he was determined to die in full consciousness and appreciation of his act.

'I wish I could flatter myself that it is for Hilda's sake,' he thought. 'But as I cannot, let this be the end.'

The castle clock began to toll the hour of noon, as he raised the revolver a second time.

CHAPTER 27

When Berbel had hidden the precious letter among her possessions, she had firmly intended to keep it for some time, before giving it to its owner, but she had not excluded from her calculations the possibility of consulting Hilda upon the matter. In the hurry and confusion of the christening day it had seemed to the good woman that she might wait an indefinite time, leaving Greif in ignorance of the writing, while he grew daily better able to bear such a sudden and vivid quickening of past horrors, as must be brought about in his mind when he should read his father's message. It appeared to Berbel both wiser and kinder to hide the letter for a long time.

The day had passed off to the satisfaction of every one, and Berbel certainly deserved a share in the success of the christening. She had been indefatigable, wise and provident in all things, just as she had been in the old times when a penny meant more than a gold piece now. She had superintended everything and everybody, from the baby Sigmund to Greif himself, from the christening cake to the potato dumplings of the labourers' feast. Nothing had escaped her quick eyes, or her ready memory, and all had gone well to the end.

But when all was over Berbel was tired, and she was fain to acknowledge that she was not the woman she had been twenty years before. She was tired with the long day's work and slept, instead of meditating upon the letter, as she had meant to do. Moreover sleep brought a wiser judgment to her refreshed brain, and when she awoke in the morning she resolved to consult Hilda without delay. Once more she opened her treasure safe and took out the sealed envelope, and looked at it attentively; not that she meant to run the risk of carrying it about with her, but because she wished to fix its appearance in her mind, in order to describe it to Hilda.

There was nothing remarkable about the outward look of the letter except, perhaps, the superscription, in which Wastei had detected something of old Greifenstein's roughness. But Berbel thought it quite natural that he should have addressed it simply, 'To my son Greif,' as he had done. To her mind it was more affectionate, and looked better than if he had written 'Seiner Hochwohlgeboren Herrn Greif von Greifenstein.' She looked closely at the thing, turning it over and examining it with the utmost attention. But there was nothing worth noticing beyond what she saw at first. The writing was large, heavy and clear, and the envelope was sealed with wax bearing the impress of the Greifenstein arms. There could not be more than one sheet of paper inside, for the letter was very thin.

Berbel was somewhat surprised to find it in such good condition, considering that it had lain between the linings of a coat for more than a year and a half, but she reflected that during that time it had been carefully preserved, most probably in a chest or drawer in the recesses of the Jew's shop, and that, after all, there was no particular reason why it should be torn, or stained, or otherwise injured, as though it had been handed about from one person to another ever since it had been written. The pristine freshness of the paper was certainly a little tarnished, and there were a few insignificant creases on its smooth surface; but, on the whole, the letter looked as though it might have been written but a few weeks before it had fallen into Berbel's hands. It struck the good woman that Hilda would certainly wish to hear the whole story of Wastei's discovery, which was strange enough, indeed; and that when she had heard it, that would not be all, for if they decided to give Greif the letter at once, he also must know whence it came.

For a moment Berbel conceived it possible that it might not, after all, contain a farewell communication, since there was nothing to show that it had really been written on the fatal night, but the idea would not bear examination, and when she laid the envelope once more in its place in her box she was firmly persuaded that it contained old Greifenstein's last words to his son. The longer she thought of this, the more she wondered how on the previous day she could have meditated keeping it from Greif for any length of time. Her motive had assuredly been to save him pain if possible, but at present she saw the whole matter in a different light.

At the most, she thought, he might be saddened for a day or two by this message from another world, but it was better that he should suffer a little at present than that he should continue to fancy that his father had forgotten him in his last moments. Berbel was by no means without her share of the national military instinct, which will face annoyance in any shape, or impose it upon others rather than allow a duty of any kind to be eluded, or the execution of its mandates postponed. Better for Greif, she thought, that the matter should be settled at once, better for herself, better for everybody. Delay might be fatal. She herself might die suddenly, and the letter would be found among her belongings.

What would be thought of her by her beloved mistress if it were discovered that she had concealed so precious a document? Or Greif might die, without ever knowing that his father had written—a hundred misfortunes might occur to prevent the letter reaching the hands for which it was destined. There was no time like the present, thought the sturdy Berbel, and no day like today for doing unpleasant things which could not be avoided.

It was necessary to find an opportunity of speaking with Hilda alone, without danger of interruption, and as soon as possible. It was yet early morning, and Hilda was in all probability still asleep, dreaming of the festivities of the previous day, but it would be important to know whether Greif was up or not, and whether he intended to leave the castle during the morning. Berbel left her room and went down to the court. The men were sure to know if Greif had meant to go into the forest or to stay at home, as he would certainly have given orders for someone to accompany him. He was not like his father, who had loved to tramp all day alone, wearying himself out, and coming home late in the evening, in the perpetual attempt to make the days seem short. Greif was by nature gregarious, and was not satisfied with the society of his dogs, but usually took a couple of men with him, when he could not prevail upon Rex to join in his expeditions.

Berbel went into the court and asked a few questions, carelessly enough. It was a warm morning and the men seemed sleepy after the carousal of the previous night. None of them had received any orders for the day, and those who had anything to do went about their occupations in a leisurely fashion, slowly and deliberately, while those who had no work sat together in a shady corner smoking their porcelain pipes, and discussing the festive reminiscences of the christening, enjoying their idleness as very strong men can, who habitually work hard and say little. It was evident that nothing would be done on that day, and it was probable that Greif would stay at home. Berbel turned away and went towards the entrance of the hall. She was about to go in when she heard footsteps behind her, and on looking round saw Wastei striding up with his long, greyhound step.

'God greet you, Frau Berbel,' he said, coming nearer.

He was no longer arrayed in his magnificent velvet coat as on the previous day. Such finery was only for the greatest festivities, and at present he wore no jacket at all, but a rough waistcoat with metal buttons, which hung loose and open over his shirt, and he had a bundle under his arm.

'Good morning, Wastei,' answered Berbel, fixing her sharp eyes upon him with a look of inquiry. She wondered why he had come.

'I have brought you something,' he remarked, standing still before her, and tapping the bundle he carried with one hand.

'More trout?' inquired Berbel with a twitching smile. 'There is no gold to be picked up today, Master Wastei.'

'Unfortunately,' he answered. 'But then one can never know,' he added reflectively.

'Out with it!' exclaimed Berbel who was not in a humour for long conversations.

'Out with it is soon said,' returned the other. 'It is a serious matter. Do you think I can chatter like a magpie without thinking of what I am to say?'

'Then think, and be quick about it, or I shall go in.'

'Oh, if you are in a hurry, you may take the bundle without any explanation,' replied Wastei, holding it out towards her. Berbel took it, and felt it, as though trying to guess what it contained.

'What is it?' she asked at length, as her imagination failed to suggest the nature of the contents.

'It is my coat,' said Wastei. 'The old wolf's coat, if you like it better.'

'And what am I to do with your coat?' inquired Berbel. In spite of the question she had thrust the bundle under one arm and held it firmly, with the evident intention of keeping it.

'When you have given the letter to the baron, you might be so kind as to mend the pocket for me,' said Wastei calmly.

'But I told you I should perhaps wait some time before giving the letter.'

'Yes—but you have thought about that in the night,' answered Wastei keenly. 'You will not wait much longer than today.'

'What makes you think that?'

'It would not be like you, Frau Berbel,' said the man, with affected indifference.

'Perhaps not,' replied Berbel, smiling unconsciously at the subtle flattery bestowed upon her scrupulously honest character. 'Perhaps not. I had thought of it, as you say.'

'And I had thought that unless the old wolf's coat were there with the hole in the pocket, Frau Berbel might not be able to make it quite clear that Master Wastei had spoken the truth. But if the truth is quite clear, why then—' he paused, as though he did not care what might happen in such a case.

Berbel looked at him for a moment, and then laughed a little, a phenomenon which with her was exceedingly unusual.

'You are really not stupid at all,' she remarked. The ghost of a smile played about Wastei's thin lips as he turned his eyes upon her. Their expression was at once keen, cunning and good-natured.

'Nobody ever said I was particularly dull,' he answered.

'Then you want me to show the coat, together with the letter?'

'Of course.'

'But when they know that it belonged to Herr von Greifenstein, they will wish to keep it, will they not?'

'Of course,' repeated Wastei.

'And then, when they find that you have bought it honestly, they will want to buy it of you.'

'Of course.'

'And you gave twenty *marks* for it?'

'Twenty *marks*.'

'And you think they will give you more for it, though I shall tell them just what it cost you at the Jew's?'

'Of course.'

'You are not stupid, Wastei. You are not stupid at all. But I thought you imagined the coat would bring you luck. I wonder that you want to part with it!'

'Do you? Is it not luck if I get more for it than it cost at the Jew's?' The man's eyes twinkled as he spoke.

'There is certainly something in what you say,' answered Berbel. 'I am not surprised that you got it so cheap. You understand a bargain, I see.'

'And you will be glad, too, Frau Berbel, when you have to explain how the letter was found,' said Wastei thoughtfully. 'You will be glad to have the coat in your hands to show, and if they like, they can go to the Jew and he will tell them that I bought it only the other day.'

'You are quite sure you are telling the truth, Wastei?'

'I always do, now that I have a gun license,' he answered. 'You see, the truth is best for people who have anything to lose.' 'Fie, Wastei!' exclaimed Berbel, half inclined to smile at his odd philosophy, but unwilling to let him see that she could appreciate a jest upon so moral a subject.

'It is true, Frau Berbel. Not that I ever lied much, either, though I have told some smart tales to the foresters in the old days, when I was a free-shot in the forest, and they were always trying to catch me with a hare in my pocket—and to you too, Frau Berbel, when I used to make you think the game was all right. What did it matter, so long as you had it to eat, you and— well, those were queer times. I suppose you have game whenever you like, now, do you not?'

'Ay, Wastei—I sometimes could not find any lead in your hares—'

'That made them lighter to carry and more wholesome to eat,' observed the other with a chuckle.

'And I had my doubts about them, of course—'

'But you did not ask many questions—not very many—did you?'

'Not always, Wastei,' answered Berbel with a twitch of the lips. 'You see I thought it best to believe you, and to treat you like an honest fellow. There were reasons—'

'Better than doubts, especially when the hare was dead and lying on your kitchen table. Well, well, those times are gone now, and if I ever shot a hare or a roebuck without lead, or pulled the trout out of the stream without making a hole in his nose, why I have forgotten it, and I will not do it again, I promise you. I am growing old, Frau Berbel, I am growing old.'

'And wise, I hope—'

'When a man is young he can do without a gun license,' observed Wastei. 'When the years begin to come, he wants that and other things too. May-wine in May, Frau Berbel, and brown beer in October.'

'And all the cherry spirits you can pick up, between times, I suppose. What are the other things?'

'A good house to live in, and a good wife to roll the potato dumplings. These are two things that are good when the grey years come.'

'You put the house before the wife, I see,' remarked Berbel.

'Because if I had a good house I could have the good wife

fast enough. Wastei is not so dull as he looks. He has looked about him in the world. Ay, Frau Berbel, now if you were thinking of being married and had your choice of two men, would you choose the one with a house or the one without? It is a simple question.'

'Very simple, Master Wastei,' answered Berbel, stiffening her stiff neck a little. 'So simple that it is of no use to think about it, nor even to ask it. When do you want your coat back?'

'I want a coat, but not that one—whenever you please. But do not hurry yourself, for I shall not catch cold, and my sweetheart does not care whether I have one or not.'

'So you have a sweetheart, have you?'

'Ay, and a treasure, too—in my waistcoat pocket,' explained Wastei, showing the shining edge of the gold piece he had received on the previous day. 'She has yellow hair, like the lady Hilda's, and a golden heart like Frau Berbel's—I only wish she were as big.'

'*Fie*, Wastei—making compliments at this time of day, and to an old woman!'

'Old friends, old logs, old spirits,' observed Wastei. 'We have known each other a long time, Frau Berbel, in good and bad days, summer and winter, and you have always been the same to me.'

'Small credit for that!' exclaimed Berbel. 'You have done me many a good turn in twenty years, and my ladies too, and you have never got much by it, that I can see—more praise to you!'

'Nonsense!' ejaculated Wastei, who was visibly affected by the speech. 'God greet you, Frau Berbel!' he added, turning away abruptly and leaving her standing alone in the court.

Berbel looked after him for a few seconds, and there was an unusually tender expression in her sharp eyes, as she watched his retreating figure. He had been a wild fellow in his day, a daring poacher, an intrepid drinker of fiery cherry spirits, always the first in a fight and the last out of it, the terror of the head forester and his men, the object of old Greifenstein's inveterate hatred, the admiration of the village maidens for twenty miles around, the central figure in a hundred adventures and hairbreadth escapes of all kinds, and yet, as though he were miraculously preserved from harm, he had always managed to keep out of trouble, and though many a time suspected of making free with the game, yet never convicted, nor even brought to a trial.

It had been impossible to catch him and impossible to prove anything against him. At last the head forester, who had a secret reverence for his extraordinary powers of endurance and unrivalled skill in woodcraft, had made terms with him and employed him as a sort of supernumerary upon the government establishment. From that day, Wastei, who would have waged war to the death with all regular foresters, had surrendered at discretion to the kindness shown him, and had given up poaching forever. Berbel could not help liking him, and being grateful to him for many a good turn he had done the poor ladies at Sigmundskron. She had often distrusted him at first, but after twenty years' acquaintance and friendship she owned, as she watched him stride away, that he had a heart of gold, as he had said of her but a few moments earlier.

It seemed as though circumstances pointed clearly to the course she had intended to pursue, for since Wastei had brought her the coat it was no longer possible to put off the execution of her purpose. She determined to obtain an interview with Hilda as soon as possible and to place both the garment and the letter in her hands. The reasoning she followed in selecting Hilda for her confidence has been sufficiently explained already. The intimacy existing between the two made such a plan seem most natural to her, Hilda's strong and sensible nature made it safe, the difficulty of the mission, so far as Greif was concerned, made it appear wisest to leave the matter to his wife's wisdom and tact. Berbel went upstairs with her bundle under her arm.

Though Hilda had not risen quite so early as her old servant, she was by this time dressed and ready for the morning walk Greif liked so much in the summer time. Berbel met them both in one of the passages, walking quickly, arm in arm, talking and laughing happily as they went. Berbel would have let them pass, seeing that Hilda was not alone, had not the latter stopped and asked a question.

'What have you got there, Berbel?' she inquired, looking at the bundle.

'It is a very important matter,' answered Berbel. 'And if you could spare me a few minutes—'

'Is it really important?' asked Hilda, leaning on her husband's arm.

'Very. And if you could spare the time—' Berbel looked at Greif.

'Very well,' said the latter. 'I have plenty to do, dear. Finish your business with Berbel and meet me on the tower—there is a man waiting for me, I believe.'

Thereupon Greif went on his way down the broad corridor, leaving Hilda and Berbel to their own devices.

'What is it?' asked Hilda, who wanted to lose no time in re-joining her husband.

'It is a very serious affair, and concerns the baron,' answered Berbel. 'Perhaps it would be better if you would come to my room.'

Hilda followed her, wondering what could have happened, and not without some presentiment of evil. When they had reached their destination Berbel carefully bolted the door and turned to her mistress. It was a small bright room, vaulted and whitewashed, simply but comfortably furnished. Hilda sat down and looked up at Berbel's face, somewhat anxiously.

'It is nothing bad,' said Berbel. 'But it will give pain to the baron, and so I consulted you. I have found a letter written to him by Herr von Greifenstein on the night he died. No one but you can give it to him.'

Hilda started slightly. Anything which recalled the fearful tragedy was necessarily painful and disturbing to the peace of her unclouded happiness.

'A letter?' she repeated in a low voice. 'Where did you find it? They searched everywhere for months. Are you quite sure?'

'They might have searched for ever, but for the merest accident,' answered Berbel, beginning to undo her bundle. 'This,' she added, unfolding the velvet garment—'this is the coat Herr von Greifenstein wore when he shot himself.'

Hilda gazed silently at the thing during several seconds, and shuddered at the thoughts it recalled, though she was by no means persuaded that Berbel was not mistaken.

'How do you know it is?' she asked at last.

'It was stolen on that night by one of those city servants who were always at Greifenstein. Your mother did not notice it. The man took it to a Jew, who kept it a year and then hung it up for sale. A few days ago Wastei bought it to wear at the christening.' 'But how did he know?' 'He guessed it, and found these marks.'

Berbel showed the collar of the coat to Hilda, putting her finger on each spot in succession.

'It looks like rust,' said Hilda.

'It is the blood of Herr von Greifenstein,' answered Berbel solemnly. 'The ball went in just below the right ear, as I have heard your mother say more than once.'

'How horrible!' exclaimed Hilda, drawing back, though her eyes remained riveted on the rusty marks.

'It is not gay,' said Berbel grimly. 'Now look here. Do you see the pocket? Yes. Well, do you see that the lining is torn just above it? Good. Herr von Greifenstein wrote his letter and slipped it into his pocket, because he was thinking of other things at that moment, and paid no attention to what he did, which was natural enough, poor gentleman. But instead of putting it into the pocket, he happened to slip it through the slit, so that it fell down between the coat and the lining. Do you see?'

'Yes—and then?'

'And then he pulled the trigger of his pistol and died. The letter was hidden in the coat, the coat was stolen, taken to the Jew's and sold to Wastei eighteen months later, with the letter still in it. And Wastei brought me the letter yesterday, and the coat today. That is the whole history.'

'Where is it—the letter?' asked Hilda in an anxious tone.

Berbel unlocked her little deal chest and withdrew the precious document, which she put into Hilda's hand. Hilda turned it over and over, and looked from it to the coat, and back again to the sealed envelope, reading the address again and again.

'It is a strange story,' she said at last. 'But I do not see that there can be any doubt. O Berbel, Berbel! What do you think there is written inside this little bit of paper?'

'A few words to say goodbye to his son, I suppose,' the woman answered.

'If it were only that—' Hilda did not finish the sentence, but her face grew slowly pale and she stared vacantly out of the window, while the hand that held the letter rested on her knee.

'I do not see that it can be anything else,' said Berbel quietly. 'It cannot be a will, for they found everything about the property. What could the poor gentleman say except "Goodbye," and "God bless you"? It seems very simple to me. Of course I knew that it would make the baron very sad to read it, and so I came to you, because I knew you could find just the right moment to give it to him, and just the right words to say, and it seemed wrong in me to keep it even a day. At first, I thought I ought to put it away and wait a year or two, until he had quite forgotten the first shock—but then—'

'Thank heaven you did not!' exclaimed Hilda.

'Well, I am glad I have pleased you,' observed Berbel in her sharp, good-natured way.

'Pleased? Oh, anything would have pleased me better than this thing! It is dreadful, after all this time has passed—'

'But, after all,' suggested Berbel, 'it is only the affair of a day or two, and the baron will be very glad, afterwards, to feel that his father had not forgotten him.'

'You do not understand,' answered Hilda with increasing anxiety. 'We never knew why they killed themselves—it is an awful secret, and the explanation is in this letter.'

'You never knew!' cried Berbel in great astonishment. It had not entered her comprehension that the real facts could be unknown, though they had never been communicated to herself.

'No—neither I nor my husband, and I had hoped that as all

has turned out happily we might never know. It would have been far better, far better!'

'Yes, far better,' echoed Berbel, whose simple calculations had been upset by the news, and who began to wish that the coat had fallen into other hands.

Hilda sat quite still, thinking what she should do. The situation was painful from its very simplicity, for it was assuredly her duty to go to her husband and give him the letter, telling him the whole truth at once. He had a right to receive the message from his dead father without a moment's delay, and she knew it, though she hesitated at the thought of what might follow. Her beautiful young face was pale with anxiety, and her bright eyes were veiled by sad thoughts. Poor Berbel was terribly distressed at the result of her discovery and tried to imagine some means of improving the situation.

'If you would let me,' she said, at last, 'I would take the letter to the baron and explain—if it would hurt you—'

'You? I?' cried Hilda almost fiercely. 'It is of him I am thinking, and of what he will suffer. What does it matter for me? It is my duty, and I must do it—am I his wife only when the sun shines and we are happy? Ah, Berbel, you should know better than that!'

'I only wanted to spare you,' said Berbel humbly.

Hilda looked up quickly and then took the old servant's hand kindly in hers.

'I know,' she said softly. 'But you must think first of him, always—if you love me. Berbel—are you perfectly sure that all this is true and real, that no wicked person is trying to do us some harm?'

'I am as sure as I can be—Wastei said I might ask the Jew, if I pleased.'

'It is true—it is Wastei. Unless he is mistaken himself there can be no doubt, then. But it is all so strange!'

It was stranger still, perhaps, that Wastei's name should be enough to dispel in Hilda's mind all doubts as to the truth of the story, and yet she would have believed the wild, kind-hearted free-shot sooner than many a respectable member of society.

'Put away the coat, Berbel,' she said after a pause. 'He will not need to see it when he has read the letter, and it would hurt him, as it hurts me.'

'Shall I give it back to Wastei?' inquired Berbel, folding it up.

'No, oh no! Put it away carefully where it will be safe, but where no one will ever see it again.'

'Wastei gave twenty *marks* for it,' observed Berbel. 'It is not fair that he should lose his money.' She could not help speaking a good word for her old friend.

'Give him forty to buy a new one. He has been honest, very honest.' Hilda sighed, thinking, perhaps, of all the pain that might have been spared, if Wastei had put the letter into the fire, instead of giving it to Berbel.

The good woman carefully folded the coat and hid it away in the recesses of a huge press that filled the end of the room. Then she rolled up the coloured handkerchief and put it into her pocket.

'It is Wastei's,' she said, as her mistress watched her.

The disappearance of the coat recalled to Hilda the duty of acting immediately, and she rose from her seat with a heavy heart. As she was about to leave the room a thought crossed her mind, and she stopped.

'Berbel,' she said, 'my mother must never know that this has been found, or at least, you must never speak of it to her or to any one, and you must tell Wastei to hold his tongue. She has had sorrow enough in her life, and we need not add any more, now that she is so happy.'

'Good,' answered Berbel. 'I will not talk about it, and as for Wastei, I would trust him with anything.'

Hilda slipped the fatal letter into the bosom of her frock and went in search of her husband.

Chapter 28

Greif had not found the man who was supposed to be waiting for him, and he himself had sat down to wait for Hilda on the shady side of the great tower. The air was warm and fragrant, even at that height, with the odour of the pines, and the sun was not yet high enough to make it unpleasantly hot. Through the bright, sunlit distance Greif could see many a familiar landmark of the forest, and as he sat there doing nothing, he amused himself half unconsciously with counting the points in the surrounding landscape which he had visited, and those he had never reached, and the number of the former greatly exceeded that of the rest.

It was a very peaceful scene, and Greif breathed in the smooth refreshing air with delight, while his eyes wandered lazily up and down the heights and along the feathery green crests of the forest's waves. For all the firs and pines were still tipped with the green of their new-grown shoots, though the autumn winds and the winter snows would soon stain the newcomers as black as the old boughs on which they grew. The time is short indeed, during which the Black Forest is not black, but takes a softer hue, and a warmer light. The autumn comes early, the spring comes late, there is but little summer, and the winter has it all to himself during the rest of the time. But though the summer days be few, they are of exquisite beauty, such as are rarely seen elsewhere in Europe.

Greif knew, as he sat by his tower, that they were nearly over, and he was the more grateful for the delight of the soft sunshine, of the green treetops, of the fragrance of the forest coming up to his nostrils over the grey ramparts, of the short whistle of the shooting swallows, that seemed to spring up like the spray of a fountain out of the abyss beneath, and after circling the highest pinnacle of the castle fell again with lightning speed into the cool depths below. Greif listened to the rushing noise of their wings, and to their short, clear cry, and he wished that Hilda were beside him, to help him to enjoy the more what already gave him such keen pleasure.

To him, indeed, Sigmundskron still had the charm of novelty. Its situation on a high and projecting crag was very different from that of Greifenstein, which latter was but the three-cornered end of a precipitous promontory, cut off from the forest by its single enormous bulwark. Sigmundskron commanded a view of many miles over the landscape below, while Greifenstein lay much lower, and a man standing on the topmost rampart could but just look over the level sea of the treetops to the higher hills in the distance beyond.

Greif was very happy. It seemed to him as though all the possible unhappiness of his life had concentrated itself into a very short time, not extending over more than a few days, from the moment when he had received news of the catastrophe in the hall at the banquet at Schwarzburg, to that in which the delirium of his fever had overtaken him. The rest had been but little troubled by the tragedy which had left him alone in the world. Nothing cuts us off from the past more effectually than a dangerous illness in which we are for the most part unconscious.

Greif had felt, when he recovered, that he was completely separated from the former time, and the sensation had itself contributed to his recovery, by deadening the sense of pain that had been with him so constantly before he broke down altogether. Rex had not been ill, and to him the past did not seem so distant; moreover he knew what Greif did not know, and had greater cause for sadness. Greif was happy, and he knew it. It appeared impossible, so far as he could see, that anything should arise out of the gloom of Greifenstein to trouble his serenity in Sigmundskron.

Every effort had been made by him and Rex together to discover some clue to the mystery, which for Rex was no mystery any longer, and nothing had been found which could cast the smallest light upon what had happened. Rex suggested the possibility of a sudden madness having overtaken one or more of the party, and Greif was so easily satisfied, and so glad to bury the past, that he accepted the idea without defining it. He reflected, indeed, that under no imaginable circumstances could his present be touched or disturbed by the true explanation of the tragedy, should it ever be found, and he was content to let the tide of years flow silently over the place those terrible deeds held in his own life.

It is no wonder that he was happy now, since all his hopes were attained and all his desires satisfied. Being also of a faithful and persistent nature, his satisfaction was solid and permanent. Apart from the one dark spot which was so rapidly fading into the dim distance, he had no regrets; no dreams of what might have been sent rays of false light through his present, no images of disappointed desires haunted him in the silent night, no shadows of a lost joy, still madly anticipated in the distorted anachronisms of a wounded heart, came between him and Hilda's glorious beauty.

That misery of humanity was unknown to him, in which the soul still looks forward with a beating, throbbing hope to what the memory knows is buried in the depth and dust of twenty years. All was real, present, glorious, happy and complete. If anyone had asked him what he most dreaded, he would have said that he dreaded death alone, death for Hilda, death for the sturdy little child that was to bear the name now his, death for himself, though for himself the fear was less than for the other two. That anything but death could bring back those days and nights of agony through which he had once passed, he did not and he could not believe.

Even as he sat beneath the shadow of the tower on that summer's morning he asked himself the question, and the answer was the same as ever. Why, indeed, should he not be left in peace? Why should he even expect the possibility of evil? Evil might come, assuredly, but it must come in some sudden, violent and unexpected shape out of the present, by accident, by illness, by death. The terrors of the past were with the past, and Greif was too strong, and young, and happy to expect misfortune in the present. He sat there, peacefully gazing at the green feathers of the firs and at the circling swallows, and almost laughing to scorn the possibility of a pain that was already near him, that was with him now, as Hilda's graceful figure emerged from the door of the tower and stood beside him.

Her face was still a little pale, but she looked almost supernaturally beautiful in her gravity. It is possible that if she had been transported into the midst of the world, of that company of half-morbid, half-enthusiastic beings which we define commonly as society, she might not have pleased those tired critics altogether as well as one of themselves, though she would assuredly have surprised them exceedingly, and perhaps when she began to grow old they would remember that they had never seen anything like her.

But here, in her natural surroundings, she was magnificent. She was dressed all in white, and the delicate shades of her colouring did not suffer by the contrast, but seemed more perfect and harmonious, blended as all the tints were by the all-pervading light of the clear mountain air in the thin, vapoury blue shadows of the old tower. And the rough grey stone was a harmonious background for her beauty and its rugged surface showed more completely the exquisite outlines of her face and figure. Greif saw her beside him, and could not repress his admiration.

'Hilda—how beautiful you are!' he exclaimed, springing to his feet and putting his arms about her.

It seemed as though her perfection had suddenly become visible out of the dream of his cloudless happiness. She smiled faintly as she kissed him, so faintly that he was surprised and drew back, looking into her face.

'Has anything happened, sweetheart?' he asked anxiously. 'Is anything the matter? You are pale, darling, tell me—'

'Something has happened, Greif, and I will tell you,' she said, sitting down upon the long stone seat that ran round the base of the tower, and touching the spot beside her with the palm of her hand, as though bidding him do likewise.

His face grew grave as he took his place at her side, still looking into her eyes.

'It is something that pains you, dear—is it not?' he asked tenderly.

'Because it will pain you,' she answered. 'You must listen to my story patiently, Greif, for it is not easy to tell, and it is not easy to hear. But I will do my best, for it is best to tell it all quite plainly from beginning to end, is it not?'

'Yes,' answered Greif nervously. 'Please tell me all quite frankly.'

'It is about your father, Greif—about all that happened on that dreadful night at Greifenstein. Yes, darling, I will try and be quick. You know when—after they were dead, my mother went over, and did what she could until you came. You know, too, that the house was full of servants, whom your father was always changing—you sent them all away last year. Well, one of those wretches stole—had the heart to steal at that fearful time—a coat—one that belonged to your father—indeed—' she hesitated.

'And you have found it,' asked Greif, whose face relaxed suddenly. He thought it was but a common theft, and was immensely relieved.

'Yes, we have found it,' continued Hilda. 'But it was not a common coat, dear—it was the very one in which—the one he had on, I mean, when—'

'I understand,' Greif said in a low voice.

Hilda looked away, and clasped her hands upon her knee, making an effort to tell her story connectedly. She knew that it would be far better that Greif should be prepared by the knowledge of the details which it would be hard to communicate to him afterwards.

'Yes,' she continued, 'and the wretched servant took it to a Jew and sold it, and the Jew hid it—I suppose because he knew it was stolen— and long afterwards, only a very few days ago, he sold it to Wastei— and Wastei gave it to Berbel, and Berbel showed it to me.'

'Is it safe?' asked Greif, almost under his breath.

'Yes—quite safe.'

'Then I do not want to see it—'

'I have not told you all, dear. There is more. If it had been only that—but there is something else. The coat was torn inside, above the pocket, so that something that had been meant for the pocket had slipped down inside. It was very strange!'

'Something of his?'

'Of his—for you. Oh, Greif—it is the letter you searched for so long and could never find!'

Greif's face turned white and his voice was thick and indistinct.

'Give it to me,' he tried to say, and he held out his hand to receive it.

Without another word Hilda drew the sealed envelope from the bosom of her frock and gave it to him, not daring to look at him. Then she rose and would have left him alone, but with one hand he caught hers and held her back.

'Together, dear,' he almost whispered.

Greif was stunned and shocked. It seemed as though the dead man had risen from his grave to deliver his message himself, to tell his own story and reveal his own secret. With trembling fingers Greif turned the envelope over and over, scarcely able to read the superscription at first, then glancing curiously at the impress on the seal, doubting, as Hilda had doubted, that it was perhaps not genuine. But his memory told him the truth. He knew the paper well, and as trivial details come before the mind in the most appalling moments of life, so he remembered instantly the whole appearance of the library at Greifenstein, the table with the huge old silver inkstand, the rack that had held that very writing paper, the heavy, clumsy seal that had sealed that envelope, and which always lay beside the blotter and next to the sealing wax. It all came back to him so vividly that, even if the letter had been a forgery, he would have believed it genuine, from the mere force of the associations it evoked. He held it in his hands and hesitated.

Within that narrow bit of folded paper was contained the secret of his father's death, of his mother's sudden end, of Rieseneck's suicide. He had not a doubt of it, though he had not realised it at first. A sort of mist veiled his eyes and darkened the glorious day. It seemed so strange that such a poor scrap of perishable rag should hold the key to so great a mystery, the solution to such a fearful question. Within that cover was a sheet of paper and on it he should see characters traced in a familiar hand. He closed his eyes and fancied that he already saw the writing, for he had often imagined how it would look, during his long search.

Again and again in his dreams, he had laid his hand upon that envelope, and had broken the seal and had read those short words of tender farewell which he felt must have been in his father's heart at the supreme moment. And now he held the reality and yet he shut out the light of day in order to call up the fancy that had so often consoled his imagination.

But the reality was not one with the dreamland shadow. In the one there had been only words of love and sad regret, in this real letter was written the secret whose effects had so nearly ruined his life, a secret so terrible, that had Hilda guessed it she would have thrust the cruel message from the dead into the flames, rather than allow it to live and stab Greif to the heart.

Hilda did not understand his hesitation, though she knew as well as he himself that the yet unread words contained the solution of the great problem. But she sat patiently by his side, her white hand resting on his shoulder, her anxious face turned towards his, her lips already parted, as though but awaiting her breath to speak words of consolation for the suffering that had not yet begun.

Greif roused himself, as though ashamed of the emotion he had shown, though indeed he had seemed outwardly calm enough. He pressed his lips together and ran his finger through the upper side of the envelope, so as not to break the seal. His hands did not tremble any longer, and with the action all his dreams vanished in the broad light of the summer morning. Carefully he withdrew the sheet and spread it out.

'Shall I go, sweetheart? Would you rather be alone?' Hilda asked once more.

'No, darling. Read it with me—let us read it together,' he answered quietly, as though he were speaking in some sacred presence.

Hilda bent her golden head forward until it was close to his, and their cheeks touched as they read together the contents.

My dear Greif, my beloved son—first of all, I remind you that you are a man and a brave one, and I solemnly enjoin upon you to act like one, and to put your trust in God. A great misfortune has befallen you, and at the moment of death I look to you to bear its burden in a manner worthy of a German gentleman. Heaven will certainly atone to you for the injustice of a cruel destiny. Your mother was the lawful wife of my brother Rieseneck. She has deceived me for five and twenty years, until his sudden coming revealed to me all her crimes within an hour. You are therefore illegitimate and nameless, and not one penny of my fortune is yours. I am utterly dishonoured by this enormous wickedness.

My brother and I have done justice upon the woman Clara Kurtz, Freiherrin von Rieseneck, after receiving her full confession, and nothing remains for us but to die decently. As for you, I need not point out your course. You will declare the truth to my cousin Therese von Sigmundskron, who is the sole heir to all my fortune and estates, being next of kin in the line of the Greifensteins. You will renounce your engagement to marry Hilda von Sigmundskron. You will enter the ranks and serve your king as a private soldier, which is the only course open to a penniless gentleman.

I know you too well to think you will hesitate a moment. My brother leaves a son by his wife, who goes by the name of Rex, and to whom he is now writing. Perhaps it is the student of whom you have spoken often to me lately. He is your brother as Rieseneck is mine, and he is rich by his father's death. But you will accept nothing from him, nor from anyone else except your sovereign, who, if he learns your story, may help you if he be graciously pleased to do so.

My son, I am about to die. I have taken the law into my own hands and I must pay the penalty by the only hand to which I can submit. If I have been at fault towards you, if I have been deceived by this woman through any carelessness of mine, I, your father, implore your forgiveness at this final moment. And so I leave you. May the God of our fathers protect and bless you, and bring you to a nobler end than mine. Though you are nameless and penniless, you can yet be a Christian man; you can be true, you can be brave, and you can give your life, which is all you have to give, to your king and your country. Farewell.

Your father,

Hugo Von Greifenstein.

Strange as it may seem, both Hilda and Greif read this long letter to the end before they paused, almost before they understood what it meant. Their two faces were livid, as they sat in the shadow of the tower, and gazed at each other with wild and staring eyes. The cold sweat of horror stood upon Greif's forehead, like the drops of moisture on a marble statue when the south wind blows.

But there was a vast difference between Greif's condition now and his state when he had broken down under the burden of his emotions eighteen months earlier. The calm and peaceful life had strengthened his character and fortified his nerves, and though Hilda expected every moment that he would sink down as he had done on that memorable day, almost unconscious with pain, he nevertheless sat upright in his seat, bracing himself, as it were, against the huge wave of his misfortunes, which had risen from the depths of the tomb to overtake him and annihilate his happiness in a single moment. His comprehension seemed to grow clearer, and he grasped the whole frightful hopelessness of his enormous calamity.

Hilda understood it too, in a measure, but she thought only of his suffering, and not of any possible consequences to herself. With womanly tenderness, she took her handkerchief, and pressed the cool linen to his wet brow, while she could see his broad chest heaving and hear the dull, short sound of his breath between his grinding teeth. Her arms went round him, and tried

to draw him to her, but he sat upright like a figure of stone, unbending as a block of granite.

'Greif!' she cried at last. 'Speak to me, dear one—'

'How can I speak to you, whom I have dishonoured?' he
asked, slowly turning his head towards her and yet trying to
draw back from her embrace.

'Dishonoured me! Ah, Greif—'

'Yes—Hilda, I am no more your husband, than my wretched
father was husband to the creature who bore me—who ruined
him and me—'

'Greif—sweetheart, beloved, are you mad?'

'Mad? No! The merciful unhinging of that rack of torture
which should be my mind, God has denied me. Mad? It were
better, for your sake. Mad? I know not what I say. You are not my
wife, nor Sigmund, Sigmund, nor I Sigmundskron, nor Greifenstein, nor Hilda's husband, nor anything that I wot of—save a
nameless vagabond who has dishonoured Hilda—'

'Greif—for the love of Heaven—'

'Ay, I must speak, and quickly. It is better that you should
know all the truth from these lips, foul from their birth—that
have kissed yours, though they be not worthy to eat the dust in
your path—these lips that kissed that vile thing they called my
mother, and that spoke words of sorrow, and uttered cries of
grief, at a death too decent for such a being—no, let me speak,
take your pure hands from me—I am not your husband! By a
name that was never mine, I took your name—thank God you
have it still! Your marriage is no marriage, your child is nameless as I am—do you know how the law would call me? One
Greif, the bastard son of a certain Herr von Greifenstein and of a
woman known as Clara Kurtz—that is the designation of all my
honours, that is the description of your child's father, of the man
you have called husband for twelve months and one day!

'The curse of God in Heaven on that wretch—she was not
woman—may the furies of hell not tire of tormenting her ac-
cursed soul throughout all ages—yes—I mean my mother, I
mean every word I say—I would say more if I knew how! She

has done all this—she brought my father to his death, my brave old father, whom I loved, and she has brought me to shame worse than death; and worse than shame or death to me, she has brought dishonour upon the only creature left me to love—oh, death was made too easy for her by those merciful men, they were a thousand times too pitiful, too kind!'

He paused, trembling in every limb with the wrathful passion for which words alone were no satisfaction. Hilda was startled at the violence of his language, and alarmed by the furious look in his eyes, but actual fear was too foreign to her nature to influence her. She understood, now, however, what had escaped her before, namely that he believed their marriage to have been no marriage at all in law. Then her love spoke out, softly at first and with a gentle accent.

'Greif, my beloved—let them rest in their graves! They cannot harm us.'

'Not harm us?' he cried. 'Do you know that every word I have told you is true—that the curse of that dead woman will pursue us to the end? Do you understand that we are not married man and wife?'

'That is not true,' answered Hilda. 'God made us man and wife—'

'Ay—but the law—'

'What is the law to us? Do we not love? Is not that law?'

'It may be in heaven—'

'And it is on earth. It is love that has made us what we are, by Heaven's help. It is neither man nor law, for my love is beyond all laws or men, save you! And this thing, what is it? A voice from the dead cries in our ears that we are not what we are, what I know we are, because a deed of shame was done long years ago of which we knew nothing, nor guessed anything until this moment. Is that justice; is that the law you fear and respect, the law you will allow to come between you and me? There is a better law than that, my beloved, the law that binds me to you with bands of steel, for good or ill, for shame or fame, for honour or dishonour—'

'Ah—the dishonour of it, Hilda, the dishonour!'

'The dishonour of what? Of a bit of paper, of a dead woman's sin and miserable death? Is that all? Or is it for name, or no name? And if it be that, what then? Do you think that if you were but a trooper in the ranks, calling yourself by any meaningless syllables that it crossed your mind to choose, if you were the poorest soldier that ever drew sword, do you think that I would not follow you, and work for you and slave for you, and live as I could, or starve, rather than leave you for one day, a thousand times rather than be Hilda von Sigmundskron and heir to all the wealth of the Greifensteins, as that thing says I am?

'Could all the laws you talk of prevent me from doing that? And you talk of my dishonour through you! I would beg for you, I would toil for you, I would wear out my body and my soul to get you bread—oh, I would almost sell the hope of heaven for your dear sake! And you say that because you have found this paper I am not your wife! A bit of paper, Greif, between you and me—a bit of paper on the one hand and my love on the other, with all it means, with all that harm or pain to you could make it mean, does make it mean, now and forever! Oh, my beloved, my beloved, have you loved me so long without knowing what love means?'

She would have twined her arm about his neck, but he hid his face in his hands and would not move. To himself, he seemed the basest of mankind, absolutely innocent as he was of every thought or intention of evil. He cursed his weakness in having yielded long ago, in having broken down into unconsciousness, to wake again, weak and enfeebled by his illness, no longer able to break through the spell that drew him towards her. He called himself, in his heart, a traitor, a coward, a weakling, a miserable wretch without strength, or faith, or honour. There were no bounds to his self-abasement, no depths to which he did not sink in his self-judgment.

He recalled that morning eighteen months ago when he had come over to Sigmundskron to fight the battle of honour, he remembered the agony of that bitter struggle, the triumph of his heart when he had made the last desperate effort and had gone forth victorious, though the fever was already on him, and he could scarcely see the road under his feet. He reproached himself bitterly with having yielded after winning such a fight, with having stooped to do the bidding of love, after having trampled down every loving instinct and every tender thought within him, in the proud consciousness of doing right for right's sake only.

If he had but been brave still when his body was so weak, all that now was could not have been. He would have cared for neither name nor fame, still less for fortune, without Hilda. But he had yielded, he had grafted the infamy of his birth upon the spotless line of her he loved, and fate had done the rest. The relentless destiny which had overtaken his father, his mother and his brother, had tracked him down and struck him within the boundaries of the false paradise his weakness had built up. He said to himself that he, too, must die, for he was the last and the lowest of living men.

'Will you not be persuaded, Greif?' asked Hilda, after a long pause. 'Do you not see that I am right, and that you are wrong— wrong only in this?'

'I see nothing,' he answered, 'unless it be that I have brought the most irretrievable dishonour upon all I love, as dishonour was brought upon me by him who loved me best.'

'And if I refuse to be dishonoured, what then?'

'What then? I do not know what then,' he answered half absently, not understanding her thoughts.

'Will you dishonour me in spite of yourself, in spite of my love?'

He did not answer this time, but buried his face in his hands once more, as though trying to shut out the sight of her from his aching eyes. The tones of Hilda's voice rose and fell faintly, as if they reached him through some thick substance that dulled their distinctness. At first he scarcely knew what she was saying, and he hardly cared.

'And if my love will not move you, then, I will tell you more,' she said, with a strong and rising intonation. 'I tell you that you have not dishonoured me, because I will not be dishonoured. You and I have done right before God, and before man until this day, and if there be wrong now it shall be right and I will make it right. I, Hilda von Sigmundskron, am your wife. I, Hilda von Sigmundskron, will not have it told to the world that I am a disgraced woman, that I am married to a nameless being, the mother of a nameless child. Your wife I am, and you are Sigmundskron and Greifenstein, and so you shall live and die, for I will make it law! There goes the law! Prove that you are a bastard if you can, and that I am a dishonoured woman!'

With a movement like a falcon swooping to the earth and soaring again to heaven, she had snatched the fallen letter from the ground. Before she had finished speaking, her desperate fingers had torn the paper to tiniest scraps and the light shreds were floating fast before the summer breeze, like snow-flakes in the sun, to the deep abyss below the castle wall.

Chapter 29

Greif sprang to his feet and seized Hilda by the wrist, his eyes and his whole expression full of horror and dismay.

'What have you done?' he cried.

'What you could not do,' answered Hilda boldly.

The colour had come back to her face, and the light to her eyes, and she met his gaze calmly and courageously. For some seconds neither moved, but stood looking at each other, he holding her tightly, she making no effort at resistance. Greif's first impression was that his wife had committed an act of sacrilege as well as a serious offence against the law. She had explained her meaning clearly enough when she tore up the letter, and he had understood all the consequences of the act at once. It would be useless to attempt a search for the fragments of paper, which were already scattered on the breeze and floating down to the deep gorge.

So far as the law was concerned, Hilda had spoken the truth. Not a shred of evidence remained to prove that he was not all today that he had been yesterday, in law as well as in fact. But there was gone with that evidence something precious to Greif, something which it had hurt him desperately to see torn to scraps and flung away. He had loved his father with all his heart, and the letter had contained his father's last solemn blessing, of which not a single word remained whole; not even if one of those bits of floating paper that whirled and floated down the precipice had preserved a syllable of the message, was it in the power of human skill or strength to save it from reaching the bottom of the abyss and being swept away to the distant river by the tumbling stream.

Nevertheless Hilda's quick and decisive action had produced the effect of a salutary shock upon her husband's mind and nerves. She, as usual, felt that absolute certainty of having done right which was a part of her strong character. 'You have destroyed it all,' said Greif at last in a reproachful tone. 'You have left no two words together—'

'And I am glad. I would do it again, if need were.'

'It cannot be undone,' Greif answered gloomily. He dropped her wrist and began to walk slowly backwards and forwards in the shadow of the tower.

'How could you do it! How could you do it!' he repeated in a low voice, as though speaking to himself and without looking at her.

'It was the only thing to be done,' she answered firmly.

'But the injustice of it—the illegality—what shall I call it?' he stopped in his walk.

'Call it what you please,' replied Hilda scornfully. 'It does not exist anymore. It may not have been a legal act, but it was an act of justice, whatever you may say; of the truest justice, and I would do it again.'

'Justice!' exclaimed Greif bitterly. 'If justice were done, I should be—'

'Stop,' said Hilda in a determined tone. 'Justice is done and you are here, and you are what you were yesterday and shall be tomorrow, not for me only, but for the whole world. That is the only justice I can understand.'

'Hilda, it is wrong,' cried Greif. 'I know it is. I have no right to throw off what has been brought upon me, what is proved so clearly—it is a wrong and a great wrong, and it must be repaired.'

'A wrong to whom?' Hilda asked, with flashing eyes. 'Whose would your fortune be if you renounced it for the sake of that thing I have destroyed? It would be my mother's—mine, would it not? The letter said so. And the name of Greifenstein, to whom would it go, if you proclaimed through the whole land that you had no right to it? To no one. It would end. No one would ever bear it, for no one has a right to dispose of it except, perhaps, my mother—'

'Yes—your mother—'

'My mother! Would you break her heart by telling her that she has given my father's name to—'

Hilda stopped short in her speech.

'To me!' exclaimed Greif in the bitterest self-reproach. 'Oh, the shame of it, Hilda, the shame of it all! You are right in that— to think that she has given the name she loves to one who has no right to any name—it would break her heart—'

'Then let her never know it, nor guess it, nor dream that it is possible, never, never, so long as she lives!'

'It is not for her only—it is for you, Hilda! That is the worst to bear—the shame, the shame!'

'For me?' The two words came slowly and distinctly from her lips, as though she were trying to make clear to him the enormity of his speech. Then she drew herself up proudly to her full height, and a wonderful smile illuminated her face.

'Not for me, Greif,' she said. 'There is no shame for me. In your love, I am above all earthly shame.'

There was something in her manner and in the accent of her speech that affected Greif very suddenly. He was gradually growing more calm and better able to reason, as well as to realise the splendid depth of his wife's love. There was a ring in her voice that told him more than her words could tell. He came to her, and took her hand, and kissed it, almost devotionally.

'You are above all earthly women,' he said simply.

'I? No. Any woman would do as much, and it is so little. If you would only think, dear, it is so very little—and it is for myself, too. Could I do anything else? Could any woman do less, even the most selfish?'

'I know none who would do as much,' Greif answered.

'Did I not tell you, that it was for my own sake that I destroyed the letter, that I would not be dishonoured, that I would not have the world say—what it might say?'

'That is not all, Hilda.'

'It is all—except my love, and that is all indeed, all there is for me.'

'Ay, that is it, that is it! And if these hideous crimes are never known to anyone but you and me, can you live beside me, day by day, year by year, and never feel one pang, one regret, one little thrust of shame? I know you love me, but that is too much to ask of any love. I know that you mean what you say, but it is too much for man or woman to say and mean. Think of it, Hilda, think of it all—there are such things here as angels could not forget!'

'I love you very, very much—my memory has no place for any other things.'

She twined her arm about his neck as they stood together, and she laid her golden head upon his shoulder, while her bright eyes looked upwards with a sidelong glance into his face. But his cheek was pale and cold, and he gazed sternly out at the distant crags, as though he would not see her. The unbearable conviction of disgrace was upon him, hopeless, endless, embracing all his existence and already extending back in his imagination to all his earlier youth. Her hands burned him, her touch was like the shock of death, as the old mystics used to say the draught of life would be to the lips of the unprepared and the impure.

'Let me go,' he said gently. 'I cannot bear it.'

But she would not. Instead of one arm, both went round him. He felt as if her strong embrace would lift him from his feet, out of himself, to bear him away from all trouble and woe to endless peace.

'I will not let you go—neither now nor ever, neither in this world nor the next.'

He knew that tone of hers, deep, ringing and clear, and he knew that she was desperate. Then the conflict began in his own soul, the struggle between that deep conviction of law and right, which was the foundation of his character, and that honest and all-sacrificing love that filled his heart.

'Give me time to think what I am doing,' he said.

He sat down upon the seat in his old place and bent down, pressing his temples with his hands. He had spoken very simply out of his great distress, for he needed time to think of what he was doing, and of what he must yet do. All was vague and moving in the vision of his mind, like a distant landscape seen through the trembling, heated air at noontide on a summer's day. Nothing was distinct, save his love for Hilda on the one side, and upon the other, the black shadow of his awful disgrace.

'Think, my beloved, if you will,' said Hilda softly. 'You will but think what I have thought already.'

Perhaps he felt, even then, that she was right, but he could not so soon be comforted, nor put aside in a moment what had presented itself so strongly as an inexorable duty. At that juncture a cunning man of law could have persuaded him more easily than the woman he loved more than all the world besides. As had happened before, in the old days, that love appeared to him in the light of a temptation, beautiful as the broad sun, eloquent as sweetest music. But there was this difference, now, that the opposite course was not as plain as it had been then.

Instead of a straight path, he saw but a confused medley of conflicting ideas, of which the whole sum represented to his mind a mysterious notion of a necessary sacrifice, but in which it was impossible to distinguish the discriminating point, the centre of action, the goal of duty. In the first place, he recognised out of this chaos, his father's injunction to act like a Christian man, to give up all that was not his, to lay aside the name he had borne and to go forth into the world with nothing but his own courage and perseverance as his weapons. That was clear enough. If the letter had come into his hands immediately, as it had been intended that it should, he would have fulfilled his father's last commands bravely in every detail of their spirit.

Even if he had received the message on the eve of his marriage, after he had begun to call himself Sigmundskron, even then he would have done the same; and though it would have been mortal agony, it would have been easy to do, so far as the mere execution of it was concerned. He would have gone to Frau von Sigmundskron, and would have told her the truth, showing her the letter, and taking the consequences. No woman alive, in such a case, would have hesitated a moment, he thought. Hilda's mother would certainly not have had the least doubt how to act, for she would have died rather than give her daughter to a man of illegitimate birth. She would have offered him his fortune, no doubt, for she was a noble and generous woman, but he would have refused to take anything. That at least would not have cost him a pang. As for the rest, his course would have been clear enough.

But now, it was a very different matter. His conscience still told him to go to Frau von Sigmundskron and tell all, but the consideration of the consequences appalled him. He knew better even than Hilda herself, what a sacrifice the good lady had made in regard to the name, and what importance she attached to it. She was perfectly happy in the existing condition of things; to tell her would be to destroy her happiness forever, to the last day of her life. Greif felt that if he were in her place he should not want to know the truth, since all reparation was now utterly impossible. And yet, to conceal it looked like a crime, or at least like an action of bad faith.

Could he meet the white-haired lady who loved him so well and who had built such hopes upon him, could he meet her daily, and call her mother, as she loved to be called, and yet feel that he was deceiving her, that he had defiled the name she had given him, and that he was living in possession of all that the law made hers? It might be true that all would be Hilda's some day, and that in the end no harm would be effected because it would go to Hilda's son. But the fortune was not Hilda's yet, and she to whom it really belonged, who had really the power to control all, and to turn Greif and her own daughter from home and hearth if she pleased, was to all intents dependent upon the generosity of both. Though she might be made to accept much, yet it seemed a positive wrong that she should be allowed to feel that she was receiving favours when she was in reality conferring them.

Greif therefore should go to her, and tell his story, and acknowledge that everything was hers and that he was beholden to her charity for the bread he ate at her table. He had the courage to do so, and he would do it, if it seemed wholly right. But if he thus satisfied his love of justice, he must also do her an injury of a very different kind. It would be cruel to disclose the truth. Even Hilda had said that it would break her mother's heart if she were told that she had given what she most prized to a nameless bastard. Hilda had not said the word, but it had been in her mind, nevertheless.

And Frau von Sigmundskron had given more than that, for she had bestowed upon him her only daughter. Should he make her declining years miserable with the shame that was upon him, in order to give her money, or should he keep what was hers in order that she might end her life in happiness and peace? It was a case of doing evil that good might come.

When such a question arises there can be but one answer. The good to be obtained must be immense and the evil must be relatively very small. If such a position could be imagined, a man would be justified in lying, stealing, or doing almost anything which could only hurt himself, for the sake of saving a nation, of preserving his country from destruction. Perhaps he would not be wrong, if it were to save a thousand innocent lives, a hundred, ten, even one, if he wronged only himself in the evil he did to attain his end. But as the ratio diminishes, the case becomes manifestly more difficult to judge, and the absolute nature of right asserts itself more strongly when it is not confronted by overwhelming odds in most exceptional circumstances.

Stealing is bad, but there is a difference between the case of the starving mother who steals a crust for her dying child, and the professional thief who lives riotously upon the proceeds of his crimes; there is a difference of degree in evil between stealing money in order to render possible the escape of a beloved sovereign from the hands of a bloodthirsty and revolutionary mob, and stealing it, under the apparent protection of the law, by deceiving thousands in the game of finance.

Nothing can be more repugnant to a man of honour than to do evil of any sort in order that good may come. To such a man as Greif, lying is but a shade less bad than murder, and stealing is many shades worse. In his judgment of the situation he was called upon both to steal and to lie, in order to secure Frau von Sigmundskron's happiness. It was true that the deception was to be practised by merely holding his tongue, and the theft by keeping what did not belong to him, but Greif made no such subtle distinctions of degree. It was lying and stealing. It was adding a disgrace by his own conduct to the shame he had inherited. It was to give up all that remained to him, which was his spotless honesty in thought and deed. The case seemed terribly strong.

There was Hilda, by his side, and she had said that she would not let him go. Suppose then that he went and told her mother the story. There would be one more person in the secret, for though she might die of grief, she would never tell a human being; she could not ever be called upon to do so, by the maddest exaggeration of the principles of honour. She would suffer horribly, but she would not take what was hers. She could have no use for the fortune, except to give it to her daughter, who had the use of it already. Her peace would be destroyed forever, and there would be no change in the conditions under which the three were living, except that Greif would have satisfied his desire to be strictly honest.

A moral satisfaction on the one hand, and the destruction of all happiness to one he loved on the other. His brain reeled, for his desire to be truthful suddenly appeared to him in the light of a selfish passion which would cause endless pain to those whom he most desired to shield from all suffering. This was another view, and a strangely unexpected one.

The chaos of his thoughts became wilder and more unsettled than ever, he dropped his hands upon his knees and leaned back against the rough stones of the tower, pale and exhausted with the struggle, but uncertain yet how he should act. Hilda sat motionless beside him, watching his movements, and to some extent understanding his thoughts, ready to give him her sympathy or her counsel, if he needed it, ready, too, to throw all the force of her undaunted nature into the contest if he should endeavour to maintain his first position. She was, indeed, terribly anxious, lest in a moment of excitement he should break away from her and go to her mother in his present frame of mind.

A long time had passed in silence, far longer than it has taken to describe the thoughts that succeeded each other in Greif's brain, but Hilda would not speak, nor interrupt the course of his reflexions. She knew that this was the decisive moment of their lives, and she understood her husband's stubbornly honourable nature well enough to give him leisure to consider all the points of his position.

At last he spoke, not looking at her and still leaning his head against the stones.

'It is hard to talk of it,' he said. 'And yet I must, for I cannot think without words. I must decide, and quickly. In another hour I may meet your mother. I must either tell her, or not tell her, and this must be final. If I do—'

'She will die,' interrupted Hilda. 'Not today, not tomorrow, perhaps not this year. But it will eat up her heart. I know her. She will spend hours in her room, alone, looking at my father's picture, and crying over his sword. All her dreams will go out, like a light extinguished in the dark, All her hopes will be broken to pieces. She will never feel again that you are a son to her, and that through you the Sigmundskrons have begun again. She will grow more silent, more thin and wan until the end; and then she will die. That is what will happen if you tell her.'

'And why should not all that happen to you, who know?' asked Greif.

'Because I love you yourself, and not an idea,' answered Hilda. 'If you were taken from me, I should die, as my mother will if you kill the idea she loves.'

'And is it better that my whole life should be a lie from this day forth, than that she should know the truth, and do what she can to meet it?'

'To whom do you owe the truth, Greif? To the woman you have married, to the mother of your child, or to someone else? What good would she get by it? Your money? She does not want money. What is money to her, compared with the memory of him she loved, as I love you, or in comparison with the honour of his name, for which she would give her blood?'

'And if you had left me alone to read that letter—would you have had me keep the truth from you too?'

'Would I have you bear alone anything that we can bear together? If you understand my love so little as to think that such a thing could change it, or weaken it, or make me what I am not—why then, I would not care what you did, nor what became of me!'

'And my shame is nothing to you?'

'Nothing, being what it is, not yours, but of others, thrust upon your innocence.'

'You would not, for your own sake, wish that we had never known of it?'

'For my sake? No. For yours—I would die to wash it out. For my sake, do you say? Oh, Greif, is one hair of your head, one look of your dear eyes less wholly mine, because your mother sinned? Are you not Greif to me, always, and nothing else?'

'And so you love me still—just as you did before?'

'Can I say more than I have said? Can I do more than I have done? Ah— then love must be too cold a word for what I mean!'

400

'You would not love me if I lied, and were a coward.'

'You would not be Greif.'

'Nor should I be my miserable self, if I acted this lie before your mother!'

'You would not be Greif, if you could kill her with the vanity of selfish truth-telling.'

'The vanity! Ay, I have thought of that. Perhaps I am vain, after all —I, who have but little left to be proud of.'

His head sank on his breast, and he sighed bitterly, wringing his fingers together. He wished he could shed tears, and cry aloud, and faint, as some women do.

'And yet—you have me—not to be proud of, but to love,' said Hilda gently.

'In spite of all! Is it really true, quite true?' He shook his head doubtfully.

'It is true.'

Hilda had no words left with which to persuade him of her unfaltering love, but perhaps at that moment the simple little phrase, with the accent she gave it, told Greif more than many protestations. It seemed to him that the course of his distress was checked suddenly, and that he felt the strain of the cable upon the firm anchor at last. It was the hour of destiny, when one word decides the future of many lives, for good or evil.

'Thank God!' Greif exclaimed in a low voice. He put out his hand and took hers. 'I will never ask you again, dear,' he said presently. 'It was hard to believe, it seemed as though I ought not to believe it.'

In spite of all, there was a happy light in his eyes, as he turned them to her and gazed into her face. After all, the terrible things told in the letter had happened long ago, and he was young, in the midst of a glorious present, in the very midst of all that love and happiness could give. It would be many a long year before he could think calmly of the hideous secret, and perhaps his whole life from that day would be more thoughtful and serious than it had been. But it was not in the power of an evil fate to follow him further than that.

The curse of the Greifensteins, as people a hundred years ago would have called that strange chain of circumstances in which his race had been involved, had run its course, and had spent itself in the conflict with a woman's love. Beyond that there was nothing but the smooth haven of rest, which no blast of evil could ruffle, and into which no overwhelming wave of calamity could break.

Greif scarcely knew how it was that the struggle ended, nor why, when it was over, he felt that he had not lost the day. But nevertheless, it was so, and peace descended upon his soul. For a long time neither he nor Hilda spoke. Very gradually, the colour returned to Greif's face, and the light to his eyes; very gradually the luminous veil of his happiness descended between him and the shades of the evil dead, not cutting off the memory of their deeds, but hiding the horror of their presence.

'And so Rex is my brother,' he said at last.

'And mine,' said Hilda.

'He does not know—or does he?'

'How could he?'

'His father wrote to him—was that letter lost too? Is that yet to come?' Greif's heart sank at the thought that all was not over yet.

'But if he had known,' said Hilda, 'could he have hidden it so long? And besides, he came with you. If there had been a letter to him, you would have known of it. Who could have given it to him, without your knowledge?'

'Your mother.'

'She never told me of it, though she often wondered that you had nothing.'

'Rex knows!' exclaimed Greif in a tone of conviction. 'And he received the letter. I have told you how it was that he confessed to me his real name. He was telling the truth then, for I know him well. He would as soon have told me that he was my brother as my cousin—'

'He would have hesitated to do that—'

'No. You do not know him. He does not value his life a straw,

402

and would as soon have taken that opportunity of parting with it as any other.'

'But how could he have concealed it since? Why should my mother have never told us that his father wrote?'

'Because she felt that I should have been pained to think that Rex had received something and I nothing. It is as clear as day. It explains many things. No one but a brother could have acted as he did all through my illness. I have often seen him looking at me strangely, and I never understood what it meant until now. He knew, and I did not. Besides—'

'What?' asked Hilda, as he stopped short.

'Well, it would explain, too, why he was so anxious that you and I should be married. If he knew—and he did, I am sure—he saw that if I persisted he would have to tell me the truth, in order that you should have the fortune. I used to wonder why he pressed me so.'

'Do you think that was it?'

'What else could he do? He must have ruined me, his brother, if the marriage had not taken place.'

'Would he have done that?' asked Hilda.

'Rex believes in nothing but honour,' Greif answered thoughtfully. 'There is nothing in heaven or earth which could keep him from doing what he thinks honourable. He would ruin me or himself with perfect indifference rather than see an injustice done by the fault of either.'

'He is a strange man.'

'He is a grand man, noble in every part of him, splendidly unselfish, magnificently brave—I wish I were like him.'

'I should not love you. He is cold as stone, though he may be all that you say, and though I am very fond of him.'

'Yes—he is cold. He never loved a woman in his life. But I admire him and respect him, though I never quite understand him. There is always something that escapes me, something beyond my reach. Perhaps that is what they call genius.'

'And yet no one has heard of him. He has never done anything with his talent. It is strange, too, for he is immensely wise.

I wonder what the reason can be.'

'He does not believe in anything—not even in greatness.' answered Greif. 'I believe his mind is so large that the greatest things seem little to him. I have heard him talk about almost everything at one time or another. The end of all his arguments is that nothing is worthwhile. And there is a reason, too. His father's disgrace has pursued him since he was a child.'

Greif's voice fell suddenly, and his face grew dark.

'And what should I be, then!' he exclaimed a moment later.

'What he is, were you in his place.' Hilda answered. 'But you are not, you see.'

'But for you, Hilda, but for you.'

'You for me, and I for you, my beloved. That is what love means.'

Their hearts were too full for either of them to speak much so soon as they approached the question which had so nearly destroyed all their happiness. For a long time they were silent, unconscious of the swift flight of the hours, little guessing what a strange drama was being enacted almost beneath their feet, in the solitary room where Rex had determined to lay down the burden of life in the cause of honour.

'I must go to him.' said Greif at last.

'To Rex?'

'Yes. I must know how much he knows—though I am sure he knows all.'

'Will you tell him if he does not know?'

'Shall I?'

'He is your brother. He will see it as I do. It is best that he should know.'

'Come then, dear,' said Greif rising from his seat.

'Shall I go with you?'

'I will bring him out of his room, if he is there, and you can wait a moment in the passage. If not, we will go on together and find him.'

'It is twelve o'clock!' exclaimed Hilda, glancing up at the great dial in the tower as she rose.

'It has not struck yet,' answered Greif carelessly.

They entered the winding staircase together and went down.

CHAPTER 30

Rex's room was situated in the upper story of the castle, at no great distance from the staircase through which Greif and Hilda descended. Greif knocked and opened the door almost simultaneously, not waiting for permission to enter. Hilda stood in the corridor outside.

With a sharp exclamation Greif sprang forward. Fortunately, his presence of mind did not forsake him, and he did not hesitate an instant. Before Rex could pull the trigger of his revolver, Greif had grappled with him and was trying to wrest the weapon from his grasp. It was an even match, or very nearly so. Neither spoke a word while they both twisted and wrenched and strained for the mastery. Greif's superior height gave him some advantage, but Rex was compactly built and very strong.

Very probably, if Greif had made a less sudden entry, Rex would have laid the pistol down with all his usual calm, and would have postponed his intention until he had got his brother out of the room. But Greif had sprung upon him very unexpectedly, and Rex knew instantly that he was detected in his purpose, and must either execute it now or give it up, and resign himself to being treated like a madman, and watched by lynx-eyed keepers day and night.

Hilda, who heard the noise of the scuffle, but had no idea that such a contest was taking place, approached the open door, supposing from the sound of shuffling feet that the two men were hunting some animal that had got into the room. Just as she stood before the threshold, and caught sight of Greif and Rex wrestling for life, Greif to take the pistol, Rex to put it to his own head, she heard a low, angry voice which she did not recognise. It was more like the growl of an angry wild beast than anything else. Rex was not getting the better in the fight, though he had not lost much. His object was to bring the muzzle of his revolver against his own head, while Greif was doing his utmost to prevent the movement.

'Let me go!' exclaimed Rex in deep, vibrating tones. 'Let me go, man—I love your wife, and I mean to die!'

With a violent effort he twisted his hand upwards, lowering his head as much as he could at the same moment. As the charge exploded, the bullet went crashing through the mirror, and the weapon was wrenched away by other hands than Greif's, whiter and smaller, but scarcely less strong. Hilda had seen the danger and had joined in the struggle at the critical moment, just in time to save Rex from a dangerous wound, if not from actual death. She had got possession of the chief object of contention, not without risk of being injured herself.

Rex's efforts ceased almost immediately. Between his anger at having been forced to relinquish his intention and his profound horror at seeing Hilda at his side almost at the moment when he had said that he loved her, Rex had no strength left. Only a supreme struggle, at once moral and physical, could have forced from his lips the words he had spoken. For a few seconds only his presence of mind failed him. Then the superiority of his nature over ordinary mankind asserted itself. He gently pushed Greif's hands away, and drew back a step in the direction of the door.

'You know my secret now,' he said, with a quiet dignity that was almost beautiful to see. 'I ask but the favour of being left alone.'

'I will not leave you for an instant—' Greif began, but Hilda interrupted him and passed him quickly.

She came to Rex and laid one hand upon his shoulder, and looked into his eyes.

'Do you love me? Is it true?' she asked earnestly, while Greif looked on amazed.

'But for your hand, I should have died with the confession on my lips,' Rex answered. 'I love you, yes.'

'Then live, for my sake!' said Hilda, holding out the hand that had saved him.

'For your sake?' Rex repeated the words as though scarcely understanding them.

'For my sake and for his,' Hilda answered, pointing to Greif.

'With that sin against him in my heart? No. I will not. It would be but a traitor's life, a dog's life. I will not.'

'You shall, and you will!' said Hilda, with that grand conviction of power she had shown more than once during her life.

'Only a man who has tried to die is worthy to live in such a case. Do you know what my husband is to you?'

'I know it better than he. I have known it long.'

'Not better than he, or than I. We have learnt the secret to-day.'

'You know!' exclaimed Rex in great surprise. 'Look at those ashes, there upon the floor—they are all I have left of it—and you know! No—you cannot, it is impossible—'

'We know that you are brothers,' said Hilda, taking his hand in spite of him. 'There is no secret any more, between us three—'

'And you know that I love you, that I love my brother's wife, and you would have me live?'

'Yes,' said Greif, who had not spoken yet. 'I would have you live, through all our lives, and I would have you two love each other with all your hearts, as I love you both.'

Rex stared at him, and then at Hilda. He raised one hand, and passed it over his eyes.

'I do not understand,' he said, in a low voice.

'It is because I understand, that I speak as I do,' Greif answered earnestly. 'It is because I know that not a nobler man than you breathes in the world. It is because there is but one Hilda in the earth, and she is mine, as I am hers.'

'You are not human, my brother,' said Rex. 'You should wish me dead.'

'If you were any other man but Rex, I might. Being what you are, I wish that we three may never part.'

'Never!' exclaimed Hilda. 'Ah, Horst, do you not see that you are my brother, too? Do you not feel that I am your sister—and should brothers and sisters such as we be made to part?'

407

'I cannot tell,' Rex answered. 'If you would have me live, I can but give you what life is left in me. You know me now. You know what I only learned of myself last night, and what I would have taken to the grave, unknown to any one, today. If in your eyes I am so far less base than in my own, if you can look upon me and not loathe me, if you can think of me and not call me traitor, why then this life is yours. And yet, I wonder that you can, seeing that I am what I am. Would you know how it came? You may know if you will, there is less shame to me in that than in the rest. I loved in a dream. I made myself the father of this Hilda in my shadowy visions; I made in my thoughts a mother for her, like her, dead long ago, whom I had loved. I talked with a shadow, I loved a shadow, and the unreal phantasm I loved grew to be like Hilda herself— so like that when I saw they were the same, last night, here upon this very spot, I knew that I must die and quickly.

'The shadow was the living wife of him for whom I would give all, of my only friend, of my only kinsman, of my only brother. And so, if you had not hindered me, I should have been but a shadow now, myself. It had been best, perhaps. But my life is yours, do with it what you will. It is yours in all honour, such as it is. It was not to escape from torment that I would have died; it was not because I feared by word or deed to break the seal and to show you what was in me. It was to rid my brother and the world of a wretch who had no claim to live.'

'More right than I, or many a better man than I am,' said Greif, laying his hand upon his brother's shoulder.

'Be wise, Greif,' answered Rex. 'Think well of what is to come. Think well whether you can trust me and trust yourself. For me—I care little. A touch of the finger, a little noise, and you would be rid of me forever. There is a safety in death, which life cannot give.'

'Do not talk any more of death, dear Horst,' said Hilda. 'It is but a year and a few months, since two brothers and one woman, three as we are, in the same bonds save one, all stood together as we stand, perhaps, and by their deeds and deaths wiped away death from our lives. Talk no more of death now—in this other home, where there are other names than those that were dishonoured. Let this be the house of life, as that was the house of death, the home of honest love, as that was the home of treachery, the dwelling of peace, as that was made at last the place of violent and desperate deeds. The hour of destiny is passed. The days without fear begin today.'

It was indeed the decisive moment in the lives of all three, and there was silence for a space after Hilda had spoken. The thoughts her words called up passed rapidly through the minds of her hearers and produced their effect on each. As she had truly said, there was a mysterious resemblance between the climax and the anti-climax of their history. As Rieseneck and Greifenstein had been half-brothers, so were Greif and Rex; as their fathers had loved one woman, so they also both loved Hilda; as the elder pair might have been, but for the woman who wrought their destruction, honourable, brave and earnest men, so were their sons in reality—the difference lay not so much between the fathers and the sons, as between one woman and the other, between Clara Kurtz and Hilda von Sigmundskron.

Instead of ruining both brothers, as Clara had done, Hilda had saved both from destruction, in the place of shame, she had brought honour, in the stead of death she had given life to both. And both looked at her during the silence and wondered inwardly at the beauty of her strength, asking themselves how it was possible that in a few short months this child of the forest, innocent and ignorant of the world, should have attained to proportions that were almost divine in their eyes, should have developed from the simple maiden to the noble woman, from the quiet, gentle girl, to the splendidly dominating incarnation of good, that had more than once overcome their mistaken impulses, and made plain their way before them by the illumination of the right, just as her golden head and gleaming eyes seemed to light up the room in which she stood.

They looked at her and wondered, both loving her beyond all earthly things, each in his own way; the one with the earnest, deep-rooted purpose to live and die in all honour for her sake, silent forever, having spoken once, doing daily homage to her innocence and loveliness, and reverently sacrificing every day for her the very love whereby he lived; the other, loving in her the wife, the mother of his sons, the source of all the glorious happiness that had come upon his early manhood in such an abundant measure, the woman who had saved him, the woman he adored, the woman who was his, as he was hers. Neither had known before how great and good she was, and from this day neither would ever forget one shade of the goodness and the greatness she had revealed to both.

A baser man than Rex would have suffered and would have foreseen suffering throughout his coming days, in dwelling beside the woman who could not be his. But he was made of better stuff than most men, and his passion had received a stern and sudden check from the force of his commanding will. It was as though Hilda had been deified before him, and had been lifted to a sphere in which he could worship her as a higher being and forget that she was a woman. He bowed his head in thought, while Hilda and Greif stood before him. They saw the white streaks in the soft hair that had been so brown and bright but yesterday, and they glanced at each other, awestruck at the thought of what he must have suffered.

'His hair is white—and it is for me!' Hilda whispered as she leaned upon her husband's shoulder.

Rex's quick ear caught the words, though they were scarcely audible. He looked up, and his stony eyes grew strangely soft and expressive.

'Yes,' he said. 'I know it—but it is not strange. I am glad it is so, for it was in a good cause. You are right, Hilda, my sister— the hour of destiny is passed. It has left its marks, but they are pledges that it will not return. The new life begins today—give me your hands, both of you—do mine tremble so? It is with happiness, not with pain—oh, not with pain, do not think it! Give me a share in your lives, since you will. I take it gladly, and you shall not regret it. You have my word that you shall never feel one sting when you look at me, you, my brother, you, my sister. I will be a brother to you both, a son to her you both call mother, though, in truth, I am too old for that—but she must be a mother to us all, in place of what none of us have ever had, save Hilda.

'And I kiss your hand, dear sister—so—it is the pledge—I take yours in mine, brother, and I know you, and you know me, and we can look each into the other's eyes and say I trust, and know that we trust well. There—it is done, and we are joined, we three, for good or evil, to stand together if there be strife still in store for us who have striven so much, to live in brotherly love and peace, if peace is to be ours, until the grey years come and we are laid side by side together.'

'So be it, and may God bless us all,' said Greif.

'God will bless us,' answered Hilda softly.

One more pressure of the hands and then Greif and Hilda turned and went away. The door closed softly behind them, and Rex was alone.

He went and took up the revolver that Hilda had laid upon the table, looked at it long, and then placed it in the drawer, and turned the key upon it. Once more he sat down where he had sat so long, and buried his face in his hands, and pressed them to his aching eyes.

The greater sacrifice was accomplished now, and he knew that it was over, and that his years would be in peace, for all was clear and honest and true as the day. He looked up at last, upwards as though searching for something above him, straining his weary sight for a vision that was not granted him.

'I have lived,' he said aloud, in a strange voice. 'I had never lived before, never in all this time. And if they are right, if You are there, You, their God—then bless me too, with them, and make me like them! Is that a prayer? Why then, I will say Amen, and be it so! It is the only prayer I could ever pray now, to be like them, to be like them—yes, only that, to be like them!'

And Rex meant what he said. He was incapable of seeing that he himself had done anything more than his plain and honourable duty. He knew that he had overcome what had seemed most base in his own eyes, but he would have been amazed if anyone had suggested that any credit was due to him for that, since he had but obeyed the law of honour, the only law he knew or recognised. In his own estimation he was not less contemptible for having harboured a thought which would have been dishonourable only if it had been base and gross, but which, being so pure and sacred, was but the natural expression of a noble heart. But he saw in Hilda and Greif a generosity which seemed boundless when confronted with the evil of which he judged himself guilty, and he felt that genuine gratitude which only a high-souled being can feel in such a case.

Perhaps, if the truth were told, Rex was himself the noblest of the three. It is certain that he had suffered most, and he had assuredly suffered bravely, and fought against what he hated in himself with an earnestness and true-hearted purpose worthy of a good man. Hilda and Greif thought so, at least, as they walked slowly away from his room.

'We have seen a strange and wonderful sight, my beloved,' said Greif, as they came out together again upon the terrace. They had returned thither instinctively in order to be alone.

'Wonderful indeed. Ah, Greif, you were right when you said that he was a grand man. I never thought that there were such men as that nowadays.'

'And we were wrong to say that he was cold.'

'You saw his hair! I was frightened when I thought of what he must have suffered, to make it change like that! Oh, Greif, is it my fault? Have I any fault in it? I should never rest again, if I thought so.'

'What fault of yours can there be?'

'Do you remember, long ago, on that day when you came to ask my mother, here, on this very terrace—I told you to speak to him?'

'Yes. What of it?'

'Perhaps it was vanity after all. Perhaps, if I had let him hate me, or dislike me, or whatever it was—all this might never have happened. It is my fault, it is, I know it is!'

'No, darling—it is not. Things could not then have gone on as they were going, and we both did right. You heard his story—you know how truthful he is. He told us exactly what had happened to him, and he told us for that very reason, in order to make it clear that he had not known it all along, but had realised it suddenly, as he said he did. If he had guessed before that he was in danger of loving you he would not have stayed a day under our roof. But it came upon him all at once, and when it came upon him it was too strong, and too great.'

'And besides, he knew that you were his brother, from the first. That made it worse. How wonderfully he has kept the secret through all this time!'

'There is nobody like him. There is only one Rex in the world,' said Greif in a tone of conviction.

'And there is only one Greif in the world,' Hilda answered.

'Fortunately. Do you know? I feel as if Rex were really going to make it easier for us.'

'Easier? How?'

'Easier to keep this thing from your mother. Hilda—it is a fearful story! As we stood there together, when you were speaking, I felt it all, I saw those other three, I heard their voices, I knew what they must have felt and thought and said, on that night. It must have been an awful scene. And here are we—two brothers, as they were—ah, the difference is in you, darling—how can I ever thank you for being Hilda!'

'By loving me, sweetheart. Do not think of that in any other way. Besides, you owe me nothing. I cannot help loving you. If I did not love you I might hate you, though I think I should admire you, all the same.'

'Admire me!' exclaimed Greif, with an honest laugh.

'You were grand today—you were so generous!'

'I do not see much generosity—'

'You are not a woman. How can you see anything! Do you think that every man would have put out his hand to another who loved his wife and said so? It was splendid—I was so proud of you.'

'What else could I have done? And then, I was not jealous, I am not now, I never shall be, of him.'

'You are right in that, dear. That is not the sort of love that a man need be jealous of. It is not love at all, as we think of love, strong as it is.'

'How much you know!'

'I know about love—yes, a great deal, for I have thought about it, ever since I first loved you, when I was little. Yes, I know much about love, much more than you would think. What Rex feels, is a sort of wild adoration, half ecstasy, half imagination, which he connects in some way with my face and the sound of my voice. That is all. It is not like what I feel for you, or you for me. He would not be sorry if I died. It would make it easier for him. He would build temples to me, and kneel before a picture of me, and be quite as happy as he is now. One sees that. And yet it is all so real, and he suffers so fearfully, that his hair has turned white. Poor fellow, and I am so very fond of him!'

'What makes you think all you say, Hilda?' asked Greif, growing interested in her strange view of the case.

'The whole thing. He is as fond of you as ever, and more so, just as you are of him. Now if it were our sort of love, you two would instinctively go and cut each other's throats, and that would be the natural ending. Instead of that, you love each other like brothers as you are. Do you not see that it must be a different kind of love from ours?'

'Yes. You are right. But it is not less real.'

'Less real? No! It seems more real to him than ours could ever seem, if he were capable of it. That is the reason why he is so grand, and true and noble—being placed as he is. If he loved me as you have always loved me, I should hate him, even if I pitied him; I should want him to go away, so that I might never see him again, nor hear of him. I should be miserable so long as he were under the roof. And instead of that—I feel that he is a dear brother and a true friend.'

'So do I.'

414

'And he will be all we expect of him. You and I must try to make his life happy, Greif. He is a very lonely man. He is much older than we are—just think! He is nearly as old as my mother. But he looked old today. Poor Rex! I would do anything to make him happy.'

'You have made him happy already.'

'How?'

'You have made him forgive himself, and you have made him feel that he is one of us, more than ever before. Only a woman could have done that, Hilda—perhaps no woman but you.'

'Do you think I did that? I should be very glad—'

'I am sure of it. He never yields unless he is convinced. He is a man of iron and steel. If he had still believed that he was to blame for all this, no earthly power would have made him consent to live. And now, he will live, and he will be happy. He owes his life to you, darling.'

'As I owe yours to him.'

'As I owe mine to you both. Surely, no three were ever so bound together as we are. It is strange and wonderful.'

'But the bond is closest here, my beloved!' exclaimed Hilda, as her arms went round him.

'Ay, closest and best!' answered Greif, as their lips met.

During that long and eventful morning Frau von Sigmund-skron had been alone. Of all the four she only knew no sadness. When she went from time to time and gazed upon her little grandson, she felt as though her heart would burst with gladness. There, in his small cradle, lay the realisation of a hope she had thought vain for nearly twenty years. There lay a little Sigmund-skron, a sturdy little baby with white hair and bright eyes and rosy mouth, his tiny hands clenched stubbornly in the first effort to feel his own mimic strength, fair as a Gothic child should be, without blemish, perfect and noble in every point. There he was, and his name was Sigmundskron as well as Sigmund, and the day would come when he should be tall and strong.

In his veins there stirred that good blood that had never known fear or dishonour, untainted still through nigh a thousand years. Not only had he the name, as Greif had—that little child had the blood also, and he would surely have the loyal heart and the strong hand. And he should have brothers, too. Never again should the fate of the ancient race hang by the single silken strand that had borne its burden so bravely. And that little child was to have not only the name and the lion's soul, and the bare walls of Sigmundskron. He was to have broad lands and princely wealth. He was to have the power, as well as the will, the worldly greatness befitting the son of such a high and lordly line.

It seemed too good to believe, too good to think, too good to see. Day after day from his birth the white-haired lady came and looked at him and never tired of the wonderful truth. All had been wonderful of late, but the rosy little Sigmund was the best of all her wonders. She had grown to care for little else. She loved them all with a great love passing words, but she loved them best for what they had given her, for what lay in the cradle in the great cool nursery.

The tears would come, and she let them flow on unheeded, day by day. But they were not the old tears of long ago, that had left cruel stains upon her cheeks and aching fires in her brain. Their soothing streams came from the fountain of a new life and washed away the pain of the grey years in their healing flood. Instead of the pale dye of grief, they left behind them soft, faint hues as of returning day; instead of fierce, smarting heat, they brought the clear light of other years to the eyes that had seen such horror of death, such misery of want, and that now gazed tranquilly on such sights of unspeakable joy.

Today, she spent long hours alone beside what she loved best in the world. The christening had given a new impulse to all she felt, and it seemed to her that the child was more her own than ever. A long time she stood with folded hands before the tiny bed, thinking, thinking always of the great deeds that little boy should one day dare and do, for God and king and country. Many times she stooped and kissed his dazzling face, that seemed to glow with light from within, and each time her cheeks were wet, as the sudden and almost unbearable thrill of certain happiness leaped through her heart. Then all at once she smiled, then turned and went out softly and entered her own room.

The glory of the summer's day streamed in through the lofty window, shedding a blaze of light upon all within, upon the smooth matting that had replaced the patched old carpet, upon the old chest that held so many of her dearest treasures, upon the broad expanse of black velvet whereon were hung the most precious things she owned, two swords in their scabbards and a leathern helmet with a gilded spike.

She went up to the place and stood a moment, looking at the three objects. Then she took down the sabre and held it in her two hands, lovingly, as she would have held the child she adored. Her white hand grasped the hilt, and the burnished blade leaped from its sheath like a meteor into the blazing sunshine.

There was not a tarnished spot upon the good steel, not a speck of dust upon its gleaming length, not a shadow along the bright bevel. But she was not satisfied. With endless care she polished the shining surface again and again, with leather and silk, as she had done every day since she had brought it back nearly twenty years ago. She sheathed it then in its scabbard, and rubbed that, and last of all the hilt. Then she was satisfied.

Once more she paused and gazed at the spot where it had hung so long, as though asking herself whether she could part with it. But her hesitation was short, and the bright smile came again to her face as she went back to her grandson's cradle. With her own hands she drove two nails into the tapestried wall above his head. As the clock struck twelve, she fastened the burnished weapon securely in its new place.

'It is the sword of his fathers,' she said softly. 'God give him strength and grace to draw it in good cause!'

The Screaming Skull

I have often heard it scream. No, I am not nervous, I am not imaginative, and I never believed in ghosts, unless that thing is one. Whatever it is, it hates me almost as much as it hated Luke Pratt, and it screams at me.

If I were you, I would never tell ugly stories about ingenious ways of killing people, for you never can tell but that someone at the table may be tired of his or her nearest and dearest. I have always blamed myself for Mrs. Pratt's death, and I suppose I was responsible for it in a way, though heaven knows I never wished her anything but long life and happiness. If I had not told that story she might be alive yet. That is why the thing screams at me, I fancy.

She was a good little woman, with a sweet temper, all things considered, and a nice gentle voice; but I remember hearing her shriek once when she thought her little boy was killed by a pistol that went off though everyone was sure that it was not loaded. It was the same scream; exactly the same, with a sort of rising quaver at the end; do you know what I mean? Unmistakable.

The truth is, I had not realized that the doctor and his wife were not on good terms. They used to bicker a bit now and then when I was here, and I often noticed that little Mrs. Pratt got very red and bit her lip hard to keep her temper, while Luke grew pale and said the most offensive things. He was that sort when he was in the nursery, I remember, and afterwards at school. He was my cousin, you know; that is how I came by this house; after he died, and his boy Charley was killed in South Africa, there were no relations left. Yes, it's a pretty little property, just the sort of thing for an old sailor like me who has taken to gardening.

One always remembers one's mistakes much more vividly than one's cleverest things, doesn't one? I've often noticed it. I was dining with the Pratts one night, when I told them the story that afterwards made so much difference. It was a wet night in November, and the sea was moaning. Hush!—if you don't speak you will hear it now. . .

Do you hear the tide? Gloomy sound, isn't it? Sometimes, about this time of year—hallo!—there it is! Don't be frightened, man—it won't eat you—it's only a noise, after all! But I'm glad you've heard it, because there are always people who think it's the wind, or my imagination, or something. You won't hear it again tonight, I fancy, for it doesn't often come more than once. Yes—that's right. Put another stick on the fire, and a little more stuff into that weak mixture you're so fond of. Do you remember old Blauklot the carpenter, on that German ship that picked us up when the *Clontarf* went to the bottom? We were hove to in a howling gale one night, as snug as you please, with no land within five hundred miles, and the ship coming up and falling off as regularly as clockwork—"*Biddy te boor beebles ashore tis night, poys!*" old Blauklot sang out, as he went off to his quarters with the sail-maker. I often think of that, now that I'm ashore for good and all.

Yes, it was on a night like this, when I was at home for a spell, waiting to take the *Olympia* out on her first trip—it was on the next voyage that she broke the record, you remember—but that dates it. Ninety-two was the year, early in November.

The weather was dirty, Pratt was out of temper, and the dinner was bad, very bad indeed, which didn't improve matters, and cold, which made it worse. The poor little lady was very unhappy about it, and insisted on making a Welsh rarebit on the table to counteract the raw turnips and the half-boiled mutton. Pratt must have had a hard day. Perhaps he had lost a patient. At all events, he was in a nasty temper.

"My wife is trying to poison me, you see!" he said. "She'll succeed some day." I saw that she was hurt, and I made believe to laugh, and said that Mrs. Pratt was much too clever to get rid of her husband in such a simple way; and then I began to tell them about Japanese tricks with spun glass and chopped horse-hair and the like.

Pratt was a doctor, and knew a lot more than I did about such things, but that only put me on my mettle, and I told a story about a woman in Ireland who did for three husbands before anyone suspected foul play.

Did you never hear that tale? The fourth husband managed to keep awake and caught her, and she was hanged. How did she do it? She drugged them, and poured melted lead into their ears through a little horn funnel when they were asleep. No—that's the wind whistling. It's backing up to the southward again. I can tell by the sound. Besides, the other thing doesn't often come more than once in an evening even at this time of year—when it happened. Yes, it was in November. Poor Mrs. Pratt died suddenly in her bed not long after I dined here.

I can fix the date, because I got the news in New York by the steamer that followed the *Olympia* when I took her out on her first trip. You had the *Leofric* the same year? Yes, I remember. What a pair of old buffers we are coming to be, you and I. Nearly fifty years since we were apprentices together on the *Clontarf*. Shall you ever forget old Blauklot? *Biddy te boor beebles ashore, poys!* Ha, ha! Take a little more, with all that water. It's the old Hulstkamp I found in the cellar when this house came to me, the same I brought Luke from Amsterdam five-and-twenty years ago. He had never touched a drop of it. Perhaps he's sorry now, poor fellow.

Where did I leave off? I told you that Mrs. Pratt died suddenly—yes. Luke must have been lonely here after she was dead, I should think; I came to see him now and then, and he looked worn and nervous, and told me that his practice was growing too heavy for him, though he wouldn't take an assistant on any account. Years went on, and his son was killed in South Africa, and after that he began to be queer. There was something about him not like other people. I believe he kept his senses in his profession to the end; there was no complaint of his having made mad mistakes in cases, or anything of that sort, but he had a look about him——

Luke was a red-headed man with a pale face when he was young, and he was never stout; in middle age he turned a sandy grey, and after his son died he grew thinner and thinner, till his head looked like a skull with parchment stretched over it very tight, and his eyes had a sort of glare in them that was very disagreeable to look at.

He had an old dog that poor Mrs. Pratt had been fond of, and that used to follow her everywhere. He was a bulldog, and the sweetest tempered beast you ever saw, though he had a way of hitching his upper lip behind one of his fangs that frightened strangers a good deal. Sometimes, of an evening, Pratt and Bumble—that was the dog's name—used to sit and look at each other a long time, thinking about old times, I suppose, when Luke's wife used to sit in that chair you've got. That was always her place, and this was the doctor's, where I'm sitting. Bumble used to climb up by the footstool—he was old and fat by that time, and could not jump much, and his teeth were getting shaky. He would look steadily at Luke, and Luke looked steadily at the dog, his face growing more and more like a skull with two little coals for eyes; and after about five minutes or so, though it may have been less, old Bumble would suddenly begin to shake all over, and all on a sudden he would set up an awful howl, as if he had been shot, and tumble out of the easy-chair and trot away, and hide himself under the sideboard, and lie there making odd noises.

Considering Pratt's looks in those last months, the thing is not surprising, you know. I'm not nervous or imaginative, but I can quite believe he might have sent a sensitive woman into hysterics—his head looked so much like a skull in parchment.

At last I came down one day before Christmas, when my ship

421

was in dock and I had three weeks off. Bumble was not about, and I said casually that I supposed the old dog was dead.

"Yes," Pratt answered, and I thought there was something odd in his tone even before he went on after a little pause. "I killed him," he said presently. "I could stand it no longer."

I asked what it was that Luke could not stand, though I guessed well enough.

"He had a way of sitting in her chair and glaring at me, and then howling," Luke shivered a little. "He didn't suffer at all, poor old Bumble," he went on in a hurry, as if he thought I might imagine he had been cruel. "I put dionine into his drink to make him sleep soundly, and then I chloroformed him gradually, so that he could not have felt suffocated even if he was dreaming. It's been quieter since then."

I wondered what he meant, for the words slipped out as if he could not help saying them. I've understood since. He meant that he did not hear that noise so often after the dog was out of the way. Perhaps he thought at first that it was old Bumble in the yard howling at the moon, though it's not that kind of noise, is it? Besides, I know what it is, if Luke didn't. It's only a noise after all, and a noise never hurt anybody yet. But he was much more imaginative than I am. No doubt there really is something about this place that I don't understand; but when I don't understand a thing, I call it a phenomenon, and I don't take it for granted that it's going to kill me, as he did. I don't understand everything, by long odds, nor do you, nor does any man who has been to sea.

We used to talk of tidal waves, for instance, and we could not account for them; now we account for them by calling them submarine earthquakes, and we branch off into fifty theories, any one of which might make earthquakes quite comprehensible if we only knew what they were. I fell in with one of them once, and the inkstand flew straight up from the table against the ceiling of my cabin. The same thing happened to Captain Lecky—I dare say you've read about it in his "Wrinkles". Very good. If that sort of thing took place ashore, in this room for instance, a nervous person would talk about spirits and levitation and fifty things that mean nothing, instead of just quietly setting it down as a "phenomenon" that has not been explained yet. My view of that voice, you see.

Besides, what is there to prove that Luke killed his wife? I would not even suggest such a thing to anyone but you. After all, there was nothing but the coincidence that poor little Mrs. Pratt died suddenly in her bed a few days after I told that story at dinner. She was not the only woman who ever died like that. Luke got the doctor over from the next parish, and they agreed that she had died of something the matter with her heart Why not? It's common enough.

Of course, there was the ladle. I never told anybody about that, and, it made me start when I found it in the cupboard in the bedroom. It was new, too—a little tinned iron ladle that had not been in the fire more than once or twice, and there was some lead in it that had been melted, and stuck to the bottom of the bowl, all grey, with hardened dross on it. But that proves nothing. A country doctor is generally a handy man, who does everything for himself, and Luke may have had a dozen reasons for melting a little lead in a ladle. He was fond of sea-fishing, for instance, and he may have cast a sinker for a night-line; perhaps it was a weight for the hall clock, or something like that. All the same, when I found it I had a rather queer sensation, because it looked so much like the thing I had described when I told them the story. Do you understand? It affected me unpleasantly, and I threw it away; it's at the bottom of the sea a mile from the Spit, and it will be jolly well rusted beyond recognizing if it's ever washed up by the tide.

You see, Luke must have bought it in the village, years ago, for the man sells just such ladles still. I suppose they are used in cooking. In any case, there was no reason why an inquisitive housemaid should find such a thing lying about, with lead in it, and wonder what it was, and perhaps talk to the maid who heard me tell the story at dinner—for that girl married the plumber's son in the village, and may remember the whole thing.

You understand me, don't you? Now that Luke Pratt is dead

and gone, and lies buried beside his wife, with an honest man's tombstone at his head, I should not care to stir up anything that could hurt his memory. They are both dead, and their son, too. There was trouble enough about Luke's death, as it was.

How? He was found dead on the beach one morning, and there was a coroner's inquest. There were marks on his throat, but he had not been robbed. The verdict was that he had come to his end "By the hands or teeth of some person or animal unknown," for half the jury thought it might have been a big dog that had thrown him down and gripped his windpipe, though the skin of his throat was not broken. No one knew at what time he had gone out, nor where he had been. He was found lying on his back above high-water mark, and an old cardboard bandbox that had belonged to his wife lay under his hand, open. The lid had fallen off. He seemed to have been carrying home a skull in the box—doctors are fond of collecting such things. It had rolled out and lay near his head, and it was a remarkably fine skull, rather small, beautifully shaped and very white, with perfect teeth. That is to say, the upper jaw was perfect, but there was no lower one at all, when I first saw it.

Yes, I found it here when I came. You see, it was very white and polished, like a thing meant to be kept under a glass case, and the people did not know where it came from, nor what to do with it; so they put it back into the bandbox and set it on the shelf of the cupboard in the best bedroom, and of course they showed it to me when I took possession. I was taken down to the beach, too, to be shown the place where Luke was found, and the old fisherman explained just how he was lying, and the skull beside him. The only point he could not explain was why the skull had rolled up the sloping sand towards Luke's head instead of rolling downhill to his feet. It did not seem odd to me at the time, but I have often thought of it since, for the place is rather steep. I'll take you there tomorrow if you like—I made a sort of cairn of stones there afterwards.

When he fell down, or was thrown down—whichever happened—the bandbox struck the sand, and the lid came off, and the thing came out and ought to have rolled down. But it didn't. It was close to his head almost touching it, and turned with the face towards it. I say it didn't strike me as odd when the man told me; but I could not help thinking about It afterwards, again and again, till I saw a picture of it all when I closed my eyes; and then I began to ask myself why the plaguey thing had rolled up instead of down, and why it had stopped near Luke's head instead of anywhere else, a yard away, for instance.

You naturally want to know what conclusion I reached, don't you? None that at all explained the rolling, at all events. But I got something else into my head, after a time, that made me feel downright uncomfortable.

Oh, I don't mean as to anything supernatural! There may be ghosts, or there may not be. If there are, I'm not inclined to believe that they can hurt living people except by frightening them, and, for my part, I would rather face any shape of ghost than a fog in the Channel when it's crowded. No. What bothered me was just a foolish idea, that's all, and I cannot tell how it began, nor what made it grow till it turned into a certainty.

I was thinking about Luke and his poor wife one evening over my pipe and a dull book, when it occurred to me that the skull might possibly be hers, and I have never got rid of the thought since. You'll tell me there's no sense in it, no doubt, that Mrs. Pratt was buried like a Christian and is lying in the churchyard where they put her, and that it's perfectly monstrous to suppose her husband kept her skull in her old bandbox in his bedroom. All the same, in the face of reason, and common sense, and probability, I'm convinced that he did. Doctors do all sorts of queer things that would make men like you and me feel creepy, and those are Just the things that don't seem probable, nor logical, nor sensible to us.

Then, don't you see?—if it really was her skull, poor woman, the only way of accounting for his having it is that he really killed her, and did it in that way, as the woman killed her husbands in the story, and that he was afraid there might be an examination some day which would betray him. You see, I told that too, and I believe it had really happened some fifty or sixty years ago. They dug up the three skulls, you know, and there was a small lump of lead rattling about in each one. That was what hanged the woman. Luke remembered that, I'm sure. I don't want to know what he did when he thought of it; my taste never ran in the direction of horrors, and I don't fancy you care for them either, do you? No. If you did, you might supply what is wanting to the story.

It must have been rather grim, eh? I wish I did not see the whole thing so distinctly, just as everything must have happened. He took it the night before she was buried, I'm sure, after the coffin had been shut, and when the servant girl was asleep. I would bet anything, that when he'd got it, he put something under the sheet in its place, to fill up and look like it. What do you suppose he put there, under the sheet?

I don't wonder you take me up on what I'm saying! First I tell you that I don't want to know what happened, and that I hate to think about horrors, and then I describe the whole thing to you as if I had seen it. I'm quite sure that it was her work-bag that he put there. I remember the bag very well, for she always used it of an evening; it was made of brown plush, and when it was stuffed full it was about the size of—you understand. Yes, there I am, at it again! You may laugh at me, but you don't live here alone, where it was done, and you didn't tell Luke the story about the melted lead. I'm not nervous, I tell you, but sometimes I begin to feel that I understand why some people are. I dwell on all this when I'm alone, and I dream of it, and when that thing screams—well, frankly, I don't like the noise any more than you do, though I should be used to it by this time.

I ought not to be nervous. I've sailed in a haunted ship. There was a Man in the Top, and two-thirds of the crew died of the West Coast fever inside of ten days after we anchored; but I was all right, then and afterwards. I have seen some ugly sights, too, just as you have, and all the rest of us. But nothing ever stuck in my head in the way this does.

You see, I've tried to get rid of the thing, but it doesn't like that. It wants to be there in its place, in Mrs. Pratt's bandbox in the cupboard in the best bedroom. It's not happy anywhere else. How do I know that? Because I've tried it. You don't suppose that I've not tried, do you? As long as it's there it only screams now and then, generally at this time of year, but if I put it out of the house it goes on all night, and no servant will stay here twenty-four hours. As it is, I've often been left alone and have been obliged to shift for myself for a fortnight at a time. No one from the village would ever pass a night under the roof now, and as for selling the place, or even letting it, that's out of the question. The old women say that if I stay here I shall come to a bad end myself before long.

I'm not afraid of that. You smile at the mere idea that anyone could take such nonsense seriously. Quite right. It's utterly blatant nonsense, I agree with you. Didn't I tell you that it's only a noise after all when you started and looked round as if you expected to see a ghost standing behind your chair?

I may be all wrong about the skull, and I like to think that I am when I can. It may be just a fine specimen which Luke got somewhere long ago, and what rattles about inside when you shake it may be nothing but a pebble, or a bit of hard clay, or anything. Skulls that have lain long in the ground generally have something inside them that rattles don't they? No, I've never tried to get it out, whatever it is; I'm afraid it might be lead, don't you see? And if it is, I don't want to know the fact, for I'd much rather not be sure. If it really is lead, I killed her quite as much as if I had done the deed myself. Anybody must see that, I should think. As long as I don't know for certain, I have the consolation of saying that it's all utterly ridiculous nonsense, that Mrs. Pratt died a natural death and that the beautiful skull belonged to Luke when he was a student in London. But if I were quite sure, I believe I should have to leave the house; indeed I do, most certainly. As it is, I had to give up trying to sleep in the best bedroom where the cupboard is

You ask me why I don't throw it into the pond—yes, but please don't call it a "confounded bugbear"—it doesn't like being called names.

There! Lord, what a shriek! I told you so! You're quite pale, man. Fill up your pipe and draw your chair nearer to the fire, and take some more drink. Old Hollands never hurt anybody yet. I've seen a Dutchman in Java drink half a jug of Hulstkamp in a morning without turning a hair. I don't take much rum myself, because it doesn't agree with my rheumatism, but you are not rheumatic and it won't damage you Besides, it's a very damp night outside. The wind is howling again, and it will soon be in the south-west; do you hear how the windows rattle? The tide must have turned too, by the moaning.

We should not have heard the thing again if you had not said that. I'm pretty sure we should not. Oh yes, if you choose to describe it as a coincidence, you are quite welcome, but I would rather that you should not call the thing names again, if you don't mind. It may be that the poor little woman hears, and perhaps it hurts her, don't you know? Ghosts? No! You don't call anything a ghost that you can take in your hands and look at in broad daylight, and that rattles when you shake it Do you, now? But it's something that hears and understands; there's no doubt about that.

I tried sleeping in the best bedroom when I first came to the house just because it was the best and most comfortable, but I had to give it up It was their room, and there's the big bed she died in, and the cupboard is in the thickness of the wall, near the head, on the left. That's where it likes to be kept, in its bandbox. I only used the room for a fortnight after I came, and then I turned out and took the little room downstairs, next to the surgery, where Luke used to sleep when he expected to be called to a patient during the night.

I was always a good sleeper ashore; eight hours is my dose, eleven to seven when I'm alone, twelve to eight when I have a friend with me. But I could not sleep after three o'clock in the morning in that room—a quarter past, to be accurate—as a matter of fact, I timed it with my old pocket chronometer, which still keeps good time, and it was always at exactly seventeen minutes past three. I wonder whether that was the hour when she died?

It was not what you have heard. If it had been that, I could not have stood it two nights. It was just a start and a moan and hard breathing for a few seconds in the cupboard, and it could never have waked me under ordinary circumstances, I'm sure. I suppose you are like me in that, and we are just like other people who have been to sea. No natural sounds disturb us at all, not all the racket of a square-rigger hove to in a heavy gale, or rolling on her beam ends before the wind. But if a lead pencil gets adrift and rattles in the drawer of your cabin table you are awake in a moment. Just so—you always understand. Very well, the noise in the cupboard was no louder than that, but it waked me instantly.

I said it was like a "start". I know what I mean, but it's hard to explain without seeming to talk nonsense. Of course you cannot exactly "hear" a person "start"; at the most, you might hear the quick drawing of the breath between the parted lips and closed teeth, and the almost imperceptible sound of clothing that moved suddenly though very slightly. It was like that.

You know how one feels what a sailing vessel is going to do, two or three seconds before she does it, when one has the wheel. Riders say the same of a horse, but that's less strange, because the horse is a live animal with feelings of its own, and only poets and landsmen talk about a ship being alive, and all that. But I have always felt somehow that besides being a steaming machine or a sailing machine for carrying weights, a vessel at sea is a sensitive instrument, and a means of communication between nature and man, and most particularly the man at the wheel, if she is steered by hand. She takes her impressions directly from wind and sea, tide and stream, and transmits them to the man's hand, just as the wireless telegraphy picks up the interrupted currents aloft and turns them out below in the form of a message.

You see what I am driving at; I felt that something started in the cupboard, and I felt it so vividly that I heard it, though there may have' been nothing to hear, and the sound inside my head

429

waked me suddenly. But I really heard the other noise. It was as if it were muffled inside a box, as far away as if it came through a long-distance telephone; and yet I knew that it was inside the cupboard near the head of my bed. My hair did not bristle and my blood did not run cold that time. I simply resented being waked up by something that had no business to make a noise, any more than a pencil should rattle in the drawer of my cabin table on board ship.

For I did not understand; I just supposed that the cupboard had some communication with the outside air, and that the wind had got in and was moaning through it with a sort of very faint screech. I struck a light and looked at my watch, and it was seventeen minutes past three. Then I turned over and went to sleep on my right ear. That's my good one; I'm pretty deaf with the other, for I struck the water with it when I was a lad in diving from the fore-topsail yard. Silly thing to do, it was, but the result is very convenient when I want to go to sleep when there's a noise.

That was the first night, and the same thing happened again and several times afterwards, but not regularly, though it was always at the same time, to a second; perhaps I was sometimes sleeping on my good ear, and sometimes not. I overhauled the cupboard and there was no way by which the wind could get in, or anything else, for the door makes a good fit, having been meant to keep out moths, I suppose; Mrs. Pratt must have kept her winter things in it, for it still smells of camphor and turpentine.

After about a fortnight I had had enough of the noises. So far I had said to myself that it would be silly to yield to it and take the skull out of the room. Things always look differently by daylight, don't they? But the voice grew louder—I suppose one may call it a voice—and it got inside my deaf ear, too, one night. I realized that when I was wide awake, for my good ear was jammed down on the pillow, and I ought not to have heard a foghorn in that position. But I heard that, and it made me lose my temper, unless it scared me, for sometimes the two are not far apart. I struck a light and got up, and I opened the cupboard, grabbed the bandbox and threw it out of the window, as far as I could.

Then my hair stood on end. The thing screamed in the air, like a shell from a twelve-inch gun. It fell on the other side of the road. The night was very dark, and I could not see it fall, but I know it fell beyond the road The window is just over the front door, it's fifteen yards to the fence, more or less, and the road is ten yards wide. There's a thick-set hedge beyond, along the glebe that belongs to the vicarage.

I did not sleep much more than night. It was not more than half an hour after I had thrown the bandbox out when I heard a shriek outside—like what we've had tonight, but worse, more despairing, I should call it; and it may have been my imagination, but I could have sworn that the screams came nearer and nearer each time. I lit a pipe, and walked up and down for a bit, and then took a book and sat up reading, but I'll be hanged if I can remember what I read nor even what the book was, for every now and then a shriek came up that would have made a dead man turn in his coffin.

A little before dawn someone knocked at the front door. There was no mistaking that for anything else, and I opened my window and looked down, for I guessed that someone wanted the doctor, supposing that the new man had taken Luke's house. It was rather a relief to hear a human knock after that awful noise.

You cannot see the door from above, owing to the little porch. The knocking came again, and I called out, asking who was there, but nobody answered, though the knock was repeated. I sang out again, and said that the doctor did not live here any longer. There was no answer, but it occurred to me that it might be some old countryman who was stone deaf. So I took my candle and went down to open the door. Upon my word, I was not thinking of the thing yet, and I had almost forgotten the other noises. I went down convinced that I should find somebody outside, on the doorstep, with a message. I set the candle on the hall table, so that the wind should not blow it out when I opened. While I was drawing the old-fashioned bolt I heard the knocking again. It was not loud, and it had a queer, hollow sound, now that I was close to it, I remember, but I certainly thought it was made by some person who wanted to get in.

It wasn't. There was nobody there, but as I opened the door inward, standing a little on one side, so as to see out at once, something rolled across the threshold and stopped against my foot.

I drew back as I felt it, for I knew what it was before I looked down. I cannot tell you how I knew, and it seemed unreasonable, for I am still quite sure that I had thrown it across the road. It's a French window, that opens wide, and I got a good swing when I flung it out. Besides, when I went out early in the morning, I found the bandbox beyond the thick hedge.

You may think it opened when I threw it, and that the skull dropped out; but that's impossible, for nobody could throw an empty cardboard box so far. It's out of the question; you might as well try to fling a ball of paper twenty-five yards, or a blown bird's egg.

To go back, I shut and bolted the hall door, picked the thing up carefully, and put it on the table beside the candle. I did that mechanically, as one instinctively does the right thing in danger without thinking at all—unless one does the opposite. It may seem odd, but I believe my first thought had been that somebody might come and find me there on the threshold while it was resting against my foot, lying a little on its side, and turning one hollow eye up at my face, as if it meant to accuse me. And the light and shadow from the candle played in the hollows of the eyes as it stood on the table, so that they seemed to open and shut at me. Then the candle went out quite unexpectedly, though the door was fastened and there was not the least draught; and I used up at least half a dozen matches before it would burn again.

I sat down rather suddenly, without quite knowing why. Probably I had been badly frightened, and perhaps you will admit there was no great shame in being scared. The thing had come home, and it wanted to go upstairs, back to its cupboard. I sat still and stared at it for a bit till I began to feel very cold; then I took it and carried it up and set it in its place, and I remember that I spoke to it, and promised that it should have its bandbox again in the morning.

You want to know whether I stayed in the room till day-break? Yes but I kept a light burning, and sat up smoking and reading, most likely out of fright; plain, undeniable fear, and you need not call it cowardice either, for that's not the same thing. I could not have stayed alone with that thing in the cupboard; I should have been scared to death, though I'm not more timid than other people. Confound it all, man, it had crossed the road alone, and had got up the doorstep and had knocked to be let in.

When the dawn came, I put on my boots and went out to find the bandbox. I had to go a good way round, by the gate near the high road, and I found the box open and hanging on the other side of the hedge. It had caught on the twigs by the string, and the lid had fallen off and was lying on the ground below it. That shows that it did not open till it was well over; and if it had not opened as soon as it left my hand, what was inside it must have gone beyond the road too.

That's all. I took the box upstairs to the cupboard, and put the skull back and locked it up. When the girl brought me my breakfast she said she was sorry, but that she must go, and she did not care if she lost her month's wages. I looked at her, and her face was a sort of greenish yellowish white. I pretended to be surprised, and asked what was the matter; but that was of no use, for she just turned on me and wanted to know whether I meant to stay in a haunted house, and how long I expected to live if I did, for though she noticed I was sometimes a little hard of hearing, she did not believe that even I could sleep through those screams again—and if I could, why had I been moving about the house and opening and shutting the front door, be-tween three and four in the morning? There was no answering that, since she had heard me, so off she went, and I was left to myself. I went down to the village during the morning and found a woman who was willing to come and do the little work there is and cook my dinner, on condition that she might go home every night.

As for me, I moved downstairs that day, and I have never tried to sleep in the best bedroom since. After a little while I got a brace of middle-aged Scotch servants from London, and things were quiet enough for a long time. I began by telling them that the house was in a very exposed position, and that the wind whistled round it a good deal in the autumn and winter, which had given it a bad name in the village, the Cornish people being inclined to superstition and telling ghost stories. The two hard-faced, sandy-haired sisters almost smiled, and they answered with great contempt that they had no great opinion of any Southern bogey whatever, having been in service in two English haunted houses, where they had never seen so much as the Boy in Grey, whom they reckoned no very particular rarity in Forfarshire.

They stayed with me several months, and while they were in the house we had peace and quiet. One of them is here again now, but she went away with her sister within the year. This one—she was the cook—married the sexton, who works in my garden. That's the way of it. It's a small village and he has not much to do, and he knows enough about flowers to help me nicely, besides doing most of the hard work; for though I'm fond of exercise, I'm getting a little stiff in the hinges. He's a sober, silent sort of fellow, who minds his own business, and he was a widower when I came here—Trehearn is his name, James Trehearn.

The Scottish sisters would not admit that there was anything wrong about the house, but when November came they gave me warning that they were going, on the ground that the chapel was such a long walk from here, being in the next parish, and that they could not possibly go to our church. But the younger one came back in the spring, and as soon as the banns could be published she was married to James Trehearn by the vicar, and she seems to have had no scruples about hearing him preach since then. I'm quite satisfied, if she is! The couple live in a small cottage that looks over the churchyard.

I suppose you are wondering what all this has to do with what I was talking about. I'm alone so much that when an old friend comes to see me, I sometimes go on talking just for the sake of hearing my own voice. But in this case there is really a connection of ideas. It was James Trehearn who buried poor Mrs. Pratt, and her husband after her in the same grave, and it's not far from the back of his cottage. That's the connection in my mind, you see. It's plain enough. He knows something; I'm quite sure that he does, though he's such a reticent beggar.

Yes, I'm alone in the house at night now, for Mrs. Trehearn does everything herself, and when I have a friend the sexton's niece comes in to wait on the table. He takes his wife home every evening in winter, but in summer, when there's light, she goes by herself. She's not a nervous woman, but she's less sure than she used to be that there are no bogies in England worth a Scotch-woman's notice. Isn't it amusing, the idea that Scotland has a monopoly of the supernatural? Odd sort of national pride, I call that, don't you?

That's a good fire, isn't it? When driftwood gets started at last there's nothing like it, I think. Yes, we get lots of it, for I'm sorry to say there are still a great many wrecks about here. It's a lonely coast, and you may have all the wood you want for the trouble of bringing it in. Trehearn and I borrow a cart now and then, and load it between here and the Spit. I hate a coal fire when I can get wood of any sort A log is company, even if it's only a piece of a deck beam or timber sawn off, and the salt in it makes pretty sparks. See how they fly, like Japanese hand-fireworks! Upon my word, with an old friend and a good fire and a pipe, one forgets all about that thing upstairs, especially now that the wind has moderated. It's only a lull, though, and it will blow a gale before morning.

You think you would like to see the skull? I've no objection. There's no reason why you shouldn't have a look at it, and you never saw a more perfect one in your life, except that there are two front teeth missing in the lower jaw.

Oh yes—I had not told you about the jaw yet. Trehearn found it in the garden last spring when he was digging a pit for a new asparagus bed. You know we make asparagus beds six or eight feet deep here. Yes, yes—I had forgotten to tell you that. He was digging straight down, just as he digs a grave; if you want a good asparagus bed made, I advise you to get a sexton to make it for you. Those fellows have a wonderful knack at that sort of digging.

Trehearn had got down about three feet when he cut into a mass of white lime in the side of the trench. He had noticed that the earth was a little looser there, though he says it had not been disturbed for a number of years. I suppose he thought that even old lime might not be good for asparagus, so he broke it out and threw it up. It was pretty hard, he says, in biggish lumps, and out of sheer force of habit he cracked the lumps with his spade as they lay outside the pit beside him; the jaw bone of the skull dropped out of one of the pieces. He thinks he must have knocked out the two front teeth in breaking up the lime, but he did not see them anywhere.

He's a very experienced man in such things, as you may imagine, and he said at once that the jaw had probably belonged to a young woman, and that the teeth had been complete when she died. He brought it to me, and asked me if I wanted to keep it; if I did not, he said he would drop it into the next grave he made in the churchyard, as he supposed it was a Christian jaw, and ought to have decent burial, wherever the rest of the body might be. I told him that doctors often put bones into quicklime to whiten them nicely, and that I supposed Dr Pratt had once had a little lime pit in the garden for that purpose, and had forgotten the jaw. Trehearn looked at me quietly.

"Maybe it fitted that skull that used to be in the cupboard upstairs, sir," he said. "Maybe Dr Pratt had put the skull into the lime to clean it, or something, and when he took it out he left the lower jaw behind. There's some human hair sticking in the lime, sir."

I saw there was, and that was what Trehearn said. If he did not suspect something, why in the world should he have suggested that the jaw might fit the skull? Besides, it did. That's proof that he knows more than he cares to tell. Do you suppose he looked before she was buried? Or perhaps—when he buried Luke in the same grave——

Well, well, it's of no use to go over that, is it? I said I would keep the jaw with the skull, and I took it upstairs and fitted it into its place. There's not the slightest doubt about the two belonging together, and together they are.

Trehearn knows several things. We were talking about plastering the kitchen a while ago, and he happened to remember that it had not been done since the very week when Mrs. Pratt died. He did not say that the mason must have left some lime on the place, but he thought it, and that it was the very same lime he had found in the asparagus pit. He knows a lot. Trehearn is one of your silent beggars who can put two and two together. That grave is very near the back of his cottage, too, and he's one of the quickest men with a spade I ever saw. If he wanted to know the truth, he could, and no one else would ever be the wiser unless he chose to tell. In a quiet village like ours, people don't go and spend the night in the churchyard to see whether the sexton potters about by himself between ten o'clock and daylight.

What is awful to think of, is Luke's deliberation, if he did it; his cool certainty that no one would find him out; above all, his nerve, for that must have been extraordinary. I sometimes think it's bad enough to live in the place where it was done, if it really was done. I always put in the condition, you see, for the sake of his memory, and a little bit for my own sake, too.

I'll go upstairs and fetch the box in a minute. Let me light my pipe; there's no hurry! We had supper early, and it's only half-past nine o'clock. I never let a friend go to bed before twelve, or with less than three glasses—you may have as many more as you like, but you shan't have less, for the sake of old times.

It's breezing up again, do you hear? That was only a lull just now, and we are going to have a bad night.

A thing happened that made me start a little when I found that the jaw fitted exactly. I'm not very easily startled in that way myself, but I have seen people make a quick movement, drawing their breath sharply, when they had thought they were alone and suddenly turned and saw someone very near them. Nobody can call that fear. You wouldn't, would you? No. Well, just when I had set the jaw in its place under the skull, the teeth closed sharply on my finger. It felt exactly as if it were biting me hard, and I confess that I jumped before I realized that I had been pressing the jaw and the skull together with my other hand. I assure you I was not at all nervous.

It was broad daylight, too, and a fine day, and the sun was streaming into the best bedroom. It would have been absurd to be nervous, and it was only a quick mistaken impression, but it really made me feel queer. Somehow it made me think of the funny verdict of the coroner's jury on Luke's death, "by the hand or teeth of some person or animal unknown". Ever since that I've wished I had seen those marks on his throat, though the lower jaw was missing then.

I have often seen a man do insane things with his hands that he does not realize at all. I once saw a man hanging on by an old awning stop with one hand, leaning backward, outboard, with all his weight on it, and he was just cutting the stop with the knife in his other hand when I got my arms round him. We were in mid-ocean, going twenty knots. He had not the smallest idea what he was doing; neither had I when I managed to pinch my finger between the teeth of that thing. I can feel it now. It was exactly as if it were alive and were trying to bite me. It would if it could, for I know it hates me, poor thing! Do you suppose that what rattles about inside is really a bit of lead?

Well, I'll get the box down presently, and if whatever it is happens to drop out into your hands, that's your affair. If it's only a clod of earth or a pebble, the whole matter would be off my mind, and I don't believe I should ever think of the skull again; but somehow I cannot bring myself to shake out the bit of hard stuff myself. The mere idea that it may be lead makes me confoundedly uncomfortable, yet I've got the conviction that I shall know before long. I shall certainly know. I'm sure Trehearn knows, but he's such a silent beggar

I'll go upstairs now and get it. What? You had better go with me? Ha, ha! do you think I'm afraid of a bandbox and a noise? Nonsense!

Bother the candle, it won't light! As if the ridiculous thing understood what it's wanted for! Look at that—the third match. They light fast enough for my pipe. There, do you see? It's a fresh box, just out of the tin safe where I keep the supply on account of the dampness. Oh, you think the wick of the candle may be damp, do you? All right, I'll light the beastly thing in the fire. That won't go out, at all events. Yes, it sputters a bit, but it will keep lighted now. It burns just like any other candle, doesn't it? The fact is, candles are not very good about here. I don't know where they come from, but they have a way of burning low occasionally, with a greenish flame that spits tiny sparks, and I'm often annoyed by their going out of themselves. It cannot be helped, for it will be long before we have electricity in our village. It really is rather a poor light, isn't it?

You think I had better leave you the candle and take the lamp, do you? I don't like to carry lamps about, that's the truth. I never dropped one in my life, but I have always thought I might, and it's so confoundedly dangerous if you do. Besides, I am pretty well used to these rotten candles by this time.

You may as well finish that glass while I'm getting it, for I don't mean to let you off with less than three before you go to bed. You won't have to go upstairs, either, for I've put you in the old study next to the surgery—that's where I live myself. The fact is, I never ask a friend to sleep upstairs now. The last man who did was Crackenthorpe, and he said he was kept awake all night. You remember old Crack, don't you? He stuck to the Service, and they've just made him an admiral. Yes, I'm off now—unless the candle goes out. I couldn't help asking if you remembered

Crackenthorpe. If anyone had told us that the skinny little idiot he used to be was to turn out the most successful of the lot of us, we should have laughed at the idea, shouldn't we? You and I did not do badly, it's true—but I'm really going now. I don't mean to let you think that I've been putting it off by talking! As if there were anything to be afraid of! If I were scared, I should tell you so quite frankly, and get you to go upstairs with me.

★★★★★★

Here's the box. I brought it down very carefully, so as not to disturb it, poor thing. You see, if it were shaken, the jaw might get separated from it again, and I'm sure it wouldn't like that. Yes, the candle went out as I was coming downstairs, but that was the draught from the leaky window on the landing. Did you hear anything? Yes, there was another scream. Am I pale, do you say? That's nothing. My heart is a little queer sometimes, and I went upstairs too fast. In fact, that's one reason why I really prefer to live altogether on the ground floor.

Wherever the shriek came from, it was not from the skull, for I had the box in my hand when I heard the noise, and here it is now; so we have proved definitely that the screams are produced by something else. I've no doubt I shall find out some day what makes them. Some crevice in the wall, of course, or a crack in a chimney, or a chink in the frame of a window. That's the way all ghost stories end in real life. Do you know, I'm jolly glad I thought of going up and bringing it down for you to see, for that last shriek settles the question. To think that I should have been so weak as to fancy that the poor skull could really cry out like a living thing!

Now I'll open the box, and we'll take it out and look at it under the bright light. It's rather awful to think that the poor lady used to sit there, in your chair, evening after evening, in just the same light, isn't it? But then—I've made up my mind that it's all rubbish from beginning to end, and that it's just an old skull that Luke had when he was a student and perhaps he put it into the lime merely to whiten it, and could not find the jaw.

I made a seal on the string, you see, after I had put the jaw in its place, and I wrote on the cover. There's the old white label on it still, from the milliner's, addressed to Mrs. Pratt when the hat was sent to her, and as there was room I wrote on the edge: "A skull, once the property of the late Luke Pratt, MD." I don't quite know why I wrote that, unless it was with the idea of explaining how the thing happened to be in my possession. I cannot help wondering sometimes what sort of hat it was that came in the bandbox. What colour was it, do you think? Was it a gay spring hat with a bobbing feather and pretty ribands? Strange that the very same box should hold the head that wore the finery—perhaps. No—we made up our minds that it just came from the hospital in London where Luke did his time. It's far better to look at it in that light, isn't it? There's no more connection between that skull and poor Mrs. Pratt than there was between my story about the lead and——

Good Lord! Take the lamp—don't let it go out, if you can help it—I'll have the window fastened again in a second—I say, what a gale! There, it's out! I told you so! Never mind, there's the firelight—I've got the window shut—the bolt was only half down. Was the box blown off the table? Where the deuce is it? There! That won't open again, for I've put up the bar. Good dodge, an old-fashioned bar—there's nothing like it. Now, you find the bandbox while I light the lamp. Confound those wretched matches! Yes, a pipe spill is better—it must light in the fire—hadn't thought of it—thank you—there we are again. Now, where's the box? Yes, put it back on the table, and we'll open it.

That's the first time I have ever known the wind to burst that window open; but it was partly carelessness on my part when I last shut it. Yes, of course I heard the scream. It seemed to go all round the house before it broke in at the window. That proves that it's always been the wind and nothing else, doesn't it? When it was not the wind, it was my imagination I've always been a very imaginative man: I must have been, though I did not know it. As we grow older we understand ourselves better, don't you know?

I'll have a drop of the Hulstkamp neat, by way of an exception, since you are filling up your glass. That damp gust chilled me, and with my rheumatic tendency I'm very much afraid of a chill, for the cold sometimes seems to stick in my joints all winter when it once gets in.

By George, that's good stuff! I'll just light a fresh pipe, now that everything is snug again, and then we'll open the box. I'm so glad we heard that last scream together, with the skull here on the table between us, for a thing cannot possibly be in two places at the same time, and the noise most certainly came from outside, as any noise the wind makes must. You thought you heard it scream through the room after the window was burst open? Oh yes, so did I, but that was natural enough when everything was open. Of course we heard the wind. What could one expect?

Look here, please. I want you to see that the seal is intact before we open the box together. Will you take my glasses? No, you have your own. All right. The seal is sound, you see, and you can read the words of the motto easily. "Sweet and low"—that's it—because the poem goes on "Wind of the Western Sea", and says, "blow him again to me", and all that. Here is the seal on my watch chain, where it's hung for more than forty years. My poor little wife gave it to me when I was courting, and I never had any other. It was just like her to think of those words—she was always fond of Tennyson.

It's no use to cut the string, for it's fastened to the box, so I'll just break the wax and untie the knot, and afterwards we'll seal it up again. You see, I like to feel that the thing is safe in its place, and that nobody can take it out. Not that I should suspect Trehearn of meddling with it, but I always feel that he knows a lot more than he tells.

You see, I've managed it without breaking the string, though when I fastened it I never expected to open the bandbox again. The lid comes off easily enough. There! Now look!

What! Nothing in it! Empty! It's gone, man, the skull is gone!

No, there's nothing the matter with me. I'm only trying to

442

collect my thoughts. It's so strange. I'm positively certain that it was inside when I put on the seal last spring. I can't have imagined that: it's utterly impossible. If I ever took a stiff glass with a friend now and then, I would admit that I might have made some idiotic mistake when I had taken too much. But I don't, and I never did. A pint of ale at supper and half a go of rum at bedtime was the most I ever took in my good days. I believe it's always we sober fellows who get rheumatism and gout! Yet there was my seal, and there is the empty bandbox. That's plain enough.

I say, I don't half like this. It's not right. There's something wrong about it, in my opinion. You needn't talk to me about supernatural manifestations, for I don't believe in them, not a little bit! Somebody must have tampered with the seal and stolen the skull. Sometimes, when I go out to work in the garden in summer, I leave my watch and chain on the table. Trehearn must have taken the seal then, and used it, for he would be quite sure that I should not come in for at least an hour.

If it was not Trehearn—oh, don't talk to me about the possibility that the thing has got out by itself! If it has, it must be somewhere about the house, in some out-of-the-way corner, waiting. We may come upon it anywhere, waiting for us, don't you know?—just waiting in the dark. Then it will scream at me; it will shriek at me in the dark, for it hates me, I tell you!

The bandbox is quite empty. We are not dreaming, either of us. There, I turn it upside down.

What's that? Something fell out as I turned it over. It's on the floor, it s near your feet. I know it is, and we must find it. Help me to find it, man. Have you got it? For God's sake, give it to me, quickly!

Lead! I knew it when I heard it fall. I knew it couldn't be anything else by the little thud it made on the hearthrug. So it was lead after all and Luke did it.

I feel a little bit shaken up—not exactly nervous, you know, but badly shaken up, that's the fact. Anybody would, I should think. After all, you cannot say that it's fear of the thing, for I went up and brought it down—at least, I believed I was bringing it down, and that's the same thing, and by George, rather than give in to such silly nonsense, I'll take the box upstairs again and put it back in its place. It's not that. It's the certainty that the poor little woman came to her end in that way, by my fault, because I told the story. That's what is so dreadful. Somehow, I had always hoped that I should never be quite sure of it, but there is no doubting it now. Look at that!

Look at it! That little lump of lead with no particular shape. Think of what it did, man! Doesn't it make you shiver? He gave her something to make her sleep, of course, but there must have been one moment of awful agony. Think of having boiling lead poured into your brain. Think of it. She was dead before she could scream, but only think of—oh! there it is again—it's just outside—I know it's just outside—I can't keep it out of my head!—oh!—oh!

★★★★★★

You thought I had fainted? No, I wish I had, for it would have stopped sooner. It's all very well to say that it's only a noise, and that a noise never hurt anybody—you're as white as a shroud yourself. There's only one thing to be done, if we hope to close an eye tonight. We must find it and put it back into its bandbox and shut it up in the cupboard, where it likes to be I don't know how it got out, but it wants to get in again. That's why it screams so awfully tonight—it was never so bad as this—never since I first——

Bury it? Yes, if we can find it, we'll bury it, if it takes us all night. We'll bury it six feet deep and ram down the earth over it, so that it shall never get out again, and if it screams, we shall hardly hear it so deep down. Quick, we'll get the lantern and look for it. It cannot be far away; I'm sure it's just outside—it was coming in when I shut the window, I know it.

Yes, you're quite right. I'm losing my senses, and I must get hold of myself. Don't speak to me for a minute or two; I'll sit quite still and keep my eyes shut and repeat something I know. That's the best way.

"Add together the altitude, the latitude, and the polar distance, divide by two and subtract the altitude from the half-sum; then add the logarithm of the secant of the latitude, the cosecant of the polar distance, the cosine of the half-sum and the sine of the half-sum minus the altitude"—there! Don't say that I'm out of my senses, for my memory is all right, isn't it?

Of course, you may say that it's mechanical, and that we never forget the things we learned when we were boys and have used almost every day for a lifetime. But that's the very point. When a man is going crazy, it's the mechanical part of his mind that gets out of order and won't work right; he remembers things that never happened, or he sees things that aren't real, or he hears noises when there is perfect silence. That's not what is the matter with either of us, is it?

Come, we'll get the lantern and go round the house. It's not raining—only blowing like old boots, as we used to say. The lantern is in the cupboard under the stairs in the hall, and I always keep it trimmed in case of a wreck.

No use to look for the thing? I don't see how you can say that. It was nonsense to talk of burying it, of course, for it doesn't want to be buried; it wants to go back into its bandbox and be taken upstairs, poor thing! Trehearn took it out, I know, and made the seal over again. Perhaps he took it to the churchyard, and he may have meant well. I dare say he thought that it would not scream any more if it were quietly laid in consecrated ground, near where it belongs. But it has come home. Yes, that's it. He's not half a bad fellow, Trehearn, and rather religiously inclined, I think. Does not that sound natural, and reasonable, and well meant? He supposed it screamed because it was not decently buried—with the rest. But he was wrong. How should he know that it screams at me because it hates me, and because it's my fault that there was that little lump of lead in it?

No use to look for it, anyhow? Nonsense! I tell you it wants to be found—Hark! what's that knocking? Do you hear it? Knock—knock—knock—three times, then a pause, and then again. It has a hollow sound, hasn't it?

445

It has come home. I've heard that knock before. It wants to come in and be taken upstairs in its box. It's at the front door.

Will you come with me? We'll take it in. Yes, I own that I don't like to go alone and open the door. The thing will roll in and stop against my foot, just as it did before, and the light will go out. I'm a good deal shaken by finding that bit of lead, and, besides, my heart isn't quite right—too much strong tobacco, perhaps. Besides, I'm quite willing to own that I'm a bit nervous tonight, if I never was before in my life.

That's right, come along! I'll take the box with me, so as not to come back. Do you hear the knocking? It's not like any other knocking I ever heard. If you will hold this door open, I can find the lantern under the stairs by the light from this room without bringing the lamp into the hall—it would only go out.

The thing knows we are coming—hark! It's impatient to get in. Don't shut the door till the lantern is ready, whatever you do. There will be the usual trouble with the matches, I suppose—no, the first one, by Jove! I tell you it wants to get in, so there's no trouble. All right with that door now; shut it, please. Now come and hold the lantern, for it's blowing so hard outside that I shall have to use both hands. That's it, hold the light low. Do you hear the knocking still? Here goes—I'll open just enough with my foot against the bottom of the door—now!

Catch it! it's only the wind that blows it across the floor, that's all—there s half a hurricane outside, I tell you! Have you got it? The bandbox is on the table. One minute, and I'll have the bar up. There!

Why did you throw it into the box so roughly? It doesn't like that, you know.

What do you say? Bitten your hand? Nonsense, man! You did just what I did. You pressed the jaws together with your other hand and pinched yourself. Let me see. You don't mean to say you have drawn blood? You must have squeezed hard by Jove, for the skin is certainly torn. I'll give you some carbolic solution for it before we go to bed, for they say a scratch from a skull's tooth may go bad and give trouble.

Come inside again and let me see it by the lamp. I'll bring the bandbox—never mind the lantern, it may just as well burn in the hall for I shall need it presently when I go up the stairs. Yes, shut the door if you will; it makes it more cheerful and bright. Is your finger still bleeding? I'll get you the carbolic in an instant; just let me see the thing.

Ugh! There's a drop of blood on the upper jaw. It's on the eyetooth. Ghastly, isn't it? When I saw it running along the floor of the hall, the strength almost went out of my hands, and I felt my knees bending, then I understood that it was the gale, driving it over the smooth boards. You don t blame me? No, I should think not! We were boys together, and we've seen a thing or two, and we may just as well own to each other that we were both in a beastly funk when it slid across the floor at you. No wonder you pinched your finger picking it up, after that, if I did the same thing out of sheer nervousness, in broad daylight, with the sun streaming in on me.

Strange that the jaw should stick to it so closely, isn't it? I suppose it's the dampness, for it shuts like a vice—I have wiped off the drop of blood, for it was not nice to look at. I'm not going to try to open the jaws, don't be afraid! I shall not play any tricks with the poor thing, but I'll just seal the box again, and we'll take it upstairs and put it away where it wants to be. The wax is on the writing-table by the window. Thank you. It will be long before I leave my seal lying about again, for Trehearn to use, I can tell you. Explain? I don't explain natural phenomena, but if you choose to think that Trehearn had hidden it somewhere in the bushes, and that the gale blew it to the house against the door, and made it knock, as if it wanted to be let in, you're not thinking the impossible, and I'm quite ready to agree with you.

Do you see that? You can swear that you've actually seen me seal it this time, in case anything of the kind should occur again. The wax fastens the strings to the lid, which cannot possibly be lifted, even enough to get in one finger. You're quite satisfied, aren't you? Yes. Besides, I shall lock the cupboard and keep the key in my pocket hereafter.

Now we can take the lantern and go upstairs. Do you know? I'm very much inclined to agree with your theory that the wind blew it against the house. I'll go ahead, for I know the stairs; just hold the lantern near my feet as we go up. How the wind howls and whistles! Did you feel the sand on the floor under your shoes as we crossed the hall?

Yes—this is the door of the best bedroom. Hold up the lantern, please. This side, by the head of the bed. I left the cupboard open when I got the box. Isn't it queer how the faint odour of women's dresses will hang about an old closet for years? This is the shelf. You've seen me set the box there, and now you see me turn the key and put it into my pocket. So that's done!

Goodnight. Are you sure you're quite comfortable? It's not much of a room, but I dare say you would as soon sleep here as upstairs tonight. If you want anything, sing out; there's only a lath and plaster partition between us. There's not so much wind on this side by half. There's the Hollands on the table, if you'll have one more nightcap. No? Well, do as you please. Goodnight again, and don't dream about that thing, if you can.

★★★★★★

The following paragraph appeared in the *Penraddon News*, 23rd November 1906:

MYSTERIOUS DEATH OF
A RETIRED SEA CAPTAIN

The village of Tredcombe is much disturbed by the strange death of Captain Charles Braddock, and all sorts of impossible stories are circulating with regard to the circumstances, which certainly seem difficult of explanation. The retired captain, who had successfully commanded in his time the largest and fastest liners belonging to one of the principal transatlantic steamship companies, was found dead in his bed on Tuesday morning in his own cottage, a quarter of a mile from the village. An examination was made at once by the local practitioner, which revealed the horrible fact that the deceased had been bitten in the throat by a human assailant, with such amazing force as to crush the windpipe and cause death. The marks of the teeth of both jaws were so plainly visible on the skin that they could be counted, but the perpetrator of the deed had evidently lost the two lower middle incisors.

It is hoped that this peculiarity may help to identify the murderer, who can only be a dangerous escaped maniac. The deceased, though over sixty-five years of age, is said to have been a hale man of considerable physical strength, and it is remarkable that no signs of any struggle were visible in the room, nor could it be ascertained how the murderer had entered the house. Warning has been sent to all the insane asylums in the United Kingdom, but as yet no information has been received regarding the escape of any dangerous patient.

The coroner's Jury returned the somewhat singular verdict that Captain Braddock came to his death "by the hands or teeth of some person unknown". The local surgeon is said to have expressed privately the opinion that the maniac is a woman, a view he deduces from the small size of the jaws, as shown by the marks of the teeth. The whole affair is shrouded in mystery. Captain Braddock was a widower, and lived alone. He leaves no children.

(Author's Note.—Students of ghost lore and haunted houses will find the foundation of the foregoing story in the legends about a skull which is still preserved in the farmhouse called Bettiscombe Manor, situated, I believe, on the Dorsetshire coast.)

The King's Messenger

It was a rather dim daylight dinner I remember that quite distinctly, for I could see the glow of the sunset over the trees in the park, through the high window at the west end of the dining-room. I had expected to find a larger party, I believe, for I recollect being a little surprised at seeing only a dozen people assembled at table. It seemed to me that in old times, ever so long ago, when I had last stayed in that house, there had been as many as thirty or forty guests. I recognized some of them among a number of beautiful portraits that hung on the walls. There was room for a great many because there was only one huge window, at one end, and one large door at the other.

I was very much surprised, too, to see a portrait of myself, evidently painted about twenty years ago by Lenbach. It seemed very strange that I should have so completely forgotten the picture, and that I should not be able to remember having sat for it. We were good friends, it is true, and he might have painted it from memory, without my knowledge, but it was certainly strange that he should never have told me about it. The portraits that hung in the dining-room were all very good indeed and all, I should say, by the best painters of that time.

My left-hand neighbour was a lovely young girl whose name I had forgotten, though I had known her long, and I fancied that she looked a little disappointed when she saw that I was beside her. On my right there was a vacant seat, and beyond it sat an elderly woman with features as hard as the overwhelmingly splendid diamonds she wore. Her eyes made me think of grey glass marbles cemented into a stone mask. It was odd that her name should have escaped me, too, for I had often met her.

The table looked irregular, and I counted the guests mechanically while I ate my soup. We were only twelve, but the empty chair beside me was the thirteenth place.

I suppose it was not very tactful of me to mention this, but I wanted to say something to the beautiful girl on my left, and no other subject for a general remark suggested itself. Just as I was going to speak I remembered who she was.

"Miss Lorna," I said, to attract her attention, for she was looking away from me toward the door. "I hope you are not superstitious about there being thirteen at table, are you?"

"We are only twelve," she said, in the sweetest voice in the world. "Yes; but someone else is coming. There's an empty chair here beside me."

"Oh, he doesn't count," said Miss Lorna quietly. "At least, not for everybody. When did you get here? Just in time for dinner, I suppose."

"Yes," I answered. "I'm in luck to be beside you. It seems an age since we were last here together."

"It does indeed," Miss Lorna sighed and looked at the pictures on the opposite wall. "I've lived a lifetime since I saw you last."

I smiled at the exaggeration. "When you are thirty, you won't talk of having your life behind you," I said.

"I shall never be thirty," Miss Lorna answered, with such an odd little air of conviction that I did not think of anything to say. "Besides, life isn't made up of years or months or hours, or of anything that has to do with time," she continued. "You ought to know that. Our bodies are something better than mere clocks, wound up to show just how old we are at every moment, by our hair turning grey and our teeth falling out and our faces getting wrinkled and yellow, or puffy and red. Look at your own portrait over there. I don't mind saying that you must have been twenty years younger when that was painted, but I'm sure you are just the same man today, improved by age, perhaps."

I heard a sweet little echoing laugh that seemed very far away; and indeed I could not have sworn that it rippled from Miss Lorna's beautiful lips, for though they were parted and smiling, my impression is that they did not move, even as little as most women's lips are moved by laughter.

"Thank you for thinking me improved," I said. "I find you a little changed, too. I was just going to say that you seem sadder, but you laughed just then."

"Did I? I suppose that's the right thing to do when the play is over, isn't it?"

"If it has been an amusing play," I answered, humouring her. The wonderful violet eyes turned to me, full of light. "It's not been a bad play. I don't complain."

"Why do you speak of it as over?"

"I'll tell you, because I'm sure you will keep my secret. You will, won't you? We were always such good friends, you and I, even two years ago when I was young and silly. Will you promise not to tell anyone till I'm gone?"

"Gone?"

"Yes. Will you promise?"

"Of course I will. But . . ." I did not finish the sentence, because Miss Lorna bent nearer to me, so as to speak in a much lower tone. While I listened, I felt her sweet young breath on my cheek.

"I'm going away tonight with the man who is to sit at your other side," she said. "He's a little late; he often is, for he is tremendously busy; but he'll come presently, and after dinner we shall just stroll out into the garden and never come back. That's my secret. You won't betray me, will you?" Again, as she looked at me, I heard that far-off silver laugh, sweet and low. I was almost too much surprised by what she had told me to notice how still her parted lips were, but that comes back to me now, with many other details.

"My dear Miss Lorna," I said, "do think of your parents before taking such a step."

"I have thought of them," she answered. "Of course they

would never consent, and I am very sorry to leave them, but it can't be helped."

At this moment, as often happens when two people are talking in low tones at a large dinner-table, there was a momentary lull in the general conversation, and I was spared the trouble of making any further answer to what Miss Lorna had told me so unexpectedly, and with such profound confidence in my discretion.

To tell the truth, she would very probably not have listened, whether my words expressed sympathy or protest, for she had turned suddenly pale, and her eyes were wide and dark. The lull in the talk at table was due to the appearance of the man who was to occupy the vacant place beside me.

He had entered the room very quietly, and he made no elaborate apology for being late, as he sat down, bending his head courteously to our hostess and her husband, and smiling in a gentle sort of way as he nodded to the others.

"Please forgive me," he said quietly. "I was detained by a funeral and missed the train."

It was not until he had taken his place that he looked across me at Miss Lorna and exchanged a glance of recognition with her. I noticed that the lady with the hard face and the splendid diamonds, who was at his other side, drew away from him a little, as if not wishing even to let his sleeve brush against her bare arm. It occurred to me at the same time that Miss Lorna must be wishing me anywhere else than between her and the man with whom she was just about to run away, and I wished for their sake and mine that I could change places with him. He was certainly not like other men, and though few people would have called him handsome there was something about him that instantly fixed the attention; rarely beautiful though Miss Lorna was, almost everyone would have noticed him first on entering the room, and most people, I think, would have been more interested by his face than by hers. I could well imagine that some women might love him, even to distraction, though it was just as easy to understand that others might be strongly repelled by

453

him, and might even fear him.

For my part, I shall not try to describe him as one describes an ordinary man, with a dozen or so adjectives that leave nothing to the imagination but yet offer it no picture that it can grasp. My instinct was to fear him rather than think of him as a possible friend, but I could not help feeling instant admiration for him, as one does at first sight for anything that is very complete, harmonious, and strong. He was dark, and pale with a shadowy pallor I never saw in any other face; the features of thrice-great Hermes were not modelled in more perfect symmetry, his luminous eyes were not unkind, but there was something fateful in them, and they were set very deep under the grand white brow. His age I could not guess, but I should have called him young; standing, I had seen that he was tall and sinewy, and now that he was seated, he had the unmistakable look of a man accustomed to be in authority, to be heard and to be obeyed. His hands were white, his fingers straight, lean, and very strong.

Everyone at the table seemed to know him, but as often happens among civilized people no one called him by name in speaking to him.

"We were beginning to be afraid that you might not get here," said our host.

"Really?" The Thirteenth Guest smiled quietly, but shook his head. "Did you ever know me to break an engagement, under any circumstances?"

The master of the house laughed, though not very cordially, I thought. "No," he answered. "Your reputation for keeping your appointments is proverbial. Even your enemies must admit that."

The Guest nodded and smiled again. Miss Lorna bent toward me.

"What do you think of him?" she asked, almost in a whisper.

"Very striking sort of man," I answered, in a low tone. "But I'm inclined to be a little afraid of him."

"So was I, at first," she said, and I heard the silver laugh again.

454

"But that soon wears off," she went on. "You'll know him better some day."

"Shall I?"

"Yes; I'm quite sure you will. Oh, I don't pretend that I fell in love with him at first sight. I went through a phase of feeling afraid of him, as almost everyone does. You see, when people first meet him they cannot possibly know how kind and gentle he can be, though he is so tremendously strong. I've heard him called cruel and ruthless and cold, but it's not true. Indeed it's not. He can be as gentle as a woman, and he's the truest friend in all the world."

I was going to ask her to tell me his name, but just then I saw that she was looking at him, across me, and I sat as far back in my chair as I could, so that they might speak to each other if they wished to. Their eyes met, and there was a longing light in both. I could not help glancing from one to the other; and Miss Lorna's sweet lips moved almost imperceptibly, though no sound came from them. I have seen young lovers make that small sign to each other even across a room, the signal of a kiss given and returned in the heart's thoughts.

If she had been less beautiful and young, if the man she loved had not been so magnificently manly, it would have irritated me, but it seemed natural that they should love and not be ashamed of it, and I only hoped that no one else at the table had noticed the tenderly quivering little contraction of the young girl's exquisite mouth.

"You remembered," said the man quietly. "I got your message this morning. Thank you."

"I hope it's not going to be very hard," murmured Miss Lorna, smiling. "Not that it would make any great difference if it were," she added more thoughtfully.

"It's the easiest thing in life," he said, "And I promise that you shall never regret it."

"I trust you," the young girl answered simply.

Then she turned away, for she no doubt felt the awkwardness of talking to him across me of a secret which she had confided to me without letting him know that she had done so. Instinctively I turned to him, feeling that the moment had come for disregarding formality and making his acquaintance, since we were neighbours at table in a friend's house and I had known Miss Lorna so long. Besides, it is always interesting to talk with a man who is just going to do something very dangerous or dramatic and who does not guess that you know what he is about.

"I suppose you motored here from town, as you said you missed the train," I said. "It's a good road, isn't it?"

"Yes, I literally flew," replied the dark man, with his gentle smile. "I hope you're not superstitious about thirteen at table?"

"Not in the least," I answered. "In the first place, I'm a fatalist about everything that doesn't depend on my own free will. As I have not the slightest intention of doing anything to shorten my life, it will certainly not come to an abrupt end by any autosuggestion arising from a silly superstition like that about thirteen."

"Autosuggestion? That's rather a new light on the old beliefs."

"And secondly," I continued, "I don't believe in death. There is no such thing."

"Really?" My neighbour seemed greatly surprised. "How do you mean?" he asked. "I don't think I understand you."

"I'm sure I don't," put in Miss Lorna, and the silver laugh followed. She had overheard the conversation, and some of the others were listening, too.

"You don't kill a book by translating it," I said, rather glad to expound my views. "Death is only a translation of life into another language. That's what I mean."

"That's a most interesting point of view," observed the Thirteenth Guest thoughtfully. "I never thought of the matter in that way before, though I've often seen the expression 'translated' in epitaphs. Are you sure that you are not indulging in a little paronomasia?"

"What's that?" inquired the hard-faced lady, with all the contempt which a scholarly word deserves in polite society.

"It means punning," I answered. "No, I am not making a pun. Grave subjects do not lend themselves to low forms of humour. I assure you, I am quite in earnest. Death, in the ordinary sense, is not a real phenomenon at all, so long as there is any life in the universe. It's a name we apply to a change we only partly understand."

"Learned discussions are an awful bore," said the hard-faced lady very audibly.

"I don't advise you to argue the question too sharply with your neighbour there," laughed the master of the house, leaning forward and speaking to me. "He'll get the better of you. He's an expert at what you call 'translating people into another language.'"

If the man beside me was a famous surgeon, as our host perhaps meant, it seemed to me that the remark was not in very good taste. He looked more like a soldier.

"Does our friend mean that you are in the army, and that you are a dangerous person?" I asked of him.

"No," he answered quietly. "I'm only a King's Messenger, and in my own opinion I'm not at all dangerous."

"It must be rather an active life," I said, in order to say something; "constantly coming and going, I suppose?"

"Yes, constantly."

I felt that Miss Lorna was watching and listening, and I turned to her, only to find that she was again looking beyond me, at my neighbour, though he did not see her. I remember her face very distinctly as it was just then; the recollection is, in fact the last impression I retain of her matchless beauty, for I never saw her after that evening.

It is something to have seen one of the most beautiful women in the world gazing at the man who was more to her than life and all it held, it is something I cannot forget. But he did not return her look just then, for he had joined in the general conversation, and very soon afterward he practically absorbed it.

He talked well; more than well, marvellously; for before long even the lady with the hard face was listening spellbound, with the rest of us, to his stories of nations and tales of men, brilliant descriptions, anecdotes of heroism and tenderness that were each a perfect coin from the mint of humanity, with dashes of daring wit, glimpses of a profound insight into the great mystery of the beyond, and now and then a manly comment on life that came straight from the heart: never, in all my long experience, have I heard poet, or scholar, or soldier, or ruler of men talk as he did that evening.

And as I listened I was more and more amazed that such a man should be but a simple King's Messenger, as he said he was, earning a poor gentleman's living by carrying His Majesty's dispatches from London to the ends of the earth, and I made some sad and sober inward reflections on the vast difference between the gift of talking supremely well and the genius a man must have to accomplish even one little thing that may endure in history, in literature, or in art.

"Do you wonder that I love him?" whispered Miss Lorna. Even in a whisper I heard the glorious pride of a woman who loves altogether and wholly believes that there is no one like her chosen man.

"No," I answered, "for it is no wonder. I only hope—" I stopped, feeling that it would be foolish and unkind to express the doubt I felt.

"You hope that I may not be disappointed," said Miss Lorna, still almost in a whisper. "That was what you were going to say, I'm sure."

I nodded, in spite of myself, and met her eyes; they were full of a wonderful light.

"No one was ever disappointed in him," she murmured— "no living being, neither man, nor woman, nor child. With him I shall have peace and love without end."

"Without end?"

"Yes. Forever and ever!"

After dinner we scattered through the great rooms in the soft evening light of mid-June, and by and by I was standing at an open window, looking out across the garden.

In the distance, Lorna was walking slowly away down the broad avenue with a tall man; and while they were still in sight, though far away, I am sure that I saw his arm steal round her as if he were drawing her on, and her head bent lovingly to his shoulder; and so they glided away into the twilight and disappeared.

Then at last I turned to my hostess. "Do you mind telling me the name of that man who came in late and talked so well?" I asked. "You all seemed to know him like an old friend."

She looked at me in profound surprise. "Do you mean to say that you do not know who he is?" she asked.

"No. I never met him before. He is a most extraordinary man to be only a King's Messenger."

"He is indeed the King's Messenger, my dear friend. His name is Death."

★★★★★★

I dreamed this dream one afternoon last summer, dozing in my chair on deck, under the double awning, when the *Alda* was anchored off Goletta, in sight of Carthage, and the cool north breeze was blowing down the deep gulf of Tunis. I must have been wakened by some slight sound from a boat alongside, for when I opened my eyes my man was standing a little way off, evidently waiting till I should finish my nap. He brought me a telegram which had just come on board, and I opened it rather drowsily, not expecting any particular news. It was from England, from a very dear friend.

Lorna died suddenly last night at Church Hadley.

That was all; the dream had been a message. "With him I shall have peace and love without end."

Thank God, I hear those words in her own voice, whenever I think of her.

Man Overboard!

Yes—I have heard "Man overboard!" a good many times since I was a boy, and once or twice I have seen the man go. There are more men lost in that way than passengers on ocean steamers ever learn of. I have stood looking over the rail on a dark night, when there was a step beside me, and something flew past my head like a big black bat—and then there was a splash! Stokers often go like that. They go mad with the heat, and they slip up on deck and are gone before anybody can stop them, often without being seen or heard.

Now and then a passenger will do it, but he generally has what he thinks a pretty good reason. I have seen a man empty his revolver into a crowd of emigrants forward, and then go over like a rocket. Of course, any officer who respects himself will do what he can to pick a man up, if the weather is not so heavy that he would have to risk his ship; but I don't think I remember seeing a man come back when he was once fairly gone more than two or three times in all my life, though we have often picked up the life-buoy, and sometimes the fellow's cap.

Stokers and passengers jump over; I never knew a sailor to do that, drunk or sober. Yes, they say it has happened on hard ships, but I never knew a case myself. Once in a long time a man is fished out when it is just too late, and dies in the boat before you can get him aboard, and—well, I don't know that I ever told that story since it happened—I knew a fellow who went over, and came back dead. I didn't see him after he came back; only one of us did, but we all knew he was there.

No, I am not giving you "sharks." There isn't a shark in this story, and I don't know that I would tell it at all if we weren't alone, just you and I. But you and I have seen things in various parts, and maybe you will understand. Anyhow, you know that I am telling what I know about, and nothing else; and it has been on my mind to tell you ever since it happened, only there hasn't been a chance.

It's a long story, and it took some time to happen; and it began a good many years ago, in October, as well as I can remember. I was mate then; I passed the local Marine Board for master about three years later. She was the *Helen B. Jackson*, of New York, with lumber for the West Indies, four-masted schooner, Captain Hackstaff. She was an old-fashioned one, even then—no steam donkey, and all to do by hand. There were still sailors in the coasting trade in those days, you remember. She wasn't a hard ship, for the old man was better than most of them, though he kept to himself and had a face like a monkey-wrench.

We were thirteen, all told, in the ship's company; and some of them afterwards thought that might have had something to do with it, but I had all that nonsense knocked out of me when I was a boy. I don't mean to say that I like to go to sea on a Friday, but I *have* gone to sea on a Friday, and nothing has happened; and twice before that we have been thirteen, because one of the hands didn't turn up at the last minute, and nothing ever happened either—nothing worse than the loss of a light spar or two, or a little canvas. Whenever I have been wrecked, we had sailed as cheerily as you please—no thirteens, no Fridays, no dead men in the hold. I believe it generally happens that way.

I dare say you remember those two Benton boys that were so much alike? It is no wonder, for they were twin brothers. They shipped with us as boys on the old *Boston Belle*, when you were mate and I was before the mast. I never was quite sure which was which of those two, even then; and when they both had beards it was harder than ever to tell them apart. One was Jim, and the other was Jack; James Benton and John Benton. The only difference I ever could see was, that one seemed to be rather more cheerful and inclined to talk than the other; but one couldn't even be sure of that. Perhaps they had moods. Anyhow, there was one of them that used to whistle when he was alone. He only knew one tune, and that was *Nancy Lee*, and the other didn't know any tune at all; but I may be mistaken about that, too. Perhaps they both knew it.

Well, those two Benton boys turned up on board the *Helen B. Jackson*. They had been on half a dozen ships since the *Boston Belle*, and they had grown up and were good seamen. They had reddish beards and bright blue eyes and freckled faces; and they were quiet fellows, good workmen on rigging, pretty willing, and both good men at the wheel. They managed to be in the same watch—it was the port watch on the *Helen B.*, and that was mine, and I had great confidence in them both. If there was any job aloft that needed two hands, they were always the first to jump into the rigging; but that doesn't often happen on a fore-and-aft schooner. If it breezed up, and the jibtopsail was to be taken in, they never minded a wetting, and they would be out at the bowsprit end before there was a hand at the down-haul. The men liked them for that, and because they didn't blow about what they could do. I remember one day in a reefing job, the downhaul parted and came down on deck from the peak of the spanker.

When the weather moderated, and we shook the reefs out, the downhaul was forgotten until we happened to think we might soon need it again. There was some sea on, and the boom was off and the gaff was slamming. One of those Benton boys was at the wheel, and before I knew what he was doing, the other was out on the gaff with the end of the new downhaul, trying to reeve it through its block. The one who was steering watched him, and got as white as cheese. The other one was swinging about on the gaff end, and every time she rolled to lee-ward he brought up with a jerk that would have sent anything but a monkey flying into space. But he didn't leave it until he had rove the new rope, and he got back all right.

I think it was Jack at the wheel; the one that seemed more

cheerful, the one that whistled *Nancy Lee*. He had rather have been doing the job himself than watch his brother do it, and he had a scared look; but he kept her as steady as he could in the swell, and he drew a long breath when Jim had worked his way back to the peak-halliard block, and had something to hold on to. I think it was Jim.

They had good togs, too, and they were neat and clean men in the forecastle. I knew they had nobody belonging to them ashore,—no mother, no sisters, and no wives; but somehow they both looked as if a woman overhauled them now and then. I remember that they had one ditty bag between them, and they had a woman's thimble in it. One of the men said something about it to them, and they looked at each other; and one smiled, but the other didn't. Most of their clothes were alike, but they had one red guernsey between them. For some time I used to think it was always the same one that wore it, and I thought that might be a way to tell them apart. But then I heard one asking the other for it, and saying that the other had worn it last. So that was no sign either. The cook was a West Indiaman, called James Lawley; his father had been hanged for putting lights in cocoa-nut trees where they didn't belong. But he was a good cook, and knew his business; and it wasn't soup-and-bully and dog's-body every Sunday. That's what I meant to say. On Sunday the cook called both those boys Jim, and on week-days he called them Jack. He used to say he must be right sometimes if he did that, because even the hands on a painted clock point right twice a day.

What started me to trying for some way of telling the Bentons apart was this. I heard them talking about a girl. It was at night, in our watch, and the wind had headed us off a little rather sud-denly, and when we had flattened in the jibs, we clewed down the topsails, while the two Benton boys got the spanker sheet aft. One of them was at the helm. I coiled down the mizzen-topsail downhaul myself, and was going aft to see how she headed up, when I stopped to look at a light, and leaned against the deck-house. While I was standing there I heard the two boys talking.

It sounded as if they had talked of the same thing before, and as far as I could tell, the voice I heard first belonged to the one who wasn't quite so cheerful as the other,—the one who was Jim when one knew which he was.

"Does Mamie know?" Jim asked.

"Not yet," Jack answered quietly. He was at the wheel. "I mean to tell her next time we get home."

"All right."

That was all I heard, because I didn't care to stand there listening while they were talking about their own affairs; so I went aft to look into the binnacle, and I told the one at the wheel to keep her so as long as she had way on her, for I thought the wind would back up again before long, and there was land to leeward. When he answered, his voice, somehow, didn't sound like the cheerful one. Perhaps his brother had relieved the wheel while they had been speaking, but what I had heard set me wondering which of them it was that had a girl at home. There's lots of time for wondering on a schooner in fair weather.

After that I thought I noticed that the two brothers were more silent when they were together. Perhaps they guessed that I had overheard something that night, and kept quiet when I was about. Some men would have amused themselves by trying to chaff them separately about the girl at home, and I suppose whichever one it was would have let the cat out of the bag if I had done that. But, somehow, I didn't like to. Yes, I was thinking of getting married myself at that time, so I had a sort of fellow-feeling for whichever one it was, that made me not want to chaff him.

They didn't talk much, it seemed to me; but in fair weather, when there was nothing to do at night, and one was steering, the other was everlastingly hanging round as if he were waiting to relieve the wheel, though he might have been enjoying a quiet nap for all I cared in such weather. Or else, when one was taking his turn at the lookout, the other would be sitting on an anchor beside him. One kept near the other, at night more than in the daytime. I noticed that. They were fond of sitting on that anchor, and they generally tucked away their pipes under it, for the *Helen B.* was a dry boat in most weather, and like most fore-and-afters was better on a wind than going free. With a beam sea we sometimes shipped a little water aft. We were by the stern, anyhow, on that voyage, and that is one reason why we lost the man.

We fell in with a southerly gale, south-east at first; and then the barometer began to fall while you could watch it, and a long swell began to come up from the south'ard. A couple of months earlier we might have been in for a cyclone, but it's "October all over" in those waters, as you know better than I. It was just going to blow, and then it was going to rain, that was all; and we had plenty of time to make everything snug before it breezed up much. It blew harder after sunset, and by the time it was quite dark it was a full gale. We had shortened sail for it, but as we were by the stern we were carrying the spanker close reefed instead of the storm trysail. She steered better so, as long as we didn't have to heave to. I had the first watch with the Benton boys, and we had not been on deck an hour when a child might have seen that the weather meant business.

The old man came up on deck and looked round, and in less than a minute he told us to give her the trysail. That meant heaving to, and I was glad of it; for though the *Helen B.* was a good vessel enough, she wasn't a new ship by a long way, and it did her no good to drive her in that weather. I asked whether I should call all hands, but just then the cook came aft, and the old man said he thought we could manage the job without waking the sleepers, and the trysail was handy on deck already, for we hadn't been expecting anything better. We were all in oilskins, of course, and the night was as black as a coal mine with only a ray of light from the slit in the binnacle shield, and you couldn't tell one man from another except by his voice.

The old man took the wheel; we got the boom amidships, and he jammed her into the wind until she had hardly any way. It was blowing now, and it was all that I and two others could do to get in the slack of the downhaul, while the others low-

465

ered away at the peak and throat, and we had our hands full to get a couple of turns round the wet sail. It's all child's play on a fore-and-after compared with reefing topsails in anything like weather, but the gear of a schooner sometimes does unhandy things that you don't expect, and those everlasting long halliards get foul of everything if they get adrift. I remember thinking how unhandy that particular job was. Somebody unhooked the throat-halliard block, and thought he had hooked it into the head-cringle of the trysail, and sang out to hoist away, but he had missed it in the dark, and the heavy block went flying into the lee rigging, and nearly killed him when it swung back with the weather roll.

Then the old man got her up in the wind until the jib was shaking like thunder; then he held her off, and she went off as soon as the head-sails filled, and he couldn't get her back again without the spanker. Then the *Helen B.* did her favourite trick, and before we had time to say much we had a sea over the quarter and were up to our waists, with the parrels of the trysail only half becketed round the mast, and the deck so full of gear that you couldn't put your foot on a plank, and the spanker beginning to get adrift again, being badly stopped, and the general confusion and hell's delight that you can only have on a fore-and-after when there's nothing really serious the matter.

Of course, I don't mean to say that the old man couldn't have steered his trick as well as you or I or any other seaman; but I don't believe he had ever been on board the *Helen B.* before, or had his hand on her wheel till then; and he didn't know her ways. I don't mean to say that what happened was his fault. I don't know whose fault it was. Perhaps nobody was to blame. But I knew something happened somewhere on board when we shipped that sea, and you'll never get it out of my head. I hadn't any spare time myself, for I was becketing the rest of the trysail to the mast. We were on the starboard tack, and the throat-halliard came down to port as usual, and I suppose there were at least three men at it, hoisting away, while I was at the beckets.

Now I am going to tell you something. You have known me, man and boy, several voyages; and you are older than I am; and you have always been a good friend to me. Now, do you think I am the sort of man to think I hear things where there isn't anything to hear, or to think I see things when there is nothing to see? No, you don't. Thank you. Well now, I had passed the last becket, and I sang out to the men to sway away, and I was standing on the jaws of the spanker-gaff, with my left hand on the bolt-rope of the trysail, so that I could feel when it was board-taut, and I wasn't thinking of anything except being glad the job was over, and that we were going to heave her to. It was as black as a coal-pocket, except that you could see the streaks on the seas as they went by, and abaft the deck-house I could see the ray of light from the binnacle on the captain's yellow oilskin as he stood at the wheel—or rather I might have seen it if I had looked round at that minute.

But I didn't look round. I heard a man whistling. It was "Nancy Lee", and I could have sworn that the man was right over my head in the crosstrees. Only somehow I knew very well that if anybody could have been up there, and could have whistled a tune, there were no living ears sharp enough to hear it on deck then. I heard it distinctly, and at the same time I heard the real whistling of the wind in the weather rigging, sharp and clear as the steam-whistle on a Dago's peanut-cart in New York. That was all right, that was as it should be; but the other wasn't right; and I felt queer and stiff, as if I couldn't move, and my hair was curling against the flannel lining of my sou'wester, and I thought somebody had dropped a lump of ice down my back.

I said that the noise of the wind in the rigging was real, as if the other wasn't, for I felt that it wasn't, though I heard it. But it was, all the same; for the captain heard it, too. When I came to relieve the wheel, while the men were clearing up decks, he was swearing. He was a quiet man, and I hadn't heard him swear before, and I don't think I did again, though several queer things happened after that. Perhaps he said all he had to say then; I don't see how he could have said anything more. I used to think nobody could swear like a Dane, except a Neapolitan or a South American; but when I had heard the old man I changed my mind. There's nothing afloat or ashore that can beat one of your quiet American skippers, if he gets off on that tack. I didn't need to ask him what was the matter, for I knew he had heard "Nancy Lee", as I had, only it affected us differently.

He did not give me the wheel, but told me to go forward and get the second bonnet off the staysail, so as to keep her up better. As we tailed on to the sheet when it was done, the man next me knocked his sou'wester off against my shoulder, and his face came so close to me that I could see it in the dark. It must have been very white for me to see it, but I only thought of that afterwards. I don't see how any light could have fallen upon it, but I knew it was one of the Benton boys. I don't know what made me speak to him. "Hullo, Jim! Is that you?" I asked. I don't know why I said Jim, rather than Jack.

"I am Jack," he answered. We made all fast, and things were much quieter.

"The old man heard you whistling 'Nancy Lee,' just now," I said, "and he didn't like it."

It was as if there were a white light inside his face, and it was ghastly. I know his teeth chattered. But he didn't say anything, and the next minute he was somewhere in the dark trying to find his sou'wester at the foot of the mast.

When all was quiet, and she was hove to, coming to and falling off her four points as regularly as a pendulum, and the helm lashed a little to the lee, the old man turned in again, and I managed to light a pipe in the lee of the deck-house, for there was nothing more to be done till the gale chose to moderate, and the ship was as easy as a baby in its cradle. Of course the cook had gone below, as he might have done an hour earlier; so there were supposed to be four of us in the watch. There was a man at the lookout, and there was a hand by the wheel, though there was no steering to be done, and I was having my pipe in the lee of the deck-house, and the fourth man was somewhere about decks, probably having a smoke too.

I thought some skippers I had sailed with would have called the watch aft, and given them a drink after that job, but it wasn't cold, and I guessed that our old man wouldn't be particularly generous in that way. My hands and feet were red-hot, and it would be time enough to get into dry clothes when it was my watch below; so I stayed where I was, and smoked. But by and by, things being so quiet, I began to wonder why nobody moved on deck; just that sort of restless wanting to know where every man is that one sometimes feels in a gale of wind on a dark night. So when I had finished my pipe I began to move about. I went aft, and there was a man leaning over the wheel, with his legs apart and both hands hanging down in the light from the binnacle, and his sou'wester over his eyes.

Then I went forward, and there was a man at the lookout, with his back against the foremast, getting what shelter he could from the staysail. I knew by his small height that he was not one of the Benton boys. Then I went round by the weather side, and poked about in the dark, for I began to wonder where the other man was. But I couldn't find him, though I searched the decks until I got right aft again. It was certainly one of the Benton boys that was missing, but it wasn't like either of them to go below to change his clothes in such warm weather. The man at the wheel was the other, of course. I spoke to him.

"Jim, what's become of your brother?"

"I am Jack, sir."

"Well, then, Jack, where's Jim? He's not on deck."

"I don't know, sir."

When I had come up to him he had stood up from force of instinct, and had laid his hands on the spokes as if he were steering, though the wheel was lashed; but he still bent his face down, and it was half hidden by the edge of his sou'wester, while he seemed to be staring at the compass. He spoke in a very low voice, but that was natural, for the captain had left his door open when he turned in, as it was a warm night in spite of the storm, and there was no fear of shipping any more water now.

"What put it into your head to whistle like that, Jack? You've been at sea long enough to know better."

He said something, but I couldn't hear the words; it sounded as if he were denying the charge.

"Somebody whistled," I said.

He didn't answer, and then, I don't know why, perhaps because the old man hadn't given us a drink, I cut half an inch off the plug of tobacco I had in my oilskin pocket, and gave it to him. He knew my tobacco was good, and he shoved it into his mouth with a word of thanks. I was on the weather side of the wheel.

"Go forward and see if you can find Jim," I said.

He started a little, and then stepped back and passed behind me, and was going along the weather side. Maybe his silence about the whistling had irritated me, and his taking it for granted that because we were hove to and it was a dark night, he might go forward any way he pleased. Anyhow, I stopped him, though I spoke good-naturedly enough.

"Pass to leeward, Jack," I said.

He didn't answer, but crossed the deck between the binnacle and the deck-house to the lee side. She was only falling off and coming to, and riding the big seas as easily as possible, but the man was not steady on his feet and reeled against the corner of the deck-house and then against the lee rail. I was quite sure he couldn't have had anything to drink, for neither of the brothers were the kind to hide rum from their shipmates, if they had any, and the only spirits that were aboard were locked up in the captain's cabin. I wondered whether he had been hit by the throat-halliard block and was hurt.

I left the wheel and went after him, but when I got to the corner of the deck-house I saw that he was on a full run forward, so I went back. I watched the compass for a while, to see how far she went off, and she must have come to again half a dozen times before I heard voices, more than three or four, forward; and then I heard the little West Indies cook's voice, high and shrill above the rest:—

"Man overboard!"

There wasn't anything to be done, with the ship hove-to and the wheel lashed. If there was a man overboard, he must be in the water right alongside. I couldn't imagine how it could have happened, but I ran forward instinctively. I came upon the cook first, half-dressed in his shirt and trousers, just as he had tumbled out of his bunk. He was jumping into the main rigging, evidently hoping to see the man, as if anyone could have seen anything on such a night, except the foam-streaks on the black water, and now and then the curl of a breaking sea as it went away to leeward. Several of the men were peering over the rail into the dark. I caught the cook by the foot, and asked who was gone.

"It's Jim Benton," he shouted down to me. "He's not aboard this ship!"

There was no doubt about that. Jim Benton was gone; and I knew in a flash that he had been taken off by that sea when we were setting the storm trysail. It was nearly half an hour since then; she had run like wild for a few minutes until we got her hove-to, and no swimmer that ever swam could have lived as long as that in such a sea. The men knew it as well as I, but still they stared into the foam as if they had any chance of seeing the lost man. I let the cook get into the rigging and joined the men, and asked if they had made a thorough search on board, though I knew they had and that it could not take long, for he wasn't on deck, and there was only the forecastle below.

"That sea took him over, sir, as sure as you're born," said one of the men close beside me.

We had no boat that could have lived in that sea, of course, and we all knew it. I offered to put one over, and let her drift astern two or three cable's-lengths by a line, if the men thought they could haul me aboard again; but none of them would listen to that, and I should probably have been drowned if I had tried it, even with a life-belt; for it was a breaking sea. Besides, they all knew as well as I did that the man could not be right in our wake. I don't know why I spoke again. "Jack Benton, are you there? Will you go if I will?"

"No, sir," answered a voice; and that was all.

By that time the old man was on deck, and I felt his hand on my shoulder rather roughly, as if he meant to shake me.

"I'd reckoned you had more sense, Mr. Torkeldsen," he said. "God knows I would risk my ship to look for him, if it were any use; but he must have gone half an hour ago."

He was a quiet man, and the men knew he was right, and that they had seen the last of Jim Benton when they were bending the trysail—if anybody had seen him then. The captain went below again, and for some time the men stood around Jack, quite near him, without saying anything, as sailors do when they are sorry for a man and can't help him; and then the watch below turned in again, and we were three on deck.

Nobody can understand that there can be much consolation in a funeral, unless he has felt that blank feeling there is when a man's gone overboard whom everybody likes. I suppose landsmen think it would be easier if they didn't have to bury their fathers and mothers and friends; but it wouldn't be. Somehow the funeral keeps up the idea of something beyond. You may believe in that something just the same; but a man who has gone in the dark, between two seas, without a cry, seems much more beyond reach than if he were still lying on his bed, and had only just stopped breathing. Perhaps Jim Benton knew that, and wanted to come back to us. I don't know, and I am only telling you what happened, and you may think what you like.

Jack stuck by the wheel that night until the watch was over. I don't know whether he slept afterwards, but when I came on deck four hours later, there he was again, in his oilskins, with his sou'wester over his eyes, staring into the binnacle. We saw that he would rather stand there, and we left him alone. Perhaps it was some consolation to him to get that ray of light when everything was so dark. It began to rain, too, as it can when a southerly gale is going to break up, and we got every bucket and tub on board, and set them under the booms to catch the fresh water for washing our clothes. The rain made it very thick, and I went and stood under the lee of the staysail, looking out. I could tell that day was breaking, because the foam was whiter in the dark where the seas crested, and little by little the black rain grew grey and steamy, and I couldn't see the red glare of the port light on the water when she went off and rolled to leeward. The gale had moderated considerably, and in another hour we should be under way again.

I was still standing there when Jack Benton came forward. He stood still a few minutes near me. The rain came down in a solid sheet, and I could see his wet beard and a corner of his cheek, too, grey in the dawn. Then he stooped down and began feeling under the anchor for his pipe. We had hardly shipped any water forward, and I suppose he had some way of tucking the pipe in, so that the rain hadn't floated it off. Presently he got on his legs again, and I saw that he had two pipes in his hand. One of them had belonged to his brother, and after looking at them a moment I suppose he recognised his own, for he put it in his mouth, dripping with water. Then he looked at the other fully a minute without moving. When he had made up his mind, I suppose, he quietly chucked it over the lee rail, without even looking round to see whether I was watching him. I thought it was a pity, for it was a good wooden pipe, with a nickel ferrule, and somebody would have been glad to have it.

But I didn't like to make any remark, for he had a right to do what he pleased with what had belonged to his dead brother. He blew the water out of his own pipe, and dried it against his jacket, putting his hand inside his oilskin; he filled it, standing under the lee of the foremast, got a light after wasting two or three matches, and turned the pipe upside down in his teeth, to keep the rain out of the bowl. I don't know why I noticed everything he did, and remember it now; but somehow I felt sorry for him, and I kept wondering whether there was anything I could say that would make him feel better. But I didn't think of anything, and as it was broad daylight I went aft again, for I guessed that the old man would turn out before long and order the spanker set and the helm up. But he didn't turn out before seven bells, just as the clouds broke and showed blue sky to leeward—"the Frenchman's barometer," you used to call it.

Some people don't seem to be so dead, when they are dead, as others are. Jim Benton was like that. He had been on my watch, and I couldn't get used to the idea that he wasn't about decks with me. I was always expecting to see him, and his brother was so exactly like him that I often felt as if I did see him and forgot he was dead, and made the mistake of calling Jack by his name; though I tried not to, because I knew it must hurt. If ever Jack had been the cheerful one of the two, as I had always supposed he had been, he had changed very much, for he grew to be more silent than Jim had ever been.

One fine afternoon I was sitting on the main-hatch, over-hauling the clock-work of the taffrail-log, which hadn't been registering very well of late, and I had got the cook to bring me a coffee-cup to hold the small screws as I took them out, and a saucer for the sperm-oil I was going to use. I noticed that he didn't go away, but hung round without exactly watching what I was doing, as if he wanted to say something to me. I thought if it were worth much he would say it anyhow, so I didn't ask him questions; and sure enough he began of his own accord before long. There was nobody on deck but the man at the wheel, and the other man away forward.

"Mr. Torkeldsen," the cook began, and then stopped.

I supposed he was going to ask me to let the watch break out a barrel of flour, or some salt horse.

"Well, doctor?" I asked, as he didn't go on.

"Well, Mr. Torkeldsen," he answered, "I somehow want to ask you whether you think I am giving satisfaction on this ship, or not?"

"So far as I know, you are, doctor. I haven't heard any complaints from the forecastle, and the captain has said nothing, and I think you know your business, and the cabin-boy is bursting out of his clothes. That looks as if you are giving satisfaction. What makes you think you are not?"

I am not good at giving you that West Indies talk, and sha'n't try; but the doctor beat about the bush awhile, and then he told me he thought the men were beginning to play tricks on him, and he didn't like it, and thought he hadn't deserved it, and would like his discharge at our next port. I told him he was a d——d fool, of course, to begin with; and that men were more apt to try a joke with a chap they liked than with anybody they wanted to get rid of; unless it was a bad joke, like flooding his bunk, or filling his boots with tar. But it wasn't that kind of practical joke. The doctor said that the men were trying to frighten him, and he didn't like it, and that they put things in his way that frightened him. So I told him he was a d——d fool to be frightened, anyway, and I wanted to know what things they put in his way. He gave me a queer answer. He said they were spoons and forks, and odd plates, and a cup now and then, and such things.

I set down the taffrail-log on the bit of canvas I had put under it, and looked at the doctor. He was uneasy, and his eyes had a sort of hunted look, and his yellow face looked grey. He wasn't trying to make trouble. He was in trouble. So I asked him questions.

He said he could count as well as anybody, and do sums without using his fingers, but that when he couldn't count any other way he did use his fingers, and it always came out the same. He said that when he and the cabin-boy cleared up after the men's meals there were more things to wash than he had given out. There'd be a fork more, or there'd be a spoon more, and sometimes there'd be a spoon and a fork, and there was always a plate more. It wasn't that he complained of that. Before poor Jim Benton was lost they had a man more to feed, and his gear to wash up after meals, and that was in the contract, the doctor said. It would have been if there were twenty in the ship's company; but he didn't think it was right for the men to play tricks like that. He kept his things in good order, and he counted them, and he was responsible for them, and it wasn't right that the men should take more things than they needed when his back was turned, and just soil them and mix them up with their own, so as to make him think—

He stopped there, and looked at me, and I looked at him. I didn't know what he thought, but I began to guess. I wasn't going to humour any such nonsense as that, so I told him to speak to the men himself, and not come bothering me about such things.

"Count the plates and forks and spoons before them when they sit down to table, and tell them that's all they'll get; and when they have finished, count the things again, and if the count isn't right, find out who did it. You know it must be one of them. You're not a green hand; you've been going to sea ten or eleven years, and don't want any lesson about how to behave if the boys play a trick on you."

"If I could catch him," said the cook, "I'd have a knife into him before he could say his prayers."

Those West India men are always talking about knives, especially when they are badly frightened. I knew what he meant, and didn't ask him, but went on cleaning the brass cogwheels of the patent log and oiling the bearings with a feather. "Wouldn't it be better to wash it out with boiling water, sir?" asked the cook, in an insinuating tone. He knew that he had made a fool of himself, and was anxious to make it right again.

I heard no more about the odd platter and gear for two or three days, though I thought about his story a good deal. The doctor evidently believed that Jim Benton had come back, though he didn't quite like to say so. His story had sounded silly enough on a bright afternoon, in fair weather, when the sun was on the water, and every rag was drawing in the breeze, and the sea looked as pleasant and harmless as a cat that has just eaten a canary. But when it was toward the end of the first watch, and the waning moon had not risen yet, and the water was like still oil, and the jibs hung down flat and helpless like the wings of a dead bird—it wasn't the same then. More than once I have started then, and looked round when a fish jumped, expecting to see a face sticking up out of the water with its eyes shut. I think we all felt something like that at the time.

One afternoon we were putting a fresh service on the jib-sheet-pennant. It wasn't my watch, but I was standing by looking on. Just then Jack Benton came up from below, and went to look

476

for his pipe under the anchor. His face was hard and drawn, and his eyes were cold like steel balls. He hardly ever spoke now, but he did his duty as usual, and nobody had to complain of him, though we were all beginning to wonder how long his grief for his dead brother was going to last like that. I watched him as he crouched down, and ran his hand into the hiding-place for the pipe. When he stood up, he had two pipes in his hand.

Now, I remembered very well seeing him throw one of those pipes away, early in the morning after the gale; and it came to me now, and I didn't suppose he kept a stock of them under the anchor. I caught sight of his face, and it was greenish white, like the foam on shallow water, and he stood a long time looking at the two pipes. He wasn't looking to see which was his, for I wasn't five yards from him as he stood, and one of those pipes had been smoked that day, and was shiny where his hand had rubbed it, and the bone mouthpiece was chafed white where his teeth had bitten it. The other was water-logged. It was swelled and cracking with wet, and it looked to me as if there were a little green weed on it.

Jack Benton turned his head rather stealthily as I looked away, and then he hid the thing in his trousers pocket, and went aft on the lee side, out of sight. The men had got the sheet pennant on a stretch to serve it, but I ducked under it and stood where I could see what Jack did, just under the fore-staysail. He couldn't see me, and he was looking about for something. His hand shook as he picked up a bit of half-bent iron rod, about a foot long, that had been used for turning an eye-bolt, and had been left on the main-hatch. His hand shook as he got a piece of marline out of his pocket, and made the water-logged pipe fast to the iron. He didn't mean it to get adrift, either, for he took his turns carefully, and hove them taut and then rode them, so that they couldn't slip, and made the end fast with two half-hitches round the iron, and hitched it back on itself. Then he tried it with his hands, and looked up and down the deck furtively, and then quietly dropped the pipe and iron over the rail, so that I didn't even hear the splash. If anybody was playing tricks on board, they weren't meant for the cook.

I asked some questions about Jack Benton, and one of the men told me that he was off his feed, and hardly ate anything, and swallowed all the coffee he could lay his hands on, and had used up all his own tobacco and had begun on what his brother had left.

"The doctor says it ain't so, sir," said the man, looking at me shyly, as if he didn't expect to be believed; "the doctor says there's as much eaten from breakfast to breakfast as there was before Jim fell overboard, though there's a mouth less and another that eats nothing. I says it's the cabin-boy that gets it. He's bu'sting."

I told him that if the cabin-boy ate more than his share, he must work more than his share, so as to balance things. But the man laughed queerly, and looked at me again.

"I only said that, sir, just like that. We all know it ain't so."

"Well, how is it?"

"How is it?" asked the man, half-angry all at once. "I don't know how it is, but there's a hand on board that's getting his whack along with us as regular as the bells."

"Does he use tobacco?" I asked, meaning to laugh it out of him, but as I spoke I remembered the water-logged pipe.

"I guess he's using his own still," the man answered, in a queer, low voice. "Perhaps he'll take someone else's when his is all gone."

It was about nine o'clock in the morning, I remember, for just then the captain called to me to stand by the chronometer while he took his fore observation. Captain Hackstaff wasn't one of those old skippers who do everything themselves with a pocket watch, and keep the key of the chronometer in their waistcoat pocket, and won't tell the mate how far the dead reckoning is out. He was rather the other way, and I was glad of it, for he generally let me work the sights he took, and just ran his eye over my figures afterwards. I am bound to say his eye was pretty good, for he would pick out a mistake in a logarithm, or tell me that I had worked the "Equation of Time" with the wrong sign, before it seemed to me that he could have got as far as "half the sum, minus the altitude." He was always right, too, and besides he knew a lot about iron ships and local deviation, and adjusting the compass, and all that sort of thing. I don't know how he came to be in command of a fore-and-aft schooner. He never talked about himself, and maybe he had just been mate on one of those big steel square-riggers, and something had put him back.

Perhaps he had been captain, and had got his ship aground, through no particular fault of his, and had to begin over again. Sometimes he talked just like you and me, and sometimes he would speak more like books do, or some of those Boston people I have heard. I don't know. We have all been shipmates now and then with men who have seen better days. Perhaps he had been in the Navy, but what makes me think he couldn't have been, was that he was a thorough good seaman, a regular old wind-jammer, and understood sail, which those Navy chaps rarely do. Why, you and I have sailed with men before the mast who had their master's certificates in their pockets,—English Board of Trade certificates, too,—who could work a double altitude if you would lend them a sextant and give them a look at the chronometer, as well as many a man who commands a big square-rigger. Navigation ain't everything, nor seamanship, either. You've got to have it in you, if you mean to get there.

I don't know how our captain heard that there was trouble forward. The cabin-boy may have told him, or the men may have talked outside his door when they relieved the wheel at night. Anyhow, he got wind of it, and when he had got his sight that morning he had all hands aft, and gave them a lecture. It was just the kind of talk you might have expected from him. He said he hadn't any complaint to make, and that so far as he knew everybody on board was doing his duty, and that he was given to understand that the men got their whack, and were satisfied. He said his ship was never a hard ship, and that he liked quiet, and that was the reason he didn't mean to have any nonsense, and the men might just as well understand that, too.

We'd had a great misfortune, he said, and it was nobody's fault. We had lost a man we all liked and respected, and he felt that everybody in the ship ought to be sorry for the man's brother, who was left behind, and that it was rotten lubberly childishness, and unjust and unmanly and cowardly, to be playing schoolboy tricks with forks and spoons and pipes, and that sort of gear. He said it had got to stop right now, and that was all, and the men might go forward. And so they did.

It got worse after that, and the men watched the cook, and the cook watched the men, as if they were trying to catch each other; but I think everybody felt that there was something else. One evening, at supper-time, I was on deck, and Jack came aft to relieve the wheel while the man who was steering got his supper. He hadn't got past the main-hatch on the lee side, when I heard a man running in slippers that slapped on the deck, and there was a sort of a yell and I saw the coloured cook going for Jack, with a carving-knife in his hand. I jumped to get between them, and Jack turned round short, and put out his hand. I was too far to reach them, and the cook jabbed out with his knife.

But the blade didn't get anywhere near Benton. The cook seemed to be jabbing it into the air again and again, at least four feet short of the mark. Then he dropped his right hand, and I saw the whites of his eyes in the dusk, and he reeled up against the pin-rail, and caught hold of a belaying-pin with his left. I had reached him by that time, and grabbed hold of his knife-hand and the other too, for I thought he was going to use the pin; but Jack Benton was standing staring stupidly at him, as if he didn't understand. But instead, the cook was holding on because he couldn't stand, and his teeth were chattering, and he let go of the knife, and the point stuck into the deck.

"He's crazy!" said Jack Benton, and that was all he said; and he went aft.

When he was gone the cook began to come to and he spoke quite low, near my ear.

"There were two of them! So help me God, there were two of them!"

I don't know why I didn't take him by the collar, and give him a good shaking; but I didn't. I just picked up the knife and gave it to him, and told him to go back to his galley, and not to make a fool of himself. You see, he hadn't struck at Jack, but at something he thought he saw, and I knew what it was, and I felt that same thing, like a lump of ice sliding down my back, that I felt that night when we were bending the trysail.

When the men had seen him running aft, they jumped up after him, but they held off when they saw that I had caught him. By and by, the man who had spoken to me before told me what had happened. He was a stocky little chap, with a red head.

"Well," he said, "there isn't much to tell. Jack Benton had been eating his supper with the rest of us. He always sits at the after corner of the table, on the port side. His brother used to sit at the end, next him. The doctor gave him a thundering big piece of pie to finish up with, and when he had finished he didn't stop for a smoke, but went off quick to relieve the wheel. Just as he had gone, the doctor came in from the galley, and when he saw Jack's empty plate he stood stock still staring at it; and we all wondered what was the matter, till we looked at the plate. There were two forks in it, sir, lying side by side. Then the doctor grabbed his knife, and flew up through the hatch like a rocket. The other fork was there all right, Mr. Torkeldsen, for we all saw it and handled it; and we all had our own. That's all I know."

I didn't feel that I wanted to laugh when he told me that story; but I hoped the old man wouldn't hear it, for I knew he wouldn't believe it, and no captain that ever sailed likes to have stories like that going round about his ship. It gives her a bad name. But that was all anybody ever saw except the cook, and he isn't the first man who has thought he saw things without having any drink in him. I think, if the doctor had been weak in the head as he was afterwards, he might have done something foolish again, and there might have been serious trouble. But he didn't. Only, two or three times I saw him looking at Jack Benton in a queer, scared way, and once I heard him talking to himself.

"There's two of them! So help me God, there's two of them!"

He didn't say anything more about asking for his discharge, but I knew well enough that if he got ashore at the next port we should never see him again, if he had to leave his kit behind him, and his money, too. He was scared all through, for good and all; and he wouldn't be right again till he got another ship. It's no use to talk to a man when he gets like that, any more than it is to send a boy to the main truck when he has lost his nerve.

Jack Benton never spoke of what happened that evening. I don't know whether he knew about the two forks, or not; or whether he understood what the trouble was. Whatever he knew from the other men, he was evidently living under a hard strain. He was quiet enough, and too quiet; but his face was set, and sometimes it twitched oddly when he was at the wheel, and he would turn his head round sharp to look behind him. A man doesn't do that naturally, unless there's a vessel that he thinks is creeping up on the quarter. When that happens, if the man at the wheel takes a pride in his ship, he will almost always keep glancing over his shoulder to see whether the other fellow is gaining. But Jack Benton used to look round when there was nothing there; and what is curious, the other men seemed to catch the trick when they were steering. One day the old man turned out just as the man at the wheel looked behind him.

"What are you looking at?" asked the captain.

"Nothing, sir," answered the man.

"Then keep your eye on the mizzen-royal," said the old man, as if he were forgetting that we weren't a square-rigger.

"Ay, ay, sir," said the man.

The captain told me to go below and work up the latitude from the dead-reckoning, and he went forward of the deck-house and sat down to read, as he often did. When I came up, the man at the wheel was looking round again, and I stood beside him and just asked him quietly what everybody was looking at, for it was getting to be a general habit. He wouldn't say anything at first, but just answered that it was nothing. But when he saw that I didn't seem to care, and just stood there as if there were nothing more to be said, he naturally began to talk.

He said that it wasn't that he saw anything, because there wasn't anything to see except the spanker sheet just straining a little, and working in the sheaves of the blocks as the schooner rose to the short seas. There wasn't anything to be seen, but it seemed to him that the sheet made a queer noise in the blocks. It was a new manilla sheet; and in dry weather it did make a little noise, something between a creak and a wheeze. I looked at it and looked at the man, and said nothing; and presently he went on. He asked me if I didn't notice anything peculiar about the noise. I listened awhile, and said I didn't notice anything. Then he looked rather sheepish, but said he didn't think it could be his own ears, because every man who steered his trick heard the same thing now and then,—sometimes once in a day, sometimes once in a night, sometimes it would go on a whole hour.

"It sounds like sawing wood," I said, just like that.

"To us it sounds a good deal more like a man whistling 'Nancy Lee.'" He started nervously as he spoke the last words. "There, sir, don't you hear it?" he asked suddenly.

I heard nothing but the creaking of the manilla sheet. It was getting near noon, and fine, clear weather in southern waters,— just the sort of day and the time when you would least expect to feel creepy. But I remembered how I had heard that same tune overhead at night in a gale of wind a fortnight earlier, and I am not ashamed to say that the same sensation came over me now, and I wished myself well out of the *Helen B.*, and aboard of any old cargo-dragger, with a windmill on deck, and an eighty-nine-forty-eighter for captain, and a fresh leak whenever it breezed up.

Little by little during the next few days life on board that vessel came to be about as unbearable as you can imagine. It wasn't that there was much talk, for I think the men were shy even of speaking to each other freely about what they thought. The whole ship's company grew silent, until one hardly ever heard a voice, except giving an order and the answer. The men didn't sit over their meals when their watch was below, but either turned in at once or sat about on the forecastle smoking their pipes without saying a word. We were all thinking of the same thing. We all felt as if there were a hand on board, sometimes below, sometimes about decks, sometimes aloft, sometimes on the boom end; taking his full share of what the others got, but doing no work for it.

We didn't only feel it, we knew it. He took up no room, he cast no shadow, and we never heard his footfall on deck; but he took his whack with the rest as regular as the bells, and—he whistled "Nancy Lee." It was like the worst sort of dream you can imagine; and I dare say a good many of us tried to believe it was nothing else sometimes, when we stood looking over the weather rail in fine weather with the breeze in our faces; but if we happened to turn round and look into each other's eyes, we knew it was something worse than any dream could be; and we would turn away from each other with a queer, sick feeling, wishing that we could just for once see somebody who didn't know what we knew.

There's not much more to tell about the *Helen B. Jackson* so far as I am concerned. We were more like a shipload of lunatics than anything else when we ran in under Morro Castle, and anchored in Havana. The cook had brain fever, and was raving mad in his delirium; and the rest of the men weren't far from the same state. The last three or four days had been awful, and we had been as near to having a mutiny on board as I ever want to be. The men didn't want to hurt anybody; but they wanted to get away out of that ship, if they had to swim for it; to get away from that whistling, from that dead shipmate who had come back, and who filled the ship with his unseen self. I know that if the old man and I hadn't kept a sharp lookout the men would have put a boat over quietly on one of those calm nights, and pulled away, leaving the captain and me and the mad cook to work the schooner into harbour.

We should have done it somehow, of course, for we hadn't

far to run if we could get a breeze; and once or twice I found myself wishing that the crew were really gone, for the awful state of fright in which they lived was beginning to work on me too. You see I partly believed and partly didn't; but anyhow I didn't mean to let the thing get the better of me, whatever it was. I turned crusty, too, and kept the men at work on all sorts of jobs, and drove them to it until they wished I was overboard, too. It wasn't that the old man and I were trying to drive them to desert without their pay, as I am sorry to say a good many skippers and mates do, even now. Captain Hackstaff was as straight as a string, and I didn't mean those poor fellows should be cheated out of a single cent; and I didn't blame them for wanting to leave the ship, but it seemed to me that the only chance to keep everybody sane through those last days was to work the men till they dropped.

When they were dead tired they slept a little, and forgot the thing until they had to tumble up on deck and face it again. That was a good many years ago. Do you believe that I can't hear "Nancy Lee" now, without feeling cold down my back? For I heard it too, now and then, after the man had explained why he was always looking over his shoulder. Perhaps it was imagination. I don't know. When I look back it seems to me that I only remember a long fight against something I couldn't see, against an appalling presence, against something worse than cholera or Yellow Jack or the plague—and goodness knows the mildest of them is bad enough when it breaks out at sea. The men got as white as chalk, and wouldn't go about decks alone at night, no matter what I said to them. With the cook raving in his bunk the forecastle would have been a perfect hell, and there wasn't a spare cabin on board. There never is on a fore-and-after. So I put him into mine, and he was more quiet there, and at last fell into a sort of stupor as if he were going to die. I don't know what became of him, for we put him ashore alive and left him in the hospital.

The men came aft in a body, quiet enough, and asked the captain if he wouldn't pay them off, and let them go ashore.

Some men wouldn't have done it, for they had shipped for the voyage, and had signed articles. But the captain knew that when sailors get an idea into their heads they're no better than children; and if he forced them to stay aboard he wouldn't get much work out of them, and couldn't rely on them in a difficulty. So he paid them off, and let them go. When they had gone forward to get their kits, he asked me whether I wanted to go too, and for a minute I had a sort of weak feeling that I might just as well. But I didn't, and he was a good friend to me afterwards. Perhaps he was grateful to me for sticking to him.

When the men went off he didn't come on deck; but it was my duty to stand by while they left the ship. They owed me a grudge for making them work during the last few days, and most of them dropped into the boat without so much as a word or a look, as sailors will. Jack Benton was the last to go over the side, and he stood still a minute and looked at me, and his white face twitched. I thought he wanted to say something.

"Take care of yourself, Jack," said I. "So long!"

It seemed as if he couldn't speak for two or three seconds; then his words came thick.

"It wasn't my fault, Mr. Torkeldsen. I swear it wasn't my fault!"

That was all; and he dropped over the side, leaving me to wonder what he meant.

The captain and I stayed on board, and the ship-chandler got a West India boy to cook for us.

That evening, before turning in, we were standing by the rail having a quiet smoke, watching the lights of the city, a quarter of a mile off, reflected in the still water. There was music of some sort ashore, in a sailors' dance-house, I dare say; and I had no doubt that most of the men who had left the ship were there, and already full of jiggy-jiggy. The music played a lot of sailors' tunes that ran into each other, and we could hear the men's voices in the chorus now and then. One followed another, and then it was "Nancy Lee," loud and clear, and the men singing "*Yo-ho, heave-ho!*"

"I have no ear for music," said Captain Hackstaff, "but it appears to me that's the tune that man was whistling the night we lost the man overboard. I don't know why it has stuck in my head, and of course it's all nonsense; but it seems to me that I have heard it all the rest of the trip."

I didn't say anything to that, but I wondered just how much the old man had understood. Then we turned in, and I slept ten hours without opening my eyes.

I stuck to the *Helen B. Jackson* after that as long as I could stand a fore-and-after; but that night when we lay in Havana was the last time I ever heard "Nancy Lee" on board of her. The spare hand had gone ashore with the rest, and he never came back, and he took his tune with him; but all those things are just as clear in my memory as if they had happened yesterday.

After that I was in deep water for a year or more, and after I came home I got my certificate, and what with having friends and having saved a little money, and having had a small legacy from an uncle in Norway, I got the command of a coastwise vessel, with a small share in her. I was at home three weeks before going to sea, and Jack Benton saw my name in the local papers, and wrote to me.

He said that he had left the sea, and was trying farming, and he was going to be married, and he asked if I wouldn't come over for that, for it wasn't more than forty minutes by train; and he and Mamie would be proud to have me at the wedding. I remembered how I had heard one brother ask the other whether Mamie knew. That meant, whether she knew he wanted to marry her, I suppose. She had taken her time about it, for it was pretty nearly three years then since we had lost Jim Benton overboard.

I had nothing particular to do while we were getting ready for sea; nothing to prevent me from going over for a day, I mean; and I thought I'd like to see Jack Benton, and have a look at the girl he was going to marry. I wondered whether he had grown cheerful again, and had got rid of that drawn look he had when he told me it wasn't his fault. How could it have been his fault, anyhow? So I wrote to Jack that I would come down and see him married; and when the day came I took the train, and got there about ten o'clock in the morning. I wish I hadn't. Jack met me at the station, and he told me that the wedding was to be late in the afternoon, and that they weren't going off on any silly wedding trip, he and Mamie, but were just going to walk home from her mother's house to his cottage. That was good enough for him, he said.

I looked at him hard for a minute after we met. When we had parted I had a sort of idea that he might take to drink, but he hadn't. He looked very respectable and well-to-do in his black coat and high city collar; but he was thinner and bonier than when I had known him, and there were lines in his face, and I thought his eyes had a queer look in them, half shifty, half scared. He needn't have been afraid of me, for I didn't mean to talk to his bride about the *Helen B. Jackson*.

He took me to his cottage first, and I could see that he was proud of it. It wasn't above a cable's-length from high-water mark, but the tide was running out, and there was already a broad stretch of hard wet sand on the other side of the beach road. Jack's bit of land ran back behind the cottage about a quarter of a mile, and he said that some of the trees we saw were his. The fences were neat and well kept, and there was a fair-sized barn a little way from the cottage, and I saw some nice-looking cattle in the meadows; but it didn't look to me to be much of a farm, and I thought that before long Jack would have to leave his wife to take care of it, and go to sea again. But I said it was a nice farm, so as to seem pleasant, and as I don't know much about these things I dare say it was, all the same. I never saw it but that once.

Jack told me that he and his brother had been born in the cottage, and that when their father and mother died they leased the land to Mamie's father, but had kept the cottage to live in when they came home from sea for a spell. It was as neat a little place as you would care to see: the floors as clean as the decks of a yacht, and the paint as fresh as a man-o'-war. Jack always was a good painter. There was a nice parlour on the ground floor, and Jack had papered it and had hung the walls with photographs of ships and foreign ports, and with things he had brought home from his voyages: a boomerang, a South Sea club, Japanese straw hats and a Gibraltar fan with a bull-fight on it, and all that sort of gear. It looked to me as if Miss Mamie had taken a hand in arranging it. There was a bran-new polished iron Franklin stove set into the old fireplace, and a red table-cloth from Alexandria, embroidered with those outlandish Egyptian letters.

It was all as bright and homelike as possible, and he showed me everything, and was proud of everything, and I liked him the better for it. But I wished that his voice would sound more cheerful, as it did when we first sailed in the *Helen B.*, and that the drawn look would go out of his face for a minute. Jack showed me everything, and took me upstairs, and it was all the same: bright and fresh and ready for the bride. But on the upper landing there was a door that Jack didn't open. When we came out of the bedroom I noticed that it was ajar, and Jack shut it quickly and turned the key.

"That lock's no good," he said, half to himself. "The door is always open."

I didn't pay much attention to what he said, but as we went down the short stairs, freshly painted and varnished so that I was almost afraid to step on them, he spoke again.

"That was his room, sir. I have made a sort of store-room of it."

"You may be wanting it in a year or so," I said, wishing to be pleasant.

"I guess we won't use his room for that," Jack answered in a low voice.

Then he offered me a cigar from a fresh box in the parlour, and he took one, and we lit them, and went out; and as we opened the front door there was Mamie Brewster standing in the path as if she were waiting for us. She was a fine-looking girl, and I didn't wonder that Jack had been willing to wait three years for her. I could see that she hadn't been brought up on steam-heat and cold storage, but had grown into a woman by the sea-shore. She had brown eyes, and fine brown hair, and a good figure.

"This is Captain Torkeldsen," said Jack. "This is Miss Brewster, captain; and she is glad to see you."

"Well, I am," said Miss Mamie, "for Jack has often talked to us about you, captain."

She put out her hand, and took mine and shook it heartily, and I suppose I said something, but I know I didn't say much.

The front door of the cottage looked toward the sea, and there was a straight path leading to the gate on the beach road. There was another path from the steps of the cottage that turned to the right, broad enough for two people to walk easily, and it led straight across the fields through gates to a larger house about a quarter of a mile away. That was where Mamie's mother lived, and the wedding was to be there. Jack asked me whether I would like to look round the farm before dinner, but I told him I didn't know much about farms. Then he said he just wanted to look round himself a bit, as he mightn't have much more chance that day; and he smiled, and Mamie laughed.

"Show the captain the way to the house, Mamie," he said. "I'll be along in a minute."

So Mamie and I began to walk along the path, and Jack went up toward the barn.

"It was sweet of you to come, captain," Miss Mamie began, "for I have always wanted to see you."

"Yes," I said, expecting something more.

"You see, I always knew them both," she went on. "They used to take me out in a dory to catch codfish when I was a little girl, and I liked them both," she added thoughtfully. "Jack doesn't care to talk about his brother now. That's natural. But you won't mind telling me how it happened, will you? I should so much like to know."

Well, I told her about the voyage and what happened that night when we fell in with a gale of wind, and that it hadn't been anybody's fault, for I wasn't going to admit that it was my old captain's, if it was. But I didn't tell her anything about what happened afterwards. As she didn't speak, I just went on talking about the two brothers, and how like they had been, and how when poor Jim was drowned and Jack was left, I took Jack for him. I told her that none of us had ever been sure which was which.

"I wasn't always sure myself," she said, "unless they were together. Leastways, not for a day or two after they came home from sea. And now it seems to me that Jack is more like poor Jim, as I remember him, than he ever was, for Jim was always more quiet, as if he were thinking."

I told her I thought so, too. We passed the gate and went into the next field, walking side by side. Then she turned her head to look for Jack, but he wasn't in sight. I sha'n't forget what she said next.

"Are you sure now?" she asked.

I stood stock-still, and she went on a step, and then turned and looked at me. We must have looked at each other while you could count five or six.

"I know it's silly," she went on, "it's silly, and it's awful, too, and I have got no right to think it, but sometimes I can't help it. You see it was always Jack I meant to marry."

"Yes," I said stupidly, "I suppose so."

She waited a minute, and began walking on slowly before she went on again.

"I am talking to you as if you were an old friend, captain, and I have only known you five minutes. It was Jack I meant to marry, but now he is so like the other one."

When a woman gets a wrong idea into her head, there is only one way to make her tired of it, and that is to agree with her. That's what I did, and she went on talking the same way for a little while, and I kept on agreeing and agreeing until she turned round on me.

"You know you don't believe what you say," she said, and laughed. "You know that Jack is Jack, right enough; and it's Jack I am going to marry."

Of course I said so, for I didn't care whether she thought me a weak creature or not. I wasn't going to say a word that could interfere with her happiness, and I didn't intend to go back on Jack Benton; but I remembered what he had said when he left the ship in Havana: that it wasn't his fault.

"All the same," Miss Mamie went on, as a woman will, without realising what she was saying, "all the same, I wish I had seen it happen. Then I should know."

Next minute she knew that she didn't mean that, and was afraid that I would think her heartless, and began to explain that she would really rather have died herself than have seen poor Jim go overboard. Women haven't got much sense, anyhow. All the same, I wondered how she could marry Jack if she had a doubt that he might be Jim after all. I suppose she had really got used to him since he had given up the sea and had stayed ashore, and she cared for him.

Before long we heard Jack coming up behind us, for we had walked very slowly to wait for him.

"Promise not to tell anybody what I said, captain," said Mamie, as girls do as soon as they have told their secrets.

Anyhow, I know I never did tell anyone but you. This is the first time I have talked of all that, the first time since I took the train from that place. I am not going to tell you all about the day. Miss Mamie introduced me to her mother, who was a quiet, hard-faced old New England farmer's widow, and to her cousins and relations; and there were plenty of them too at dinner, and there was the parson besides. He was what they call a Hardshell Baptist in those parts, with a long, shaven upper lip and a whacking appetite, and a sort of superior look, as if he didn't expect to see many of us hereafter—the way a New York pilot looks round, and orders things about when he boards an Italian cargo-dragger, as if the ship weren't up to much anyway, though it was his business to see that she didn't get aground.

That's the way a good many parsons look, I think. He said grace as if he were ordering the men to sheet home the topgallant-sail and get the helm up. After dinner we went out on the *piazza*, for it was warm autumn weather; and the young folks went off in pairs along the beach road, and the tide had turned and was beginning to come in. The morning had been clear and fine, but by four o'clock it began to look like a fog, and the damp came up out of the sea and settled on everything. Jack said he'd go down to his cottage and have a last look, for the wedding was to be at five o'clock, or soon after, and he wanted to light the lights, so as to have things look cheerful.

"I will just take a last look," he said again, as we reached the house. We went in, and he offered me another cigar, and I lit it and sat down in the parlour. I could hear him moving about, first in the kitchen and then upstairs, and then I heard him in the kitchen again; and then before I knew anything I heard somebody moving upstairs again. I knew he couldn't have got up those stairs as quick as that. He came into the parlour, and he took a cigar himself, and while he was lighting it I heard those steps again overhead. His hand shook, and he dropped the match.

"Have you got in somebody to help?" I asked.

"No," Jack answered sharply, and struck another match.

"There's somebody upstairs, Jack," I said. "Don't you hear footsteps?"

"It's the wind, captain," Jack answered; but I could see he was trembling.

"That isn't any wind, Jack," I said; "it's still and foggy. I'm sure there's somebody upstairs."

"If you are so sure of it, you'd better go and see for yourself, captain," Jack answered, almost angrily.

He was angry because he was frightened. I left him before the fireplace, and went upstairs. There was no power on earth that could make me believe I hadn't heard a man's footsteps overhead. I knew there was somebody there. But there wasn't. I went into the bedroom, and it was all quiet, and the evening light was streaming in, reddish through the foggy air; and I went out on the landing and looked in the little back room that was meant for a servant girl or a child. And as I came back again I saw that the door of the other room was wide open, though I knew Jack had locked it. He had said the lock was no good. I looked in. It was a room as big as the bedroom, but almost dark, for it had shutters, and they were closed. There was a musty smell, as of old gear, and I could make out that the floor was littered with sea chests, and that there were oilskins and stuff piled on the bed. But I still believed that there was somebody upstairs, and I went in and struck a match and looked round. I could see the four walls and the shabby old paper, an iron bed and a cracked looking-glass, and the stuff on the floor. But there was nobody there. So I put out the match, and came out and shut the door and turned the key. Now, what I am telling you is the truth. When I had turned the key, I heard footsteps walking away from the door inside the room. Then I felt queer for a minute, and when I went downstairs I looked behind me, as the men at the wheel used to look behind them on board the *Helen B.*

Jack was already outside on the steps, smoking. I have an idea that he didn't like to stay inside alone.

"Well?" he asked, trying to seem careless.

"I didn't find anybody," I answered, "but I heard somebody moving about."

"I told you it was the wind," said Jack, contemptuously. "I ought to know, for I live here, and I hear it often."

There was nothing to be said to that, so we began to walk down toward the beach. Jack said there wasn't any hurry, as it would take Miss Mamie some time to dress for the wedding. So we strolled along, and the sun was setting through the fog, and the tide was coming in. I knew the moon was full, and that when she rose the fog would roll away from the land, as it does sometimes. I felt that Jack didn't like my having heard that noise, so I talked of other things, and asked him about his prospects, and before long we were chatting as pleasantly as possible.

I haven't been at many weddings in my life, and I don't suppose you have, but that one seemed to me to be all right until it was pretty near over; and then, I don't know whether it was part of the ceremony or not, but Jack put out his hand and took

Mamie's and held it a minute, and looked at her, while the parson was still speaking.

Mamie turned as white as a sheet and screamed. It wasn't a loud scream, but just a sort of stifled little shriek, as if she were half frightened to death; and the parson stopped, and asked her what was the matter, and the family gathered round.

"Your hand's like ice," said Mamie to Jack, "and it's all wet!" She kept looking at it, as she got hold of herself again.

"It don't feel cold to me," said Jack, and he held the back of his hand against his cheek. "Try it again."

Mamie held out hers, and touched the back of his hand, timidly at first, and then took hold of it.

"Why, that's funny," she said.

"She's been as nervous as a witch all day," said Mrs. Brewster, severely.

"It is natural," said the parson, "that young Mrs. Benton should experience a little agitation at such a moment."

Most of the bride's relations lived at a distance, and were busy people, so it had been arranged that the dinner we'd had in the middle of the day was to take the place of a dinner afterwards, and that we should just have a bite after the wedding was over, and then that everybody should go home, and the young couple would walk down to the cottage by themselves. When I looked out I could see the light burning brightly in Jack's cottage, a quarter of a mile away. I said I didn't think I could get any train to take me back before half-past nine, but Mrs. Brewster begged me to stay until it was time, as she said her daughter would want to take off her wedding dress before she went home; for she had put on something white with a wreath, that was very pretty, and she couldn't walk home like that, could she?

So when we had all had a little supper the party began to break up, and when they were all gone Mrs. Brewster and Mamie went upstairs, and Jack and I went out on the *piazza*, to have a smoke, as the old lady didn't like tobacco in the house.

The full moon had risen now, and it was behind me as I looked down toward Jack's cottage, so that everything was clear and white, and there was only the light burning in the window. The fog had rolled down to the water's edge, and a little beyond, for the tide was high, or nearly, and was lapping up over the last reach of sand, within fifty feet of the beach road.

Jack didn't say much as we sat smoking, but he thanked me for coming to his wedding, and I told him I hoped he would be happy; and so I did. I dare say both of us were thinking of those footsteps upstairs, just then, and that the house wouldn't seem so lonely with a woman in it. By and by we heard Mamie's voice talking to her mother on the stairs, and in a minute she was ready to go. She had put on again the dress she had worn in the morning, and it looked black at night, almost as black as Jack's coat.

Well, they were ready to go now. It was all very quiet after the day's excitement, and I knew they would like to walk down that path alone now that they were man and wife at last. I bade them good-night, although Jack made a show of pressing me to go with them by the path as far as the cottage, instead of going to the station by the beach road. It was all very quiet, and it seemed to me a sensible way of getting married; and when Mamie kissed her mother goodnight I just looked the other way, and knocked my ashes over the rail of the *piazza*. So they started down the straight path to Jack's cottage, and I waited a minute with Mrs. Brewster, looking after them, before taking my hat to go. They walked side by side, a little shyly at first, and then I saw Jack put his arm round her waist. As I looked he was on her left, and I saw the outline of the two figures very distinctly against the moonlight on the path; and the shadow on Mamie's right was broad and black as ink, and it moved along, lengthening and shortening with the unevenness of the ground beside the path.

I thanked Mrs. Brewster, and bade her goodnight; and though she was a hard New England woman her voice trembled a little as she answered, but being a sensible person she went in and shut the door behind her as I stepped out on the path. I looked after the couple in the distance a last time, meaning to go down to the road, so as not to overtake them; but when I had made a few steps I stopped and looked again, for I knew I had seen something queer, though I had only realised it afterwards. I looked again, and it was plain enough now; and I stood stock-still, staring at what I saw.

Mamie was walking between two men. The second man was just the same height as Jack, both being about a half a head taller than she; Jack on her left in his black tail-coat and round hat, and the other man on her right—well, he was a sailor-man in wet oilskins. I could see the moonlight shining on the water that ran down him, and on the little puddle that had settled where the flap of his sou'wester was turned up behind: and one of his wet, shiny arms was round Mamie's waist, just above Jack's. I was fast to the spot where I stood, and for a minute I thought I was crazy. We'd had nothing but some cider for dinner, and tea in the evening, otherwise I'd have thought something had got into my head, though I was never drunk in my life. It was more like a bad dream after that.

I was glad Mrs. Brewster had gone in. As for me, I couldn't help following the three, in a sort of wonder to see what would happen, to see whether the sailor-man in his wet togs would just melt away into the moonshine. But he didn't.

I moved slowly, and I remembered afterwards that I walked on the grass, coming. I suppose it all happened in less than five minutes after that, but it seemed as if it must have taken an hour. Neither Jack nor Mamie seemed to notice the sailor. She didn't seem to know that his wet arm was round her, and little by little they got near the cottage, and I wasn't a hundred yards from them when they reached the door. Something made me stand still then. Perhaps it was fright, for I saw everything that happened just as I see you now.

Mamie set her foot on the step to go up, and as she went forward I saw the sailor slowly lock his arm in Jack's, and Jack didn't move to go up. Then Mamie turned round on the step, and they all three stood that way for a second or two. She cried out then,—I heard a man cry like that once, when his arm was taken off by a steam-crane,—and she fell back in a heap on the little *piazza*.

I tried to jump forward, but I couldn't move, and I felt my hair rising under my hat. The sailor turned slowly where he stood, and swung Jack round by the arm steadily and easily, and began to walk him down the pathway from the house. He walked him straight down that path, as steadily as Fate; and all the time I saw the moonlight shining on his wet oilskins. He walked him through the gate, and across the beach road, and out upon the wet sand, where the tide was high. Then I got my breath with a gulp, and ran for them across the grass, and vaulted over the fence, and stumbled across the road. But when I felt the sand under my feet, the two were at the water's edge; and when I reached the water they were far out, and up to their waists; and I saw that Jack Benton's head had fallen forward on his breast, and his free arm hung limp beside him, while his dead brother steadily marched him to his death. The moonlight was on the dark water, but the fog-bank was white beyond, and I saw them against it; and they went slowly and steadily down. The water was up to their armpits, and then up to their shoulders, and then I saw it rise up to the black rim of Jack's hat. But they never wavered; and the two heads went straight on, straight on, till they were under, and there was just a ripple in the moonlight where Jack had been.

It has been on my mind to tell you that story, whenever I got a chance. You have known me, man and boy, a good many years; and I thought I would like to hear your opinion. Yes, that's what I always thought. It wasn't Jim that went overboard; it was Jack, and Jim just let him go when he might have saved him; and then Jim passed himself off for Jack with us, and with the girl. If that's what happened, he got what he deserved. People said the next day that Mamie found it out as they reached the house, and that her husband just walked out into the sea, and drowned himself; and they would have blamed me for not stopping him if they'd known that I was there. But I never told what I had seen, for they wouldn't have believed me. I just let them think I had come too late.

When I reached the cottage and lifted Mamie up, she was raving mad. She got better afterwards, but she was never right in her head again.

Oh, you want to know if they found Jack's body? I don't know whether it was his, but I read in a paper at a Southern port where I was with my new ship that two dead bodies had come ashore in a gale down East, in pretty bad shape. They were locked together, and one was a skeleton in oilskins.

LEONAUR

ALSO FROM LEONAUR

AVAILABLE IN SOFTCOVER OR HARDCOVER WITH DUST JACKET

THE FIRST BOOK OF AYESHA *by H. Rider Haggard*—Contains *She & Ayesha: the Return of She.*

THE SECOND BOOK OF AYESHA *by H. Rider Haggard*—Contains *She and Allan & Wisdom's Daughter.*

QUATERMAIN: THE COMPLETE ADVENTURES—1 *by H. Rider Haggard*—Contains *King Solomon's Mines & Allan Quatermain.*

QUATERMAIN: THE COMPLETE ADVENTURES—2 *by H. Rider Haggard*—Contains *Allan's Wife, Maiwa's Revenge & Marie.*

QUATERMAIN: THE COMPLETE ADVENTURES—3 *by H. Rider Haggard*—Contains *Child of Storm & Allan and the Holy Flower.*

QUATERMAIN: THE COMPLETE ADVENTURES—4 *by H. Rider Haggard*—Contains *Finished & The Ivory Child.*

QUATERMAIN: THE COMPLETE ADVENTURES—5 *by H. Rider Haggard*—Contains *The Ancient Allan & She and Allan.*

QUATERMAIN: THE COMPLETE ADVENTURES—6 *by H. Rider Haggard*—Contains *Heu-Heu or, the Monster & The Treasure of the Lake.*

QUATERMAIN: THE COMPLETE ADVENTURES—7 *by H. Rider Haggard*—Contains *Allan and the Ice Gods, Four Short Adventures & Nada the Lily.*

TROS OF SAMOTHRACE 1: WOLVES OF THE TIBER *by Talbot Mundy*—55 B.C.--an adventurer set during the Roman invasion of Britain.

TROS OF SAMOTHRACE 2: DRAGONS OF THE NORTH *by Talbot Mundy*—55 B.C. —Caesar plots, Britons war among themselves and the Vikings are coming.

TROS OF SAMOTHRACE 3: SERPENT OF THE WAVES *by Talbot Mundy*—55 B.C.--Caesar is poised to invade Britain—only a grand strategy can foil him!.

TROS OF SAMOTHRACE 4: CITY OF THE EAGLES *by Talbot Mundy*—54 B.C.—Rome—Tros treads in the streets of his sworn enemies!.

TROS OF SAMOTHRACE 5: CLEOPATRA *by Talbot Mundy*—Tros and the Roman Empire turn to the Egypt of the Pharaohs.

TROS OF SAMOTHRACE 6: THE PURPLE PIRATE *by Talbot Mundy*—The epic saga of the ancient world—Tros of Samothrace—draws to a conclusion in this sixth—and final—volume.

LEONAUR

ALSO FROM LEONAUR
AVAILABLE IN SOFTCOVER OR HARDCOVER WITH DUST JACKET

THE PRISONER OF ZENDA & ITS SEQUEL RUPERT OF HENTZAU *by Anthony Hope*—Two famous novels of high adventure in one volume.

THE GLADIATORS *by G. J. Whyte Melville*—A Classic Novel of Ancient Rome—Three Volumes in One Special Edition.

THE COMPLETE CAPTAIN DANGEROUS *by George Augustus Sala*—The Adventures of a Soldier, Sailor, Merchant, Spy, Slave and Bashaw of the Grand Turk.

ORTHERIS, LEAROYD & MULVANEY *by Rudyard Kipling*—The Complete Soldiers Three stories.

SIR NIGEL & THE WHITE COMPANY *by Arthur Conan Doyle*—Two Classic Novels of the 100 Years' War.

THE ILLUSTRATED & COMPLETE BRIGADIER GERARD *by Arthur Conan Doyle*—All 18 Stories with the Original Strand Magazine Illustrations by Wollen and Paget.

THE OHIO RIVER TRILOGY 1: BETTY ZANE *by Zane Grey*—The land along the Ohio River is newly settled. Indomitable men and women—Col. Zane and his family, the McCollochs, Wetzel, the "Death Wind" Indian killer, among them—have hewn a life out of the frontier wilderness.

THE OHIO RIVER TRILOGY 2: THE SPIRIT OF THE BORDER *by Zane Grey*—Fort Henry still stands as a bastion for the settlers on the frontier along the Ohio River. More pioneers are now moving west to carve new lives out of the wilderness.

THE OHIO RIVER TRILOGY 3: THE LAST TRAIL *by Zane Grey*—This final volume of Zane Grey's Ohio River Trilogy is a gripping finale to a great series—another thrilling story of life and death on the early American frontier and a classic in the tradition of Drums Along the Mohawk.

THE NAPOLEONIC NOVELS: VOLUME 1 *by Erckmann-Chatrian*—This book comprises two linked novels—*The Conscript & Waterloo*—about the adventures a young conscript in the French Army. during the Napoleonic wars.

THE NAPOLEONIC NOVELS: VOLUME 2 *by Erckmann-Chatrian*—*The Blockade of Phalsburg & The Invasion of France in 1814*—the events portrayed in these two novels of the Napoleonic period properly fit in time between those of the first volume. They appear together here since each—unlike the other two in this series—is a stand alone work.

LEONAUR

ALSO FROM LEONAUR
AVAILABLE IN SOFTCOVER OR HARDCOVER WITH DUST JACKET

THE CIVIL WAR NOVELS: 1 *by Joseph A. Altsheler*—*The Guns of Bull Run &*
The Guns of Shiloh—the first and second novels of a series of eight adventures which
follow the momentous events, campaigns and battles of the great American Civil War
between the Northern and Southern states.

THE CIVIL WAR NOVELS: 2 *by Joseph A. Altsheler*—*The Scouts of Stonewall*
& The Sword of Antietam—the third and fourth novels of a series of nine adventures
which follow the momentous events, campaigns and battles of the great American
Civil War between the Northern and Southern states.

THE CIVIL WAR NOVELS: 3 *by Joseph A. Altsheler*—*The Star of Gettysburg*
& The Rock of Chickamauga—the fifth and sixth novels of a series of nine adventures
which follow the momentous events, campaigns and battles of the great American
Civil War between the Northern and Southern states.

THE CIVIL WAR NOVELS: 4 *by Joseph A. Altsheler*—*The Shades of the Wil-*
derness & The Tree of Appomattox—the seventh and eighth novels of a series of nine
adventures which follow the momentous events, campaigns and battles of the great
American Civil War between the Northern and Southern states.

THE CIVIL WAR NOVELS: 5 *by Joseph A. Altsheler*—*Before the Dawn: a Story*
of the Fall of Richmond—the last of a series of nine adventures which follow the momentous events, campaigns and battles of the great American Civil War between the
Northern and Southern states.

THE FRENCH & INDIAN WAR NOVELS: 1 *by Joseph A. Altsheler*—*The*
Hunters of the Hills & The Shadow of the North—In this three volume, six novel set the
story of the war, with many of its real life characters, is told through the adventures
of its principal characters, Robert Lennox, the hunter Willet and his Indian companion Tayoga.

THE FRENCH & INDIAN WAR NOVELS: 2 *by Joseph A. Altsheler*—*The*
Rulers of the Lakes & The Masters of the Peaks—In this three volume, six novel set the
story of the war, with many of its real life characters, is told through the adventures
of its principal characters, Robert Lennox, the hunter Willet and his Indian companion Tayoga.

THE FRENCH & INDIAN WAR NOVELS: 1 *by Joseph A. Altsheler*—*The Lords*
of the Wild & The Sun of Quebec—In this three volume, six novel set the story of the
war, with many of its real life characters, is told through the adventures of its principal
characters, Robert Lennox, the hunter Willet and his Indian companion Tayoga.

LEONAUR

ALSO FROM LEONAUR
AVAILABLE IN SOFTCOVER OR HARDCOVER WITH DUST JACKET

THE LONG PATROL *by George Berrie*—A Novel of Light Horsemen from Gallipoli to the Palestine campaign of the First World War.

NAPOLEONIC WAR STORIES *by Arthur Quiller-Couch*—Tales of soldiers, spies, battles & sieges from the Peninsular & Waterloo campaingns.

THE FIRST DETECTIVE *by Edgar Allan Poe*—The Complete Auguste Dupin Stories—The Murders in the Rue Morgue, The Mystery of Marie Rogêt & The Purloined Letter.

THE COMPLETE DR NIKOLA—MAN OF MYSTERY: 1 *by Guy Boothby*—*A Bid for Fortune* & *Dr Nikola Returns*—Guy Boothby's Dr.Nikola adventures continue to fascinate readers and enthusiasts of crime and mystery fiction because—in the manner of Raffles, the gentleman cracksman—here is character far removed from the uncompromising goodness of Holmes and Watson or the uncompromising evil of Professor Moriarty.

THE COMPLETE DR NIKOLA—MAN OF MYSTERY: 2 *by Guy Boothby*—*The Lust of Hate, Dr Nikola's Experiment* & *Farewell, Nikola*—Guy Boothby's Dr.Nikola adventures continue to fascinate readers and enthusiasts of crime and mystery fiction because—in the manner of Raffles, the gentleman cracksman—here is character far removed from the uncompromising goodness of Holmes and Watson or the uncompromising evil of Professor Moriarty.

THE CASEBOOKS OF MR J. G. REEDER: BOOK 1 *by Edgar Wallace*—*Room 13, The Mind of Mr J. G. Reeder* and *Terror Keep*—Edgar Wallace's sleuth—whose territory is the London of the 1920s—is an unlikely figure, more bank clerk than detective in appearance, ever wearing his square topped bowler, frock coat, cravat and muffler, Mr Reeder is usually inseparable from his umbrella.

THE CASEBOOKS OF MR J. G. REEDER: BOOK 2 *by Edgar Wallace*—*Red Aces, Mr J. G. Reeder Returns, The Guv'nor* and *The Man Who Passed*—Edgar Wallace's sleuth—whose territory is the London of the 1920s—is an unlikely figure, more bank clerk than detective in appearance, ever wearing his square topped bowler, frock coat, cravat and muffler, Mr Reeder is usually inseparable from his umbrella.

THE COMPLETE FOUR JUST MEN: VOLUME 1 *by Edgar Wallace*—*The Four Just Men, The Council of Justice* & *The Just Men of Cordova*—disillusioned with a world where the wicked and the abusers of power perpetually go unpunished, the Just Men set about to rectify matters according to their own standards, and retribution is dispensed on swift and deadly wings.

LEONAUR

ALSO FROM LEONAUR
AVAILABLE IN SOFTCOVER OR HARDCOVER WITH DUST JACKET

MR MUKERJI'S GHOSTS *by S. Mukerji*—Supernatural tales from the British Raj period by India's Ghost story collector.

KIPLINGS GHOSTS *by Rudyard Kipling*—Twelve stories of Ghosts, Hauntings, Curses, Werewolves & Magic.